The EVERYTHING YOU WANT TO KNOW ABOUT SPORTS ENCYCLOPEDIA

EDITED BY NEIL COHEN

A *Sports Illustrated For Kids* Book

THE EVERYTHING YOU WANT TO KNOW ABOUT SPORTS ENCYCLOPEDIA (Special Book Club Edition)

SPORTS ILLUSTRATED FOR KIDS and [KIDS logo] are registered trademarks of Time Inc.

Cover and Interior Design by Pegi Goodman
Computer Graphics by Dixon Rohr
Illustrations by Marc Rosenthal
All rights reserved. Special Book Club Edition, copyright © 1996 Time Inc.

The Everything You Want to Know About Sports Encyclopedia, Special Book Club Edition is published by SPORTS ILLUSTRATED FOR KIDS, a division of Time Inc. Its trademark is registered in the U.S. Patent and Trademark Office and in other countries. SPORTS ILLUS-TRATED FOR KIDS, 1271 Avenue of the Americas, New York, NY 10020

ISBN 0-553-48166-5

PRINTED IN THE UNITED STATES OF AMERICA

Front cover photographs by (from top): Dave Black, Indy 500 Photos, Manny Millan/Sports Illustrated. Back cover photographs (from left to right): National Baseball Hall of Fame, Peter Read Miller/Sports Illustrated.

The Everything You Want to Know About Sports Encyclopedia, Special Book Club Edition is a production of SPORTS ILLUSTRATED FOR KIDS Books: Cathrine Wolf, Editorial Director; Margaret Sieck, Senior Editor (Project Editor); Jill Safro, Associate Editor; Sherie Holder, Assistant Editor

Time Inc. New Business Development: David Gitow, Director; Stuart Hotchkiss, Associate Director; Pete Shapiro, Assistant Director; Mary Warner McGrade, Fulfillment Director; Bob Fox, Jahn Sandklev, Development Managers; John Calvano, Editorial Operations Manager; Donna Miano-Ferrara, Production Manager; Mike Holahan, Allison Weiss, Associate Development Managers; Dawn Weland, Assistant Development Manager; Charlotte Siddiqui, Marketing Assistant

To JAKE
For: CRAMS/GRANDPA
8-29-16

A book is a team effort. This one could not have been done without the heroic efforts of our all-stars: Pegi Goodman, who designed the book; David Fischer, Brad Herzog, John Rolfe, Stephen Thomas, Scott Wapner, and Ben Kaplan, who researched and wrote the chapters; Margaret Sieck and Jeanine Bucek, who helped with the editing; and Bill Kispert, who guided it all to the finish. Thanks to all.

This book is for you, the reader. Enjoy!

TABLE OF CONTENTS

CYCLING:
PAGE 92

BASEBALL:
PAGE 26

FIGURE
SKATING:
PAGE 104

WRESTLING:
PAGE 282

INTRODUCTION

WHAT THIS BOOK IS

The Everything You Want To Know About Sports Encyclopedia (Special Book Club Edition) is a sports fan's ultimate resource: You can use it to look up facts you didn't know *or* you can read it just for fun.

The book is divided into 28 chapters. Each chapter is made up of sections that look at different parts of a sport: history, how the sport is played, rules, equipment and playing field, records, legends, and champions. There are fun facts, photos and illustrations, and most chapters also have a *glossary* (definitions of terms often used in the sport). You'll even find addresses of where to write for more information or to contact your favorite athlete.

HOW TO USE IT

• To find a sport you want to read about, turn to the Table of Contents on the previous two pages.
• To find a section (Records, Legends) within a long chapter (more than six pages), turn to the guide on the first page of the chapter.

WHY IT'S FUN

All together, there are more than 25 sports covered here. Boggle your brain. Fascinate your friends. Dazzle your dad and mom. Open to any page, and you'll discover something about sports you never knew before!

KEEP IN MIND. . .

●Words that are part of the language of a sport are shown in *italics*. If they are not defined right away, you can find them in the glossary at the back of the chapter.
●We have used the pronoun *he* in explaining what athletes do in a sport. This does not mean that women cannot participate, too.
●The Soviet Union broke up into independent republics in 1991. These republics competed together at the 1992 Olympics as the Unified Team. East Germany and West Germany became one Germany in 1990.
●Chinese and Korean people write their last name first.
●Many countries use the metric system of measurement. A meter is equal to about nine-tenths of a yard. A kilometer is around six-tenths of a mile.
●This book was updated in February 1996. Records are as of that date.

ARCHERY

A rchery is the sport of shooting with a bow and arrow. The bow and arrow was first used in prehistoric times for hunting. That makes archery one of the oldest sports in the world.

SHARP POINTS

The recurve bow can send arrows flying at more than 150 miles per hour.

●

When an archer drives the tip of one arrow deep into the end of another arrow already in the bull's-eye, it is called a "robin hood."

History

In 1879, the first target archery tournament was held in the United States, and the National Archery Association was formed.

Target archery became an Olympic sport in 1900, but was dropped after the 1920 Games. In 1931, an international governing body for archery was formed: Federation Internationale de Tir a l'Arc (FITA). That year, the first archery world championships were held. In 1972, archery returned to the Olympics.

Equipment

Most bows are made of wood, fiberglass, and carbon. There are many types.

The *straight* bow looks like a straight line when it is unstrung. It was once the most popular type of bow, but today the recurve bow is more popular.

The *recurve* bow has tips that curve away from the archer, giving him more leverage.

The *compound* bow includes cables and pulleys that make it easier to *draw* (pull back) the string.

The *shaft* or body of the arrow can be made of fiberglass, aluminum, carbon, or wood. There are feathers attached to the end of the arrow to stabililize it. These are called *vanes*.

Events

In *target archery*, archers shoot at targets from different distances. Each target is divided into five colored circles separated into 10 rings. The middle ring — or bull's-eye — is worth 10 points, and each ring's point value

TEXT BY BRAD HERZOG

Denise Parker of the United States finished fifth in the individual competition at the 1992 Olympics.

CHAMPIONS

Denise Parker has been America's best female archer for a long time — and she's only 22 years old. She has won six national indoor championships, two national target titles, two Pan American gold medals, and a bronze team medal at the 1988 Olympics.

Among America's top male archers are two-time Olympic gold medalist Darrell Pace, 1988 gold medalist and six-time national field champion Jay Barrs, and nine-time national outdoor target champion Rick McKinney.

decreases from the bull's-eye out. Tournaments are held both indoors and outdoors.

Field archery tests accuracy from various distances and often with challenging target placements. Competitions are held in freestyle (using any bow), barebow (using no aiming devices, called *sights*), and compound. Targets with three scoring rings are used.

In *flight shooting*, the competitors shoot for distance, instead of accuracy.

Clout shooting tests both distance and accuracy. Archers aim at a huge (15 meters in diameter) target outlined on the ground. The target is 165 meters away for men and 125 meters for women. (A meter is 39.37", slightly longer than a yard, which is 36".)

Other types of archery include *crossbow shooting* (using a short, powerful bow with a trigger), *ski-arc* (a combination of archery and cross-country skiing in which competitors ski long distances before and after shooting at small targets), and *archery golf* (in which the bow replaces the club and the arrow replaces the ball).

Where to Write

National Archery Association, 1 Olympic Plaza, Colorado Springs, CO 80909

1992 OLYMPIC CHAMPIONS

Men	**Sebastian Flute, France**
Team	**Spain**
Women	**Cho Youn Jeong, Korea**
Team	**Korea**

U.S. CHAMPIONS

1995 Indoor Target

Men	**Butch Johnson**
Women	**Denise Parker**

1995 Outdoor Target

Men	**Justin Huish**
Women	**Jessica Carlson**

1995 Freestyle Field

Men	**Jay Barrs**
Women	**Janet Barrs**

9

AUTO RACING

Automobile racing is exciting but dangerous. It tests the performance of both the car and the driver. Some racing events take 24 hours and cover 2,500 miles. Others last five seconds over a quarter-mile track.

History

The automobile, as we know it today, was probably born in 1885, when German engineer Gottlieb Daimler perfected an *internal-combustion* engine, which worked by burning kerosene.

In an internal-combustion engine, the fuel is burned inside the engine rather than outside, as it is with a furnace or steam engine. The first car powered by an internal-combustion engine to be developed in the U.S. is credited to Charles and J. Frank Duryea in Springfield, Massachusetts, in 1892.

It was only natural that soon after automobiles were built, contests were held to determine whose car was the fastest.

The first American automobile race is thought to have taken place in 1895 in Chicago. The 54-mile race was won by J. Frank Duryea, driving a Duryea car, at an average speed of 7 ½ miles per hour!

Later, Henry Ford, a pioneer of car manufacturing and the founder of the Ford Motor Company, built a race car called the "999." In 1903 his test driver, Barney Oldfield, became the first person to drive a mile a minute — that's 60 miles per hour!

The American Automobile Association (AAA) began *sanctioning* major automobile races in the U.S. in 1904. From 1904–16, the AAA ran the Vanderbilt Cup race, on an open road course on Long Island, New York. It was the country's biggest motor race. The first Grand Prix race *(see Formula One, page 14)* took place in 1906, near LeMans, France.

TEXT BY DAVID FISCHER

A. J. Foyt and Number 14 make a pit stop at the Indy 500. A. J. won Indy four times in his career.

Professional Auto Racing

Today, there are five major types of auto racing. They are stock car, Formula One, IndyCar, sports car, and drag racing.

STOCK CAR

Stock car racing is the most popular form of auto racing in the United States, with attendance in 1993 of more than four million people. Stock cars are American-made automobiles that look much like the cars driven by your parents, with one exception: Stock cars have powerful engines that enable them to

CHAMPIONS

Here are the most recent driving champions in each of the five types of auto racing.

WINSTON CUP (NASCAR)

1995 Jeff Gordon
1994 Dale Earnhardt
1993 Dale Earnhardt
1992 Alan Kulwicki

INDYCAR (CART)

1995 Jacques Villeneuve
1994 Al Unser, Jr.
1993 Nigel Mansell
1992 Bobby Rahal

FORMULA ONE (GRAND PRIX)

1995 Michael Schumacher, Germany
1994 Michael Schumacher
1993 Alain Prost, France
1992 Nigel Mansell, Great Britain

IMSA

1995 Fermin Velez
1994 Wayne Taylor
1993 Juan-Manuel Fangio II
1992 Juan-Manuel Fangio II

DRAG RACING (NHRA)

TOP FUEL
1995 Scott Kalitta
1994 Scott Kalitta
1993 Eddie Hill
1992 Joe Amato

FUNNY CAR
1995 John Force
1994 John Force
1993 John Force
1992 Cruz Pedregon

PRO STOCK
1995 Darrell Alderman
1994 Warren Johnson
1993 Warren Johnson
1992 Warren Johnson

COOL FACTS

During an IndyCar race, the driver's heart rate can accelerate to 195 beats per minute — that's faster than an astronaut's heart rate at blast-off! Drivers keep up a rate of 175 beats per minute for the three-hour race, about the same pace as an Olympic marathon runner.

●

Joe Gibbs is a winner in any sport. As an NFL coach, Joe led the Washington Redskins to three Super Bowl championships. As a stock car owner, Joe watched his Chevrolet win the 1993 Daytona 500 with Dale Jarrett behind the wheel.

reach speeds of 200 miles per hour.

The cars have a front engine, fenders, doors, windshield, and rear-view mirror. Unlike regular cars, they don't have brake lights, upholstery, seats (except for the driver's), or a speedometer (although they do have a *tachometer*). Stock cars are made of steel, and are heavy. They weigh 3,700 pounds. (An Indy car weighs 1,550 pounds).

Races are held on oval asphalt tracks. The distance around the track can range from ⅕ of a mile to 2 ⅔ miles at *superspeedways*. A superspeedway has wide turns with high-banking curves. Most championship races run 200 to 600 miles.

Stock car racing began as an organized sport in December 1947, when a group of stock car officials met in Daytona Beach, Florida. Led by Bill France, Sr., a stock car racer and promoter, these officials formed the National Association for Stock Car Auto Racing (NASCAR). Bill France was president of NASCAR through 1972.

The first NASCAR race, held in February 1948 at Daytona, was won by Red Byron, driving a Ford *modified* car. Red was the first NASCAR driving champion, in 1949. That year also saw the first-ever Grand National race, now called the Winston Cup. Raced at the Charlotte (North Carolina) Fairgrounds, it was won by Jim Roper, driving a Lincoln.

The first asphalt superspeedway in the United States was opened in 1950: the 1.366-mile Darlington International Raceway in Darlington, South Carolina. The first race on the track, called the Southern 500, was won by Johnny Mantz in a Plymouth at an average speed of 76.26 miles per hour. The 1993 winner, Mark Martin, won in a Ford at an average speed of 137.93 miles per hour.

The most famous NASCAR superspeedway, Daytona (Florida) International Speedway, opened in 1959. The 2.5-mile *trioval* (a track

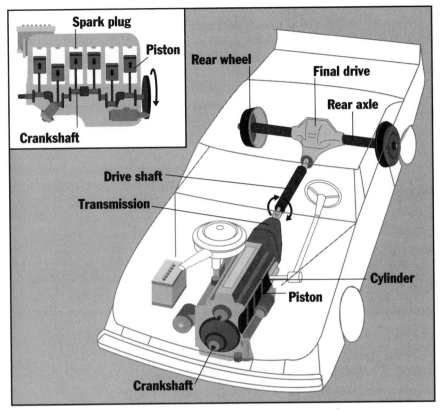

that looks like a triangle with rounded corners) hosts the Daytona 500, which is 200 laps around high-banked turns. The first Daytona 500 was won by Lee Petty in an Oldsmobile at an average speed of 135.52 miles per hour. The track record of 177.60 m.p.h. was set by 1980 winner Buddy Baker, also in an Oldsmobile.

In 1960, the 1.5-mile Charlotte Motor Speedway in Charlotte, North Carolina, opened to host the World 600. Joe Lee Johnson won in a Chevy, averaging 107.75 miles per hour. In 1993, Dale Earnhardt won in a Chevy, averaging 145.50 miles per hour.

The Alabama International Motor Speedway, now called Talladega Speedway, opened in 1969. At 2 ⅔ miles, Talladega is the world's largest motorsports oval. The first Talladega

HOW A CAR WORKS

When the driver steps on the accelerator, the throttle opens, letting gas and air into the cylinders. Electricity from the battery starts the spark plugs, which ignite the air-fuel mixture with timed sparks. These small explosions start the pistons pumping. The pistons turn the crankshaft, which takes the engine's power to the transmission. When a gear is chosen, the power from the transmission goes to the drive shaft. The drive shaft carries the power to the final drive, which turns the rear wheels.

AMAZING FEATS

British driver Nigel Mansell made history in 1993 by becoming the first rookie to win the IndyCar championship. Nigel was also the 1992 Formula One World Driving Champion, making him the first driver ever to win both titles in consecutive seasons.

●

Roger Penske is the owner of the most successful Indy car racing team in history. Entering 1994, Penske Racing teams had won a record 79 Indy car races, including nine Indy 500s and eight IndyCar championships.

500 was won by Richard Brickhouse in a Dodge at 153.78 miles per hour. Ernie Irvan won in a Chevy in 1992 at 176.31 mph.

The R. J. Reynolds Tobacco Company, for its Winston cigarettes, began to sponsor NASCAR in 1971. The Grand Nationals had its name changed to the Winston Cup Series, which currently consists of 31 races.

Besides competing in individual races, NASCAR drivers also compete to become Winston Cup champion for the year. Points are awarded after each race, based on how the driver finished (175 for first place, 170 for second place, 165 for third, and so on). The top 25 point-getters at year's end receive prize money. The driver with the most points is the champion and receives $1.25 million.

Winston also offers a $1 million bonus to any driver who wins three of NASCAR's top four events in the same season. These races are the Daytona 500 (which offers the most prize money), the Winston 500 (which has the fastest average speed), the Coca-Cola 600 (which is the longest race, at 600 miles), and the Southern 500 (which is the oldest race on the circuit). No driver has ever won all four races in one year, but three drivers have won three: LeeRoy Yarbrough in 1969, David Pearson in 1976, and Bill Elliott in 1985.

FORMULA ONE

It costs more money to build a Formula One car than any other type of racing car. That's because the design of a Formula One car is similar to the design of an airplane.

The *fuselage*, or body, is made of special lightweight aluminum and carbon material. The car has one seat, no roof (called an *open cockpit*), and no fenders (*open wheels*). The car features front and rear *wings*. When the car is moving, the wings make the air flow over and under the wings. This produces an effect called *downforce*, which means the wind presses the car downward to the pavement. The downforce actually holds the car on the road. The downforce effect is similar to "lift" on airplanes, only in reverse.

Like stock cars, Formula One cars run on gasoline. Their engine is in the rear.

Outside of the United States, Formula One is the most popular form of auto racing in the world. The Federation Internationale de l'Automobile (FIA), in Paris, France, governs Formula One racing. FIA was established in 1904. The most famous Formula One races are Grand Prix *[grahn PREE]* races. *Grand Prix* is a French term meaning "large prize."

Grand Prix races are contested on challenging road courses throughout Europe. The races run from 150 to 200 miles in length, and the cars travel at speeds of more than 200 m.p.h. on straightaways and as slow as 30 m.p.h. around sharp turns.

In 1993, a total of 35 drivers took part in the 16 Grand Prix events. Points are awarded only to the first six finishers. The Formula One World Championship driver's title is awarded to the driver who scores the highest number of points over the racing season.

INDY CAR

Indy cars look a lot like Formula One cars. They have one seat, an open cockpit (no roof), and open wheels (no fenders). The car's body, which cannot be longer than 16 ¼ feet, is made of fiberglass, aluminum, and carbon fiber. Indy cars weigh a minimum of 1,550 pounds. The fuel used to propel an Indy Car is called *methanol.*

Indy cars have a *turbocharged engine.* Turbocharging increases the power of a small engine. The energy from the engine's exhaust gases are pumped back into the car's engine by a propellor-like pump. The mixture of air and fuel is burned in the *combustion chamber.* The more fuel and air in the com-

GREAT RACE! STOCK CAR

The 1976 Daytona 500 is remembered for the wildest finish in stock car history. During the race, there were 36 lead changes by 10 different drivers. But at the end, it turned into a duel between David Pearson and Richard Petty, the sport's two most successful drivers.

David had never won at Daytona. Richard had won the race five times and wanted more. On the final lap, David's Mercury was right on the tail of Richard's Dodge. Richard hit the gas hard and jumped his car into the lead on the back straightaway.

Richard tried to recover the lead in turn four, but he was barely in control, and his right rear fender knocked David's left front fender. Both cars smashed into the wall and spun out — just a few feet from the finish line.

David had been able to keep his engine running, but Richard had not. David easily crossed the finish line the winner. Richard needed a push from his crew to finish in second place.

15

QUICK HITS

Besides the Indy 500, the U.S. Auto Club oversees the world's fastest cars. These cars, called land-speed racers, are jet-powered vehicles that look like missiles — and travel almost as fast! These vehicles don't race against each other; they attempt to break the world land speed record at the Bonneville Salt Flats in Utah. The record of 633.468 m.p.h. was set in 1983 by British driver Richard Noble.

●

A Top Fuel dragster leaves the starting line with a force five times greater than gravity — the same force needed by the space shuttle when it takes off from the launching pad at Cape Canaveral, Florida.

bustion chamber, the faster the car can go.

An Indy car can go from 0 to 100 m.p.h. in 4.2 seconds. The cars are often clocked at 240 m.p.h., a speed greater than a Boeing 747 jumbo jet taking off!

Indy cars are raced on four different types of tracks: superspeedways longer than one mile, short ovals shorter than a mile, temporary road courses (usually built on closed-off downtown streets of major cities), and permanent road courses (laid out over the natural countryside). The turns are often described by their names: *ess*, *hairpin*, and *dogleg*.

The Indianapolis 500 is the most famous Indy car race and annually draws the largest crowd of any sporting event in the world, over 300,000 people. The race is 200 laps around the 2.5-mile course at the Indianapolis Motor Speedway. Built in 1909 in Indianapolis, Indiana, the Speedway is called "The Brickyard" because the track surface was made from more than three million paving bricks.

The United States Auto Club (USAC) has run the Indy 500 since USAC was formed in 1955. USAC used to supervise all Indy car racing. But as the cost of Indy car ownership increased, prize money did not. In 1978, Indy car owners created their own organization, Championship Auto Racing Teams (CART), and their own racing series. IndyCar is the name of the racing series. (USAC still presents about 150 events in sprint car and midget car racing.)

The first IndyCar season was a 13-race schedule in 1979. The next year, PPG Industries became the sponsor. The season now consists of 16 races, ranging from 150 miles to 500 miles. Points are awarded to drivers based on their order of finish. The driver with the most points at the end of the season wins the PPG Cup trophy. Al Unser won the closest battle for the title in history, edging out his son, Al Unser, Jr., by one point in 1985.

SPORTS CAR

The Sports Car Club of America (SCCA) was founded in 1944 by a group of amateur motorsports enthusiasts. Today, it has more than 50,000 members, and sponsors more than 2,000 amateur and professional races each year.

The amateur racing circuit is called *club racing*. Club racing is a stepping-stone to becoming a pro driver. The SCCA sponsors over 250 club races each year. By racing safely in regional and national races, drivers can attain their pro driving license.

In pro racing, the SCCA's most famous event is the Trans-Am Championships, now in its 29th season. The Trans-Am Championship circuit consists of 14 races, with total prize money of $1.5 million. Most events are sprint races 100 miles long.

The winner and runners-up in each race earn points. The driver who earns the most points at the end of the season wins the Trans-Am drivers' championship.

The top model cars competing in Sports Car racing are the Pontiac Trans Am, Chevrolet Camaro, and Ford Mustang. These cars can go as fast as 200 m.p.h. on an extended straightaway.

The sports car engine is the standard engine used for the street model. To make races as competitive as possible, each car is assigned a weight based on the power of the car's engine. For example, cars with higher-horsepower engines must weigh more than cars with lower-horsepower engines.

ENDURANCE RACING

Sports cars also compete in endurance racing. In a 24-hour endurance race, the winner is the team that drives the most miles in the 24 hours. Three to five drivers act as a team and take turns driving the car. The two most famous endurance races

GREAT RACE! FORMULA ONE

Argentina's Juan-Manuel Fangio won 24 Formula One races in just 51 starts. But his greatest victory may have come in his final race, in 1957, at Nurburgring, West Germany.

Juan-Manuel knew that he was one minute behind before the race even started. He would be driving against Ferraris that could go the 310-mile distance without stopping. His Maserati would need to make a pit stop for fuel.

Juan-Manuel decided to start the race with his fuel tank only half full, to make his car lighter and faster. He drove his car to a 28-second lead before he was forced to make a refueling stop, where he fell nearly a minute behind.

In the next few laps, Juan-Manuel seemed to hold back, fooling the Ferrari team. Then he increased his speed over the next 10 laps, gaining at a rate of six seconds per lap. On the second to last lap, he rocketed to the lead and held on to win. Then, Juan-Manuel Fangio retired from racing.

COOL FACT

A new Indy car costs $420,000 — and that's without an engine. A racing engine can cost between $40,000 and $140,000. Most engines need to be rebuilt after 500 miles of use, at a cost of $25,000. The usual IndyCar team starts a season with about eight engines per race car. A set of four tires costs $1,200, and a set of tires are changed at least seven times per race. Add in the fuel costs, spare parts, transportation, etc., and it takes $2.5 million to make an Indy car race-ready!

are the 24 Hours of Daytona and the 24 Hours of LeMans.

A driving team will cover more than 2,500 miles during the 24 Hours of Daytona. Held at the Daytona International Speedway, the 24 Hours of Daytona is the opening event for the International Motor Sports Association (IMSA) sports car season.

IMSA was started in 1969. Its races are professional road races on permanent road courses or temporary street circuits. The nine-race Exxon World Sports Car Championship is the highlight of the IMSA season.

The 24 Hours of LeMans is the most important international road-racing event. It is to road racing what the Indy 500 is to track racing. The race is held on a difficult 8.5-mile run over the public roads of LeMans, France. During the race, a driving team will cover more than 1,000 miles.

The 24 Hours of Le Mans is unique because the prize goes to the car, not the driver. Ferrari cars won at LeMans in 1949, 1954, 1958, and every year from 1960 to 1965. Porsche cars won 10 times in 12 years, from 1976 to 1987. Peugeots won in 1992 and 1993.

DRAG RACING

Drag racing is a high-speed contest between two cars racing from a standing start over a straight, quarter-mile paved track called a *drag strip*. The fastest cars reach a speed of 300 m.p.h. and can travel the quarter-mile distance in less than five seconds!

A drag-racing event, called a *drag meet*, consists of a series of elimination races. Cars compete two at a time. The loser is eliminated and the winner advances to the next round. The winner of the final round is the meet champion. Last year, more than 1.6 million people attended drag meets.

The National Hot Rod Association (NHRA) oversees the major drag races in the United

Formula One legend Alain Prost leads the field over the road course at the Monaco Grand Prix.

GREAT RACE! INDY 500

Racing is in Al Unser, Jr.'s blood. His father, Al Sr., has won the Indy 500 four times; his uncle Bobby has won three times. At Indy in 1992, it was Little Al's turn.

This particular Indy was scarred with accidents. Of the 33 cars to start the race, only 12 would finish. Little Al was careful to stay out of trouble, as was Scott Goodyear. After 190 of the 200 laps, the two were neck and neck. Al was in first place, but Scott was just off his back fender.

Scott searched desperately for a way to pass Al. But Al, at 220 m.p.h., smartly swerved his car from side to side, refusing to allow Scott room to pass.

With 100 yards to go, Scott swept inside Al's car in a final effort to snatch victory. It was not enough. Little Al took the checkered flag a heartbeat ahead of Scott, winning by .043 of a second. After racing for 500 miles, Little Al was about half a car length better than Scott. It was the closest finish ever at the Indy 500.

States, such as the U.S. Nationals in Indianapolis, Indiana; the Winternationals in Pomona, California; and the Gatornationals in Gainesville, Florida.

Drivers compete on the NHRA Winston Drag Racing Series tour, which consists of 18 events. Drivers earn points based on how they finish in each race. The winner of an event gets 1,000 points, the runner-up 800 points, the semi-finalists 600, and so on. The driver with the most points at the end of the season is the season champion.

The NHRA was founded in 1951 to establish drag racing rules and safety standards. Today, the NHRA has 77,000 members, including 26,000 licensed drivers, making it the world's largest motorsports organization.

The three most popular types of cars in professional drag racing are Top Fuel, Funny Car, and Pro Stock.

Top Fuel: These cars, called *dragsters*, can accelerate faster than any other machine in the world. Top Fuel dragsters accelerate from 0 to 100 m.p.h. in less than one second, and

QUICK HIT

The only way for race officials to communicate with drivers during a race is by visual signs. There is an international code of motor racing signals, using flags. A green flag is used to start the race. A yellow flag is a caution signal to indicate danger (such as an accident on the course). When there is a yellow flag, passing is not allowed. Another green flag indicates that the road is now clear. A red flag is like a traffic light signal: All cars must stop at once. A black flag signals a driver to make a pit stop. And a black-and-white checkered flag signals victory for the driver who crosses the finish line first.

exceed 250 miles per hour in just 660 feet!

These dragsters have custom-built, 5,000-horsepower (about 35 times that of the average street car), rear engines that burn *nitromethane*. The car's frame is shaped like a cigar, with small front tires and large, 17" rear tires. Car and driver together must weigh at least 1,975 pounds.

An electronic device, called a *Christmas tree*, is used at the starting line. This is a set of lights that acts as a visual countdown for the drivers. A series of lights flash on to indicate the start.

At the start of a drag race, the car's front wheels lift up off the ground as the driver accelerates from a standing start. The front wheels remain inches off the ground for the first 100' of the race. At the finish, the driver uses a hand control inside the cockpit to open two parachutes that serve as brakes.

Funny Car: The engine in a Funny Car is the same as a Top Fuel engine, except it is located in front of the driver. A Funny Car looks like an ordinary passenger car but has a fiberglass body. The minimum weight of a Funny Car, including driver, is 2,225 pounds.

Pro Stock: Pro Stock cars are 1989, or newer, two-door sedans from Oldsmobile, Dodge, Pontiac, Ford, or Chevrolet, but with a 500 cubic-inch engine instead of the usual 140–250 cubic-inch engine. These engines produce about 1,200 horsepower, or eight times that of the average street car.

Safety

Race car drivers, like airplane pilots, are highly skilled and have excellent reflexes. Unfortunately, accidents do happen at top speeds, endangering both drivers and spectators. To make the sport of auto racing as safe as possible for the fans, strong guardrails and high fences protect the crowd from an out-of-control car and any parts of the car that may happen to fly free during the accident.

There are safety measures for drivers, too. They must wear a helmet, safety belts, and flame-resistant clothing in case of fire. To help prevent fires, the fuel for the car is stored in a *fuel cell*. The rubbery fuel cell looks like a hot water bottle. Inside is a sponge-like material that will absorb any fuel that might leak out from a crash.

The driver is also protected if the car should turn over. A car with an open cockpit has a *roll bar*, a metal bar that stretches over the driver's head. A car that has a roof is equipped with a *roll cage*, a metal frame that keeps the roof from collapsing.

The Pits

There is a special area alongside the track called the *pits*. Here, drivers make a pit stop during the race to refuel, change tires, or make any repairs needed to keep the car racing. A group of highly-trained mechanics, called the *pit crew*, work furiously to make the necessary adjustments.

The pit crew can change four tires and fill the car with gas in about the same time it takes you to read this sentence! A delay in the pits of just a few seconds can be the difference between winning and losing a race.

Records

STOCK CAR (NASCAR)

Most wins, season: 27, by Richard Petty of the United States, in 1967 (out of 48 races).

Most wins, career: 200, Richard Petty, U.S., 1958–92.

Most driving titles won, career: 7, Richard Petty, U.S., 1958–92.

FORMULA ONE (GRAND PRIX)

Most wins, season: 8, Ayrton Senna, Brazil, 1988.

Most wins, career: 51, Alain Prost, France, 1980–93.

GREAT RACE! DRAG RACING

For a long time, drag racers had dreamed of reaching 300 m.p.h. on a quarter-mile run. On March 20, 1992, Kenny Bernstein made that dream come true.

Competing in a qualifying heat at the NHRA's Gatornationals, Kenny knew his run had been very fast when it took his Budweiser King Top Fuel dragster a longer time than usual to come to a stop. Workers at the end of the track held up three fingers, and Kenny thought he had qualified in third place.

Kenny had misunderstood — and how! The three fingers were a signal that the 300-m.p.h. barrier had been broken. Kenny's dragster had gone 301.70 m.p.h.

NHRA rules require a record run be backed up with another run within 1 percent of the record speed. In the second round, Kenny clocked 299.30 m.p.h., within the required 1 percent, and his record went into the books. Since Kenny's record run, the 300-m.p.h. mark has been reached more than 40 times.

AWESOME ATHLETES

In 1977, Janet Guthrie became the first woman to race in the Indianapolis 500. In 1978, she finished ninth in the race. In 1992, Lyn St. James became only the second woman to qualify for the Indy 500. That year, Lyn finished the race in 11th place to become the first female Indy 500 Rookie of the Year.

●

Shirley Muldowney, a drag racer, won the Top Fuel Winston World Championship three times — in 1977, 1980, and 1982.

Most driving titles won, career: 5, Juan-Manuel Fangio, Argentina, 1951, 1954–57.

INDYCAR (CART)
Most wins, season: 10, A. J. Foyt, U.S., 1964 (out of 13 races).
Most wins, career: 67, A. J. Foyt, U.S., 1957–92.
Most driving titles won, career: 7, A. J. Foyt, U.S., 1957–92.

SPORTS CAR
Most Trans-Am wins, season: 10, Mark Donohue, U.S., 1968.
Most Trans-Am wins, career: 29, Mark Donohue, U.S., 1966–73.
Most driving titles won, career: 2, done five times, most recently by Scott Sharp, 1991 and 1993.

DRAG RACING (NHRA)
Most consecutive years winning driving title: four, by Don Prudhomme, 1975–78; and Kenny Bernstein, 1985–88.
Fastest Top Fuel speed: 314.46 m.p.h., Kenny Bernstein, October 30, 1994.
Fastest Funny Car speed: 306.43 m.p.h., Al Hofmann, October 15, 1995.
Fastest Pro Stock speed: 199.15 m.p.h., Warren Johnson, March 10, 1995.

Legends
Mario Andretti, U.S.: The most versatile driver racing has ever known, Mario has won races on paved ovals, road courses, and dirt tracks in the same season four different times. He is the only driver in history to win the Daytona 500 (1967), the Indianapolis 500 (1969), and the Formula One World Driving Championship (1978). Mario's 52 IndyCar victories is second on the all-time list, and he also won 12 Formula One races. During his career, Mario was Indy car driving champion four times. Mario's son, Michael, placed second at Indy in 1991.

Dale Earnhardt, U.S.: The all-time lead-

Richard Petty, stock car racing's all-time winner, takes the checkered flag at the 1979 Daytona 500.

OTHER CARS

A midget car is slightly larger than a go-kart. It has open wheels and an open cockpit. Cars race around banked dirt or asphalt quarter-mile or half-mile ovals. Races are usually no more than 25 miles. Cars go as fast as 115 miles per hour.

A sprint car is longer than a midget car. It has a powerful front engine and open wheels. Sprint cars race much like midget cars.

A Super Vee looks like a small Indy car, but has a Volkswagen engine. (That's where it gets its name.) Super Vees race on asphalt ovals or road-racing courses, and can hit 160 miles per hour.

Off-road races are usually long-distance events run on rough, desert terrain. Small trucks are often used in these races.

Rally races can be either road rallies or pro rallies. Road rallies are held on public roads. Pro rallies are held on back roads, which can be pretty bumpy, hilly, and dirty. Rally cars, some of which have four-wheel drive, are just like street models.

ing money-winner in the history of motorsports, Dale has won more than $25 million during his NASCAR career. He was the 1979 Rookie of the Year and the 1980 driving champion — the first driver to win both awards in consecutive years. Dale has won seven driving titles. Entering the 1996 season, he had won 68 races, sixth on the all-time list.

A. J. Foyt, U.S.: The rancher from Texas is the only driver to have won the Indianapolis 500, the 24 Hours of LeMans, the Daytona 500, and the 24 Hours of Daytona. A. J. is the first driver to win the Indy 500 four times and the only driver to win the Indy car championship seven times. He is the all-time leader in IndyCar victories with 67 and holds the record for most wins (10) in a season. A. J.'s famous car, Number 14, qualified for a record 35 Indy 500s in a row from 1958 to 1992, completing 4,914 laps for 12,285 miles!

Don Garlits, U.S.: The man fellow drag racers call "Big Daddy" knows only one speed — fast. Don was the first Top Fuel driver to surpass 170 m.p.h. (1957), 180 m.p.h.

BLAST FROM THE PAST

The first go-kart was made in 1956 by Art Ingles, a professional race-car designer from Southern California. Art knew how to make fast big cars — he had helped build cars that raced in the Indy 500 in the 1950's — but he also wanted to make fast little cars. Art's first go-kart was made with a lawn mower engine and a frame of metal tubing. Sitting with his knees bent so they almost touched his chin, Art sped around the parking lot of the Rose Bowl, in Pasadena, California, at 30 miles per hour! A crowd gathered in amazement, and karting was born.

(1958), 190 m.p.h. (1963), 200 m.p.h. (1964), 240 m.p.h. (1973), 250 m.p.h. (1975), and 270 m.p.h. (1986). Don drove his "Swamp Rat" dragsters to victory in 35 NHRA Top Fuel events, fourth on the all-time list. He was NHRA champion three times, becoming the first ever to win back-to-back titles, which he did in 1985-86 when he was 54 years old!

Rick Mears, U.S.: Rick went from racing motorcycles in the California desert to setting speed records in IndyCar racing. His greatest successes came at the Indy 500, where he had a record six *pole* starts. Between 1979 and 1991, Rick won Indy four times, tying A. J. Foyt and Al Unser for most victories. Rick's 29 IndyCar victories ranks fifth on the all-time list. He was driving champion three times, and in 1991 became the first driver to top $10 million in career earnings.

Richard Petty, U.S.: The winningest stock car racer in history, Richard's car, Number 43, took the checkered flag a record 200 times, almost twice as often as his closest competitor. In 1,185 starts during his 35-year career, from 1958 to 1992, Richard was a Top 10 finisher 60 percent of the time! "The King" won the Daytona 500 and the NASCAR championship seven times, more than any other driver. He also set records by winning 27 races in a single season (1967) and by becoming the first stock car racer to pass $1 million in career earnings. Richard's father, Lee, won the first Daytona 500 and was NASCAR champion three times; Richard's son, Kyle, is a leading driver today.

Alain Prost, France: Alain retired after the 1993 season as the most successful driver in Grand Prix history. During his 13 years of Formula One racing, he won more times, 51, than any other driver. A master of racing tactics, "The Professor" won the driving championship four times (one shy of the record) and was runner-up four times.

Jackie Stewart, Scotland: During his nine-year career, Jackie was Formula One driving champion three times and runner-up twice. A very safe driver, he was sometimes criticized for not taking risks. Still, he retired from racing with a record 27 victories, which now ranks third on the all-time list.

Glossary

Cylinder: The chamber in which a piston moves.

Modified: A racing car with a closed cockpit but open wheels.

Pole position: The position on the inside of the front row at the start of a race. It usually goes to the driver with the fastest qualifying time for a race.

Sanctioned: A race that is declared official by the governing body of the sport.

Tachometer: An instrument, like a speedometer, that measures engine revolutions per minute (r.p.m.). It lets the driver know how hard the engine is working, and when to shift gears.

Transmission: A car's collection of gears, through which power is transmitted from the engine to the driving axle.

Where to Write

National Association for Stock Car Auto Racing, P.O. Box 2875, Daytona Beach, FL 32120-2875

National Hot Rod Association, 2035 East Financial Way, Glendora, CA 91741

Championship Auto Racing Teams, 390 Enterprise Ct., Bloomfield Hills, MI 48302

International Motor Sports Association, 3502 Henderson Blvd., Tampa, FL 33609

Sports Car Club of America, P.O. Box 3278, Englewood, CO 80112-2150

U.S. Auto Club, 4910 West 16th St., Indianapolis Speedway, IN 46224

ONE MORE THING

The first Indy 500, in 1911, was won by Ray Harroun, driving a Marmon Wasp (see photograph on cover) at an average speed of 74.602 miles per hour. It took 14 years for a driver to break the 100-m.p.h. barrier in average speed. Here are some of the milestone speeds at Indy over the years:

YEAR	WINNER
1925	Peter DePaolo
	101.130 m.p.h.
1937	Wilbur Shaw
	113.580
1949	Bill Holland
	121.327
1954	Bill Vukovich
	130.840
1962	Rodger Ward
	140.293
1965	Jim Clark
	150.686
1972	Mark Donohue
	162.962
1986	Bobby Rahal
	170.722
1990	Arie Luyendyk
	185.981

BASEBALL

Baseball has been called "America's national pastime" for almost 140 years. It was one of America's first popular team games and it has produced more famous athletes, memorable moments, and colorful expressions than any other sport.

History

Baseball is based on an English game called *rounders*. In rounders, players hit a pitched ball, run to bases (in the opposite direction from the way we do it today in baseball), and are "out" if the ball is caught before it hits the ground.

In 1744, the rules for "base-ball" were published in England and, later, in the British colonies that would soon become the United States of America. By the early 1800's, a version called *town ball* had become popular in states in the Northeast. Town ball was much like baseball, but the games were informal. Different sets of rules were used in different towns and states. Fielders did not play set positions, and there were 20 or more players on each team.

The first set of standard rules for baseball was written in 1845 by the Knickerbocker Base Ball Club of New York. The club was created by Alexander Cartwright, a bank teller and volunteer fireman from New York City. At first, the Knickerbockers were mostly a social club. The members met twice a week to play baseball and have dinner after the games. They designed their own uniforms: blue wool pants, white flannel shirts, and straw hats.

The Knickerbocker rules included:

• Bases that were set 90' apart in a diamond pattern.

• A place for the pitcher to throw from that was 45' from the batter. (Today, the major league pitching distance is 60' 6".)

TEXT BY JOHN ROLFE

Babe Ruth, nicknamed "The Sultan of Swat," hit 60 home runs in one season and 714 in his career.

•Nine defensive players at set positions: pitcher, catcher, first baseman, second baseman, third baseman, shortstop (a roving infielder who now plays between second and third), and three outfielders.

•A set batting order in which players took turns hitting. Each team got a turn to bat during an *inning* and the first team to score 21 points was the winner.

In 1857, that last rule was changed and games became nine innings long. Other rules were changed or added through the years. By 1900, baseball was being played almost exactly the way it is now.

When other ball clubs adopted the Knickerbocker rules, formal games became common. The first organized baseball game was held

HOW TO PLAY

The object of baseball is to score runs, by advancing runners around the four bases. The team that scores the most runs by the end of nine innings is the winner.

Each inning, a team bats until three of its players are out. The pitcher's goal is to get the batter out; the batter's goal is to get on base. A player can get on base by hitting the ball, getting hit by a pitch, or by walking. A walk occurs when the pitcher fails to get the ball in the strike zone. This is called a ball. After four balls, the batter walks to first.

Outs are most often made by striking out (if the batter swings and misses or if the ball passes through the strike zone and the batter doesn't swing; three strikes make an out), hitting a ball that is caught in the air, being tagged with the ball while off base, and being forced to run to a base that's been touched by a player holding the ball.

When the player makes it safely around all the bases, he scores a run for his team.

COOL FACTS

on June 19, 1846 at the Elysian Fields in Hoboken, New Jersey. The Knickerbockers were beaten at their own game, 23–1, in four innings, by the New York Base Ball Club.

Formal rules and organized games helped make baseball popular all over the United States. It is now played in countries around the world. In 1992, baseball was made an official medal sport in the Summer Olympics.

Equipment

Baseball is played with a ball, a bat, and a fielder's glove. On the field, there are bases, which are square canvas bags (15" by 15") filled with sand or sawdust. Home plate is a rubber slab with five sides. It is 17" wide and 17" deep.

Baseballs are made of two pieces of cowhide stitched together over a ball of tightly wound yarn. At the center is a small round cork coated with rubber. A baseball weighs between 5 and 5 ¼ ounces, and is between 9" and 9 ¼" around.

Bats are usually made out of wood from northern white ash trees. Metal bats made of aluminum are also common, but they are not allowed in the major leagues. That is because balls hit with aluminum bats can travel so hard and fast that pitchers would be in danger of being struck by the ball before they could protect themselves. Bats are made in different lengths and weights. Major leaguers commonly use bats that weigh 30 to 35 ounces and are 33" to 35" long.

Fielders' gloves have been used since the 1870's. Back then, they were no more than a thin piece of leather that covered and protected the palm of the hand. Holes were cut out for each finger. Today's gloves are much larger and usually made from cowhide. They come in different sizes and styles:

•A regular fielder's glove has four separate fingers connected to the thumb by a leather

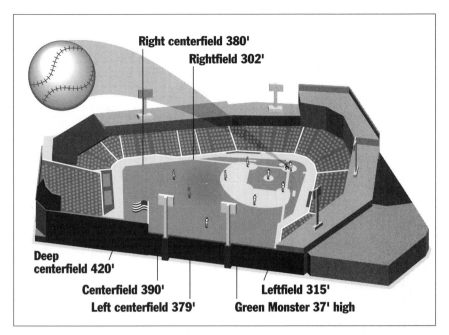

Right centerfield 380'
Rightfield 302'
Deep centerfield 420'
Centerfield 390'
Left centerfield 379'
Leftfield 315'
Green Monster 37' high

web or pocket. Outfielders generally use larger gloves that give them more reach.

• A first baseman's glove resembles a large mitten that is connected between the thumb and fingers. It is long and wide to help first basemen scoop a thrown ball out of the dirt.

• A catcher's glove is round and thick with padding to protect the catcher's hand from the impact of fast pitches.

The Major Leagues

More than 60 million people attend major league games in the United States and Canada each year. There are two major leagues, the American and the National, and each has 14 teams *(see Major League Teams, page 33)*.

The roots of big league baseball go back to that first organized game in 1846. After that, new teams sprouted up and their games began to attract crowds of spectators.

In the 1850's, stories about games appeared regularly in newspapers. Sportswriter Henry Chadwick of the *New York Clipper*

A BALLPARK

A baseball field is called a diamond because it is a square turned on its edge with a base located at each corner. The distance between the bases on a big league field is always 90' and the pitcher's rubber is always 60' 6" from home plate. But the outfield distances may vary. Shown here is Fenway Park, home of the Boston Red Sox. It opened in 1912, and is one of the oldest ballparks in the major leagues. It's famous for the 37'-high "Green Monster" wall in leftfield that's only 315' from home plate. Anything hit off the wall is in play.

BLAST FROM THE PAST

Harry Wright is known as the "Father of Professional Baseball." Harry played outfield for the Knickerbocker club in 1858. With baseball's first pro team, the Red Stockings, he was an outfielder, a pitcher, and a manager. Harry made the Red Stockings a terrific team by emphasizing teamwork and strategy. He was the first manager to use coaching signals during games. He also introduced the pants that are still a standard part of baseball uniforms.

helped make baseball even more popular by writing many articles and books about it.

In 1858, the National Association of Base Ball Players (NABBP) was formed by 22 teams in the New York City area. That year, the first known games which fans paid to watch were held at Fashion Race Course on Long Island. The admission fee was 50¢. The money was used to maintain the field for three games between all-star teams from New York City and the borough of Brooklyn. About 1,500 fans attended the first game.

By 1868 there were almost 350 NABBP teams all over the United States. The players were supposed to be unpaid amateurs, but as more teams were formed, the demand for good players grew. Some teams had begun paying top players to play for them.

THE FIRST PROFESSIONALS

In 1869, the Cincinnati Red Stockings became the first professional team when they began paying all their players. The Red Stockings traveled around the United States that year and had a record of 56 wins, no losses, and 1 tie. Their success made other cities want pro teams of their own.

The first major pro league, the National Association of Professional Base Ball Players, was formed in 1871. It had 10 teams its first season, but Cincinnati's Red Stockings weren't among them. (The Red Stockings had started losing games — and losing fans. Ticket sales dwindled, and their best players left. The team went out of business in 1870.)

The National Association introduced important changes to the game, such as fielders' gloves and called strikes by umpires. (Until then, batters did not have to swing unless they wanted to.) Trick pitches such as curveballs and change-ups became common, but pitchers were required to throw underhand.

The National Association collapsed after

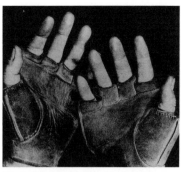

Early baseball gloves were designed only to protect the palms.

five seasons. It had tried to grow quickly and allowed too many new teams to join. Fan support wasn't strong enough to keep all of them in business. However, a new pro league was formed in 1876: the National League, today known as the "Senior Circuit."

THE NATIONAL LEAGUE

The National League did a lot to make big league baseball what it is today. Pitchers were allowed to throw overhand. Batters were allowed three strikes for an out or four balls for a walk. Games were played in stadiums at which fans could buy food and drinks.

The National League started with only eight teams, and all were in cities that could supply plenty of fan support and media attention. The league struggled during its first few years, but new magazines and newspapers about baseball helped make national heroes of some of the players.

Baseball became so popular that poems and songs were written about it. The famous poem "Casey at the Bat" was written by Ernest Lawrence Thayer in 1888.

THE AMERICAN LEAGUE

The National League was challenged by several rival leagues that came and went between 1877 and 1892. In 1901, a second major league arrived for good: the American League. It survived by putting eight teams in big cities and offering National League stars lots of money to switch leagues.

QUICK HITS

A major league game was broadcast on the radio for the first time by station KDKA of Pittsburgh on August 5, 1921. In that game, the Pirates beat the Phillies in Philadelphia, 8–5.

●

The first televised major league game was broadcast by NBC on an experimental station called W2XBS on August 26, 1939. (Most people did not own TVs until the 1950's.) The game was played by the Cincinnati Reds and the Brooklyn Dodgers at Ebbets Field in Brooklyn.

Major league baseball grew in popularity during the early 1900's. There were no other pro sports that could compete with it.

HERE COMES BABE RUTH

The biggest baseball star of all time exploded onto the scene in 1920. He was outfielder Babe Ruth of the New York Yankees. Luckily for Babe, that year also marked the end of the "dead ball era."

Baseballs had been made without the cork center and home runs were rare. Only a few players had ever hit more than 25 homers in a season.

Starting in 1920, a new ball was used that was harder and could be hit farther. Babe was able to whack a record 54 home runs in 1920. The next season, he hit 59.

Babe's power hitting helped create a new style of play. Sluggers who could blast the ball out of the park overshadowed the pitchers, who had been dominating the game for many years.

Fans loved the excitement of home runs, and Babe was the greatest home run hitter of his era. He was a colorful character and loved kids. He became famous around the world.

RADIO, TV, AND NIGHT GAMES

During the 1920's, radio broadcasts of games brought baseball into the homes of millions of old and new fans. Night games were introduced in 1935 so people could go to the ballpark without having to miss work or school. In 1939, a game was shown on TV for the first time.

The growth of major league baseball was interrupted in the 1940's by World War II, but it began to spread again in the 1950's. During that decade, several East Coast teams moved to the Midwest, and two to California. For the first time, there were big-league teams in cities from coast to coast.

THE CHANGING GAME

Major league baseball has come a long way from the first game at Elysian Fields and is still changing. The 1960's and 1970's were a time of growth and new ideas:

•Ten new teams were created, including two in Canada: the Montreal Expos in 1969 and the Toronto Blue Jays in 1977. (Two more teams, the Colorado Rockies and the Florida Marlins, joined the National League in 1993.)

•In 1965, the Houston Astros became the first team to play its home games in a domed stadium: the Astrodome. Five big-league stadiums now have domes or a roof that can be opened and closed.

•The Astrodome was the first stadium to have a field covered with plastic grass called "AstroTurf." Now there are 10 teams playing in stadiums that have artificial turf.

•Speedy base runners and fielders became more important because balls roll faster and bounce higher on artificial turf.

•Some teams began stealing more bases because their newer stadiums were bigger and harder to hit home runs in.

•Relief pitchers started playing a more important role during games.

•In 1973, American League teams began using a "designated hitter" to take the pitcher's regular turn at bat. The first DH was Ron Blomberg of the New York Yankees, playing on April 6, 1973.

•In 1975, players won the right to leave their teams when their contracts end and join new teams that offer them more money. These players are called *free agents*. Free agency caused salaries to skyrocket.

AWARDS

After each season, members of the Baseball Writers Association of America vote for the players and pitchers they feel were the

MAJOR LEAGUE TEAMS

AMERICAN LEAGUE

East Division
- Baltimore Orioles
- Boston Red Sox
- Detroit Tigers
- New York Yankees
- Toronto Blue Jays

Central Division
- Chicago White Sox
- Cleveland Indians
- Kansas City Royals
- Milwaukee Brewers
- Minnesota Twins

West Division
- California Angels
- Oakland Athletics
- Seattle Mariners
- Texas Rangers

NATIONAL LEAGUE

East Division
- Atlanta Braves
- Florida Marlins
- Montreal Expos
- New York Mets
- Philadelphia Phillies

Central Division
- Chicago Cubs
- Cincinnati Reds
- Houston Astros
- Pittsburgh Pirates
- St. Louis Cardinals

West Division
- Colorado Rockies
- Los Angeles Dodgers
- San Diego Padres
- San Francisco Giants

AMAZING FEATS

Only 11 players in major league history have won the Triple Crown, which means they led their league in homers, RBIs, and batting average during the same season. The last to do it was Carl Yastrzemski of the Boston Red Sox in 1967. Two players won the Triple Crown twice: Rogers Hornsby of the St. Louis Cardinals in 1922 and 1925, and Ted Williams of the Red Sox in 1942 and 1947.

best in each league. The major awards are:

Most Valuable Player (MVP): Originally called the Chalmers Award, it is usually given to a player who plays every day, but 19 pitchers have also won it a total of 22 times. Eight players have been chosen MVP as many as three times. MVP awards are also given to the best players in the All-Star Game, the League Championship Series playoffs, and the World Series.

Rookie of the Year: This is given to the best player or pitcher who played his first season in the majors. It was first awarded in 1947 to one rookie chosen from either league. Since 1949, one from each league has been chosen. The Dodgers have had more players (13) win the award than any other team.

Cy Young Award: This is given to either starting or relief pitchers. From 1956 through 1966, only one big-league pitcher was chosen. Now, a pitcher from each league is picked. Steve Carlton of the Philadelphia Phillies won the award a record four times. Gaylord Perry is the only pitcher to win it in each league (with Cleveland in 1972 and with San Diego in 1978).

Manager of the Year: This award has been given since 1983. It usually goes to the manager whose team achieves the most surprising success. Tony La Russa has won it a record three times — with the Chicago White Sox in 1983 and with the Oakland A's in 1988 and 1992.

Gold Glove: Since 1957, this award for fielding excellence has been given by the managers and coaches of each league to one player at each position.

MARKS OF EXCELLENCE

Success in baseball is most often measured by statistics. Here are some numbers and totals that major league players strive to reach or top each season:

A .300 batting average: This means a player gets 3 hits every 10 times at bat. The very best hitters bat about .330 or higher, but batting .400 (4 hits per 10 at-bats) for an entire season is rare. The last player to do it was Ted Williams of the Boston Red Sox, who batted .406 in 1941.

30 home runs: Top sluggers occasionally hit 40. Only 11 players in major league history have ever hit 50 or more.

30 homers and 30 stolen bases: Few players have both power and speed. Only 14 major leaguers have ever reached or topped the "30-30" mark in the same season. Only one has ever reached "40-40": Jose Canseco of the Oakland A's in 1988.

100 runs batted in (RBIs): A few players have driven in as many as 150 runs, but no major leaguer has ever had 200 RBIs in a single season.

20 wins: A starting pitcher usually starts about 35 games each season. He must win in almost two out of every three starts to win 20. Only one pitcher since 1934 has won 30 or more games in a season: Denny McLain, who won 31 for the Detroit Tigers in 1968.

3.00 earned run average (ERA): This means a pitcher gives up three *earned* runs per nine innings. (Runs that score because of errors are usually not "earned" because they are not the pitcher's fault.) The best pitchers have ERAs between 2.00 and 3.00.

300 strikeouts: Most starters pitch about 200 to 250 innings per season, so they must strike out more than one batter each inning to reach this total.

40 saves: Relief pitchers *save* games by protecting leads in the late innings. Relievers usually pitch about 65 times each season, so they must be successful in more than half of their appearances. Dennis Eckersley of the Oakland A's is the only reliever ever to save 40 or more games in a season four times.

SPRING TRAINING

Each February and March, big-league teams prepare for the upcoming season by training and playing exhibition games. Twenty teams train in Florida and make up what is called the "Grapefruit League." Eight train in Arizona in the "Cactus League."

The exhibition games are played in small stadiums, and players can be approached more easily for autographs.

Spring training began in 1870 when the Chicago White Stockings and Cincinnati Red Stockings set up camps in New Orleans, Louisiana. Other teams trained by touring the South, where the weather in early spring is warm enough for baseball. In 1888, the Washington Statesmen became the first team to train in Florida.

AWESOME ATHLETES

Pitcher Jim Abbott was born without a right hand, but still became a successful major leaguer. On September 4, 1993, Jim pitched a no-hitter for the New York Yankees against the Cleveland Indians at Yankee Stadium.

●

Also in 1993, Greg Maddux of the Atlanta Braves became only the fifth pitcher ever to win the Cy Young Award in two straight seasons. He became only the second pitcher to win the award with two different teams. He won the Cy Young in 1992 with the Chicago Cubs.

Major League Records
BATTING

Highest average, season: .438, by Hugh Duffy of the Boston Braves, in 1894.

Highest average, career: .367, Ty Cobb, 1905–28.

Most hits, season: 257, George Sisler, St. Louis Browns, 1920.

Most hits, career: 4,256, Pete Rose, 1963–86.

Most home runs, season: 61, Roger Maris, New York Yankees, 1961.

Most home runs, career: 755, Hank Aaron, 1954–76.

Most RBIs, season: 190, Hack Wilson, Chicago Cubs, 1930.

Most RBIs, career: 2,297, Hank Aaron, 1954–76.

PITCHING

Most wins, season: 41, Jack Chesbro, New York Highlanders (later the New York Yankees), 1904.

Most wins, career: 511, Cy Young, 1890–1911.

Most saves, season: 57, Bobby Thigpen, Chicago White Sox, 1990.

Most saves, career: 471, Lee Smith (through the 1995 season), 1980–present.

Lowest earned run average, season: 1.01, Dutch Leonard, Boston Red Sox, 1914.

Lowest earned run average, career: 1.82, Eddie Walsh, 1904–17.

Most strikeouts, season: 383, Nolan Ryan, California Angels, 1973.

Most strikeouts, career: 5,714, Nolan Ryan, 1966–93.

BASERUNNING

Most stolen bases, season: 130, Rickey Henderson, Oakland A's, 1982.

Most stolen bases, career: 1,149, Rickey Henderson (through the 1995 season), 1979–present.

Nolan Ryan pitched in a record 27 big league seasons, before retiring in 1993 at the age of 46.

The World Series

Each October, the American and National League champions play each other in the World Series to decide the championship of major league baseball.

The first "World's Championship Series" was held in 1882. The Cincinnati Reds of the American Association played two games against the Chicago White Stockings of the National League before a dispute between the two leagues canceled the remaining games.

It wasn't until 1903 that the first modern World Series was held. The owners of the first-place teams in the American and National Leagues agreed to a series of post-season championship games. The Boston Pilgrims defeated the National League champion Pittsburgh Pirates, five games to three.

THE ALL-STAR GAME

The best players in the American and National leagues compete in the All-Star Game each July. The game is played in a different big-league city every year. The starting position players are chosen by fans, who vote using official ballots. Pitchers and substitutes are chosen by the managers of the two teams that played in the World Series the previous year.

The first All-Star Game was played in 1933 in Chicago's Comiskey Park. Babe Ruth hit the first home run. The idea for the game came from sportswriter Arch Ward of the Chicago Tribune as a one-time event, but it was so popular it has been played every year since, except in 1945. (There were two All-Star Games held each season from 1959 to 1963.)

A notable All-Star moment: In the 1934 game, National League pitcher Carl Hubbell struck out five future Hall of Famers in a row: Babe Ruth, Lou Gehrig, Jimmie Foxx, Al Simmons, and Joe Cronin.

BLASTS FROM THE PAST

The earliest known night game took place between two amateur teams in Hull, Massachusetts, on September 2, 1880. The first major league night game was held on May 24, 1935 at Crosley Field in Cincinnati. (The Reds beat the Phillies, 2-1.)

●

Umpires began using hand signals for "strike," "out," "safe," and other calls in the 1890's. The signals were created for outfielder William Hoy, who was deaf and unable to hear an umpire's call.

●

The World Series had been played for 89 straight seasons until 1994. The major league team owners cut the 1994 season short after the players went out on strike.

The following year, the series was canceled when owner John Brush of the New York Giants refused to let his team play the American League champion Pilgrims, whom he thought inferior. Mr. Brush's refusal created an uproar. Officials from each league met and made a formal agreement to hold a World Series each year. Part of the agreement required a team to win four games, instead of five, in order to win the series.

From 1905 through 1968, a team only had to finish first in its league to reach the series. In 1969, each league split into two divisions. The first-place teams in each divison met in a five-game League Championship Series. The winner of each playoff series advanced to the World Series.

In 1985, the league playoffs were changed to a best-of-seven series. In 1994, each league split into three divisions. The first-place finisher in each qualified for the playoffs, along with one *wild card* team that had the best record while finishing second.

The Minor Leagues

The minor leagues are where players begin their pro careers. They get training that helps them develop their skills until they are good enough to play in the major leagues. For that reason, the minor leagues are known as major league baseball's *farm system*.

There are 175 farm teams in 18 minor leagues. The leagues are ranked according to their level of competition. The best players compete in Class AAA. The next-best level is Class AA. The third level is Class A and the Rookie Leagues are the lowest.

Each year, major league teams draft promising high school and college players and assign them to farm teams. Most players start out in Class A or Rookie Leagues. As they improve, they are promoted to teams in a more highly ranked league. Very few players are good enough to go straight to the majors without spending any time in the minors. However, John Olerud of the Toronto Blue Jays and Dave Winfield of the Minnesota Twins are two current stars who did.

The minor leagues were organized in 1901 so players who weren't in the big leagues had a place to play. Some teams played in the country, so far away from big cities that the minors became known as the *bush leagues.*

In 1926, general manager Branch Rickey of the St. Louis Cardinals came up with the idea of using the minor leagues to develop big-league players. Minor league baseball has become very popular. Fans who do not live near a big league city can see the big-league stars of the future. In 1988, a record total of 21.6 million people attended minor league games.

The Negro Leagues

Between the years 1887 and 1947, African-Americans were forbidden to play in the major leagues. Although African-Americans had been freed from slavery in 1863, bigotry and racism often forced them to live apart from white people. In southern states, laws required blacks to eat in different restaurants, drink from different water fountains, and stay in different hotels than white people. (Keeping races apart is called *segregation.*)

Segregation existed in baseball, too. Before 1887, there were about 75 black players in the pro leagues. The first black major leaguer was catcher Moses Fleetwood Walker of the Toledo Blue Stockings. Unfortunately, many white players started to refuse to play with or against blacks, so team owners made a rule that only whites could play in the big leagues.

Because of this terrible injustice, hundreds of talented black players were left with no place to play. It wasn't until 1920 that Andrew "Rube" Foster founded the first black league: the Negro National League. It had

THE HALL OF FAME

The National Baseball Hall of Fame and Museum opened in 1939 to honor the sport's all-time greats. More than 200 players, managers, team owners, umpires, broadcasters, and sportswriters have now been honored.

Players become eligible for the Hall five years after they retire (although exceptions are made). They are chosen by the Baseball Writers Association of America. There is also a special veterans committee that chooses worthy players who have been overlooked by the writers.

The Hall of Fame is located in Cooperstown, New York. Cooperstown was chosen because a research committee had decided baseball had been invented there by Abner Doubleday in 1839. This was later found to be untrue.

The Hall of Fame is a baseball lover's dream. It features plaques with players' pictures and achievements; old uniforms, bats, and balls used during great moments; and a library full of baseball information.

AMAZING FEATS

Outfielder Barry Bonds of the San Francisco Giants is one of only eight major leaguers ever to win three MVP awards. Barry's father, Bobby, was a big-league star from 1968 to 1981. He set a record by topping 30 homers and 30 stolen bases in a season five times.

●

First baseman Cecil Fielder of the Detroit Tigers is only the second player ever to lead the major leagues in RBIs three years in a row (1990, 1991, and 1992). Babe Ruth was the first.

eight teams. In 1923, the Eastern Colored League was created. The Negro American League came along in 1937.

The Negro leagues held their own World Series and All-Star Games. Some teams even played in major league stadiums such as the Polo Grounds in New York and Forbes Field in Pittsburgh. Exhibition games between Negro league stars and major leaguers were played and the black players often won.

In time, white fans and major league players and owners began to recognize how talented many black players were, and how unjust it was to exclude them. In 1943, the Negro League All-Star Game attracted a crowd of 51,000 people. In 1945, general manager Branch Rickey of the Brooklyn Dodgers decided the time had come to give those players a chance in the big leagues.

Mr. Rickey signed Jackie Robinson of the Kansas City Monarchs to a minor league contract. In 1947, Jackie made history when he joined the Dodgers and became the first black to play in the big leagues in 60 years. Other Negro league players such as Hank Aaron, Willie Mays, and Ernie Banks later followed him to the majors and to the Hall of Fame.

More than 2,600 players played in the Negro leagues from 1920 until 1960, when the leagues went out of business. In 1971, the Hall of Fame began to honor black stars who never got a chance to play in the majors. Here are four of the greatest:

James "Cool Papa" Bell: A speedy runner who is said to have once stolen 175 bases in fewer than 200 games, Cool Papa played in the Negro, Mexican, and Dominican leagues for 27 years, from 1922 to 1948. A teammate once joked that Cool Papa was so fast he could get out of bed, flip a light switch, and be back in bed before the light went out!

Josh Gibson: Josh was a power-hitting catcher for the Homestead Grays and Pitts-

Blacks were banned from the majors for 60 years before Jackie Robinson joined the Dodgers in 1947.

burgh Crawfords from 1930 to 1946. Exact statistics weren't kept, but he is believed to have hit almost 1,000 homers and had a career .362 batting average.

Walter "Buck" Leonard: The first baseman and captain of the Homestead Grays, Buck played from 1934 to 1948. His career batting average was .328 and, with Josh Gibson, he led the Grays to nine straight Negro league championships.

Leroy "Satchel" Paige: The great slugger Joe DiMaggio once said Satchel was the best and the fastest pitcher he ever faced. Satchel is believed to have won more than 2,000 games between 1926 and 1947. He got his first taste of major league action in 1948, when he joined the Cleveland Indians at age 42. He won six games that season and helped the Indians reach and win the World Series. He made his last appearance in the big leagues in 1965 with the Kansas City A's at the age of 59!

Legends

Henry "Hank" Aaron: "Hammerin' Hank" averaged almost 33 homers and 100 RBIs each season from 1954 to 1976. On April 8,

CHAMPIONS

In major league baseball history, the New York Yankees have won more league pennants (33) and World Series (22) than any other team. The St. Louis Cardinals have won the most pennants (15) and World Series (9) of any National League team.

In 1994, the players went on strike on August 12. The season later was canceled and no World Series played.

Here are recent league and world champions of major league baseball.

AMERICAN LEAGUE

1995 Cleveland Indians
1994 None
1993 Toronto Blue Jays
1992 Toronto Blue Jays

NATIONAL LEAGUE

1995 Atlanta Braves
1994 None
1993 Philadelphia Phillies
1992 Atlanta Braves

WORLD SERIES

1995 Atlanta Braves
1994 Canceled
1993 Toronto Blue Jays
1992 Toronto Blue Jays

COOL FACTS

"Take Me Out to the Ball-game" was written in 1908 by Jack Norworth and Harry von Tilzer. At the time, neither man had even seen a baseball game!

•

The custom of playing "The Star-Spangled Banner" before baseball games began in 1942. It was meant to honor the American soldiers fighting in World War II. (When the Montreal Expos or Toronto Blue Jays play, the Canadian national anthem, "O Canada," is also played.)

1974, he broke Babe Ruth's major league career record of 714 homers. Hank finished his career with 755. He played the outfield for the Milwaukee/Atlanta Braves and the Milwaukee Brewers, and participated in 24 All-Star Games. He was elected to the Hall of Fame in 1982.

Lawrence "Yogi" Berra: A catcher, Yogi won three American League MVP awards playing for the New York Yankees from 1946 to 1963. He played in more World Series (14) and for more World Series championship teams (10) than anyone else in history. He is also famous for his sayings, such as "It ain't over 'til it's over." Yogi was elected to the Hall of Fame in 1972.

Roberto Clemente: Roberto was a native of Puerto Rico who starred in the outfield for the Pittsburgh Pirates from 1955 to 1972. He won four National League batting titles and batted over .300 in a season 13 times. He died tragically in a plane crash while flying food, clothing, and medicine to earthquake victims in the Central American country of Nicaragua on New Year's Eve in 1972. Roberto was elected to the Hall of Fame in 1973.

Ty Cobb: Ty was called "The Georgia Peach," but he wasn't sweet! He was a fierce competitor who often fought with players and fans. From 1905 to 1928, mostly with the Detroit Tigers, he batted .350 or higher 16 times and won 12 batting titles, including a record 9 in a row. An outfielder, Ty was elected to the Hall of Fame in 1936.

Joe DiMaggio: "Joltin' Joe" had a .325 career batting average with the Yankees from 1936 to 1951. In 1941, he set a big-league record by getting at least one hit in 56 consecutive games. He also had 100 or more RBIs in a season nine times and led the Yankees to nine World Series championships. His grace as an outfielder also earned him the nickname "The Yankee Clipper." (A "Yankee

Satchel Paige was the greatest pitcher in Negro league history.

Clipper" is a type of sailing ship.) Joe was elected to the Hall of Fame in 1955.

Bob Feller: Bob threw blazing fastballs for the Cleveland Indians from 1936 to 1956. He won seven American League strikeout titles and threw 12 one-hitters and three no-hitters. In the 1940's, Bob missed almost four full seasons while serving in the navy during World War II. He still finished his career with 266 wins and was elected to the Hall of Fame in 1962.

Lou Gehrig: Lou became known as "The Iron Horse" by playing in a record 2,130 games in a row for the Yankees from June 1, 1925 to April 30, 1939. During that time, the first baseman batted .340 and averaged 33 homers and 133 RBIs per season. Lou's streak and later his life were ended by a disease that crippled his nerves and muscles. The disease, amyotrophic lateral sclerosis, came to be called "Lou Gehrig's disease." Lou was elected to the Hall of Fame in 1939.

Reggie Jackson: Reggie was called "Mr. October" for his heroics in post-season play. In the final game of the 1977 World Series, he blasted three homers in a row to lead the Yankees to victory. In all, he belted 563 regular-season homers and was a member of 11 league playoff and 5 World Series teams with

GREAT GAMES!

Back-to-Back No-Hitters: On June 15, 1938, pitcher Johnny Vander Meer of the Cincinnati Reds pitched a no-hitter against the Brooklyn Dodgers. It was his second no-hitter in a row. (He had also throw one on June 11.) Johnny is still the only pitcher in big-league history to accomplish that feat.

The Shot Heard Around the World: Bobby Thomson of the New York Giants made history on October 3, 1951. In the deciding third game of the playoffs, Bobby hit a three-run homer in the bottom of the ninth inning off Ralph Branca of the Brooklyn Dodgers. It gave the Giants a 5–4 victory and the National League pennant.

The Ryan Express: On May 1, 1991, pitcher Nolan Ryan of the Texas Rangers pitched a no-hitter against the Toronto Blue Jays. It was the seventh no-hitter of his career (a record) and made him the oldest man (44) to throw a no-hitter in the big leagues.

COOL FACTS

Presidents of the United States having been throwing out the first ball on Opening Day since 1910. The first to do it was William Howard Taft at National Park in Washington, D.C. The only president who did not was Jimmy Carter, who was in office from 1976 to 1980.

●

No one knows exactly when the "Seventh-Inning Stretch" became a tradition. However, manager Harry Wright of the Cincinnati Red Stockings noticed fans standing and stretching before the second half of the seventh inning of a game in 1869. He figured they were uncomfortable from sitting on hard benches for an hour or so. By around 1920, people were doing it every game.

the Yankees, Oakland A's, and California Angels. An outfielder and designated hitter, he was elected to the Hall of Fame in 1993.

Walter Johnson: The speed and power of Walter's fastball earned him the nickname "The Big Train." He averaged almost 20 wins per season for the Washington Senators from 1907 to 1927 and struck out a total of 3,508 batters. He finished his career with 416 wins and was elected to the Hall of Fame in 1936.

Sandy Koufax: Sandy had a losing record as a pitcher his first six seasons. Then he learned to control his fastball and was dazzling. From 1961 to 1966, his record was 125–47 and he pitched four no-hitters for the Los Angeles Dodgers. He also topped 300 strikeouts in a season three times, won three Cy Young Awards, and was the 1963 National League MVP. His career ended after the 1966 season due to an arthritic elbow. Sandy was elected to the Hall of Fame in 1971.

Connie Mack: Connie, whose real name was Cornelius McGillicuddy, managed in the major leagues for a record 53 seasons between 1894 and 1950. He retired at age 87 and was the last manager to wear regular clothes in the dugout during games. He holds the record for most wins by a manager (3,731), and his Philadelphia A's won five World Series. He was elected to the Hall of Fame in 1937.

Mickey Mantle: Mickey was a slugging outfielder for the Yankees from 1951 to 1968. He belted 536 career homers and won three American League MVP awards. His best season was in 1956, when he won the "Triple Crown" by leading the league in homers (52), RBIs (130), and batting average (.353). He played in 12 World Series and was elected to the Hall of Fame in 1974.

Willie Mays: From 1951 to 1973, "The Say Hey Kid" thrilled fans with his power, speed, and spectacular catches in the outfield. In

Connie Mack, who managed for 53 years and won 3,731 games, didn't wear a uniform at work.

1956, he became the first National League player ever to hit 30 or more home runs and steal 30 or more bases in one season. He hit 660 career homers, most of them for the San Francisco Giants, and was a member of 24 All-Star teams. He was elected to the Hall of Fame in 1979.

Jackie Robinson: In 1947, Jackie became the first black player in modern major league history. He was taunted by prejudiced fans and players, but he replied by batting .297 and was chosen Rookie of the Year. In 1949, he was the league's MVP. In 10 seasons, he batted .311 and led the Brooklyn Dodgers to six World Series. An infielder, Jackie was elected to the Hall of Fame in 1962.

Pete Rose: Pete's fiery spirit earned him the nickname "Charlie Hustle." From 1963 to 1986, he batted over .300 a total of 15 times and set a career record with 4,256 hits. He played in 16 All-Star Games (at five positions) and 6 World Series as a member of the Cincinnati Reds, Philadelphia Phillies, and Montreal Expos. He later became a manager, but was banned from the major leagues for life in 1989 because of his betting activities.

George "Babe" Ruth: Babe is the most famous baseball player of all time. He began his career in 1914 as a pitcher for the Boston Red Sox and won 89 games in six seasons. In 1920, he was sold to the Yankees, where he

GREAT WORLD SERIES GAMES!

The Perfect Game: In Game 5 of the 1956 World Series, Don Larsen of the New York Yankees pitched a perfect game (no runner reached base) to beat the Brooklyn Dodgers, 2-0. It is still the only perfect game ever pitched in the World Series.

The Series-Winning Homer: In the seventh game of the 1960 World Series, Bill Mazeroski of the Pittsburgh Pirates hit a home run in the bottom of the ninth inning to defeat the Yankees, 10-9, and win the World Series. The only other player to end a World Series with a homer is Joe Carter of the Toronto Blue Jays in 1993.

Mr. October: In Game 6 of the 1977 World Series, Reggie Jackson of the New York Yankees hit three homers in a row off three different Dodger pitchers. He hit the first pitch each time. The Yankees won the Series and Reggie picked up the nickname "Mr. October" for his Fall Classic heroics.

BLASTS FROM THE PAST

In Game 3 of the 1932 World Series, Babe Ruth is said to have pointed at the centerfield bleachers in Chicago's Wrigley Field before belting a long home run to that exact spot. He may have been gesturing at the jeering crowd or holding up two fingers to acknowledge he had two strikes on him. Still, Babe's "Called Shot" remains one of the most legendary home runs in World Series history.

•

It was possibly the biggest upset in World Series history: The Baltimore Orioles were upset by the underdog New York Mets in 1969, four games to one. It was the Mets' first winning season, and they became known as the "Miracle Mets."

became an outfielder and gained fame as "The Sultan of Swat" for his power hitting. He led the American League in home runs 10 times in his next 15 seasons. In 1927, he batted .356 with 60 homers and 164 RBIs. He also led the Yankees to seven World Series. Because of Babe, Yankee Stadium is called "The House That Ruth Built." He was elected to the Hall of Fame in 1936.

Nolan Ryan: In 1974, Nolan's blazing fastball, "The Ryan Express," was timed at a world-record speed of 100.9 miles per hour. He struck out more than 300 batters in a season six times and set career records for strikeouts (5,714) and no-hitters (7). He also pitched in a record 27 big-league seasons and won 324 games with the New York Mets, California Angels, Houston Astros, and Texas Rangers. Nolan retired in 1993 at age 46.

Casey Stengel: From 1949 to 1960, Casey managed the Yankees to seven World Series titles, but people loved him most for his zany antics. When he was a player, he once tipped his cap to a jeering crowd and a bird flew out from under the cap! When his Mets lost 120 games in 1962, Casey called them the "Amazin' Mets" and asked his players, "Can't anybody here play this game?" He was elected to the Hall of Fame in 1966.

Ted Williams: Ted was called "The Splendid Splinter" because of his thin body and splendid hitting: 521 homers and a .344 career batting average. He played the outfield for the Red Sox from 1939 to 1943, then served in the navy for three years during World War II. He returned to baseball, but missed most of the 1952 and 1953 seasons while serving as a fighter pilot during the Korean War. He played until 1960. Ted won six batting titles and led the American League in homers and RBIs four times. He was elected to the Hall of Fame in 1966.

Denton "Cy" Young: Cy pitched from

1890 to 1911 for five different teams and won a total of 511 games. It is a big-league record that may never be broken. He also threw three no-hitters and is the only pitcher ever to win 200 or more games in each league. The "Cy Young Award" is named after him. He was elected to the Hall of Fame in 1937.

Glossary

Assist: Assists are credited to fielders when they throw runners out. Catchers get assists after strikeouts.

Balk: There are several kinds of balks, but the most common is called if a pitcher fails to throw the ball after beginning his windup. All runners then advance one base.

Batter's box: The 6' by 4' rectangle on each side of home plate in which batters must stand when they are hitting.

Bullpen: The area where pitchers warm up before and during games, usually located behind the outfield wall.

Bunt: A soft hit resulting from the batter holding the bat out and letting the ball hit it instead of swinging the bat.

Change-up: A slow pitch that is usually thrown after several fast ones to throw off the timing of a batter's swing.

Cleanup: The fourth batter in a lineup is called the cleanup hitter because there are often runners on base for him to drive in and, in that way, "clean up" the bases.

Curveball: A pitch that curves as it reaches the plate. It is thrown by snapping the wrist sharply away from the body as the pitch is released, so the ball spins rapidly and veers to the left (if thrown with the right hand) or right (if thrown left-handed).

Cycle: When a player hits a single, double, triple, and home run in one game.

Cutoff man: An infielder who intercepts a throw from an outfielder when runners are on base. The cutoff man then chooses to

THE WOMEN'S LEAGUE

In 1992, a popular movie called *A League of Their Own* was released. It was about a professional baseball league in which all the players were women. It was based on the All-American Girls Professional Baseball League.

The league was formed in 1942 by Philip Wrigley, the owner of the Chicago Cubs, because many big-league players had been drafted by the armed forces to serve in World War II.

The All-American Girls league started playing games in 1943 with four teams in the Midwest. Uniforms included skirts and several rules were different: The ball was larger, pitchers threw underhand, and the distance between the bases was shortened.

The league attracted enough fans to add 11 new teams during the next few years. It stayed in business until 1954.

In 1994, a women's pro team, the Colorado Silver Bullets, began playing games against men's teams made up of some former major and minor leaguers.

47

AWESOME ATHLETES

The only player to win the Most Valuable Player award in both leagues is outfielder Frank Robinson. He was National League MVP in 1961 with the Cincinnati Reds and American League MVP in 1966 with the Baltimore Orioles. In 1975, Frank became the first black manager in major league history. He was hired by the Cleveland Indians, and later managed the San Francisco Giants and the Orioles.

•

Julie Croteau was the first woman to start for a men's NCAA baseball team. She played first base for St. Mary's College. Outfielder Kendra Hanes is the first woman on a minor league team. She joined the Class A Kentucky Rifles in May 1994.

throw the ball home, to a base, or hold it.

Double: A hit on which the batter reaches second base safely.

Earned run: A run scored because of a hit or walk that is charged to a pitcher's earned run average. Runs that score because of errors or interference are unearned.

Earned run average (ERA): The average number of earned runs a pitcher allows in a nine-inning game. You can calculate it by dividing a pitcher's earned runs by his innings pitched and multiplying the total by nine.

Error: A misplay by a fielder that allows a runner to reach base safely or score.

Fastball: A straight pitch that is thrown with great speed and power.

Forkball: A pitch thrown by holding the ball with the first and second fingers spread apart on top and the thumb on the bottom. Forkballs sink sharply because they have little spin on them.

Grand slam: A home run with the bases loaded.

Ground rule double: When a batter is awarded two bases on a hit that lands in fair territory and bounces over the fence or is interfered with by fans.

Home run: A four-base hit.

Infield fly rule: If a batter hits a catchable fly ball above the infield while runners are on first and second or on all three bases with less than two outs, the batter is automatically out. The runners may run to the next base at the risk of being thrown out by a fielder.

Knuckleball: A slow pitch that is thrown by gripping the ball with the knuckles or fingertips. The ball barely spins after it is released, so breezes and air currents cause it to flutter and jump in unpredictable ways.

No-hitter: When a pitcher or pitchers on the same team do not allow a base hit during a game.

Passed ball: When a catcher fails to stop a

pitch he could have caught, allowing a baserunner to advance. If a passed ball comes on a third strike, the batter can run to first.

Pepper: A common pre-game exercise in which one player bunts brisk grounders and line drives to a group of fielders who are standing about 20 feet away. The fielders try to catch the ball and throw it back as quickly as possible. The batter hits the return throw.

Perfect game: When a pitcher does not let a runner reach base for an entire game.

Putout: A fielder is credited with a putout for catching a fly ball, pop-up, line drive, or throw that gets an opposing player out. A catcher receives a putout for catching a strikeout.

Rookie: A player in his first season. A player is *not* officially a rookie if he has pitched more than 50 innings or gone to bat more than 130 times in the major leagues before his first full season.

Sacrifice: A bunt or fly ball that allows a runner to score or advance to another base at the expense of the batter, who is out.

Save: A pitcher gets credit for a save by finishing a close game while protecting his team's lead. If his team has a big lead, he can get a save by pitching the last three innings.

Screwball: A pitch that usually curves in toward a batter. A pitcher throws it by snapping his wrist in the direction of his body.

Shutout: When a team loses a game without scoring.

Single: A one-base hit.

Slider: A pitch that is gripped more loosely than a curve so that the ball "slides" out of the pitcher's hand. It looks like a fastball but curves sharply just as it reaches the plate.

Slugging average: This is calculated by dividing the total number of bases a player has reached on singles, doubles, triples, and home runs by his number of times at bat.

Spitball: An illegal pitch thrown with sali-

LITTLE LEAGUE

In 1939, Carl Stotz of Williamsport, Pennsylvania, had the idea for an organized "little league" for kids, with uniforms, umpires, and real equipment. Carl mentioned his idea to George and Bert Bebble. The three men then rounded up 41 kids and put together three teams to form the "The Williamsport Little League."

Today, more than two million kids, ages 8 to 12, in 33 countries play Little League Baseball. They play on fields two thirds the size of big-league diamonds. Some rules are different: Most games last six innings instead of nine; base-stealing is not allowed in many leagues.

Each summer, the Little League World Series is held in Williamsport. Teams from all over the world compete in a tournament that lasts five days. The final game is televised.

Although there are other programs, Little League is the largest and most well-known organized baseball program for kids.

49

QUICK HITS

va, sweat, or any slippery substance on the ball that makes it break more sharply. Spitballs were once legal in the major leagues. They were banned in 1920, but that year 17 spitball pitchers were allowed to continue throwing them until they retired. The last legal spitball pitcher was Burleigh Grimes of the Yankees in 1934.

Squeeze play: When a batter attempts to score a runner from third base by bunting the ball. The play is called a *suicide squeeze* if the runner takes off before the ball is bunted, because if the batter misses the pitch, the runner will most likely be tagged out.

Strike zone: The area over the plate from the batter's knees up to his armpits. If a pitch passes through this area and the batter doesn't swing, the umpire calls a strike.

Triple: A three-base hit.

Where to Write

Major League Baseball/American League Office/National League Office, 350 Park Avenue, New York, NY 10022

Atlanta Braves, P.O. Box 4064, Atlanta, GA 30302

Baltimore Orioles, Oriole Park at Camden Yards, 333 W. Camden St., Baltimore, MD 21201

Boston Red Sox, Fenway Park, 4 Yawkey Way, Boston, MA 02215

California Angels, P.O. Box 2000, Anaheim, CA 92803

Chicago Cubs, 1060 West Addison St., Chicago, IL 60613

Chicago White Sox, Comiskey Park, 333 W. 35th Street, Chicago, IL 60616

Cincinnati Reds, 100 Riverfront Stadium, Cincinnati, OH 45202

Cleveland Indians, Indians Park, 2401 Ontario, Cleveland, OH 44114

Colorado Rockies, Suite 2100, 1700 Broadway, Denver, CO 80290

Detroit Tigers, Tiger Stadium, Detroit, MI 48216

Florida Marlins, P.O. Box 407018, Fort Lauderdale, FL 33340-7018

Houston Astros, The Astrodome, P.O. Box 288, Houston, TX 77001-0288

Kansas City Royals, P.O. Box 419969, Kansas City, MO 64141-6969

Los Angeles Dodgers, 1000 Elysian Park Avenue, Los Angeles, CA 90012

Milwaukee Brewers, Milwaukee County Stadium, P.O. Box 3099, Milwaukee, WI 53201-3099

Minnesota Twins, 501 Chicago Ave. South, Hubert H. Humphrey Metrodome, Minneapolis, MN 55415

Montreal Expos, P.O. Box 500, Station M, Montreal, Quebec, Canada H1V 3P2

New York Mets, 126th St. and Roosevelt Ave., Flushing, NY 11368

New York Yankees, Yankee Stadium, Bronx, NY 10451

Oakland Athletics, Oakland-Alameda County Coliseum, Oakland, CA 94621

Philadelphia Phillies, P.O. Box 7575, Philadelphia, PA 19101

Pittsburgh Pirates, P.O. Box 7000, Pittsburgh, PA 15212

St. Louis Cardinals, 250 Stadium Plaza, St. Louis, MO 63102

San Diego Padres, P.O. Box 2000, San Diego, CA 92112-2000

San Francisco Giants, Candlestick Park, San Francisco, CA 94124

Seattle Mariners, P.O. Box 4100, Seattle, WA 98104

Texas Rangers, 1000 Ballpark Way, Arlington, TX 76011

Toronto Blue Jays, 1 Blue Jays Way, Suite 3200, Toronto, Ontario, Canada M5V 1J1

National Baseball Hall of Fame and Museum, Box 590, Cooperstown, NY 13326

ONE MORE THING

The darkest chapter in baseball history occurred in 1919 when eight players from the Chicago White Sox accepted money from gamblers to lose the World Series to the Cincinnati Reds. The players became known as the "Black Sox." The eight, including outfielder "Shoeless" Joe Jackson, were tried in a court for accepting $100,000 from the gamblers. They were found innocent because of a lack of evidence. However, the baseball owners, fearing that the game was in danger of being destroyed, hired the sport's first commissioner, a tough judge named Kenesaw Mountain Landis, to clean things up. Judge Landis banned all eight players from the game for life.

BASKETBALL

Basketball is one of the most popular sports in the world. The game is played by millions of people in more than 100 nations, but it was born in a small gym in Massachusetts.

History

Baseball and football developed from other games. But basketball was the invention of one man: Dr. James Naismith.

Dr. Naismith was a physical education (P.E.) teacher at a school for men in Springfield, Massachusetts, that later became Springfield College. The head of the school's P.E. department noticed that students were bored with the usual indoor winter activities, calisthenics and gymnastics. He asked Dr. Naismith to come up with something new.

In December 1891, Dr. Naismith created a game using a round ball and two goals. He asked a custodian to find boxes to use as goals, but all he could come up with were peach baskets. The peach baskets were nailed to a balcony at each end of the gym. Today, we call the goals *baskets* because in the beginning that's what they really were!

When the students returned from their winter vacation, they saw that Dr. Naismith had posted rules for the new game. Because there were 18 students in the class, the first basketball game had nine players on a side. There was no *dribbling* or *free throws*.

The game caught on quickly among both men and women. Some people suggested that it be called Naismith ball, but Dr. Naismith called it "basket ball."

Basketball made its first public appearance on March 11, 1892. The students at the school competed against their instructors in front of about 200 people. The students won by a score of 5–1.

TEXT BY BRAD HERZOG

Over the years, basketball has had many rule changes. Free throws were introduced to the game in 1894. Dribbling (bouncing the ball as you move) was started by players at Yale University in 1896, but didn't become the part of the game it is today until 1929.

Other changes were made to speed up the game and increase scoring. These included a 10-second rule (1933), which requires the offensive team to bring

Dr. James Naismith, basketball's inventor, with an early ball and basket.

the ball past midcourt within 10 seconds; a 3-second limit for standing in the free throw lane (in the 1930's); and the elimination of a center jump after every basket (1938).

In 1954, professional basketball began using a 24-second shot clock to make teams shoot more quickly. College basketball added a shot clock (45 seconds for men, 30 seconds for women) in the late 1980's.

Equipment

The court: A regulation basketball court is 94' long and 50' wide. Courts for high school games are usually 84' long. Most courts are made of wood and have markings that divide them into sections (see The Court, page 55).

In basketball's early days, the courts were often much smaller. Sometimes, they were dance hall floors, which were waxed and slippery. Some courts even had pillars or posts in the middle!

HOW TO PLAY

A team scores by shooting the ball into the basket, and wins by scoring more points than its opponent.

The ball is moved by dribbling or passing to a teammate. Field goals (baskets) count as two points, and free throws (foul shots) as one. Long-range field goals are worth three points.

Teams consist of two guards, two forwards, and a center. The guards are usually the smallest and quickest players. A point guard, often a team's best ball handler, runs the offense. A shooting guard is often a team's best shooter.

Forwards usually play from the corners of the court to the foul lane. A power forward is often a strong rebounder, while a small forward may be a better scorer. The center, often the tallest player, plays near the basket.

Pro teams play four 12-minute quarters, high school teams play four 8-minute quarters, and college teams play two 20-minute halves.

If the score is tied at game's end, teams play overtime periods until a winner is determined.

BLASTS FROM THE PAST

The University of Chicago and the University of Iowa are believed to have played the first basketball game with five-man teams, on January 16, 1896 (Chicago won 15–12).

•

Basketball players are often called cagers. That term comes from the first few decades of basketball, when many courts were surrounded by cages made of wire, steel, or rope. The ball often bounced off the side of the cage — and the players did, too.

The ball: The ball that was used in the first basketball game was a soccer ball! The first basketballs appeared in 1894, but for many years they had thick laces and lost their shape easily.

Today, basketballs are orange or brown inflated balls that are usually made of leather. The ball for boys' and men's games is about 30" around and weighs 20–22 ounces. Girls and women use a slightly smaller ball, that is about 29" around and weighs 18–20 ounces.

The basket: In early games, a player had to climb a ladder to remove the ball from the peach basket after each score. *Backboards* were introduced in 1894, and baskets with bottomless nets came into use around 1913.

Modern baskets include a cast-iron rim, a net, and a fiberglass, metal, or wooden backboard. The rim measures 18" across and is mounted 10' above the floor.

In college and NBA basketball, the backboard is a rectangle that measures 72" wide and 48" high. High school teams use rectangular or fan-shaped backboards.

The uniform: Early professional basketball players wore long tights and velvet shorts. The game was rough in its early years, so many players wore pads on their knees, shins, and elbows.

The modern uniform generally consists of a sleeveless shirt, shorts, white socks, and lightweight sneakers. Players on an NBA team go through one pair of basketball shoes per game. The visiting team usually wears a darker-colored uniform than the home team.

Professional Basketball

The first professional basketball game was played in Trenton, New Jersey, in 1896. Each player earned $15. Today, players in the National Basketball Association earn an average salary of more than $1 million per year.

The first pro basketball players were orga-

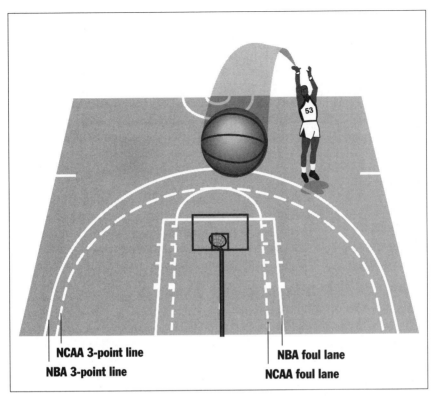

NCAA 3-point line
NBA 3-point line

NBA foul lane
NCAA foul lane

nized as teams, not leagues. Two of these were the Original Celtics and the New York Renaissance Five. These teams would tour the country and challenge local teams to games for a share of the money from tickets sold. This is known as *barnstorming*.

There were several attempts to start pro leagues, but the leagues didn't last long. The American Basketball League, formed in 1925 with nine teams, was the first truly national league, but it didn't survive the Great Depression of the 1930's. The National Basketball League was formed in 1937, and the Basketball Association of America in 1946. In 1949, the two leagues merged to form the National Basketball Association (NBA).

The NBA

Because of the merger, the NBA had 17

THE COURT

Basketball courts are different at different levels of play. In college play in the NCAA, the free throw lane is 12' wide and 19' long. In pro games in the NBA, the free throw lane is 16' wide. In international play, the free throw lane is also 16' wide, but it widens to 19' at the end lines. There are similar differences in 3-point shots. In the NCAA, the 3-point field goal line is 19' 9" from the center of the basket. In international play, it is 20' 6", and in the NBA, it is 23' 9".

AWESOME ATHLETES

Wilt Chamberlain averaged a record 50.4 points per game during the 1961–62 season! But he was not named the NBA's Most Valuable Player for the season. That honor went to Bill Russell of the Boston Celtics. Bill used his defensive skills to lead the Celtics to the NBA title.

●

The 1971–72 Los Angeles Lakers won a record 69 regular-season games. From November 5 to January 9, the Lakers won 33 games in a row, the longest winning streak in league history.

teams in its first season. Many of those were in cities that did not have enough fans to support a team. By 1954, the NBA was down to eight teams *(see Blast from the Past, page 74)*.

The NBA made some of its rules different from those of the college game in order to attract fans. It allowed each player to commit six fouls (compared to five in college), to keep star players in the game longer. Most importantly, it introduced the 24-second shot clock *(see History, page 52)*.

In the 1950's, 1960's, and 1970's, star players like George Mikan, Wilt Chamberlain, and Julius Erving brought more fans to the game. Some teams moved to different cities, searching for fans who would support them.

The NBA grew to be enormously popular in the 1980's and 1990's under the guidance of commissioner David Stern. The league also has had the help of popular stars such as Michael Jordan, Charles Barkley, David Robinson, and Shaquille O'Neal. During the 1993–94 season, the NBA drew nearly 18 million spectators.

Today, the NBA is made up of 29 teams, 15 in the Eastern Conference and 14 in the Western Conference. Two new Canadian franchises, in Vancouver and Toronto, were added for the 1995–96 season. Each conference is divided into two divisions. Teams play 82 games in the regular season, and the eight teams in each conference with the best records make the playoffs.

New players join the NBA each year through an annual draft of college stars. The teams with the league's worst records are allowed to draft first *(see Awesome Athletes, page 70)*. Some NBA players started out in the Continental Basketball Association, a 16-team "minor league." Others played for one of the many pro leagues that have started up in Europe and elsewhere around the world *(see The International Game, page 67)*.

The ABA

In 1967, a new pro basketball league began play. It was called the American Basketball Association (ABA) and had 10 teams. The ABA lasted only nine seasons, but it made important contributions to professional basketball. It featured an All-Star Slam-Dunk Contest, and it introduced the 3-point shot more than a decade before the NBA.

The league had many stars, such as Julius Erving and Artis Gilmore. Julius was the ABA's Most Valuable Player in the league's last three seasons (he shared the 1975 award with George McGinnis).

The league went out of business in 1976, but four of its teams — the Denver Nuggets, Indiana Pacers, New York (now New Jersey) Nets, and San Antonio Spurs — were invited to join the NBA. The Pacers (1970, 1972, and 1973) and the Nets (1974 and 1976) had won ABA championships. None of the former ABA teams has yet won an NBA championship.

NBA Records

SCORING

Most points scored, game: 100, by Wilt Chamberlain of the Philadelphia Warriors, on March 2, 1962.

Most points scored, season: 4,029 (50.4 points per game), Wilt Chamberlain, Philadelphia Warriors, 1961–62.

Most points scored, career: 38,387, Kareem Abdul-Jabbar, 1969–89.

Highest scoring average, career: 32.2 points per game, Michael Jordan, 1984–95.

Most scoring titles: 7, Michael Jordan, 1987–93; and Wilt Chamberlain, 1960–66.

Most 50-point games: 118, Wilt Chamberlain, 1959–73.

REBOUNDS

Most rebounds, game: 55, Wilt Chamberlain, Philadelphia Warriors, November 24, 1960.

INSIDE THE NBA

There are 29 teams in the National Basketball Association. They are divided into two conferences, and each conference is divided into two divisions.

EASTERN CONFERENCE

Atlantic Division
- Boston Celtics
- Miami Heat
- New Jersey Nets
- New York Knickerbockers
- Orlando Magic
- Philadelphia 76ers
- Washington Bullets

Central Division
- Atlanta Hawks
- Charlotte Hornets
- Chicago Bulls
- Cleveland Cavaliers
- Detroit Pistons
- Indiana Pacers
- Milwaukee Bucks
- Toronto Raptors

WESTERN CONFERENCE

Midwest Division
- Dallas Mavericks
- Denver Nuggets
- Houston Rockets
- Minnesota Timberwolves
- San Antonio Spurs
- Utah Jazz
- Vancouver Grizzlies

Pacific Division
- Golden State Warriors
- Los Angeles Clippers
- Los Angeles Lakers
- Phoenix Suns
- Portland Trail Blazers

AMAZING FEATS

The triple double (when a player reaches double figures in three statistical categories in one game) was invented in 1980. But during the 1961–62 season, Oscar Robertson of the Cincinnati Royals averaged a triple double: 30.8 points, 12.5 rebounds, and 11.4 assists per game!

●

Only four NBA players have ever had a quadruple double: Nate Thurmond (22 points, 14 rebounds, 13 assists, 12 blocks for the Chicago Bulls on October 18, 1974); Alvin Robertson (20 points, 11 rebounds, 10 assists, 10 steals for the San Antonio Spurs on February 18, 1986); Hakeem Olajuwon (18 points, 16 rebounds, 10 assists, and 11 blocks for the Houston Rockets on March 29, 1990); and David Robinson (34 points, 10 rebounds, 10 assists, and 10 blocks for the San Antonio Spurs on February 17, 1994).

Highest rebounding average, season: 27.2 rebounds per game, Wilt Chamberlain, Philadelphia Warriors, 1960–61.

Most rebounds, career: 23,924, Wilt Chamberlain, 1959–73.

Most rebound titles: 11, Wilt Chamberlain, 1959–73.

ASSISTS

Most assists, game: 30, Scott Skiles, Orlando Magic, December 30, 1990.

Highest assists average, season: 14.5 assists per game, John Stockton, Utah Jazz, 1989–90.

Most assists, career: 10,394, John Stockton, 1984–95.

Highest assists average, career: 11.6, John Stockton, 1984–present.

Most assist titles: 8, Bob Cousy, 1950–70.

BLOCKED SHOTS

Most blocked shots, game: 17, Elmore Smith, Los Angeles Lakers, October 28, 1973.

Highest blocked-shot average, season: 5.56, Mark Eaton, Utah Jazz, 1984–85.

Most blocked shots, career: 3,189, Kareem Abdul-Jabbar, 1969–89.

STEALS

Most steals, game: 11, Larry Kenon, San Antonio Spurs, December 26, 1976.

Highest steals average, season: 3.67 per game, Alvin Robertson, San Antonio Spurs, 1985–86.

Most steals, career: 2,310, Maurice Cheeks, 1978–93.

SHOOTING

Highest field goal percentage, season: .727, Wilt Chamberlain, Los Angeles Lakers, 1972–73.

Highest field goal percentage, career: .599, Artis Gilmore, 1971–88.

Highest free throw percentage, season: .958, Calvin Murphy, Houston Rockets, 1980–81.

Best free throw percentage, career:

Rival centers Wilt Chamberlain *(left)* and Bill Russell were the giants of the NBA in the 1960's.

NBA CHAMPIONS

The two most successful teams in NBA history have been the Celtics and the Lakers. The Boston Celtics have appeared in the NBA Finals 19 times and have won a record 16 titles. Boston won eight straight championships from 1959-66.

The Minneapolis Lakers won five championships in six years (1949–54). The team moved to Los Angeles in 1960, where it has won six more titles. In all, the Lakers have been in a record 24 NBA Finals and have won 11 titles. Here are the last 10 NBA champions:

1995	Houston Rockets
1994	Houston Rockets
1993	Chicago Bulls
1992	Chicago Bulls
1991	Chicago Bulls
1990	Detroit Pistons
1989	Detroit Pistons
1988	L.A. Lakers
1987	L.A. Lakers
1986	Boston Celtics

.906, Mark Price, 1986–present.

Best 3-point field goal percentage, season: .522, Jon Sundvold, Miami Heat, 1988–89.

Best 3-point field goal percentage, career: .467, Steve Kerr, 1988–present.

GAMES

Most seasons played: 20, Kareem Abdul-Jabbar, 1969–89.

Most games played: 1,560, Kareem Abdul-Jabbar, 1969–89.

Most consecutive games played: 906, Randy Smith, February 16, 1972–March 13, 1983.

Most minutes played: 57,446, Kareem Abdul-Jabbar, 1969–89.

OTHERS

Most Most Valuable Player awards:

59

QUICK HIT

After every college basketball season, several awards are presented to the nation's top male player. These include the Wooden Award, the Naismith Award, the Eastman Award, the United Press International Award, the U.S. Basketball Writers Association Award, and the Rupp Trophy. Since 1977, the first year all six awards existed, eight players have swept them all in a season: Marques Johnson (1977), Larry Bird (1979), Ralph Sampson (1982 and 1983), Michael Jordan (1984), David Robinson (1987), Lionel Simmons (1990), Calbert Cheaney (1993), and Glenn Robinson (1994).

6, Kareem Abdul-Jabbar, 1969–89.

Most consecutive MVP awards: 3, Bill Russell (1961–63), Wilt Chamberlain (1966-68), and Larry Bird (1984–86)

Most triple doubles, career: 136, Magic Johnson, 1979–91.

Coaching victories (including playoffs): 1,037, Red Auerbach, 1946–66.

PLAYOFFS

Most playoff appearances: 18, Kareem Abdul-Jabbar, 1969–89.

Most games played: 237, Kareem Abdul-Jabbar, 1969–-89.

Most points, game: 63, Michael Jordan, Chicago Bulls, April 20, 1986.

Most 3-point field goals, game: 8, Dan Majerle, Phoenix Suns, June 1, 1993.

Highest scoring average, career: 34.4, Michael Jordan, 1984–95.

Most points, career: 5,762, Kareem Abdul-Jabbar, 1969–89.

Most rebounds, game: 41, Wilt Chamberlain, Philadelphia 76ers, April 5, 1967.

Most rebounds, career: 4,104 (24.9 per game), Bill Russell, 1956–69.

Most assists, game: 24, Magic Johnson, Los Angeles Lakers, May 15, 1984; and John Stockton, Utah Jazz, May 17, 1988.

Most assists, career: 2,320 (12.5 per game), Magic Johnson, 1979–91.

College Basketball

For many years after it was invented, basketball was more popular in YMCAs and high schools than in colleges. Basketball then was a rough game that caused many injuries. After rule changes (such as a limit to the number of fouls each player could commit in a game) reduced the number of injuries, college basketball became very popular.

A sportswriter named Ned Irish helped the game by promoting college basketball doubleheader games at New York City's Madison

Square Garden in the 1930's. The games allowed local college teams to compete against college teams from other parts of the country in front of thousands of fans.

Many basketball innovations started in the colleges. For example, until about 1936, there were two basic types of basketball shots: the *layup* and the two-handed *set shot*. But in a game at Madison Square Garden between Stanford University and Long Island University (LIU), Stanford's Angelo "Hank" Luisetti showed East Coast observers a new method of shooting: the one-handed shot. Hank used his new shot to help end LIU's 43-game winning streak.

The college game also introduced the *jump shot*, which was developed by players like Kenny Sailors of the University of Wyoming and "Jumpin'" Joe Fulks of Murray State in the 1940's.

College Tournaments

Approximately 750 colleges and universities in the National Collegiate Athletic Association (NCAA, a governing body for college sports) sponsor men's basketball teams. The NCAA is divided into Divisions I, II, and III. In general, schools with the largest number of students compete in Division I.

There are two major championship tournaments for Division I men's basketball. The National Invitational Tournament (NIT) began in 1938. The NCAA began holding its own tournament one year later.

For a long time, the NIT was the more important of the two tournaments and attracted the top teams in the country. The NCAA was a minor tournament that followed the NIT. City College of New York is the only school to win the NIT and NCAA in the same season.

Today, the NIT is held both at the beginning and the end of the season, but the NCAA tournament is the one that deter-

MEN'S NCAA CHAMPIONS, DIVISION I

The most successful college basketball team of all time is the University of California at Los Angeles (UCLA) Bruins. In the 12 years from 1964–75, UCLA won an incredible 10 national titles in 12 years, including seven in a row! The Bruins' streak included four perfect 30–0 seasons and an 88-game winning streak from 1971–74.

Here are the NCAA Division I men's champions of the past 10 years:

1995	UCLA
1994	Arkansas
1993	North Carolina
1992	Duke
1991	Duke
1990	Nevada-Las Vegas
1989	Michigan
1988	Kansas
1987	Indiana
1986	Louisville

AWESOME ATHLETES

Only six schools have won back-to-back NCAA Division I men's basketball championships: Duke (1991–92), UCLA (1967–73, 1964–65), Cincinnati (1961–62), San Francisco (1955–56), Kentucky (1948–49), Oklahoma A&M (1945–46).

mines which school is the national champion.

The NCAA tournament is a playoff among 64 teams. The semi-finals of the tournament is called the Final Four and is a sports event as eagerly awaited as the Super Bowl and the World Series.

The men's Division II and Division III tournaments feature 32 teams. About 500 smaller schools belong to the National Association of Intercollegiate Athletics (NAIA), which holds Division I and Division II national tournaments. The National Junior College Athletic Association also has a national championship playoff.

Men's NCAA Division I Records

SCORING

Most points scored in a game against a Division I team: 72, by Kevin Bradshaw of U.S. International, on January 7, 1991.

Most points scored against a non-Division I team: 100, Frank Selvy, Furman, February 13, 1954.

Most 3-point field goals, game: 14, Dave Jamerson, Ohio, December 21, 1989.

Most points scored, season: 1,381 (44.5 per game), Pete Maravich, Louisiana State, 1970.

Most points scored, career: 3,667, Pete Maravich, Louisiana State, 1967–70.

Highest scoring average, career: 44.2, Pete Maravich, Louisiana State, 1967–70.

REBOUNDS

Most rebounds, game: 51, Bill Chambers, William & Mary, February 14, 1953.

Most rebounds, season: 734, Walt Dukes, Seton Hall, 1953.

Highest rebounding average, season: 25.6 per game, Charlie Slack, Marshall, 1955.

Most rebounds, career: 2,201, Tom Gola, La Salle, 1951–55.

Highest rebound average, career: 22.7, Artis Gilmore, Jacksonville, 1969–71.

ASSISTS

Most assists, game: 22, Tony Fairley, Baptist, 1987; Avery Johnson, Southern, 1988; and Sherman Douglas, Syracuse, 1989.

Most assists, season: 406, Mark Wade, Nevada-Las Vegas, 1987.

Highest assists average, season: 13.3 per game, Avery Johnson, Southern, 1988.

Most assists, career: 1,076, Bobby Hurley, Duke, 1989–93.

Highest assists average, career: 8.91, Avery Johnson, Cameron/Southern, 1985–88.

BLOCKED SHOTS

Most blocked shots, game: 14, David Robinson, Navy, 1986; and Shawn Bradley, Brigham Young, 1990.

Most blocked shots, season: 207 (5.91 per game), David Robinson, Navy, 1986.

Most blocked shots, career: 453, Alonzo Mourning, Georgetown, 1989–92.

Highest blocked-shot average, career: 5.24, David Robinson, Navy, 1985–87.

STEALS

Most steals, game: 13, Mookie Blaylock, Oklahoma, December 13, 1987 and December 17, 1988.

Most steals, season: 150, Mookie Blaylock, Oklahoma, 1988.

Highest steals average, season: 4.96, Darron Brittman, Chicago State, 1985–86.

Most steals, career: 376, Eric Murdock, Providence, 1988–91.

Highest steals average, career: 3.80 per game, Mookie Blaylock, Oklahoma, 1987–89.

SHOOTING

Highest field goal percentage, season: .746, Steve Johnson, Oregon State, 1981.

Highest 3-point field goal percentage, season: .634, Glenn Tropf, Holy Cross, 1988.

Highest free throw percentage, season: .950, Craig Collins, Penn State, 1985.

Highest field goal percentage, career: .690, Ricky Nedd, Appalachian St., 1991–94.

CHAMPIONS

NCAA DIVISION II

1995	Southern Indiana
1994	Cal-State Bakersfield
1993	Cal-State Bakersfield
1992	Virginia Union
1991	North Alabama

NCAA DIVISION III

1995	Wisconsin-Platteville
1994	Lebanon Valley, PA
1993	Ohio Northern
1992	Calvin, MI
1991	Wisconsin-Platteville

NAIA

1995	Birmingham-Southern, AL (Division I) Bethel, IN (Div. II)
1994	Oklahoma City (I) Eureka, IL (II)
1993	Hawaii Pacific (I) Williamette, OR (II)
1992	Oklahoma City (I) Grace, IN (II)
1991	Oklahoma City

63

Highest 3-point field goal percentage, career: .497, Tony Bennett, Wisconsin-Green Bay, 1988–92.

Highest free throw percentage, career: .909, Greg Starrick, Kentucky/South Illinois, 1968–72.

AMAZING FEATS

In 1984, 6' 7" center Georgeann Wells of the University of Charleston (West Virginia) became the first woman ever to dunk during a game.

●

Before women's basketball became popular at large universities, it was dominated by teams from small schools. The first three AIAW championships were won by tiny Immaculata College, of Philadelphia, Pennsylvania. The next three were won by Delta State (Mississippi), now a Division II school. Delta State has won more national championships than any other school, six (including three in Division II).

Women's College Basketball

There are some differences between men's and women's basketball. For example, women use a smaller ball *(see Equipment, page 53)* and a 30-second clock (instead of the 45-second clock in men's college basketball). But those are nothing compared to the way women's basketball used to be played.

Soon after the first men's game was played in Springfield, Massachusetts, Senda Berenson, a P.E. instructor at nearby Smith College, created her own version of the rules. She divided the court into three sections, and the players had to stay in their sections. Stealing the ball and taking more than three dribbles were not allowed.

The game spread throughout the country, played according to a wide variety of rules. In 1938, a version was developed in which the court was split in half, with three players on offense and three on defense. This game of six-person basketball was popular in Iowa until fairly recently .

Women's basketball became much faster in 1966, when unlimited dribbling was finally allowed. Five years later, the game officially became a five-player, full-court game similar to men's basketball.

Women's Tournaments

The first women's national tournament was organized by Carol Eckman, coach at West Chester College in Pennsylvania, in 1969.

In 1972, a law was passed called Title IX of the Education Amendments. It paved the way to give girls and women the same oppor-

Nancy Lieberman led Old Dominion to two Division I women's basketball titles.

tunities in sports as boys and men. That same year, the Association of Intercollegiate Athletics for Women (AIAW) hosted a national tournament. The AIAW tournament was held until 1982, when an NCAA tournament replaced it as the official playoff for the national title.

Today, about 550 colleges and universities sponsor women's teams. There are national tournaments in three divisions of the NCAA, two divisions of the NAIA, and the NJCAA.

Women's NCAA Div. I Records

Most points in a game: 60, by Cindy Brown, Long Beach State, on February 16, 1987.

Highest scoring average, season: 33.6 points per game, Patricia Hoskins, Mississippi Valley State, 1989.

Highest scoring average, career: 28.4 points per game, Patricia Hoskins, Mississippi Valley State, 1985–89.

Highest rebounding average, career: 16.1 per game, Wanda Ford, Drake, 1982–86.

Most coaching victories: 654, Jody Conradt, Texas, 1969–present.

Women's Pro Basketball

Women's professional basketball teams

CHAMPIONS

In 14 seasons of NCAA women's championships, 10 different schools have won Division I national titles. Four have won the national championship twice: Stanford (1990 and 1992), Tennessee (1989 and 1991), USC (1983–84), and Louisiana Tech (1982 and 1988). Here are the champions of women's college basketball of the past five years.

NCAA Division I

1995	Connecticut
1994	North Carolina
1993	Texas Tech
1992	Stanford
1991	Tennessee

NCAA Division II

1995	North Dakota State
1994	North Dakota State
1993	North Dakota State
1992	Delta State, MS
1991	North Dakota State

NCAA Division III

1995	Capital, OH
1994	Capital, OH
1993	Central Iowa
1992	Alma, MI
1991	St. Thomas, MN

NAIA

1995	So. Nazarene, OK (Division I)
	W. Oregon State (Div. II)
1994	So. Nazarene (I)
	No. State, SD (II)
1993	Arkansas Tech (I)
	No. Montana (II)
1992	Arkansas Tech (I)
	No. State, SD (II)
1991	Ft. Hayes State, KS

toured the United States from 1936 through 1974. Just like the early men's pro teams, they traveled from town to town, playing any team that wanted to challenge them, for a share of the tickets sold. Some played more than 200 games over six months, often against men's teams. The most famous of these were the All-American Red Heads (a team that existed from 1936 to 1974) and the Arkansas Travelers (1949–65).

Later women's professional leagues have been less successful. In 1978, an eight-team professional league called the Women's Basketball League was founded. By the following year it was up to 14 teams, but it only lasted through the 1980–81 season. Four years later, another league, called the Women's American Basketball Association, was formed but it lasted only one month.

In 1993, the eight-team Women's Basketball Association (WBA) completed its second season. The league follows NBA rules, but uses a college 3-point line. The WBA's teams are located mainly in the Midwest. They are the Indiana Stars, Nebraska Express, Iowa Twisters, Oklahoma Flames, Kansas City Mustangs, Kansas Marauders, Memphis Blues, and St. Louis River Queens.

High School

Basketball is the most popular sport in U.S. high schools. About 17,000 schools sponsor boys' basketball teams and only slightly fewer offer girls' teams.

Most states hold separate championship tournaments for schools of different sizes. Some have separate tournaments for public and private schools.

High school basketball is perhaps most popular in Indiana, where all schools compete in a single tournament. Some large cities, such as New York City, Chicago, and Philadelphia, have their own tournaments.

There are several organizations around the U.S. that choose high school All-America basketball teams, but the most well-known are named by *USA Today*, *Parade* magazine, and McDonald's. Most states also award a Mr. Basketball and Miss Basketball trophy to the top male and female player in the state.

The International Game

Basketball has become popular all over the world. Men's basketball has been part of the Summer Olympic Games since 1936. Women's basketball made its first appearance at the Games in 1976.

There are strong men's professional basketball leagues in countries such as Italy, Israel, Spain, and France. Hundreds of top college players and former NBA players compete overseas, and a handful of foreign players play in the NBA. There are women's professional and semi-professional leagues in Europe, Japan, and South America.

The rules for international basketball differ slightly from American rules *(see The Court, page 55)*. For example, there is a 30-second shot clock and players are allowed to touch the ball while it is on the rim, which is a *goaltending* violation in the U.S.

Hall of Fame

The Naismith Memorial Basketball Hall of Fame opened in 1968 in basketball's birthplace, Springfield, Massachusetts. The Hall of Fame honors players, coaches, referees, and contributors from every level of the sport — professional, college, high school, amateur, and the Olympics.

Dr. James Naismith, Hank Luisetti, and George Mikan were among the first group to be inducted into the Hall of Fame.

Legends

Kareem Abdul-Jabbar: In 1965, Kareem,

THE HARLEM GLOBETROTTERS

Black players were not allowed to play with whites in the early years of pro basketball.

In 1927, a white man named Abe Saperstein organized an all-black pro team and began to travel around the country to play games. He called the team the Harlem Globetrotters.

The team easily defeated most white pro teams it faced. The "Globies" combined basketball skill with a sense of humor. They would spin the ball on their fingers, bounce it off their heads into the basket — anything to amuse the crowd.

It took awhile before black players were invited into serious pro ball. The first African-American player drafted by the NBA was Charles Cooper, by the Boston Celtics in 1950.

Earl Lloyd was the first black player to play in a game, for the Washington Capitols on October 31, 1950.

Meanwhile, the Globetrotters carry on today, having entertained close to 100 million people in nearly 100 countries.

67

BLASTS FROM THE PAST

The United States won the first-ever Olympic gold medal in basketball at the 1936 Summer Olympics in Berlin, Germany. The final game, which the U.S. won 19–8 over Canada, was played outside in the rain!

●

At the 1972 Games in Munich, West Germany, the United States men failed to win the Olympic gold medal for the first time since basketball was made an Olympic sport. Playing against the Soviet Union, the U.S. team was ahead with no time left to play. But in a controversial decision, the Soviet Union was given the ball and time was put back on the clock. In fact, it happened twice. The Soviets scored, winning the game and the gold medal.

then called Lew Alcindor, scored 56 points in his first college basketball game for the University of California at Los Angeles (UCLA). The 7' 2" center went on to be named College Player of the Year three times. His teams lost only two games in his college career. Lew changed his name to Kareem Abdul-Jabbar in 1971. He led the Milwaukee Bucks to one NBA title and then led the Los Angeles Lakers to five more. In his 20-year career, Kareem set many records, including most points scored (38,387).

Red Auerbach: Arnold "Red" Auerbach of the Boston Celtics is the winningest coach in NBA history. His teams won a record 938 regular-season games, 99 playoff games, and nine NBA titles, including eight straight from 1959–66. Red has been involved with the Celtics — as coach, general manager, and team president — since 1950. The Coach of the Year trophy is named after him.

Elgin Baylor: Elgin was the first NBA player who seemed to defy gravity. A 6' 5" forward, he spent 14 seasons in the league (1958–72), 12 of them with the Los Angeles Lakers. Elgin was an 11-time All-Star who averaged 27.4 points per game. He scored 71 points in one game in 1960.

Larry Bird: Larry almost single-handedly led the 1979 Indiana State University team to the NCAA championship. Eventually, his team lost to Michigan State, led by Magic Johnson, in the final game. A great all-around player, Larry led the Boston Celtics to three NBA titles and earned three straight MVP awards from 1984 to 1986.

Carol Blazejowski: When women's college basketball began to take off in the 1970's, Carol was one of its stars. "The Blaze" played for Montclair State College in New Jersey. In three seasons, Carol scored 3,199 points. That's an average of 31.7 points per game.

Bill Bradley: Bill was named College

Michael Jordan tied a record by leading the NBA in scoring seven straight times.

Player of the Year in 1965, when he led Princeton University to the Final Four. He scored 58 points in the final college game of his career, lifting his team to third place in the tournament. Bill went on to play 10 seasons with the New York Knicks, helping the team win two NBA titles. He has gone on to even bigger accomplishments, and is now a United States senator from New Jersey.

Wilt Chamberlain: At 7' 1" and 275 pounds, Wilt was probably the most dominant offensive player in basketball history. He spent three years at the University of Kansas and one year with the Harlem Globetrotters before joining the NBA in 1959. "The Big Dipper" led the league in scoring seven straight times, a feat matched only by Michael Jordan. For his career, Wilt averaged 30.1 points and a record 22.9 rebounds per game. He averaged 50.4 points during the 1961–62 season, and scored 100 points in one game *(see Great Games!, page 71)*.

Julius Erving: His name was Julius Winfield Erving II, but everybody called him "Doctor J." Julius starred at the University of Massachusetts and in the American Basketball Association before joining the NBA's Philadelphia 76ers in 1976. He spent 11 years with the 76ers, averaging more than 20

DREAM TEAM

The United States basketball team that will compete at the 1996 Summer Olympic Games in Atlanta, Georgia, may be one of the greatest teams ever put together. The team has been called Dream Team III because it is the third team of its kind, the kind fans "dream" about watching.

The first Dream Team won the gold medal at the 1992 Olympics. It was the first time NBA players were allowed to compete in the Olympics. Before that, the U.S. Olympic team had been made up of the best college players in the country. The second Dream Team won the 1994 World Championship of Basketball.

The United States has dominated Olympic basketball. U.S. men won the gold medal at the first seven Olympics and 10 times in 13 tries. U.S. women have won the gold medal twice (in 1984 and 1988), second only to the former Soviet Union (which won the gold three times, once as the Unified Team in 1992).

AWESOME ATHLETES

The NBA holds a lottery after each regular season to determine which of the teams with the poorest records gets the first pick in the draft. The lottery began in 1985, when the league feared that teams would lose games on purpose to get the first pick in the draft. The number 1 pick in 1985? Patrick Ewing, selected by the New York Knicks.

●

In 1993, Shaquille O'Neal was a rookie with the Orlando Magic. Shaq joined David Robinson, Hakeem Olajuwon, Patrick Ewing, and Alonzo Mourning to form perhaps the best group of centers in NBA history. Shaq was Rookie of the Year, averaging 23.4 points and 13.9 rebounds per game.

points per game and leading his team to an NBA championship in 1983.

Magic Johnson: Earvin "Magic" Johnson is the only basketball player to win a high school state championship (in Michigan, in 1977), an NCAA title (with Michigan State, in 1979), an NBA title (five times with the Los Angeles Lakers), and an Olympic gold medal (with the "Dream Team" in 1992). Magic retired from the NBA in 1991 when he discovered that he had acquired the HIV virus, which causes AIDS. He came out of retirement and rejoined the Lakers on January 30, 1996.

Michael Jordan: Michael Jordan is regarded by many as the best player in history. He was a two-time College Player of the Year at the University of North Carolina. Michael led the NBA in scoring each season from 1986–93, averaging a record 32.3 points per game. In 1988, he was named NBA MVP, All-Star Game MVP, and Defensive Player of the Year. He also earned league MVP honors in 1991 and 1992. From 1991–93, he led the Bulls to three straight NBA titles. He played on the U.S. teams that won Olympic gold medals in 1984 and 1992. He retired from the NBA from October 1993 to March 1995 and played baseball. He then led the Bulls to an NBA-record 41–4 start in the 1995–96 season.

Nancy Lieberman: Nancy was a 5' 10" guard who was named Collegiate Woman Athlete of the Year in 1979 and 1980. In both seasons, she led Old Dominion University to national titles. Nancy played professionally in the Women's Basketball League. In 1986, she played in the United States Basketball League, becoming the first woman to play in a men's professional game.

Pete Maravich: The highest-scoring player in college basketball history, "Pistol Pete" averaged between 43 and 45 points per game in each of his three varsity seasons at Louisi-

Before he became a senator, Bill Bradley starred for Princeton and the Knicks.

ana State University (1967–70). Pete scored a record 3,667 points in his college career. The flashy 6' 5" sharpshooter averaged 24.2 points per game in 10 NBA seasons.

George Mikan: George was basketball's first dominant big man. Before he arrived as a 6' 10" freshman at DePaul University in 1942, most people thought big men were too clumsy to play basketball. George had few skills when he started out, but he became a three-time All-America and then the NBA's first superstar. He led the NBA in scoring three times and helped the Minneapolis Lakers win five championships over six seasons.

Oscar Robertson: While playing for the University of Cincinnati, "The Big O" was College Player of the Year, All-America, and NCAA scoring leader each season from 1958–60. He spent 14 seasons in the NBA and was one of the best all-around players ever. The 6' 5" guard recorded 26,710 points, 7,804 rebounds, and 9,887 assists during his NBA career. That averages out to 25.7 points, 7.5 rebounds, and 9.5 assists per game. He teamed with Kareem Abdul-Jabbar to win an NBA title with the Milwaukee Bucks in 1971.

Bill Russell: Bill changed basketball by showing how a player could dominate a game

GREAT GAMES!

Philadelphia Warriors vs. New York Knicks, March 2, 1962: Wilt Chamberlain put on the greatest one-man show in NBA history. He had 41 points by halftime, and broke his own single-game record by scoring his 79th point with more than seven minutes remaining. His final shot was a slam dunk for his 100th point of the game.

New York Knicks vs. Los Angeles Lakers, May 8, 1970: Just before the opening tip-off of Game 7 of the NBA Finals, Knick star Willis Reed hobbled onto the court despite a leg injury that had forced him to miss Game 6. Willis scored the first two baskets of Game 7, and his return sparked New York to a 119–99 win.

Los Angeles Lakers vs. Philadelphia 76ers, May 16, 1980: The Lakers led the Sixers three games to two in the Finals, but center Kareem Abdul-Jabbar was hurt. Rookie point guard Magic Johnson, 6' 8" tall, played center and had 42 points, 15 rebounds, and 7 assists to give the Lakers the title.

QUICK HITS

During the 1987–88 season, the smallest player in NBA history, 5' 3" Muggsy Bogues, and the tallest player in league history, 7' 7" Manute Bol, were teammates on the Washington Bullets.

●

Hall of Famer Rick Barry, one of the NBA's all-time free throw percentage leaders (.893), shot his foul shots underhanded.

by playing spectacular defense. He led the University of San Francisco to two national championships in 1955–56, then took the Boston Celtics to 11 NBA titles in 13 seasons. In 1966, the 6' 9" center took over as the player-coach of the Celtics and became the first African-American to coach a major league professional team in any sport.

Dean Smith: Dean has coached at the University of North Carolina since 1962 and had 802 career victories through the 1993–94 season. Only former Kentucky coach Adolph Rupp won more games (876). Coach Smith has led the Tar Heels to 24 NCAA tournament appearances, nine trips to the Final Four, and national titles in 1982 and 1993.

John Wooden: John is the only person to be selected to the Basketball Hall of Fame twice — as a player (in 1960) and as a coach (in 1972). As a player, he was a three-time All-America at Purdue University. As a coach, he led the University of California at Los Angeles (UCLA) to 10 national titles, including seven in a row. No other coach has won more than four NCAA championships.

Glossary

Assist: A pass that results in a basket.

Box out: To get good position under the basket in preparation for a rebound, with the opposing player behind you.

Charging: A personal foul, committed when a player with the ball runs into an opponent who has established his defensive position.

Dunk: To slam the ball into the basket from above the rim.

Fast break: When the team on offense moves the ball up the court before the opposing team can organize its defense.

Foul: Illegal contact by an opposing player.

Free throw: A free shot from the foul line by a player who has been fouled. It is also called a *foul shot.*

At 6' 10", George Mikan towered over the competition and was the NBA's first star.

Full-court press: A defensive strategy in which one team closely guards the opposing team all over the court.

Hook shot: A high-arcing shot, using a sweeping motion.

Jump shot: A shot taken from medium to long range at the top of a jump. The jump allows the shooter to free himself from the defender and gives the shot more power.

Lane: The area from the free throw line inside the two parallel lines that extend to the baseline at each end of the court. It is also called the *paint,* because it is usually painted in the home team's colors.

Layup: A shot from close range, often banked off the backboard.

Man-to-man defense: When each defensive player is assigned an offensive player to cover, no matter where that player goes.

Post: The area where the center usually sets up on offense, with his back to the basket.

Set shot: A two-handed shot from the chest taken with both feet on the ground. It is rarely used in today's games.

Three-point play: When a player is fouled making a basket and then makes the free throw.

GREAT GAMES!

North Carolina vs. Kansas, March 23, 1957: The NCAA tournament final game had gone to triple overtime. Wilt Chamberlain's Kansas Jayhawks led undefeated North Carolina, 53–52, as the seconds ticked down. Then, North Carolina's Joe Quigg was fouled. He sank both free throws to give Carolina the title.

UCLA vs. Memphis State, March 26, 1973: In this NCAA final, UCLA's star center, three-time College Player of the Year Bill Walton, made 21 of 22 field goal attempts and scored 44 points. The Bruins won 87–66 for their seventh consecutive NCAA title.

North Carolina State vs. Houston, April 4, 1983: The North Carolina State Wolfpack was a heavy underdog as it took on the top-ranked Houston Cougars in the NCAA tournament final. Houston was nicknamed Phi Slamma Jamma for its dunking ability, but it was a dunk by N.C. State's Lorenzo Charles as the buzzer sounded that gave the Wolfpack a 54–52 victory.

BLAST FROM THE PAST

Only two of the NBA's original teams are still in their original cities: the New York Knicks and the Boston Celtics. Five other original franchises are still playing, but in different places. These are the Warriors (who started in Philadelphia but now play in Golden State/California), Lakers (who went from Minneapolis, Minnesota, to Los Angeles), Kings (who started in Rochester, New York, as the Royals, but now play in Sacramento), Pistons (from Ft. Wayne, Indiana, to Detroit), and 76ers (from Syracuse, New York, as the Nationals, to Philadelphia).

Tip-in: A field goal made by tipping a rebound into the basket.

Turnover: When the offensive team loses possession of the ball without taking a shot.

Zone defense: When the defensive players are assigned to cover a specific area (or zone) of the court, rather than covering a particular offensive player. Zone defenses are not permitted in the NBA.

Where to Write

National Basketball Association, 645 Fifth Ave., New York, NY 10022

Atlanta Hawks, 1 CNN Center, South Tower, Suite 405, Atlanta, GA 30303

Boston Celtics, 151 Merrimac St., 5th Floor, Boston, MA 02114

Charlotte Hornets, 100 Hive Drive, Charlotte, NC 28217

Chicago Bulls, 1901 W. Madison St., Chicago, IL 60612

Cleveland Cavaliers, 1 Center Court, Cleveland, OH 44115

Dallas Mavericks, Reunion Arena, 777 Sports St., Dallas, TX 75207

Denver Nuggets, 1635 Clay St., Denver, CO 80204

Detroit Pistons, The Palace of Auburn Hills, 2 Championship Dr., Auburn Hills, MI 48326

Golden State Warriors, The Coliseum, 7000 Coliseum Way, Oakland, CA 94621

Houston Rockets, The Summit, 10 Greenway Plaza, Houston, TX 77046

Indiana Pacers, 300 East Market St., Indianapolis, IN 46204

Los Angeles Clippers, L.A. Sports Arena, 3939 S. Figueroa St., Los Angeles, CA 90037

Los Angeles Lakers, Great Western Forum, 3900 West Manchester Blvd., Inglewood, CA 90306

Miami Heat, Miami Arena, Miami, FL 33136

Milwaukee Bucks, Bradley Center, 1001 N. Fourth St., Milwaukee, WI 53203

Minnesota Timberwolves, Target Center, 600 First Avenue N., Minneapolis, MN 55403

New Jersey Nets, Meadowlands Arena, 405 Murray Hill Pkwy., East Rutherford, NJ 07073

New York Knickerbockers, Madison Square Garden, 2 Penn Plaza, New York, NY 10121

Orlando Magic, Orlando Arena, 1 Magic Pl., Orlando, FL 32801

Philadelphia 76ers, Veterans Stadium, Box 25040, Philadelphia, PA 19148

Phoenix Suns, 201 E. Jefferson, Phoenix, AZ 85004

Portland Trail Blazers, One Center Court, Suite 200, Portland, OR 97232

Sacramento Kings, ARCO Arena, 1 Sports Pkwy., Sacramento, CA 95834

San Antonio Spurs, Alamodome, 100 Montana St., San Antonio, TX 78203

Seattle SuperSonics, Key Arena, 190 Queen Anne Ave. N., Seattle, WA 98109

Toronto Raptors, SkyDome, WaterPark Place, 20 Bay St., Toronto, Ont., Canada M5J 2N8

Utah Jazz, Delta Center, 301 West South Temple, Salt Lake City, UT 84101

Vancouver Grizzlies, General Motors Place, 800 Griffiths Way, Vancouver, B.C., Canada VB 6G1

Washington Bullets, US Air Arena, 1 Harry S. Truman Dr., Landover, MD 20785

Continental Basketball Association, 425 South Cherry St., Denver, CO 80222

USA Basketball (for Olympic basketball), 5465 Mark Dabling Blvd., Colorado Springs, CO 80918

Naismith Memorial Basketball Hall of Fame, 1150 West Columbus Ave., Springfield, MA 01105

NCAA, 6201 College Blvd., Overland Park, KS 66211

ONE MORE THING

The first NBA All-Star Game, between teams representing the Eastern Conference and the Western Conference, took place in 1951. Through 1996, the Eastern Conference leads the series, 29–17.

Kareem Abdul-Jabbar holds All-Star Game records for most appearances (18) and most points (251). Wilt Chamberlain's 42 points in 1962 are the most in a single game.

In 1984, the All-Star Game was expanded into an All-Star Weekend, and today the game is surrounded by events such as a Slam-Dunk Championship, a Long-Distance Shootout, and a Rookies Game. The 1986 Slam-Dunk Championship was won by 5' 7" guard Spud Webb.

BOWLING

Bowling is the name of several kinds of games in which players try to knock down pins with a ball. It is one of the most popular sports in the United States, played by more than 79 million people each year.

KID STUFF

"Pin boys" set up pins by hand until 1952, when the automatic pin-setting machine was invented. These brave teenagers would pick up the fallen pins after the first ball, reset the pins after the second ball — and run for cover in between!

History

Bowling has probably been around as long as people have thrown stones to knock things down. Items similar to bowling equipment — nine pieces of stone to be set up as pins and a stone "ball" — were found in the tomb of an Egyptian child buried in 5200 B.C.

Bowling was later played by the Germans around 200 or 300 A.D. They tossed stones at nine wooden clubs, called *kegels*. Bowlers today are sometimes called "keglers."

The game of nine-pins spread through Europe and came to America with the Dutch. In the 1800's, nine-pins became very popular in New England. People bet heavily on the outcome of matches, so in 1841 the Connecticut state government made the game illegal. Bowlers changed their game so they could continue playing, by adding a 10th pin. This game, tenpin bowling, is the form of bowling we are most familiar with today. *(For other forms of bowling, see Bowl-a-rama, page 81.)*

How to Play

The object of bowling is to roll a ball the length of the *lane* to try to knock down all 10 pins. In indoor bowling, a ball is rolled on a wooden *alley,* or lane, for 60' to where the 10 pins are set up in a triangle.

The lane is 42" wide. Along each side is a shallow channel, called a *gutter*, which is 9" wide. A misfired ball will roll into the gutter.

The game is played in 10 *frames,* or turns, and each bowler is allowed two rolls in each frame. Points are scored by knocking down

TEXT BY DAVID FISCHER

Don Carter, voted the Greatest Bowler of All Time, was known for his bent-elbow delivery.

HOW IT WORKS

At the bowler's end of the lane is a 15-foot *approach* area. There, the bowler steps up to roll his ball. Separating the approach area from the lane itself is the *foul line*. If the bowler touches or crosses the foul line when rolling the ball, it is a *foul*, and the ball does not count.

In bowling, the ball itself hits only three or four pins, which in turn knock down the other pins. To get a strike, the ball must hit the *pocket*, which is the area between the 1-pin and 3-pin for right-handers, and the 1-pin and 2-pin for lefthanders.

Strikes are difficult to get, so there often will be pins left standing for the second roll. To score well, a bowler must *pick up* (make) the spares.

If the pins left standing after the first roll are spaced far apart, it is called a *split*. A split is named by the numbers of the pins left standing. For example, a 7-10 split means that the two pins farthest from each other, the 7-pin and 10-pin, are still standing. Making a 7-10 split is the toughest shot in bowling.

pins, and the winner is the player with the highest score at the end of the game.

Scoring

When a bowler knocks down all 10 pins with the first roll, it is called a *strike* and the second roll is not necessary. A strike is worth 10 pins, or points, plus the total of the next two rolls from the next frame. A strike is marked on the scoresheet with an *X*.

When a bowler knocks down all 10 pins with two rolls, it is called a *spare*. A spare is also worth 10 points, but the bonus is determined by the number of pins knocked down only with the first roll of the next frame. A spare is marked on the scoresheet with a /.

If neither a strike nor a spare is scored, then the number of pins knocked down is the score for that frame, and no scoring is carried

AMAZING FEAT

In bowling, a perfect game is a score of 300 points. To achieve a perfect game, a bowler must roll 12 strikes in a row — one strike in each of the 10 frames, plus one strike with each of the two extra rolls. Walter Ray Williams, Jr., bowled four 300 games in one tournament in Mechanicsburg, Pennsylvania, in 1993. Walter Ray is nicknamed "Deadeye" because he's also a five-time men's and three-time junior world horseshoe-pitching champion.

over to the next frame. If no pin is knocked down on a roll, it is called an *error* and the frame is *open*. The error is marked on the scoresheet with a —.

If a bowler scores a spare in the 10th frame, one extra roll is taken. A strike scored in the 10th frame earns two extra rolls.

Equipment

A bowling ball is made of hard rubber with a hard enamel or urethane covering and weighs between 6 and 16 pounds. The ball is normally 27" around. Three finger holes are drilled into the ball. To grip the ball, the thumb is placed in the bottom hole and the middle and ring fingers in the top holes.

Bowling pins are made of wood covered with plastic. Each pin is 15" tall and weighs about 3 ½ pounds.

Pins are placed on spots within a 36" triangle. Each spot is 12" apart. The pins are numbered from 1 to 10, beginning with the 1-pin, called the *headpin*, and counting each row from left to right.

League Bowling

The American Bowling Congress (ABC) was organized in 1895. It sets up playing rules and establishes guidelines for balls, pins, and lanes. When it began, the ABC had 300 members participating in 10 leagues. Today, more than 2.5 million bowlers compete in over 100,000 leagues.

The Women's National Bowling Association was formed in 1916 by 40 women to create rules and standards for women league bowlers. That organization is now called the Women's International Bowling Congress (WIBC), and is the largest women's sports organization in the world. The WIBC has about 2.5 million members who compete in some 110,000 leagues.

Boys and girls under age 21 participate in

the Young American Bowling Alliance. The YABA accredits local regional leagues. It conducts two major tournaments: the Intercollegiate Bowling Championship and the Coca-Cola Youth Bowling Championship.

Professional Bowling

The Professional Bowlers Association (PBA) was formed in 1958, with 33 members. The next year, 1959, the PBA's first tour traveled to three cities for prize money of $49,500. Today, there are 3,600 members who compete in 30 tour stops for nearly $8 million in prize money.

The pro tour's Triple Crown consists of the PBA National Championship (held in February), the U.S. Open (formerly called the All-Star Tournament; held in early April), and the General Tire Tournament of Champions (late April). No bowler has ever won all three in the same year, but three bowlers have won them all in a career: Billy Hardwick, Johnny Petraglia, and Pete Weber. The PBA also has a Senior Tour, which had 14 events and offered $2 million in prize money in 1994.

Like the PBA, the Professional Woman Bowlers Association (PWBA) was founded in 1958, but the group went through several name changes. In 1978, the PWBA became the Women Professional Bowlers Association (WPBA). The WPBA folded in 1981 and was replaced by the Ladies Pro Bowlers Tour (LPBT). The LPBT featured 21 events in 1994. The biggest events on the women's tour are the WIBC Queens (in early May), the U.S. Open (late May), and Sam's Town Invitational (November).

PBA Records

Most titles won, season: 8, by Mark Roth, in 1978.

Most titles won, career: 41, Earl Anthony, 1970–83.

CHAMPIONS

The Bowling Writers Association of America (BWAA) has been choosing a Bowler of the Year for men since 1942 and for women since 1948. The PBA began selecting a player of the year in 1963, and the LPBT began selecting a player of the year in 1983, but usually the choices are the same.

MALE BOWLER OF THE YEAR

1995	Mike Aulby
1994	Norm Duke
1993	Walter Ray Williams, Jr.
1992	Dave Ferraro
1991	David Ozio
1990	Amleto Monacelli
1989	Mike Aulby Amleto Monacelli (PBA)

FEMALE BOWLER OF THE YEAR

1995	Tish Johnson
1994	Anne Marie Duggan
1993	Lisa Wagner
1992	Tish Johnson
1991	Leanne Barrette
1990	Tish Johnson Leanne Barrette (LPBT)
1989	Robin Romeo

AWESOME ATHLETE

At age 11, Dede Davidson set the record for best score by a girl in her age group, when she bowled a 299! She followed that up by bowling a 300 game at the age of 16. Dede is now a pro on the LPBT tour.

Most 300 games, season: 7, Amleto Monacelli, 1989; and Walter Ray Williams, Jr., 1993.

High season average: 222.98, Walter Ray Williams, Jr., 1993.

LPBT Records

Most titles won, season: 7, Patty Costello, 1976.

Most titles won, career: 29, Lisa Wagner, 1980–present.

Most 300 games, season: 7, Tish Johnson, 1993.

High season average: 215.76, Tish Johnson, 1993.

Legends

Earl Anthony: Earl won a record 41 career PBA titles, including the PBA National Championship six times, more than any other bowler. In 1975 Earl became the first bowler to win $100,000 in a year, and in 1982 he became the first to surpass $1 million in career prize money. Earl, a left-hander noted for his smooth delivery, was voted Bowler of the Year six times.

Don Carter: Don was almost unbeatable during the 1950's, and in 1970 he was voted by bowling writers as the Greatest Bowler of All Time. He was the first bowler to win the four top tournaments of his time: the All-Star Tournament (now the U.S. Open), the World Invitational, the ABC Masters Championship, and the PBA National Championship. Don, who had a unique bent-elbow delivery, was selected as Bowler of the Year six times.

Marion Ladewig: In 1973 Marion was voted the Greatest Woman Bowler of All Time. Between 1949 and 1963, Marion won the All-Star Tournament eight times and was voted Bowler of the Year nine times, a feat unmatched by any other bowler, man or woman.

Dick Weber: A mailman who became a professional bowler, Dick dominated the sport during the 1960's. In a six-year span, he won four All-Star Tournament titles and was voted Bowler of the Year three times. Called the sport's goodwill ambassador because he traveled the world to promote bowling, Dick won 26 PBA titles during his career. Including the Senior Tour, Dick has won titles in every decade from the 1950's to the 1990's. Dick's son, Pete, is the top career money winner in PBA history.

Glossary

Bedposts: A 7-10 split.

Brooklyn: When a right-handed bowler's ball hits to the left of the headpin, or when a left-handed bowler's ball hits to the right of the headpin.

Cherry: When a front pin is knocked down but doesn't knock down any other pins.

Dead wood: The pins that are knocked down by a first ball and left lying in the lane.

Double: Two consecutive strikes.

Headpin: The front pin in the triangular set of pins. It is also called the 1-pin.

Pocket: The area between the 1-pin and 3-pin for right-handers and the 1-pin and 2-pin for left-handers.

Rack: A setup of 10 pins, ready to be knocked over.

String: A game.

Turkey: Three consecutive strikes.

Where to Write

American Bowling Congress/Women's International Bowling Congress/Young American Bowling Alliance, 5301 South 76th St., Greendale, WI 53129

Professional Bowlers Association, 1720 Merriman Rd., Box 5118, Akron, OH 44334

Ladies Pro Bowlers Tour, 7171 Cherryvale Blvd., Rockford, IL 61112

BOWL-A-RAMA

There are regional forms of bowling that differ from tenpin. **Duckpins**: Duckpin bowling is popular in the eastern United States. It is played on a regular tenpin lane, but the pins are shorter and the ball is smaller and has no holes. A game consists of 10 frames, but bowlers get three rolls per frame. Scoring is the same as in tenpins. Fallen pins are left on the lane when the bowler tries to make a spare. **Candlepins**: Popular in New England, this game is also played on a regular tenpin lane, except that the pins are taller and thinner. Bowlers use a ball that is a little smaller and lighter than a duckpin ball. Bowlers get three rolls each frame. **Lawn bowling**: Very popular in Canada, this game is played on a very smooth grass surface. Players use a small ball and teams compete in trying to roll balls as close as possible to a target ball, known as a *jack ball*. Bocce *(see Other Sports, page 391)* is a form of lawn bowling that began in Italy.

BOXING

Today, boxers face off in front of huge audiences with millions of dollars on the line. Long before that, matches were contested for nothing more than bragging rights over who was the toughest in the land.

History

Boxing's history can be traced back to the ancient Greeks and Romans. Fighters would battle each other with leather straps over their hands until one of them was too hurt to continue. After a while, the Romans outlawed this form of the sport.

The modern style of boxing began in England in the early 1700's, when a man named James Figg opened a school of boxing in London. He taught his students bare-knuckle fighting, in which fighters didn't wear gloves. There were no rounds either. Boxers would fight without rest until one fighter couldn't go on any longer. In 1743, one of the students, Jack Broughton, drew up the first official set of boxing rules. One of the rules stated that a fight was over when one man was knocked down and couldn't get up within 30 seconds.

Boxing's first organized group, the Pugilistic Club, was formed in 1814. In 1838, the London Prize Ring Rules were established. This set of rules was accepted in both the United States and Europe.

By the 1860's, boxers had begun wearing boxing gloves. An English sportsman, the Marquess of Queensbury, came up with a set of 12 rules for the sport. His rules required boxers to wear gloves and called for rounds to be three minutes long, with one minute of rest between each round. The rules also stated that when a man was knocked down, he had 10 seconds to get back up on his feet. With a few changes, these are the rules that

TEXT BY SCOTT WAPNER

Muhammad Ali screams at Sonny Liston after knocking him out in May 1965.

are used today. The last bare-knuckle fight took place in 1889, when the champion, an American named John L. Sullivan, successfully defended his title against Jake Kilrain, in 75 rounds! In 1892, John L., as he was called, fought James "Gentleman Jim" Corbett to decide the heavyweight champion under the new Queensbury rules. John L. was knocked out in the 21st round. Gentleman Jim was successful largely because of a new punch he invented, which was called a *jab*. It was a short, straight punch used to keep the opponent away.

For a time, boxing was illegal in the United States because it was thought to be too brutal. But, in 1920, the U.S. government enacted the Walker Law, which allowed public prizefighting, and boxing quickly became very popular as a spectator sport.

Who Runs Boxing

Boxing has no national or international governing body that controls the sport, sets the rules, or determines the champions. Instead, there are many different regulating bodies that act separately from one another, each choosing its own champion. Most fights are made based on verbal agreements or written contracts between fighters and *promoters*, based on which bout will bring everyone the most money.

The World Boxing Council (WBC), the In-

HOW IT WORKS

A boxer can win a fight in four ways. A *knockout* (KO) happens when one fighter gets knocked down and does not get up within 10 seconds.

A *technical knockout* (TKO) occurs when a fighter is hurt and no longer able to continue. A fight may be stopped by either the referee, ringside doctor, fight official, or even the fighter's own corner.

A *decision* is the result of a fight that goes the scheduled number of rounds with neither fighter getting knocked out. The decision is then up to the three judges who sit at ringside.

A *disqualification* occurs when a referee has to warn a boxer three times for committing such fouls as hitting below the belt, hitting with an open glove, or hitting on the break.

AWESOME ATHLETES

Leon and Michael Spinks were boxing's most successful brothers. Both won gold medals at the 1976 Olympics, Leon as a light-heavyweight and Michael as a middleweight. Both later became world champions. Leon won the heavyweight title in 1977 and Michael won the light-heavyweight title in 1981.

●

Evander Holyfield and Riddick Bowe, back-to-back heavyweight champions of the world, both boxed at the Olympics (Evander in 1984 and Riddick in 1988), but neither won gold medals.

ternational Boxing Federation (IBF), and the World Boxing Association (WBA) are the major organizations in boxing. These groups are responsible for presiding over and *sanctioning* fights. They determine which boxers will be recognized as champions and who the champions must defend their titles against. Often, different organizations recognize different champs *(see Champions, page 89).*

These groups also put out *rankings,* which are lists of the best fighters in all of the weight classes. The rankings are used to match up the fighters.

In addition, each state has an athletic commission, which either approves or rejects the bouts. These commissions also provide licenses to the fighters and make sure that they are in proper physical shape to fight.

In the Corner

A fighter must surround himself with a strong support team to be successful.

The *trainer* is like a coach. He makes sure that the fighter is in shape and knows what he has to do to fight an opponent.

The *manager* oversees the fighter's business interests and tries to find the best opponent for his fighter.

The *promoter* makes the fight happen. He works with arena and television people to set up *bouts* that will be best for the fighter and most appealing to the public. He then tries to create interest in the fight among the public and the media.

A *cut man* works in the boxer's corner during a fight. The *corner* is the area (corner) of the ring in which a boxer sits between rounds and discusses fight strategy with his trainer. The boxer may need a towel or a drink of water, or to have a cut treated. The cut man knows how to stop the bleeding from a cut. A fighter who is bleeding can lose by a technical knockout *(see How It Works, page 83).*

The **basic stance** allows the boxer to move quickly forward and back and side to side. The hands are held high, ready to punch or protect.

The **straight right** is a power punch. The boxer swings his whole right side forward and extends his arm all the way as the punch lands.

The **uppercut** is a short punch, delivered with an upward motion, usually when the boxers are close to each other.

The **left jab** is a punch, delivered with a straight arm and a snap of the left fist. It is used often, to keep an opponent on the defensive.

The **left hook** is thrown with the left arm in an arc from the side.

The **defensive position** is used when a fighter is under attack. The boxer holds his hands up to protect his face and keeps his elbows close together to protect his body.

Equipment

Before his *boxing gloves* are put on, a boxer's hands are wrapped in a soft, cloth-like tape. The gloves are made of soft, cushioned leather, and weigh between 6 and 12 ounces each. They help to protect the fighter's hands as well as the opponent from severe injury. Boxers use gloves with the thumbs attached to the hand. This protects the opponent from getting "thumbed" in the eye.

Boxer shorts (that's how the underwear got its name) are 14-18" long and made of satin. All boxers wear a plastic, protective cup un-

THE PUNCHES

Here are some basic boxing positions and punches (for right-handed fighters; reverse for lefties). Punches are often thrown in combinations, to keep opponents off-balance. The great boxers have the speed, grace, and strength to throw powerful punches while dodging those of their opponents in the ring.

AMAZING FEAT

der their shorts to protect them from low blows. Boxing shoes, which look like boots, are light in weight and made of leather.

Protective *headgear*, made of leather and hard plastic, must be worn by amateurs in all bouts. The pros wear the headgear while training, but are not required to wear it during fights. Most fighers today also wear a plastic *mouthpiece* to protect their teeth.

The Ring

The boxing *ring* is a roped-in stage where the fight takes place. It is 16-20' square for amateur bouts and 16-24' square for professional fights. The ring floor is three to four feet higher than the arena floor. The floor is padded and covered with *canvas*. The corner posts, which hold the *ropes* that surround the ring, are 58" high and also padded.

Rounds

Most professional championship boxing matches are scheduled for 12 rounds. But, it was not always this way. Not long ago, most championship bouts were 15 rounds long.

Each round lasts for three minutes. There is a one-minute rest period in between each round. Amateur fights and Olympic fights are three rounds long.

Golden Gloves

Many boxing champions have come up through Golden Gloves, a competition for amateur boxers. The National Golden Gloves program holds 32 tournaments across the United States. Fighters from age 16 to 32 compete in 12 weight classes for the right to go to the National Golden Gloves championships in April.

Fighters who have been Golden Gloves champions and gone on to become professional world champions include Joe Louis, Muhammad Ali, Thomas Hearns, Michael

Spinks, Sugar Ray Leonard, Mike Tyson, and Evander Holyfield.

The Olympics

Boxing has been part of the Olympic Games since 1904. Olympic boxing has 12 weight divisions, and matches are three rounds long.

Several United States Olympic gold medalists have become professional world champions. They are listed below, along with the year they won in the Olympics and the year they won their first professional title:

- **Cassius Clay**, later Muhammad Ali (1960 Olympic light-heavyweight champion, 1964 world heavyweight champ);
- **Joe Frazier** (1964 Olympic heavyweight, 1968 world heavyweight);
- **George Foreman** (1968 Olympic heavyweight, 1973 world heavyweight);
- **Sugar Ray Leonard** (1976 Olympic light-welterweight, 1979 world welterweight and other titles);
- **Leon Spinks** (1976 Olympic light-heavyweight, 1977 world heavyweight);
- **Michael Spinks** (1976 Olympic middleweight, 1981 world light-heavyweight);
- **Mark Breland** (1984 Olympic welterweight, 1987 world welterweight);
- **Pernell Whitaker** (1984 Olympic lightweight, 1988 world lightweight);
- **Meldrick Taylor** (1984 Olympic featherweight, 1988 world welterweight).

Records

Most wins, professional career: 222, by Young Stribling, from 1921–33.

Most knockouts, career: 145, Archie Moore.

Longest fight (with gloves): 7 hours and 19 minutes, Andy Bowen vs. Jack Burke, 1893.

Shortest fight: 7 seconds, Al Carr vs. Lew Massey, 1936.

TIPPING THE SCALES

Boxers compete against one another depending upon how much they weigh. The pro weight classes are:

Heavyweight: any weight above 195 pounds;

Cruiserweight: up to 195 pounds;

Light heavyweight: up to 175 pounds;

Super middleweight: up to 168 pounds;

Middleweight: up to 160 pounds;

Junior middleweight: up to 154 pounds;

Welterweight: up to 147 pounds;

Junior welterweight: up to 140 pounds;

Lightweight: up to 135 pounds;

Junior lightweight: up to 130 pounds;

Featherweight: up to 126 pounds;

Junior featherweight: up to 122 pounds;

Bantamweight: up to 118 pounds;

Junior bantamweight: up to 115 pounds;

Flyweight: up to 112 pounds;

Junior flyweight: up to 108 pounds.

BLAST FROM THE PAST

Joe Louis of the United States and Max Schmeling of Germany fought two of the biggest fights in history. A lot of tension surrounded their fights because World War II was about to begin. In 1936, Max defeated Joe. But, in 1938, Joe knocked out Max in the first round of their rematch, and the United States helped knock out Nazi Germany in World War II.

Longest fight (without gloves): 6 hours, 15 minutes, James Kelly vs. Jonathan Smith, 1855.

Longest heavyweight reign: 12 years (1937–49), Joe Louis.

Most wins by a heavyweight champion without a defeat: 49, Rocky Marciano.

Legends

Muhammad Ali, U.S.: Ali was the only boxer to win the heavyweight title three different times (1964, 1974, and 1978). He was born Cassius Marcellus Clay, Jr. in Louisville, Kentucky, and was nicknamed the "Louisville Lip" because of his talkative, bragging style. He often said, "I am the greatest!" He was big and fast, and would glide around the ring, teasing his opponents to hit him. One of his handlers said Ali would "float like a butterfly, sting like a bee." Ali's career record was 56–5, with 37 knockouts.

Julio César Chávez, Mexico: A welterweight, Julio has been called the best pound-for-pound fighter in the world because of his amazingly strong, yet small body. He has fought more than 95 times and lost only once.

Jim Corbett, U.S.: "Gentleman Jim" won the first heavyweight championship fight in which gloves were used. He fought only 19 times, and was heavyweight champ from September 1892 to March 1897.

Jack Dempsey, U.S.: The "Manassa Mauler," from Manassa, Colorado, won 62 of his 78 professional bouts, knocking out 25 opponents in the first round! Jack's real name was William Dempsey but he took the name of his older brother, who was also a fighter.

Roberto Duran, Panama: Roberto is called "Hands of Stone." His great punching power has enabled him to win 92 of his 102 career fights. He is a four-time world champion in four different weight classes.

Joe Frazier, U.S.: "Smokin' Joe" was

Champion Rocky Marciano *(right)* gave Joe Louis a pounding when they fought in October 1951.

heavyweight champion from 1970 to 1973. He was one of the hardest punchers ever to enter the ring. His three battles with Muhammad Ali, including the "Thrilla in Manila," are part of boxing legend *(see Great Fights, page 91)*.

Evander Holyfield, U.S.: Evander started out professionally as a light-heavyweight and a cruiserweight. As a heavyweight, he weighed much less than his opponents. Evander first became heavyweight champion in 1990, when he knocked out then-champ James "Buster" Douglas. After losing the title to Riddick Bowe in 1992, Evander came back to defeat Riddick and regain the title in 1993. He then lost the title to Michael Moorer in April 1994.

Jack Johnson, U.S.: Jack was the first African American to win the heavyweight championship, in 1908. But, he wasn't allowed to fight in the United States because he was black. He had to travel to Australia to fight — and defeat — defending champion Tommy Burns of Canada.

"Sugar Ray" Leonard, U.S.: Sugar Ray was quick on his feet and an explosive puncher. A gold medalist at the 1976 Olympics, he captured his first world title just three years later. He won world cham-

CHAMPIONS

HEAVYWEIGHT
BRUCE SEDON (WBA)
FRANK BRUNO (WBC)
CRUISERWEIGHT
NATE MILLER (WBA)
MARCELLO DOMINGUEZ (WBC)
ALFRED COLE (IBF)
LIGHT HEAVYWEIGHT
VIRGIL HILL (WBA)
FABRICE TIOZZO (WBC)
HENRY MASKE (IBF)
SUPER MIDDLEWEIGHT
FRANK LILES (WBA)
NIGEL BENN (WBC)
ROY JONES (IBF)
MIDDLEWEIGHT
JORGE CASTRO (WBA)
QUINCY TAYLOR (WBC)
BERNARD HOPKINS (IBF)
JUNIOR MIDDLEWEIGHT
CARL DANIELS (WBA)
TERRY NORRIS (WBC)
PAUL VADEN (IBF)
WELTERWEIGHT
IKE QUARTEY (WBA)
PERNELL WHITAKER (WBC)
FELIX TRINIDAD (IBF)
JUNIOR WELTERWEIGHT
JUAN MARTIN COGGI (WBA)
JULIO CESAR CHAVEZ (WBC)
KONSTANTIN TSZYU (IBF)
LIGHTWEIGHT
ORZUBEK NAZAROV (WBA)
MIGUEL GONZALEZ (WBC)
PHILIP HOLIDAY (IBF)
JUNIOR LIGHTWEIGHT
GABRIEL RUELAS (WBC)
TRACY PATTERSON (IBF)
FEATHERWEIGHT
ELOY ROJAS (WBA)
MANUEL MEDINA (WBC)
TOM JOHNSON (IBF)
JUNIOR FEATHERWEIGHT
ANTONIO CERMENO (WBA)
HECTOR ACERO SANCHEZ (WBC)
VUYANI BUNGU (IBF)
BANTAMWEIGHT
ALIMI GOITIA (WBA)
HIROSHI KAWASHIMA (WBC)
CARLOS SALAZAR (IBF)
JUNIOR BANTAMWEIGHT
VEERAPHOL SAHAPROM (WBA)
WAYNE MCCULLOUGH (WBC)
MBULELO BOTILE (IBF)
FLYWEIGHT
CHOI HI-YONG (WBA))
SAMAN SORJATURONG (WBC, IBF)
JUNIOR FLYWEIGHT
CHANA PORPAOIN (WBA)
RICARDO LOPEZ (WBC)
RATANAAPOL SOW VORAPHIN (IBF)

QUICK HITS

Angelo Dundee was the trainer of two of the greatest fighters ever: Muhammad Ali and Sugar Ray Leonard. Other legendary trainers include Eddie Futch and Ray Arcel. Eddie has trained 6 heavyweight champions, and 18 champions overall, including Joe Frazier and Michael Spinks. Ray trained 22 champions, from the 1920's until the 1990's.

●

The most famous referee today is Mills Lane, who works days as a judge in the courts of the state of Nevada. Judge Lane has officiated at 71 championship fights, including 15 heavyweight championship bouts.

pionships in a record five weight classes during his career.

Joe Louis, U.S.: The "Brown Bomber" was heavyweight champion of the world from 1937 to 1949, during which he defended his crown a record 25 times. His reign as champ was the longest in boxing history. During World War II, Joe served as a sergeant in the army.

Rocky Marciano, U.S.: The "Brockton Blockbuster" is the only heavyweight champion in history to win all of his professional fights. His 49 victories in 49 fights remains a record today.

Archie Moore, U.S.: Archie was the oldest man (age 49) to hold a world title at any weight. He won the light-heavyweight championship in 1952, and held it for a record nine years. He fought for the heavyweight title twice, but was defeated both times, first by Rocky Marciano and then by Floyd Patterson.

"Sugar Ray" Robinson, U.S.: The original Sugar Ray fought an amazing 201 professional fights, and won 174 of them. He won the world-welterweight title in 1946, and the world-middleweight title in 1951. In 1952, he retired to become a singer/dancer, but two years later he returned to the ring, and won the middleweight title for a third time.

Glossary

Canvas: The floor of a ring.

Card: The scoresheet used by a judge to score a fight. Or, a listing of several fights scheduled to take place at the same place on the same day.

Counterpunch: To punch back while defending yourself against an opponent's punches.

Going the distance: A fight or a fighter lasting the scheduled number of rounds.

Heavy bag: A large stuffed training bag that is usually hung from the ceiling and used by a boxer to develop punching force.

Neutral corner: Either of the two diagonally opposite corners of the ring not occupied by one of the boxers and his handlers between rounds.

Outpoint: To win a decision on points.

Sanction: To recognize as an official fight, possibly with a championship at stake.

Sparring: Practicing against another fighter (sometimes a training partner) in preparation for an upcoming fight.

Speed bag: An inflated, teardrop-shaped punching bag that bounces back quickly when struck. It is hit repeatedly in training to develop speed and coordination.

Split decision: A decision agreed to by a majority, but not all, of the judges.

Standing-eight count: A count up to eight that the referee gives to a boxer when he decides the boxer is on the verge of being injured or knocked out. The referee can stop the bout during the count at any time.

Ten-count: The count from 1 to 10 given to a boxer who has been knocked down. A fighter who cannot get up by the count of 10 is considered knocked out.

Ten-point must system: A scoring system in which the winner of a round is given 10 points and the loser any number less than 10. If the round is scored even, each boxer is given 10 points.

Undercard: The other fights accompanying the main bout on a boxing *card*.

Weigh-in: The official weighing of two boxers who will compete against each other. This is to make sure they weigh no more than the limit for their weight class.

Where to Write

USA Boxing, 1 Olympic Plaza, Colorado Springs, CO 80909

National Boxing Hall of Fame, 1 Hall of Fame Dr., Canastota, NY 13032

GREAT FIGHTS!

Gene Tunney vs. Jack Dempsey, 1927: In the "Battle of the Long Count," Jack knocked down Gene, the heavyweight champion, in the seventh round. But instead of moving to a *neutral corner*, Jack stood over Gene. The referee did not start the 10-count until Jack moved. Finally, after he had been on the canvas for about 16 seconds, Gene got up. He went on to win a decision and retain the title he had won from Jack the year before.

Joe Louis vs. Billy Conn, 1941: Billy, the light-heavyweight champion, bravely traded blows with Joe, the heavyweight champion for most of the fight. But Billy eventually was knocked out, in the 13th round.

Muhammad Ali vs. Joe Frazier, 1975: After splitting their two previous matches, Ali and Joe met in the "Thrilla in Manila" (in the Philippines). The fight was a war for 14 rounds, until a battered and weary Smokin' Joe couldn't answer the bell for the final round.

C ompetitive cycling is a lot more than pedaling as fast as you can. It is a sport of strategy and endurance, too.

BIKER MIGHT

CYCLING

History

The bicycle was invented in the early 1790's. But it didn't resemble today's bike: The wheels were made of solid metal, there were no pedals (it was propelled by pushing with the feet!), and there was no way to steer it. By the mid-1800's, however, pedals and a steering bar were added, which made these contraptions much easier to ride.

In the 1860's, a type of bike called a *velocipede* became popular in Europe. The velocipede's pedals were attached to the front wheel. That meant that the bigger the front wheel, the faster a bicycle would go. Soon, high bikes were being built with huge front wheels, which were 5' 6" high, and tiny rear wheels, which were just 17" high! This made the bikes unstable and difficult to ride.

By the 1880's, bikes stopped getting bigger and started getting better. In this period, there were many technical improvements, such as solid rubber tires instead of metal wheels. Some bikes even had lever-operated, four-speed *gears*.

In 1885, the *safety bike* was introduced. The safety bike had brakes and two wheels that were almost the same size. It was powered by pedals that were attached to the rear wheel by a chain. By the mid-1890's, almost all bicycles were safety bikes. In fact, most of today's modern bicycles use the same basic design as the safety bike.

By the end of the 1800's, millions of people in the United States and Europe were riding safety bikes. It wasn't expensive and it al-

TEXT BY STEPHEN THOMAS

Greg LeMond of the U.S. won the Tour de France in 1986, 1989, and 1990 (above).

lowed people to travel from place to place much more easily than they had before.

People started racing bicycles as far back as the 1860's. They started out racing on roads, although most roads weren't in very good condition in those days. Crowds would gather by the side of the roads to watch a portion of the race. There was a cycling event for men, the individual road race, at the first modern Olympic Games, in 1896. (Women's cycling did not become an Olympic event until 1984.)

Race organizers realized that it would be more exciting for the spectators if they could see the whole race, so they began holding races in enclosed areas. Eventually, indoor tracks (now called *velodromes*) were built. From the early 1900's until the late 1930's, cycling was a popular spectator sport in the United States and Europe.

As the automobile became more popular, people lost interest in cycling as a means of transportation. In the United States, bikes were sold as toys for kids. They didn't become really popular with people for recreation until the 1970's.

On the other hand, cycling remained very popular in Europe, which is where almost all the important road races take place.

YOUR BIKE AND A RACING BIKE

The biggest difference between your bike and a racing bike is weight. No rider wants to pedal any extra weight up a mountain. Many racing bikes are made from *titanium*, a very light, strong, and expensive material. Most street bikes are made of steel.

Today's racing bikes are very sophisticated. Racers will have one bike for *time trials* and one for *road races.* Some time-trial bikes have a very small front wheel, which helps the rider stay in a low, *aerodynamic* position.

Some racing bikes have electronic shifting: All the rider has to do is push one of two buttons, and he can switch *gears.*

What does a bike like this cost? Anywhere from $3,500 to $5,000.

Serious cyclists also wear special shoes that have a cleat on the bottom. The cleat fits into a slot on the pedals, which are called *clipless pedals.*The cyclist can generate more power by keeping his feet attached to the pedals throughout the pedaling motion.

QUICK HIT

Competition

There are two types of bicycle races: *road races*, which are held for both professionals and amateurs; and *track races*, which take place on a banked track, or velodrome, and in which only amateurs compete.

ROAD RACING

In a road race, all contestants start at the same time. Most of the bikes have as many as 16 gears to help the riders with the hills. Men and women compete separately in road races.

There are two kinds of road races: *stage races* and *classics*. Stage races, like the *Tour de France*, can last as long as three weeks and cover more than 2,000 miles. Each day, there is a new race, or stage, but the overall winner of the race is the person who rides all the stages in the least time.

The men's Tour de France started in 1903 and the first women's Tour de France was held in 1984. The Tour du Pont, the most important road race in the United States, is also a stage race.

Classics, like Paris-Roubaix, are one-day races. The world championship, which is held every year, is a one-day race.

Road racing is a team sport. Generally, each team has between six and eight riders, one of whom is the team leader. The other riders are known as *domestiques*, and their job is to protect their leader.

If the leader is feeling tired while racing, the domestiques might surround him and protect him from the wind, making his ride easier. Or if the leader must stop to fix a flat tire, some domestiques will stay with him and help him catch up to the pack of riders (the *peloton*). The domestiques help their leader by breaking the wind for him, pacing him back to the front, or even giving him their bike to ride.

94

Time trials: The time trial, which is ridden both on the roads and on the track, is the hardest race in cycling. It is known as "the race of truth" because the winner is simply the fastest rider.

There is little strategy and no teamwork in time trials. Races are run at varying distances. Cyclists start at one- or two-minute intervals and ride alone over the course. The rider with the fastest time wins.

TRACK RACING

These races are held on a velodrome. Velodromes are steeply banked in order to help riders maintain their speed. They are usually 250 or 333 meters (273 or 364 yards) long. The bikes used in these races have one gear and no brakes.

Men and women compete in separate races. The five kinds of track races are:

Match sprint: Two or three racers compete in the match sprint, which is usually 1,000 meters long. The first one across the finish line wins, and only the final 200 meters of the race is timed.

The match sprint is a very tactical race. Many riders would rather be in second place heading into the final lap so they can *draft*, and slingshot past the leader at the end of the race. Sometimes two riders will come to almost a complete stop on the track, in the hopes of making the other rider take the lead.

Individual pursuit: In this race, two riders start on opposite sides of the track and literally chase each other around the track. A rider wins by either passing his opponent or having the fastest time over the distance of the race. Men's races are four kilometers (2.48 miles) long, women's are three kilometers (1.86 miles).

Team pursuit: Each team is made up of four riders who circle the track in single file.

CHAMPIONS

Here are the recent winners of cycling's biggest events.

1995 TOUR DE FRANCE
Miguel Indurain, Spain

1995 WORLD CHAMPION
Abraham Olano, Spain

1992 OLYMPICS

ROAD RACING CHAMPIONS
Men's 194-kilometer
  Fabio Casatelli, Italy
Women's 81-kilometer
  Kathryn Watt, Australia
TRACK CHAMPIONS
One-kilometer time trial
  Jose Moreno, Spain
Match sprint
  Men: Jens Fiedler, Germany
  Women: Erika Salumae,
    Estonia
Individual Pursuit
  Men (4,000-meter):
    Chris Boardman,
    Great Britain
  Women (3,000-meter):
    Petra Rossner, Germany
Men's Team Pursuit
  (4,000-meter): Germany
50k points race
  Giovanni Lombardi, Italy
100k team time trial
  Germany

BLAST FROM THE PAST

In the 1890's, indoor cycling races were so popular that race promoters wanted to come up with new races to draw fans. So they thought up six-day races, during which riders pedaled for as long as they could, rested a bit, and pedaled some more. In 1898, Charlie Miller rode 2,093.4 miles in six days, and some of his competitors collapsed from exhaustion. The next year, teams of two riders rode for six days. Six-day races were pretty much gone by 1940, although they made a brief comeback in the 1960's. Today's big endurance race is the Race Across America — 2,910 miles, from Irvine, California, to Savannah, Georgia.

The rules for the team pursuit are the same as for individual pursuit. The winning team is determined when the third rider of the team crosses the finish line, or when the third rider draws even with the other team's third rider. The men's race is four kilometers; women do not compete in this event.

Points race: The points race is usually between 15 and 50 kilometers. Every third or fifth lap is a sprint, and points are awarded to the first four riders. In addition, the final lap is a bonus lap, and the points awarded are doubled. The rider who accumulates the most points wins the race.

One-kilometer time trial: This is the most difficult race for the riders; it is sometimes called the "killermeter." There are individual and team events.

In the individual race, one rider at a time tries to ride one kilometer as fast as possible. The fastest time wins. In the team event, a group of four riders works together to ride as fast as possible. Throughout the race, different riders take turns riding in front, pacing the team.

Legends

Bernard Hinault, France: Bernard was known as the Badger because he was such a tough rider. He won five Tours de France, and he was one of only a few riders to win the three most important stage races during his career: the Tour de France (1978, '79, '81, '82, '85), the Tour of Spain (1978, '83), and the Tour of Italy (1980, '82, '85).

Greg LeMond, U.S.: In 1986, Greg became the first American to win the Tour de France. He missed the 1987 and 1988 Tours due to serious injury, but came back to win in 1989 and 1990. Greg is also a two-time world champion.

Jeanne Longo, France: Many people consider Jeanne the greatest women's cyclist ever. She has won four world championships on the road and four on the track. In 1989, Jeanne won her third straight women's Tour de France.

Eddy Merckx, Belgium: Eddy may have been the greatest cyclist ever. He was a strong time-trial rider, a strong climber, and he could out-sprint most riders. From the late 1960's until the mid-1970's, he won the Tour de France and the Tour of Italy five times each, and was world champion three times. In 1974, Eddy won the Tours of France, Italy, and Spain. Only three other riders have ever done that in the same year.

Glossary

Aerodynamic: Riding in such a way that you cut through the air with as little wind resistance as possible.

Drafting: An important part of racing strategy, this is when a cyclist rides directly behind another rider, allowing the leader to block the wind. Without the wind in his face, the drafting rider can move quickly without having to work so hard, saving energy for a big push later in the race.

Gear: One of a group of small, toothed wheels located on the rear wheel of the bicycle. By shifting gears, the rider changes how easy or hard it is to turn the pedals. This helps him go fast on flats and downhills, and makes climbing hills easier.

Peloton: The large pack of riders who ride close together in a race.

Tribars: Handlebars designed by a triathlete in the 1980's, they help the rider maintain an *aerodynamic* position.

Where to Write

U.S. Cycling Federation, 1750 East Boulder, Colorado Springs, CO 80909

U.S. Bicycling Hall of Fame, 166 West Main St., Somerville, NY 08876

MOUNTAIN BIKING

The mountain bike was invented in California in the mid-1970's by Charlie Kelly and Gary Fisher, cyclists who wanted to do more than just ride on paved streets. Today, mountain bikes are the most popular bikes around.

Professional mountain bike races for men and women are held all over the world. There are three important events. The *downhill* event is run just like the downhill skiing event: A rider rides down a course as quickly as he can. The fastest time wins. The *cross-country* event is run over a rough mountain course. In the *dual slalom*, two competitors ride side by side down two courses. The biker with the fastest overall time after two runs wins.

There is a racing season, and competitors receive points based on how well they finish in races. The point leaders for 1993 were Greg Herbold and Penny Davidson in downhill, David Wiens and Juli Furtado in cross-country, and Mike King and Kim Sonier in dual slalom.

DIVING

Diving is a kind of flying gymnastics — in which the athletes land in a pool. Not surprisingly, it was gymnasts who invented the sport!

HIGHER, FASTER

Off the 10-meter platform, divers travel at a speed of around 35 miles per hour before entering the water.

●

The highest dive ever was 176' 10" inches, by Oliver Favre at Villers-le-lac, France, in 1987. He dove off a cliff in order to break the high-dive record.

History

One of the most graceful of all sports, diving was first developed in the 1600's in Germany and Sweden. Gymnasts went to the beach to practice their moves and flips over the water because it was safer if they fell.

In the late 1800's, diving developed into a sport, rather than just a practice exercise for gymnasts. In 1893 in England, diving became popular when the plunging championships were established. The plunge was a headfirst crouching dive. It remained popular until 1947 (see Blast from the Past, page 102).

Diving, as we know it, became an Olympic sport at the 1904 Olympic Games in St. Louis, Missouri. Divers from Germany and Sweden dominated the early Olympic events.

Diving in the United States owes much to two men: Ernst Bransten and Mike Peppe. Ernst came to the U.S. from Sweden in the 1920's, and shared the Swedish diving techniques with the Americans. Mike coached at Ohio State University in the early 1930's and produced a number of national college champions. Because of these two men, diving became a popular sport in the United States.

How It's Done

Two types of diving are performed in national and international meets: *springboard* and *platform*. Both refer to the surface from which the competitor dives.

Springboard: A springboard is a diving board. A triangular support piece (called a *fulcrum)* under one end of the board lets the

TEXT BY SCOTT WAPNER

There are five basic groups of dives for both platform and springboard competition.

Forward: In a forward dive, the diver faces the water. Dives may vary from a simple front dive to a four-and-a-half somersault.

Back: In a back dive, the diver starts at the end of the board or platform with his back to the water.

Reverse: The diver takes off facing the water, then does a back half-somersault to enter the water, headfirst, facing the board or platform.

Inward: The diver starts in the same position as for a back dive. He then jumps up and out and turns toward the board or platform, to enter the pool facing the water.

Twisting: A twisting dive can be any forward, back, inward, or reverse dive with a twist between the *takeoff* and the *entry*.

Greg Louganis of the U.S. won Olympic gold in both springboard and platform diving in 1984 and 1988.

other end of the board bounce under the weight of the diver. This allows the diver to jump high off the board and perform complex maneuvers in the air.

Springboard was the form of diving at the 1904 Olympics. Springboard meets are competed on boards that are 16' long, 20" wide, and either 1 or 3 meters (about 3' or about 10') above the water. The board is mounted on the side of the pool so that it extends about 6' out over the water.

Platform: Platform diving was added to the Olympics in 1908. In platform, a diver jumps from a fixed surface that offers no bounce at all. Instead, the platform is high above the water so that the diver has lots of air space to do his moves. The platform commonly used is 10 meters (about 33') off the ground and is reached by ladder. Diving platforms must be at least 20' long and 6' 6" wide. The water in the pool is usually 16–18' deep.

Parts of a Dive
Approach: In a forward dive, the approach

COOL FACT

At the 1928 Olympics, the most difficult dive performed was a forward 1 ½ somersault with a full twist off the three-meter board. Today that dive is considered simple. The toughest springboard dive at the 1992 Olympics was the reverse 3 ½ somersault. Divers can do more somersaults today because springboards, which used to be made of wood, are now made of aluminum. This gives divers more spring, thus more height and time to do more somersaults.

must be smooth and straight. The diver should take no fewer than three steps before what is called the *hurdle*. The hurdle is the point of the approach when both feet hit the board at the same time. A diver loses points from the judges if he takes fewer than three steps.

Takeoff: The takeoff from the board or the platform must be from both feet at the same time. If the diver is performing a back takeoff (with his back to the water), he may not lift his feet from the board before takeoff. In platform diving, divers sometimes use an *arm-stand takeoff*, in which the diver starts the dive by doing a handstand at the end of the platform.

Elevation: The height that a diver gets will greatly affect the success of a dive. A higher jump normally gives the diver a better chance to perform a dive successfully.

Execution: A diver's technique, timing, and form, together called the *execution*, must be correct or the judges will deduct points from his score.

Entry: This is the moment when the diver enters the water. The diver should have his toes pointed as he enters the water. He wants to make as small a splash as possible.

Competition

Men and women compete separately, but they perform the same dives and are scored in the same way. The number of dives is different, however. In national and international springboard meets, men must perform a series of 11 dives in the preliminary and final rounds. These include 5 required dives and 6 optional dives. Women must perform 10 dives, including 5 required and 5 optional.

Men and women must perform one required and one optional dive from each of the five groups of acceptable dives (*see Types of Dives, page 99*). The men's sixth optional dive

Half-twist (straight)

Forward 1 ½ (tuck)

Inward (pike)

TAKING THE PLUNGE

All dives may be performed in one of three basic positions: *straight, pike,* or *tuck.*

Straight: The straight position allows no bending at the waist or knees.

Pike: In the pike position, the legs are straight and the body is bent at the waist.

Tuck: The tuck position requires that the body be bent at both the waist and the knees. The diver's thighs are pulled tight to the chest, and the heels are close to the buttocks.

A diver can also choose a *free* position, which includes one or more of the above three positions.

can be from any class.

In national and international platform meets, men perform four required and six optional dives, while the women perform four required and four optional dives.

Each diver's program is selected by the diver and his coach from 82 springboard and 87 platform dives recognized by the International Diving Federation, the governing body of the sport.

BLAST FROM THE PAST

One of the earliest diving competitions was the British plunging championships. The plunge was a headfirst crouching dive. Once in the water, the diver was to float motionless and face downward as far up the pool as possible within a minute. Fat men were particularly good at this sport. Plunging was popular from 1893 until 1947, and was even included as part of the diving competition in the 1904 Olympics.

Scoring

A panel of five to seven judges (seven in the Olympics) gives each dive a score of 0–10 points. The highest and lowest scores are tossed out, and the remaining three or five scores are added up. That total is then multiplied by ⅗, or .6. To get the dive's final score, that figure is multiplied by a number assigned each dive based on its difficulty. This is called the *degree of difficulty* of the dive; the harder the dive, the higher the number. The degree of difficulty can be from 1.1 to 3.5.

For example, let's say a diver does a dive with a degree of difficulty of 3.0 and receives scores of 5-5-5-6-3-4-4. The numbers 6 and 3 are thrown out, and the remaining scores are added up (23), then multiplied by .6 (to get 13.8). That number is multiplied by 3.0 (degree of difficulty) to get a final score of 41.4 for the dive. The diver with the highest total score for all of his dives wins the competition.

Big Events

Diving is regulated by the same governing body as swimming, the Federation International de Natation Amateur (FINA). Most countries hold major national championships each year.

In the United States, there are two annual national championships, one indoor and one outdoor. Another major competition is the HTH Classic, also held annually. At the Classic, the top members of the U.S. national team compete against each other.

Besides the Summer Olympics, the most important international competitions are the world championships, Goodwill Games, and Pan American Games. They all are held every four years (but not in the same years). A World Cup diving competition is held every two years, with three events each for men and women.

Records

Most Olympic medals: 5, by Klaus Dibiasi of Italy in 1968, 1972, and 1976; and Greg Louganis of the U.S. in 1976, 1984, and 1988.

Most Olympic medals, country: 122, United States.

Most world championships: 5, Greg Louganis, United States.

Legends

Greg Louganis, U.S.: Greg is the greatest American diver ever. He won 4 gold medals and 1 silver in Olympic competition. He also won 5 world championships and 47 national titles in his career. From 1982–87, Greg won 19 consecutive international competitions. He was the first male diver ever to win both the Olympic springboard and platform events in two Olympics in a row (1984 and 1988).

Pat McCormick, U.S.: Pat was the first female diver to win both Olympic diving events twice in a row (1952 and 1956). She also won three international championships and 26 national titles.

Mark Lenzi, U.S.: At the 1992 Olympic Games, Mark won the only U.S. diving gold medal, in springboard. Mark has won two World Cup titles, seven national titles, and a Pan American Games gold medal.

Klaus Dibiasi, Italy: Klaus was Europe's most successful diver ever. He won the men's platform gold medal in three straight Olympic Games from 1968 to 1976. He also won two Olympic silver medals, in platform in 1964 and in springboard in 1968.

Where to Write

United States Diving Association, Pan American Plaza, Suite 430, 201 South Capitol Ave., Indianapolis, IN 46225

International Swimming Hall of Fame, 1 Hall of Fame Dr., Fort Lauderdale, FL 33316

CHAMPIONS

Here are the Olympic gold medalists from the past three Summer Games. The United States and China have been the teams to beat in men's and women's diving. Fu Mingxia, the 1992 platform champion, won her gold when she was 12 years old!

MEN

Springboard

1992	Mark Lenzi, U.S.
1988	Greg Louganis, U.S.
1984	Greg Louganis, U.S.

Platform

1992	Sun Shuwei, China
1988	Greg Louganis, U.S.
1984	Greg Louganis, U.S.

WOMEN

Springboard

1992	Gao Min, China
1988	Gao Min, China
1984	Sylvie Bernier, Canada

Platform

1992	Fu Mingxia, China
1988	Xu Yanmei, China
1984	Zhou Jihong, China

FIGURE SKATING

Skating began in ancient times, when people discovered that they could move across ice by tying animal bones to their feet. That slow, sliding movement turned into figure skating, one of the most graceful sports in the world.

History

The word *skate* comes from the German word "schake," which means leg bone. The practice of moving across ice on animal bones probably dates back to the prehistoric hunters of what is now northern Europe. The earliest known reference to skating for recreation is 1175, when some residents of London, England, "skated" with polished animal bones attached to their boots, using sticks to push themselves along.

Gradually, better skates were invented, which resulted in better skaters. The world's first skating club was formed in Edinburgh, Scotland, in the early 1700's. The first club in the United States was established in 1849 in Philadelphia, Pennsylvania.

Originally, figure skating consisted mostly of rigid, robot-like routines. It was more scientific than artistic. Skaters traced patterns — like the "figure eight" — slowly on the ice.

But an American named Jackson Haines changed the sport into a stylish version of ballet on ice, using music and colorful costumes. Jackson was a ballet dancer from New York City. He toured Europe in 1864 to popularize his "international style" of skating, which became accepted around the world.

Figure skating became an Olympic sport in 1908, before the Olympics were split into winter and summer competitions in 1924.

Equipment

It is likely that the first skates with iron blades attached to wooden soles appeared in

TEXT BY BRAD HERZOG

Sonja Henie won three Olympic gold medals, the first when she was just 15 years old.

There are nine judges at figure skating competitions. Each judge rates a skater from 0 to 6 according to this scale:

0 = did not skate
1 = very poor
2 = poor
3 = average
4 = good
5 = excellent
6 = perfect

Decimal points are used, so a skater might score 4.9 or 5.6.

Many people believe that the high and low scores for each skater are dropped and that all the marks are added together. That is not true. Instead, the scores from each judge are compared. The skater who receives the highest mark from a particular judge is placed first by that judge. The skater who receives the most first-place rankings is the winner.

the Netherlands in the 1200's or 1300's. Because iron is stronger than bone, skaters could push themselves without using sticks.

During the mid-1800's, iron blades were replaced by steel, which stayed sharper longer. Soon after, Jackson Haines created the first *single-unit skate* (a blade screwed to the sole of a boot).

Figure skates are different from hockey skates and speed skates. Figure skates have a higher top, to provide ankle support during jumps. The skate blade is ⅛" thick and about 12" long, which is much shorter than the blade of a speed skate.

Unlike the blades on other skates, the blade of a figure skate also has several teeth at the front, called a *toe pick*. This helps skaters perform jumps and spins. (The skater uses the toe pick to get better height on jumps and to stop.) In addition, the blade has

an inside edge and an outside edge. Competitors skate on one edge at a time.

Competition

Fifty countries belong to the International Skating Union (ISU), which governs international figure skating. The ISU supervises competition at the world championships, the world junior championships, the European championships, and the Winter Olympics.

Each country oversees competition at the national level through its own organization. The United States Figure Skating Association was formed in 1921. There are competitions at eight different skill levels: preliminary, juvenile, intermediate, novice (two levels), junior (two levels), and senior.

Each senior competition features four different types of figure skating: men's singles, women's singles, pair skating, and ice dancing. Ice dancing first became an Olympic sport in 1976. The other three figure skating divisions were part of the first Olympic program in 1908. Two less common forms of figure skating are *precision skating* (teams performing movements in unison) and *fours* (a combination of two pairs).

SINGLES

In top-level skating competition, the rules for singles events are similar for both the men's and women's divisions. The competition is divided into two parts: a technical or *original* program and a *free skating* program.

The technical program, also called the short program, includes eight required moves (three jumps, three spins, and two footwork moves). Each skater selects his or her own music and performs the moves in any order in a routine of 2 minutes and 40 seconds.

In the free skating program, also called the long program, the men skate for 4 ½ minutes and the women skate for 4 minutes. There

Triple Axel: The only jump that takes off from the forward position. The skater leaps off one foot, spins three and half times, and lands on the opposite foot, skating backward.

Triple Toe Loop: The skater slides backward on a curve, jumps off both feet, turns three times, and lands on one foot, continuing in the direction of the curve.

Triple Lutz: After approaching backward, the skater makes three full turns in the opposite direction of the original curve and lands on the takeoff foot gliding backward.

are no required elements, and the skaters choose their own music and theme. They try to display their technical and artistic skills by *choreographing* the different moves into their program. Judges look at the skaters' creativity, how they present their program, and the difficulty of the moves they choose to perform.

In both programs, judges award two marks.

THE JUMPS

The jump is the most exciting part of skating. Skaters have become more acrobatic. Single or double jumps (two turns in the air) have given way to triple and quadruple jumps. Some of the more difficult jumps are shown above.

107

COOL FACTS

Hayes and David Jenkins are the only two brothers to have won Olympic figure skating gold medals. Hayes won the singles title in 1956, and David won it in 1960. The duo combined for eight straight national titles from 1953 to 1960.

●

Hayes Jenkins and Carol Heiss are the only Olympic singles gold medalists to marry each other. Carol won the women's singles in 1960, and the pair were married later that year.

Skaters are judged on *technical merit* (how well each move is performed) and *artistic impression* (an evaluation of the entire program). The free skate counts for two thirds of a skater's total score and the technical program counts for one third.

For many years, the singles events at figure skating competitions included a part called the *compulsory*, or *school, figures.* Skaters would carefully trace patterns on the ice to show their control, balance, and precision.

In 1990, the ISU voted to eliminate compulsory figures from the singles competition. It is still occasionally done as a separate event.

PAIR SKATING

Pair skating first appeared in Vienna, Austria, in the late 1880's. Partners danced together on the ice, but in those days they were often two men or two women. Today, pair skating includes one man and one woman.

Pair skating is both beautiful and athletic. The partners perform many difficult moves in unison, as well as dangerous lifts and throws. Pair skating has similar scoring and time limits to singles skating.

The required elements in pair skating's technical program include overhead lifts, *synchronized* solo spins, side-by-side solo jumps, pair spins, and footwork. The free skate may include daring double and triple solo jumps, throw jumps, and many types of original lifts and spins *(see Lifts, page 113).*

ICE DANCING

Ice dancing is different from pair skating. Rules limit the types of lifts and jumps ice dancers may use and the amount of time they may skate apart from each other. Instead, ice dancing emphasizes rhythm, musical interpretation, creativity, and precise steps. It is less athletic but more theatrical than pairs.

An ice dancing competition is made up of four parts: two compulsory dances (each worth 10 percent of the final score), a two-minute original dance (30 percent), and a four-minute free dance (50 percent). In the compulsory dances, each pair performs specific dance routines, such as a tango or a waltz. Because teams perform the same dances, the judges may easily compare them. Skaters receive a technical merit mark for each dance.

In the original dance, the skaters are again given a specific rhythm to follow, but this time they design an original version of the dance. In the free dance, skaters have four minutes to display all their skills and create any mood. They may design any dance to any rhythm. In both dances, skaters are scored on technical merit and artistic impression.

Records
WOMEN
Most U.S. championships won: 9, by Maribel Vinson.

Most world championships won: 10, Sonja Henie, Norway.

Most Olympic gold medals won: 3, Sonja Henie, Norway

MEN
Most U.S. championships won: 7, Roger Turner and Dick Button.

Most world championships won: 10, Ulrich Salchow, Sweden.

Most Olympic gold medals won: 3, Gillis Grafström, Sweden.

Professionals
Many champion figure skaters turn professional after their competitive careers are over. They earn money by coaching other skaters, skating in professional competitions, and joining ice shows, such as the "Ice Capades" and "Walt Disney World on Ice."

Until 1993, skaters who turned profession-

GREAT SKATES!
Tenley Albright at the 1956 Olympics: While practicing right before the Games, Tenley struck a hole in the ice. As she fell, the edge of the blade on her left skate cut through her right boot, severing a vein and scraping a bone. Tenley still competed, and became the first American woman to win an Olympic gold medal.

Torvill and Dean at the 1984 Olympics: Skating to the music of *Bolero*, by Maurice Ravel, these British ice dancers performed a bold routine that ended with them both throwing themselves onto the ice like lovers leaping to their death. They were awarded six 5.9's and three 6.0's for technical merit and nine 6.0's for artistic impression!

Battle of the Brians, 1988 Olympics: Brian Boitano of the U.S. had been world champion in 1986 and would be again in 1988. Brian Orser of Canada had been world champion in 1987. At the Games, both skated to military music. Brian B. put on the show of his life to edge Brian O. for Olympic gold.

AWESOME ATHLETES

At the women's singles competition at the 1994 Olympics, two young women overcame great obstacles to battle for the gold medal. Oksana Baiul suffered a collision in practice the day before the finals and needed stitches in her right leg. Nancy Kerrigan of the United States was hit on the knee with a club by an attacker a month earlier at the U.S. championships. Both Nancy and Oksana skated beautifully, but the judges awarded the gold to Oksana by one of the slimmest margins in Olympic figure skating history.

al were banned from Olympic competition. But that year many former gold medalists, such as Brian Boitano and Katarina Witt, were reinstated by the ISU in time to prepare for the 1994 Games.

Legends

Tenley Albright, U.S.: Tenley overcame polio as a child to become the first American woman to win the world championship (in 1953) and an Olympic gold medal (in 1956). She also won five U.S. championships. After winning her last national title, she gave up skating and became a surgeon.

Oksana Baiul, Ukraine: Oksana was an orphan at age 13. She overcame a difficult life to win the world championship in 1993 at the age of 15 and the Olympic gold medal in 1994 at 16.

Brian Boitano, U.S.: Brian was the first man ever to land a triple *Axel* in competition. He won four U.S. championships and two world titles, as well as the 1988 Olympic gold medal. After turning professional, Brian returned to the Olympics in 1994, where he finished sixth in the men's singles competition.

Dick Button, U.S.: In 1943, at age 16, Dick became the youngest U.S. men's champion ever (at age 16). He won the national title seven times and the world title five times. In 1948, he became the first American skater to win an Olympic gold medal. He won another four years later. Dick pioneered an athletic and acrobatic style of skating. He was the first to do a double Axel and a triple loop in competition *(see The Jumps, page 107)*. Today, he is a TV commentator for skating events.

Peggy Fleming, U.S.: Peggy was a graceful skater who made difficult moves look easy. In 1964, when she was just 15, Peggy became the youngest person ever to win the U.S. championship. She went on to win five

Kristi Yamaguchi struck Olympic gold in women's singles in 1992.

national titles, three world titles, and an Olympic gold medal in 1968.

Dorothy Hamill, U.S.: In 1976, Dorothy earned a skating triple crown by winning a U.S. championship, a world championship, and an Olympic gold medal. Thousands of girls copied her famous "wedge" haircut. She also invented her own spin, now known as the Hamill *camel.* She and her husband run the Ice Capades, which they once owned.

Scott Hamilton, U.S.: Scott was sickly as a child, but he overcame his poor health to win four straight national and world titles from 1981 to 1984. Scott believed male skaters should dress like athletes, so when he skated in the 1984 Olympics, he wore a plain stretch suit rather than the glittery costumes most men wore until then. The 5' 3" skater won the gold medal and changed the way men dressed for competition.

Carol Heiss, U.S.: Carol won five straight world titles from 1956 to 1960 and four straight national titles from 1957 to 1960. In 1959, she won the U.S. championship, while her sister, Nancy, was second. In 1960, Carol won an Olympic gold medal.

Sonja Henie, Norway: Sonja first skated in the Winter Olympic Games in 1924 when she was just 11 years old. She finished last in the women's singles events, but went on to become the sport's only three-time Olympic champion. She won the gold medal

CHAMPIONS

In Olympic competition, the United States has won 31 medals in singles figure skating, more than any other country. The former Soviet Union (and the countries it broke up into) have won the pairs gold medal at every Olympics since 1964, and all but one gold medal in ice dancing from 1976-94. Here are the winners from the 1994 Olympics.

MEN'S SINGLES

Gold: Alexei Urmanov, Russia
Silver: Elvis Stojko, Canada
Bronze: Philippe Candeloro, France

WOMEN'S SINGLES

Gold: Oksana Baiul, Ukraine
Silver: Nancy Kerrigan, U.S.
Bronze: Chen Lu, China

PAIRS

Gold: Ekaterina Gordeeva and Sergei Grinkov, Russia
Silver: Natalia Mishkoutienok and Artur Dmitriev, Russia
Bronze: Isabelle Brasseur and Lloyd Eisler, Canada

DANCE

Gold: Oksana Gritschuk and Evgeni Platov, Russia
Silver: Maia Usova and Alexander Zhulin, Russia
Bronze: Jayne Torvill and Christopher Dean, Great Britain

AMAZING FEATS

Maribel Vinson Owen was one of America's greatest skaters, winning nine national titles between 1928 and 1937. When her skating career was over, she became one of the country's best skating coaches. One of her pupils was Tenley Albright, the first American woman to win a world championship and an Olympic gold medal. Unfortunately, Maribel's life ended tragically. On February 15, 1961, Maribel and 16 other members of the U.S. skating team, including her daughters, were killed in a plane crash in Brussels, Belgium.

in 1928, 1932, and 1936, as well as 10 world championships. Sonja was one of the world's most famous athletes when she retired in 1932. She went on to star in her own ice show and in American movies.

Nancy Kerrigan, U.S.: Nancy finished third in the U.S. championships in 1991, second in 1992, and first in 1993. She won a bronze medal at the 1992 Olympics. In January of 1994, just before the national championships, a man attacked her and injured her knee. Nancy couldn't compete, but she was named to the Olympic team anyway. At the 1994 Olympics, she won a silver medal.

The Protopopovs, Soviet Union: Oleg and Ludmila Protopopov were probably the greatest Soviet pair skaters. They won the Olympic gold medal in 1964 and 1968. They focused on the beauty and artistry of pair skating, turning it from an athletic event to a combination of grace and skill.

Torvill and Dean, England: Jayne Torvill and Christopher Dean changed ice dancing with their technical perfection and the imaginative way they interpreted music on the ice. In 1981, they became the first non-Russian couple since 1969 to win the world championship. They went on to win three more and the 1984 Olympic gold medal. They added a bronze medal at the 1994 Olympics.

Katarina Witt, Germany: Beautiful Katarina received 35,000 fan letters and dozens of marriage proposals after winning the Olympic gold medal for East Germany at the 1984 and 1988 Olympics. Only she and Sonja Henie have repeated as women's singles gold medalists. A four-time world champion, she turned professional but returned to the Olympics in 1994, finishing seventh.

Kristi Yamaguchi, U.S.: In 1989 and 1990, Kristi was part of a national champion pairs duo, as well as being a national singles silver medalist. In 1991, she won the world singles championship for the first time, and in 1992 she won an Olympic gold medal.

Glossary

Axel: The only jump made as the skater moves forward. In a single Axel, a skater jumps off one foot, turns 1 ½ times in the air, and lands on the back outside edge of the opposite foot, skating backward. (In a triple Axel, the skater spins 3 ½ times.) The jump is named for Axel Paulsen, who introduced it in the early 1900's.

Camel spin: A spin in which one leg is extended out and up.

Choreography: The combining of required skating moves with the skater's choice of music.

Grand slam: When a skater (or pair) wins all the major competitions in one skating season, such as the nationals, the worlds, and the Olympics.

Lutz: A difficult jump in which the skater begins by skating backward on a curve, jumps, and makes a full turn in the opposite direction of the original curve, and lands gliding backward. It is named for Alois Lutz, who first completed the jump in 1918.

Presentation: Also known as artistic impression, it is the way a skater choreographs his or her program to interpret the music and incorporate various moves.

Salchow: A basic jump, in which the skater, moving backward, jumps off one foot, makes a full turn in the air, and lands on the other foot. It is named after skater Ulrich Salchow, the 1908 Olympic gold medalist.

Synchronized: Making the same moves at the same time, as pair skaters do.

Where to Write

U. S. Figure Skating Association/Figure Skating Hall of Fame and Museum, 20 First St., Colorado Springs, CO 80906

LIFTS

In ice dancing, the man is not allowed to lift the woman over his head. But lifts are a very important part of pair skating. In pairs, the man may not only lift his partner over his head but even throw and catch her. Here are some common lifts:

Hand-to-hand loop lift: The man raises his partner above his head. She is facing in the same directon as he is, in a sitting position with her hands behind her.

Hydrant lift: The man throws the woman over his head while skating backward, turns to face the other way, and catches her facing him.

Lateral twist: The man throws the woman over his head. She rotates once, parallel to the ice, before she is caught.

Platter lift: The man raises his partner over his head with his hands on her hips, while she is parallel to the ice.

Toe overhead lift: The man swings his partner from one side of his body, around behind his head, and up into the air, holding her in a split position. Wow!

FLYING DISK

The first flying disk was actually an empty pie plate, made by the Frisbie Pie Company of New Haven, Connecticut.

OUT OF THE PARK

Top flying-disk players can toss a disk more than 400'. That's the distance from home plate to the center-field fence in many major league baseball parks.

History

In the early 1920's, students at Yale University began playing catch with tin pie plates made by a local pie company. Soon, the game of *Frisbee*, or flying disk, caught on.

The modern flying disk was developed by Fred Morrison in 1948. His disk was made of plastic and called the Flying Saucer. Soon afterward, the Wham-O Manufacturing Company of San Gabriel, California, bought the patent and began producing Fred's disk.

Games and Rules

Many games can be played with a flying disk. One of the most popular is *ultimate Frisbee*, or Frisbee football. Ultimate Frisbee was invented at Columbia High School in Maplewood, New Jersey, in 1967. The first match between two colleges was in 1972 when Rutgers faced off against Princeton.

The game is played by two teams of seven players on a field 60 yards long by 40 yards wide, with a 30-yard end zone on each side. The object is to move the flying disk down the field and into the end zone by passing it from teammate to teammate.

Guts is a game for two teams of one to five players each. The object is to pass the disk over the goal line into the scoring zone. If the disk is thrown so hard that the receivers cannot catch it, the throwers get a point.

In *freestyle Frisbee*, teams perform routines to music while throwing and catching a flying disk. They are scored on execution, difficulty, variety, and presentation.

TEXT BY SCOTT WAPNER

Ultimate Frisbee is part of the World Flying Disk Championships and World Ultimate Championships.

There is also *Frisbee golf*, played on a golf course, with each hole ending when the disk hits a certain pole on the green. In *double disk court*, two teams with two players each play with two disks. You try not to have both disks in your court at once. *Discathlon* players throw their disks while running around a twisting one-kilometer course.

Big Events

While flying disk is not included in the Olympic Games, it does have major international competitions. These are the annual U.S. Flying Disk Open, the World Junior Frisbee Disk Championships (for kids ages 15 and under), and the World Ultimate Championships (which includes other disk events).

The World Flying Disk Federation in Sweden holds the World Flying Disk Championships each year.

Where to Write

World Flying Disk Federation, Gnejsvagen 24, 853 57 Sundsvall, Sweden

Wham-O Manufacturing Co., 835 East El Monte St., San Gabriel, CA 91778

HOW TO PLAY

Here are three ways to throw a disk, and five ways to catch one.

Backhand: The thumb should be on top of the disk, and the index finger under the rim. The ring finger and pinkie should be curled back against the rim. Start by extending the arm toward the target. Bring your arm back and then extend it, releasing the disk when your arm is fully extended.

Sidearm: Hold the disk with your thumb on top and your index and middle fingers below. Your wrist should be tilted backward. To throw, swing your arm down at a 30-degree angle and snap your wrist forward.

Overhand: Hold the disk with your thumb underneath and fingers on top. Tilt your wrist backward. Swing your arm forward at shoulder level. Snap your wrist at the point of release.

Catches: There are five that can be used: between the legs, behind the head, behind the back, finger catch, and tipping. Tipping is when the Frisbee is tapped lightly in the center just before it is caught.

FOOTBALL

Football is often thought of as war. As in military battles, the object is to gain possession of the enemy's territory. Teams blitz and throw the bomb. They use speed, strength, and strategy to win.

History

The sport Americans call football began as a game played mostly with the feet — 25 to 30 players on each team trying to kick a ball across the opponent's goal line. The first organized football game was this soccer-like game. It was played in New Jersey on November 6, 1869, between Princeton University and Rutgers University. Rutgers won, 6–4.

As rugby became popular in North America, football began to look more like that sport. Players picked up the ball and ran with it until they were tackled. The first game of *this* type of football was played in 1874, when a team from McGill University, in Canada, visited Harvard University. The game ended in a scoreless tie.

Many colleges, especially in the Northeast, favored the rougher game. Leading the way in creating rules for the game was Walter Camp, a former player at Yale who became known as the "Father of American Football."

During the late 1880's, Mr. Camp came up with changes that made football the sport we know today. These included having 11 players per side, a system of *downs* and *yards to gain*, and the *center snap*.

Having downs and yards to gain meant the field had to be marked with yard lines. Using the center snap instead of the rugby *scrum* let the offense run set plays and use strategy.

In the early 1900's, football was still played mainly by colleges. Running, blocking, and tackling were rough stuff, and protective equipment was not yet worn. Players were

TEXT BY DAVID FISCHER

The greatest running back in football history, Jim Brown never missed a game in his pro career.

getting injured so often that, in 1905, President Theodore Roosevelt asked that the game be made safer.

The next year, football introduced the forward pass, with the idea that it would spread the players over the field. At first, teams ignored this new play. It was not until 1913, when Notre Dame beat Army thanks to several long passes to end Knute Rockne, that the forward pass became an acceptable offensive strategy. Modern football was born.

Scoring

Points in football are scored four ways: *touchdown, point after touchdown, field goal,* and *safety.* When the offense runs or passes the ball across the opponent's goal line, it is a touchdown (TD). A touchdown is worth six points. The defense can also score a touchdown by running an interception or a fumble into the end zone *(see Turnovers, page 123).*

After a touchdown, the placekicker attempts the point after touchdown (PAT), or *conversion.* This is also called the *extra point,*

HOW TO PLAY

The object of football is to score a touchdown by running or passing the ball over the opponent's goal line. The team that scores the most points wins.

Professional and college football games are 60 minutes long; high school games last 48 minutes. A game is divided into two halves, and each half is divided into two quarters. After each quarter the teams change direction.

The field is 100 yards long by 53 ½ yards wide. Each end zone is 10 yards long. On the back line of the end zone are two goalposts 18 ½' apart connected by a crossbar 10' off the ground.

The field is marked with solid white yard lines every five yards and yard numbers every 10 yards. Short dotted white lines, called *hash marks,* mark each yard. The hash marks form two rows of lines parallel to the sideline, near the center of the field. After a play, the ball is placed on the nearest hash mark. That keeps the ball near the center of the field.

AWESOME ATHLETES

Dallas Cowboy running back Emmitt Smith made history in 1992 by becoming the first player to win the rushing title and the Super Bowl in the same season. Emmitt and the Cowboys did it again in 1993 and in 1996!

●

Opposing quarterbacks don't have a prayer against Reggie White. The defensive lineman for the Green Bay Packers leads the lead in career sacks. He has made 157 sacks in 168 games — that's almost a sack a game! No wonder Reggie, who is also a Baptist preacher, is called the "Minister of Defense."

because it is worth one additional point. The ball is placed on the two-yard line and snapped back eight yards to the *holder*, who catches the ball and places it on its tip. The placekicker must kick the ball over the crossbar and between the goalposts. A team may also try a two-point conversion. The ball is placed on the three-yard line and, if the offense can run or pass the ball over the goal line successfully, it scores another two points.

If the offense moves the ball deep into its opponent's territory, it may try to kick a *field goal*. The placekicker kicks the ball from seven to eight yards behind the line of scrimmage, over the crossbar, and through the goalposts. A field goal is worth three points.

A *safety* is only scored by the defense and counts for two points. The defense earns a safety by tackling an offensive player who has the ball in his own end zone.

The Players

Professional and college teams have separate offensive and defensive teams — that is, players who play only on offense, and players who play only on defense. At other levels, players play both on offense and defense.

At the start of each play, the offense and defense face each other along the *line of scrimmage*. This is an imaginary line that marks the spot where the last play ended.

THE OFFENSIVE TEAM

The offensive team consists of the *offensive linemen*, *backfield*, and *receivers*.

The offensive linemen are usually five big and strong players who line up along the scrimmage line. These are the *center*, two *guards*, and two *tackles*. Their main job is to block on running plays and passing plays. The center also snaps the ball, through his legs, back to the quarterback to start the play. Offensive lineman are usually the

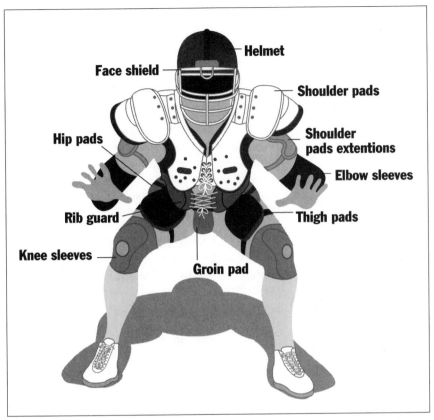

Helmet

Face shield

Shoulder pads

Shoulder pads extentions

Hip pads

Elbow sleeves

Rib guard

Thigh pads

Knee sleeves

Groin pad

biggest players on the team. Some pro offensive linemen weigh more than 300 pounds.

The *backfield* consists of the *quarterback* and the *running backs*. The quarterback is the offense's leader. He calls the *signals*, a code that tells his teammates what the play is. He can run with or *pass* (throw) the ball, or *hand off* to a running back.

The running backs stand about five yards behind the quarterback. Running backs run with the ball and must be strong and fast. However, they can also catch passes. Sometimes, one of the running backs is called a *fullback* and the other is called a *halfback*. The fullback is normally a good blocker. The halfback is usually a faster runner.

The receivers, called *wide receivers* or *split*

UNDER-GEAR

Football players wear protective equipment to help prevent injury. Each player wears a <u>helmet</u> to protect his head. A <u>chin strap</u> holds the helmet securely. The helmet has a <u>face mask</u> to protect the face. Teeth can be protected with a <u>mouthpiece</u>.

Under his jersey, a player wears <u>shoulder pads</u>, which also extend down to protect the chest. Under the pants are <u>hip pads</u>, <u>thigh pads</u>, and <u>knee sleeves</u>. The pads are filled with urethane foam.

COOL FACTS

Although a football is sometimes called a pigskin, it is really made of four pieces of leather stitched over a rubber lining, which is where the air goes in. A football is 11" long and 7" wide in the middle. When filled with air, it weighs 14–15 ounces (slightly less than one pound).

●

The football field is often called a *gridiron*, because the pattern of the lines looks like a cooking griddle that meat is broiled on.

ends, stand along the scrimmage line but a few yards away from the linemen. They are fast runners who catch passes thrown by the quarterback. Often, another receiver, called the *tight end*, is used. He lines up like a blocker but can also catch passes.

OFFENSIVE STRATEGY

The offense tries to move the ball down the field toward the opponent's goal line. The offense has four *downs* (plays) in which it must gain at least 10 yards. If a first-down play gains, say, 5 yards, then the next play situation would be second down and 5 yards to go. Gaining at least 10 yards gives the offense a new first down and four more plays.

Before each play, the offense will *huddle* together in a circle to call a play. Each play has been planned and practiced before the game. The offensive team then lines up along the line of scrimmage in *formation*, which is how it will be positioned for this play. The offense must have seven men on the scrimmage line.

The play starts when the center snaps the ball to the quarterback. At that moment, the offense and defense may make contact.

If the play is a running play, the quarterback can run with the ball himself or hand off or *pitch* (toss) the ball to a running back. The runner may follow his blockers around either end or up the middle.

If the play is a passing play, the blockers will form a *pocket*, or semi-circle, in front of the quarterback, to protect him from the defensive linemen while he throws the ball.

To throw a forward pass, the quarterback must be behind the scrimmage line. The pass can only be thrown to an *eligible receiver* — a player who is allowed to catch passes. These are usually the wide receivers, running backs, or tight end.

The receivers run specific *pass patterns*. A pass attempt that is caught is a *completed*

The Super Bowl trophy is named for coach Vince Lombardi *(left)*.

pass. A pass attempt that is not caught is *incomplete.* If the offense does not gain 10 yards after three plays, it can try to gain the needed yardage on fourth down or *punt* (kick) the ball away to its opponent *(see Special Teams, page 122).* If a team "goes for it" and doesn't pick up the yardage, the other team takes over where the play is stopped.

THE DEFENSIVE TEAM

The defensive team consists of the *defensive linemen, linebackers,* and *secondary.* The defensive linemen are usually four players, called the *front four*: two *tackles* and two *ends.* On passing plays, the defensive linemen rush the quarterback, trying to *sack* (tackle) him behind the scrimmage line for a loss of yardage. On running plays, the linemen hope to tackle the ballcarrier.

The linebackers are usually three players: a middle linebacker and two outside linebackers. Linebackers line up three to five yards behind the linemen. They usually make the most tackles on a team, because they defend against the run and the pass. Linebackers are very strong and also run fast.

The *secondary,* or *defensive backfield,* is made up of the *defensive backs*: two *cornerbacks* and two *safeties.* Each cornerback lines up on the scrimmage line, directly opposite a wide receiver. The safeties play 10 to 15 yards deeper to protect against the long pass.

The main job of defensive backs is to cover

HOW IT WORKS

In all, seven officials work a game, each with his own job.

The *referee,* who stands about 10 yards behind the quarterback, is the final authority on the rules and gives signals on penalties. The *umpire,* positioned five yards behind the defensive line, is responsible for watching for scrimmage line violations.

The *head linesman* stands on the sideline at one end of the scrimmage line. He marks where the ball is to be placed after each play and keeps track of the downs and the yards needed for a first down.

The *line judge* stands opposite the head linesman and is the official timekeeper. The *back judge, side judge,* and *field judge* all stand downfield watching for penalties on pass plays.

121

AWESOME ATHLETES

pass receivers, but if a running back slips past the linemen and linebackers, they are the defense's last chance to make the tackle.

DEFENSIVE STRATEGY

The job of the defense is to stop the offense from gaining a first down. The defense described above is called the "4-3 defense": four down linemen and three linebackers.

Some teams, however, play a "3-4 defense": three down linemen and four linebackers. In this defense, the three linemen consist of a *nose tackle* and two ends, and the four linebackers consist of two inside linebackers and two outside linebackers.

The secondary may play a *man-to-man* defense or a *zone* defense. In a man-to-man defense, a defensive back is assigned to cover a particular receiver. In a zone defense, he is responsible only for a receiver in his assigned area of the field.

If the offensive team has a very talented receiver, like a Jerry Rice, then the secondary may put a cornerback and a safety on him and use *double coverage*. When the defense knows the offense will try a long pass, it may substitute an additional safety for a linebacker or a lineman.

SPECIAL TEAMS

When one team has to kick or punt the ball to the other, the *special teams* go to work.

The *kickoff* starts each half, and a team also kicks off after it scores points. (A coin toss determines which team will kick off first to start the game.) The kickoff is from the 30-yard line in the pros, and from the 35-yard line in college and high school.

The ball is placed on a rubber or plastic *tee* so that it stands up on its point. The members of the kicking team spread out in a line, and when the ball is kicked they run downfield and try to make the tackle. The receiving team is scattered about the field to block for the *return* man, who waits near the goal line to catch the ball.

If the kick travels beyond the end zone, it is ruled a *touchback*, and the receiving team takes over on offense at the 20-yard line. If the return man catches the kick, he can run until he's tackled. At that spot, his team starts on offense.

If the offense is forced to punt the ball on fourth down, the *punter* comes in. He stands about 15 yards behind the line of scrimmage, takes the snap, and punts the ball by dropping it on his instep as he swings his leg. Pro punters usually kick the ball 35 to 40 yards past the line of scrimmage.

When the ball is kicked or punted, the kicking team runs down the field to try to tackle the returner. A punt returner may call for a *fair catch*, meaning he is allowed to catch the ball without being hit, but cannot try to run with the ball. If he tries to return the punt, the spot where he is tackled is where his team begins on offense.

Turnovers

A turnover is a mistake by the offensive team that gives the ball to the defense. It can be a *fumble* or an *interception.*

A fumble occurs when the ball is knocked loose from the ballcarrier before he goes down. If the defense *recovers* the fumble, it goes on offense at that spot. However, if a defender is able to scoop up the fumble, he may run with it until he is tackled.

An interception is when a defensive player catches a pass intended for a receiver. A defender who has made an interception may run with the ball until he is tackled.

Penalties

If a player breaks the rules, a penalty is called by an official. The official signals this

NFL TEAMS

AFC

East Division
  Buffalo Bills
  Indianapolis Colts
  Miami Dolphins
  New England Patriots
  New York Jets

Central Division
  Cincinnati Bengals
  Cleveland Browns
  Houston Oilers
  Jacksonville Jaguars
  Pittsburgh Steelers

West Division
  Denver Broncos
  Kansas City Chiefs
  Los Angeles Raiders
  San Diego Chargers
  Seattle Seahawks

NFC

East Division
  Dallas Cowboys
  New York Giants
  Philadelphia Eagles
  Phoenix Cardinals
  Washington Redskins

Central Division
  Chicago Bears
  Detroit Lions
  Green Bay Packers
  Minnesota Vikings
  Tampa Bay Buccaneers

West Division
  Atlanta Falcons
  Carolina Panthers
  Los Angeles Rams
  New Orleans Saints
  San Francisco 49ers

AMAZING FEATS

Tom Flores and Mike Ditka are the only people to have won Super Bowl rings as a player, assistant coach, and head coach.

●

Marcus Allen and Roger Staubach are the only players to win the Heisman Trophy in college, the NFL Player of the Year award, and the Super Bowl MVP award.

by throwing a *flag* made of yellow cloth into the air. Teams that commit penalties are punished with a loss of yardage and, in some cases, the loss of a down.

Most penalties occur during a play. When the play ends, the official announces what the penalty is and gives the team that has not committed the violation the choice of accepting or declining the penalty. If the penalty yardage is more than the yards gained on the play, the team will usually accept.

Some common penalty calls are holding, offsides, pass interference, and clipping. *Holding* is called against a blocker who uses his hands to grab an opponent. It results in a 10-yard loss. *Offsides* is called when a player crosses the line of scrimmage before the ball is snapped. It is a 5-yard penalty. If a pass receiver is bumped, pushed, or tackled while attempting to catch the ball, *pass interference* is called. This is a costly penalty, because the offense gets the ball and a first down at the spot of the foul. *Clipping* is a 15-yard penalty for an illegal block from behind.

Professional Football

The first professional football game was played on August 31, 1895, when the Latrobe YMCA beat the Jeannette Athletic Club 12–0. In the early days of pro football, college players played for their school on Saturday and then played for a pro team on Sunday.

Many pro football leagues came and quickly went. But in 1920, the 14-team American Professional Football Association (APFA) was formed at a meeting in Canton, Ohio. Legendary player Jim Thorpe was named president. Two years later the APFA changed its name to the National Football League (NFL).

The NFL

In the beginning, the NFL was not as popular as college football. But in 1925, former college star Red Grange joined the NFL's Chicago Bears (formerly the Decatur Staleys) and large crowds came to see his spectacular touchdown runs. The NFL was beginning to get the public's attention.

Each season, the team with the best regular-season record was named champion of the league. In 1933, at the urging of Bear owner George Halas, the NFL split its 10 teams into two divisions and held its first championship game. That game was won by the Bears over the New York Giants, 23–21. The first draft of college players was held in 1936. Teams selected players in reverse order of finish.

In 1946 a rival league, called the All-America Football Conference (AAFC), began play with eight teams. The Cleveland Browns, coached by Paul Brown, dominated the AAFC, and won four championships. Three AAFC teams — Cleveland, the Baltimore Colts, and the San Francisco 49ers — joined the NFL in 1950 after the AAFC went out of business. The Browns won the NFL title in their first year in the league.

In 1950, the Los Angeles Rams became the first NFL team to have all of its games broadcast on television. Television played an important role in the NFL's increasing popularity during the 1950's.

In 1960, another professional league of eight teams, called the American Football League (AFL), was formed. The NFL and the AFL competed separately until the 1966 season, when the two leagues agreed to play a championship game, later to be called the Super Bowl (*see Cool Facts, page 130*). Led by coach Vince Lombardi, the Green Bay Packers beat the Kansas City Chiefs, 35–10, in the first Super Bowl.

In 1970, the NFL and AFL merged to become one league, dividing into two conferences, the National Football Conference (NFC) and the American Football Conference

GREAT GAMES!

The 1958 NFL Championship Game: Called "The Greatest Game Ever Played," the title game between the Baltimore Colts and the New York Giants ended in a 17–17 tie, forcing the first *sudden-death overtime* to decide a league champion. After 8 minutes and 15 seconds, Colt fullback Alan Ameche scored on a one-yard plunge for a 23-17 Colts victory.

Super Bowl III: The matchup for the January 12, 1969 game didn't seem fair. The Baltimore Colts of the NFL were picked to beat the New York Jets of the AFL by two or three touchdowns. So when Jet quarterback Joe Namath guaranteed victory for his team, everybody laughed. But Joe delivered on his promise and led the Jets to a 16–7 upset triumph.

The Greatest Comeback in NFL History: In the January 3, 1993 AFC wild-card playoff game, the Buffalo Bills trailed the Houston Oilers, 35–3, in the third quarter. The Bills rallied to beat the Oilers, 41–38, in overtime.

BLASTS FROM THE PAST

On October 7, 1916, the most lopsided game in football history was played between Georgia Tech and Cumberland College. Georgia Tech destroyed Cumberland by the score of 222–0! Georgia Tech scored 63 points in the first quarter, 63 more in the second quarter, 54 in the third, and 42 in the fourth!

●

The most lopsided game in NFL history was a championship game. In the 1940 NFL title game, the Chicago Bears demolished the Washington Redskins 73–0!

(AFC). Today, each conference has three divisions: East, Central, and West.

The NFL consists of 30 teams, having added two in 1995: the Carolina Panthers, in Charlotte, North Carolina, and the Jacksonville Jaguars, in Jacksonville, Florida. Each team plays 16 games. The three division winners and two *wild-card* teams (second-place finishers with the best record) from each conference make the playoffs.

The playoffs are a single-elimination tournament (if a team loses, it's out of competition). The winners of the NFC and AFC Championship Games meet in the Super Bowl to play for the Vince Lombardi Trophy. Following the Super Bowl, the league's best players compete in the Pro Bowl, an all-star game played every year in Hawaii.

NFL Records

SCORING

Most points scored, game: 40, by Ernie Nevers of the Chicago Cardinals, on November 28, 1929.

Most points scored, season: 176, Paul Hornung, Green Bay Packers, 1960.

Most points scored, career: 2,002, George Blanda, 1949–75.

Most touchdowns scored, game: 6, done three times; most recently by Gale Sayers of the Chicago Bears, December 12, 1965.

Most touchdowns scored, season: 24, John Riggins, Washington Redskins, 1983.

Most touchdowns scored, career: 156, Jerry Rice, San Francisco, 1985–95.

PASSING

Most yards passing, game: 554, Norm Van Brocklin, Los Angeles Rams, September 28, 1951.

Most yards passing, season: 5,084, Dan Marino, Miami Dolphins, 1984.

Most yards passing, career: 47,003, Fran Tarkenton, 1961–78.

In 1924, football teams, like the Columbus (Ohio) Panhandles, wore helmets without face masks.

Most consecutive passes completed: 22, Joe Montana, San Francisco 49ers, 1987.

Most touchdown passes, game: 7, done five times; most recently by Joe Kapp of the Minnesota Vikings, September 28, 1969.

Most touchdown passes, season: 48, Dan Marino, Miami Dolphins, 1984.

Most touchdown passes, career: 342, Fran Tarkenton, 1961–78.

Most consecutive games throwing a touchdown pass: 47, John Unitas, Baltimore Colts, 1956–60.

RUSHING

Most yards rushing, game: 275, Walter Payton, Chicago Bears, November 20, 1977.

Most yards rushing, season: 2,105, Eric Dickerson, Los Angeles Rams, 1984.

Most yards rushing, career: 16,726, Walter Payton, Chicago Bears, 1975–87.

Most rushing touchdowns, game: 6, Ernie Nevers, Chicago Cardinals, November 28, 1929.

Most rushing touchdowns, season: 24, John Riggins, Washington Redskins, 1983.

Most rushing touchdowns, career: 110, Walter Payton, Chicago Bears, 1975–87.

CANADIAN FOOTBALL LEAGUE

Football is also very popular in Canada. The Canadian Football League (CFL) has 12 professional teams: 8 in Canada and 4 in the United States (Las Vegas Posse, Shreveport Pirates, Sacramento Goldminers, and Baltimore Stallions).

Canadian football is played by 12 men per side instead of 11. The extra man is usually in the backfield on offense and in the secondary on defense. The offense has only three downs to make a first down. And the playing field is large — 160 yards long by 65 yards wide.

The Canadian version of the Super Bowl is called the Grey Cup, which has been played since 1909. Here are the past five winners.

1995	Baltimore Stallions
1994	British Columbia Lions
1993	Edmonton Eskimos
1992	Calgary Stampeders
1991	Toronto Argonauts

AWESOME ATHLETE

Dallas Cowboy running back Tony Dorsett dashed 99 yards for a touchdown against the Minnesota Viking defense in 1983. It was the longest run from scrimmage in NFL history. The record might someday be equaled, but it can never be broken.

RECEIVING

Most receptions, game: 18, Tom Fears, Los Angeles Rams, December 3, 1950.

Most receptions, season: 122, Cris Carter, Minnesota Vikings, 1994.

Most receptions, career: 934, Art Monk, Washington Redskins, N.Y. Jets 1980–94.

Most consecutive games with a reception: 180, Art Monk, Washington Redskins, 1980–1993, N.Y. Jets 1994.

Most touchdown receptions, game: 5, done three times; most recently by Jerry Rice, San Francisco 49ers, October 14, 1990.

Most touchdown receptions, season: 22, Jerry Rice, San Francisco 49ers, 1987.

Most touchdown receptions, career: 156, Jerry Rice, San Francisco 49ers, 1985–present.

Most consecutive games with a touchdown reception: 13, Jerry Rice, San Francisco 49ers, 1986–87.

Most receiving yards gained, game: 336, Willie "Flipper" Anderson, Los Angeles Rams, November 26, 1989.

Most receiving yards gained, season: 1,746, Charley Hennigan, Houston Oilers, 1961.

Most receiving yards gained, career: 14,004, James Lofton, 1978–93.

DEFENSE

Most sacks, game: 7, Derrick Thomas, Kansas City Chiefs, November 11, 1990.

Most sacks, season: 22, Mark Gastineau, New York Jets, 1984.

Most sacks, career: 157, Reggie White, 1985–present.

Most interceptions, game: 4, done 16 times; most recently by Deron Cherry, Kansas City Chiefs, September 29, 1985.

Most interceptions, season: 14, Dick "Night Train" Lane, Los Angeles Rams, 1952.

Most interceptions, career: 81, Paul Krause, 1964–79.

SPECIAL TEAMS

Longest field goal: 63 yards, Tom Dempsey, New Orleans Saints, November 8, 1970.

Most field goals, career: 373, Jan Stenerud, 1967–85.

Longest punt: 98 yards, Steve O'Neal, New York Jets, September 21, 1969.

Longest punt return for a touchdown: 98 yards, done four times; most recently by Terance Mathis, New York Jets, November 4, 1990.

Longest kickoff return for a touchdown: 106 yards, done three times; most recently by Roy Green, St. Louis Cardinals, October 21, 1979.

The Super Bowl

The powerful Green Bay Packers of the NFL won the first two Super Bowls. They were led by coach Vince Lombardi and quarterback Bart Starr, the MVP of both games.

When the AFL's New York Jets won Super Bowl III *(see Great Games!, page 125)*, the new league showed that it was good enough to merge with the NFL. The AFC then won 9 of the next 11 Super Bowls.

In the 1970's, Don Shula coached the Miami Dolphins to two Super Bowl victories. The Pittsburgh Steelers, with running back Franco Harris, receiver Lynn Swann, and quarterback Terry Bradshaw, won four. The Dallas Cowboys, led by quarterback Roger Staubach, gave the NFC its only two Super Bowl victories during this decade.

The NFC has dominated Super Bowl play from the 1980's to today. The San Francisco 49ers won four times, led by Joe Montana, who earned a record three MVP awards. The Washington Redskins won three Super Bowls using three different quarterbacks! The New York Giants had two wins, and the Troy Aikman–Emmitt Smith combination gave the

SUPER BOWL CHAMPIONS

The past 10 Super Bowls have been won by NFC teams. Here are the past 10 winners and AFC champions. (Super Bowls are referred to with Roman numerals. The game is played in January of the year following the season.)

XXX (1996)
Dallas Cowboys
XXIX (1995)
San Francisco 49ers
XXVIII (1994)
Dallas Cowboys
XXVII (1993)
Dallas Cowboys
XXVI (1992)
Washington Redskins
XXV (1991)
New York Giants
XXIV (1990)
San Francisco 49ers
XXIII (1989)
San Francisco 49ers
XXII (1988)
Washington Redskins
XXI (1987)
New York Giants

AFC CHAMPIONS

1995	Pittsburgh Steelers
1994	San Diego Chargers
1993	Buffalo Bills
1992	Buffalo Bills
1991	Buffalo Bills
1990	Buffalo Bills
1989	Denver Broncos
1988	Cincinnati Bengals
1987	Denver Broncos
1986	Denver Broncos

COOL FACTS

The first two Super Bowls were actually called the AFL-NFL Championship Game. Lamar Hunt, the owner of the Kansas City Chiefs of the AFL, got the idea to name the game the Super Bowl from his children's favorite toy: the Super Ball. The term *Super Bowl* became official with Super Bowl III.

●

The price of a ticket to the first Super Bowl, in 1967, was $12. The best seat in the house for Super Bowl XXX, in January 1996, cost $350!

Cowboys Super Bowl wins in 1993 and 1994.

Super Bowl Records

PASSING

Most touchdown passes, game: 5, Joe Montana, San Francisco 49ers, Super Bowl XXIV (January 28, 1990).

Most touchdown passes, career: 11, Joe Montana, San Francisco 49ers, four games.

Most yards passing, game: 357, Joe Montana, San Francisco 49ers, Super Bowl XXIII (January 22, 1989).

Most yards passing, career: 1,142, Joe Montana, San Francisco 49ers, four games.

RUSHING

Most touchdowns rushing, game: 2, done 10 times; most recently by Emmitt Smith, Dallas Cowboys, Super Bowl XXVIII (January 30, 1994).

Most touchdowns rushing, career: 4, Franco Harris, Pittsburgh Steelers, 4 games.

Most yards rushing, game: 204, Timmy Smith, Washington Redskins, Super Bowl XXII (January 31, 1988).

Most yards rushing, career: 354, Franco Harris, Pittsburgh Steelers, four games.

RECEIVING

Most receptions, game: 11, Jerry Rice, San Francisco 49ers, Super Bowl XXIII (January 22, 1989); and Dan Ross, Cincinnati Bengals, Super Bowl XVI (January 24, 1982).

Most receptions, career: 27, Andre Reed, Buffalo Bills, four games.

Most yards receiving, game: 215, Jerry Rice, San Francisco 49ers, Super Bowl XXIII (January 22, 1989).

Most yards receiving, career: 364, Lynn Swann, Pittsburgh Steelers, four games.

Other Professional Leagues

There have been several other attempts to start pro football leagues. The World Football

Johnny Unitas threw a touchdown pass in a record 47 straight games.

League began in 1974, but it folded the next season. The United States Football League (USFL) was formed to play in the spring instead of the fall, when football is traditionally played. The USFL existed from 1983–85.

The Arena Football League was formed in 1987 as an indoor league playing on a 50-yard field. In 1996, it has 15 teams playing a season that runs from April until September.

In 1990, the NFL sponsored the formation of the 10-team World League of American Football (WLAF), which included teams in Europe, where American-style football has become popular. The WLAF now has six teams that play only in Europe from April to June.

College Football

There are minor differences between the NFL and college football. In college football, the hash marks are slightly closer to the middle of the field and the goalposts are wider apart. The most significant difference in the college game had been the two-point conversion *(see Scoring, page 117)*. However, the NFL will add a two-point conversion in 1994.

College sports are governed by the National Collegiate Athletic Association (NCAA) and the National Association of Intercollegiate Athletics (NAIA). There are about 700 col-

BOWL GAMES

Several bowl games offer automatic berths to the champions of certain conferences. But the sponsors of the bowl games always try to line up the best teams in the country. The Rose, Orange, Cotton, and Sugar Bowls tend to get the best games. Here are the winners for the past five years.

Rose Bowl
1996	Southern California
1995	Penn State
1994	Wisconsin
1993	Michigan
1992	Washington

Orange Bowl
1996	Florida State
1995	Nebraska
1994	Florida State
1993	Florida State
1992	Miami

Sugar Bowl
1996	Virginia Tech
1995	Florida State
1994	Florida
1993	Alabama
1992	Notre Dame

Cotton Bowl
1996	Colorado
1995	Southern California
1994	Notre Dame
1993	Notre Dame
1992	Florida State

QUICK HITS

The University of Oklahoma Sooners, coached by Bud Wilkinson, won a record 47 games in a row from 1953–57. The longest *losing* streak belongs to Columbia University, which dropped 44 straight from 1983–88.

•

The University of Southern California has won the most Rose Bowls, with 20. The University of Oklahoma has won the most Orange Bowls, with 11.

leges that field football teams. The largest play NCAA Division I-A competition.

Most teams belong to a *conference* in their part of the country. They play their regular-season games against other teams in the conference. Those that are not in a conference are called *independents*, and play against other independents around the country.

After the season, which usually lasts 11 games, the teams with the best records are invited to play in the *bowl games*. There are 18 bowl games. The oldest ones are the Rose Bowl (1902) and the Orange Bowl (1933).

College Football Records

SCORING

Most touchdowns scored, game: 8, by Howard Griffith of Illinois, on September 22, 1990.

Most touchdowns scored, season: 39, Barry Sanders, Oklahoma State, 1988.

Most touchdowns scored, career: 65, Anthony Thompson, Indiana, 1986–89.

PASSING

Most passing touchdowns, game: 11, David Klingler, Houston, November 17, 1990.

Most passing touchdowns, season: 54, David Klingler, Houston, 1990.

Most passing touchdowns, career: 121, Ty Detmer, Brigham Young, 1988–91.

Most yards passing, game: 716, David Klingler, Houston, December 1, 1990.

Most yards passing, season: 5,188, Ty Detmer, Brigham Young, 1990.

Most yards passing, career: 15,031, Ty Detmer, Brigham Young, 1988–91.

RUSHING

Most yards rushing, game: 396, Tony Sands, Kansas, November 23, 1991.

Most yards rushing, season: 2,628, Barry Sanders, Oklahoma State, 1988.

Most yards rushing, career: 6,082, Tony Dorsett, Pittsburgh, 1973–76.

Dick Butkus terrorized quarterbacks as a linebacker for the University of Illinois and the Chicago Bears.

Most rushing touchdowns, game: 8, Howard Griffith, Illinois, September 22, 1990.

Most rushing touchdowns, season: 37, Barry Sanders, Oklahoma State, 1988.

Most rushing touchdowns, career: 64, Anthony Thompson, Indiana, 1986–89.

RECEIVING

Most receptions, game: 23, Randy Gatewood, UNLV, September 17, 1994.

Most receptions, season: 142, Emmanuel Hazard, Houston, 1989.

Most receptions, career: 266, Aaron Turner, Pacific, 1989–92.

Most touchdown receptions, game: 6, Tim Delaney, San Diego State, November 15, 1969.

Most touchdown receptions, season: 22, Emmanuel Hazard, Houston, 1989.

Most touchdown receptions, career: 43, Aaron Turner, Pacific, 1989–92.

Most yards receiving, game: 363, Randy Gatewood, UNLV, September 17, 1994.

NATIONAL CHAMPIONS

Division I-A football does not have a championship tournament, so the selection of which team is Number 1 is often a matter of opinion. The Associated Press polls sportswriters for their choice. Some newspapers and TV networks also have polls.

The other NCAA divisions play a national championship tournament and their champion is the winner of that competition. Here are all the NCAA champs of the past five seasons.

DIVISION I-A
1995	Nebraska
1994	Nebraska
1993	Florida State
1992	Alabama
1991	Miami

DIVISION I-AA
1995	Montana
1994	Youngstown State
1993	Youngstown State
1992	Marshall University
1991	Youngstown State

DIVISION II
1995	North Alabama
1994	North Alabama
1993	North Alabama
1992	Jacksonville State
1991	Pittsburg State

DIVISION III
1995	Wisconsin-La Crosse
1994	Albion
1993	Mount Union
1992	Wisconsin-La Crosse
1991	Ithaca College

BLASTS FROM THE PAST

The Heisman Trophy is named after John Heisman, the coach who led Georgia Tech to the national championship in 1917. The winner of the first Heisman Trophy in 1935 was Jay Berwanger, a halfback from the University of Chicago. The only player to win the Heisman Trophy twice is Archie Griffin, running back at Ohio State, who won in his junior and senior seasons of 1974 and 1975. Notre Dame has had more Heisman Trophy winners, seven, than any other school.

Most yards receiving, season: 1,779, Howard Twilley, Tulsa, 1965.

Most yards receiving, career: 4,357, Ryan Yarborough, Wyoming, 1990–1993.

SPECIAL TEAMS RECORDS

Longest field goal: 67 yards, done three times; most recently by Joe Williams, Wichita State, October 21, 1977.

Most field goals, career: 80, Jeff Jaeger, Washington, 1983–86.

Longest punt: 99 yards, Pat Brady, Nevada, 1950.

Longest punt return for touchdown: 100 yards, done seven times; most recently by Richie Luzzi, Clemson, September 28, 1968.

Longest kickoff return for touchdown: 100 yards, done 166 times; most recently by Fred Montgomery, New Mexico State, November 9, 1991.

Legends

Doc Blanchard and Glenn Davis: "Mr. Inside" and "Mr. Outside" led Army to three consecutive undefeated seasons from 1944–46 and national championships in 1944 and 1945. Doc won the Heisman Trophy in 1945, and Glenn won it in 1946.

Jim Brown: Jim was the greatest running back ever. In nine seasons with the Cleveland Browns, from 1957–65, Jim never missed a game. By the time he retired, he held just about every rushing record. Jim played when the season was only 12 games long, and many of his records have since been broken. But his eight rushing titles and career average of 5.22 yards per carry still stand.

Paul "Bear" Bryant: The Bear coached at three other colleges during his career, from 1945–82, but it was at Alabama that he compiled the majority of his 323 wins, the most among Division I-A coaches. His Alabama teams won 6 national titles, 15 bowl games, and had 4 undefeated seasons.

Emmitt Smith led the Cowboys to two straight Super Bowl wins.

George Halas: Between 1920 and his death in 1983, "Papa Bear" served the Chicago Bears as owner, coach, and player! He coached the Bears for 40 years and won seven NFL titles. When he retired in 1967, his 324 wins were the most by any coach. He remained owner of the Bears until his death.

Leon Hart: Leon was the last lineman to win the Heisman Trophy, which he did in 1949. The Notre Dame end was a member of three national championship teams. In his four years with the Fighting Irish, they never lost a game. Later, he helped the Detroit Lions win three NFL titles.

Vince Lombardi: In his nine seasons as head coach of the Green Bay Packers, Vince led the Packers to five NFL championships, including victories in Super Bowl I and II. Known for his dedication to winning above all else, Vince had a career winning percentage of .736, the best in NFL history.

Joe Montana: Joe led the San Francisco 49ers to four Super Bowl victories during the 1980's, taking home the MVP award three times. He is the Super Bowl leader in all major passing categories. In his four Super Bowl games, Joe threw 11 touchdown passes and had no interceptions. In regular-season play, he has the highest passer rating in history.

Walter Payton: No runner in football his-

HEISMAN TROPHY WINNERS

The college football player of the year is awarded the Heisman Trophy. Other awards are the Maxwell Award, also to the nation's outstanding player; the Outland Trophy, to the best lineman; the Butkus Award, to the best linebacker; the Davey O'Brien Award, to the best quarterback; and the Jim Thorpe Award, to the best defensive back.

The most important award is the Heisman, and it is presented by the Downtown Athletic Club of New York City every year on the second Saturday of December. These are the past five winners.

1995 Eddie George,
Ohio State, tailback
1994 Rashaan Salaam,
Colorado, running back
1993 Charlie Ward,
Florida State, quarterback
1992 Gino Torretta,
Miami, quarterback
1991 Desmond Howard,
Michigan, receiver

AWESOME ATHLETE

Quarterback/placekicker George Blanda played professional football until he was 48 years old! He played more seasons (26), in more games (340), and scored more points (2,002) than anyone else in NFL history.

tory rushed for more yards (16,726) than Walter Payton. "Sweetness," as he was called, also set NFL records for most rushing touchdowns (110), most rushing attempts (3,838), most games gaining 100 or more yards (77), most seasons gaining 1,000 or more yards (10), and most rushing yards in a single game (275). Walter led the league in rushing five straight seasons from 1976–80.

Jerry Rice: The San Francisco 49er wide receiver is the all-time leader in touchdown catches (156) and holds the record for most consecutive games catching a touchdown pass (13). Jerry set a Super Bowl record with 215 receiving yards on 11 catches in Super Bowl XXIII to win the MVP award. In the next year's Super Bowl, he set another record with three touchdown catches in the game.

Knute Rockne: The head coach at the University of Notre Dame from 1918–30, Knute was famous for his halftime speeches ("Win one for the Gipper!"). During those 13 years, the Fighting Irish won three national championships and went undefeated five times. His career winning percentage of .881 is the best in college football history.

Don Shula: Don Shula retired at the end of the 1995 season, having won 347 games with the Baltimore Colts and Miami Dolphins. That made him the NFL's all-time winningest coach. He led the Dolphins to the only undefeated season in NFL history in 1972, when Miami won the first of two straight Super Bowls. His teams also reached four other Super Bowls, giving him more Super Bowl appearances (six) than any other coach.

Jim Thorpe: Jim Thorpe could do it all. This Native American was a football All-America at the Carlisle Indian School in Pennsylvania, and in 1912 led Carlisle to an upset victory over Army. At the 1912 Olympics, Jim won gold medals in the pentathlon and decathlon. After playing professional baseball from 1913 to 1919, he returned to football (becoming the first president of the league that would become the NFL) and was a star until his retirement in 1926. Jim was the first man elected to the Pro Football Hall of Fame, in 1963.

Johnny Unitas: The quarterback known for his black high-top shoes guided the Baltimore Colts to three championships, including the 1958 NFL title. When he retired, Johnny U. held six quarterbacking records, including most passes completed, most touchdown passes, and most yards passing. He threw a TD pass in a record 47 straight games.

Glossary

Blitz: A defensive play in which linebackers and defensive backs charge across the scrimmage line at the snap, hoping to tackle the quarterback before he can pass.

Bomb: A long pass thrown deep downfield.

Draw: A play in which the quarterback fades back as if to pass but then hands off to a running back.

Hang time: The amount of time a punt stays in the air.

Onside kick: A squib kick that travels at least 10 yards and can be recovered by the kicking team to keep possession of the ball.

Option: A play in which the quarterback runs along the scrimmage line with the choice of keeping the ball himself or pitching it back to a halfback.

Play action: When the quarterback fakes a handoff, then throws a pass to a receiver.

Rollout: When the quarterback sprints toward the sideline, away from the defenders, to give himself more time to find a receiver.

Screen pass: A short pass thrown behind the line of scrimmage to a back who is behind many blockers.

Stunt: A defensive play in which two linemen switch rushing routes, confusing the of-

GREAT GAMES!

Illinois vs. Michigan, October 18, 1924: Michigan had won 20 games in a row, but Illinois had running back Red Grange — the "Galloping Ghost." The first four times Red touched the ball he ran for touchdowns of 95, 67, 56, and 44 yards. He gained 402 yards, as Illinois won 39–14.

Harvard vs. Yale, November 23, 1968: Both teams entered the game with a record of 8–0, and the Ivy League title at stake. Yale led, 29–13, with 42 seconds left to play. Harvard scored two touchdowns and made two two-point conversions to tie Yale with no time showing on the clock. The two schools shared the Ivy title.

Boston College vs. Miami, November 23, 1984: Miami had scored a touchdown with 28 seconds left in the game to take a 45–41 lead. On fourth down at the 48-yard line, B.C. quarterback Doug Flutie threw a "Hail Mary" pass far into the end zone. The ball came down in the arms of receiver Gerard Phelan, and B.C. had a miraculous, 47–45 win.

QUICK HIT

He wasn't a player or a coach, but Pete Rozelle probably did more to make the NFL successful than any player or coach in the league. Pete was the fourth commissioner of the NFL. During his term, from 1960 to 1989, the league grew from 12 to 28 teams and the league merged with the AFL to create the Super Bowl. Pete also worked closely with TV, allowing, for example, the introduction of *Monday Night Football*.

fensive linemen about whom to block.

Sudden-death overtime: An extra period (or periods) played when a game ends in a tie. The first team to score wins.

Three-point stance: The crouching stance most players take just before the ball is snapped. They touch the ground at three points: two feet and one hand.

Where to Write

National Football League, 410 Park Ave., New York, NY 10022

Atlanta Falcons, I-85 and Suwanee Rd., Suwanee, GA 30174

Buffalo Bills, 1 Bills Dr., Orchard Park, NY 14127

Carolina Panthers, 227 West Trade St., Suite 1600, Charlotte, NC 28202

Chicago Bears, 250 N. Washington Rd., Lake Forest, IL 60045

Cincinnati Bengals, 200 Riverfront Stadium, Cincinnati, OH 45202

Cleveland Browns, 80 First St., Berea, OH 44017

Dallas Cowboys, 1 Cowboys Pkwy., Irving, TX 75063

Denver Broncos, 13665 Broncos Pkwy., Englewood, CO 80112

Detroit Lions, 1200 Featherstone Rd., Pontiac, MI 48342

Green Bay Packers, 1265 Lombardi Ave., Green Bay, WI 54307-0628

Houston Oilers, 6910 Fannin St., Houston, TX 77030

Indianapolis Colts, P.O. Box 535000, Indianapolis, IN 46253

Jacksonville Jaguars, 1 Stadium Pl., Jacksonville, FL 32202

Kansas City Chiefs, 1 Arrowhead Dr., Kansas City, MO 64129

Los Angeles Raiders, 332 Center St., El Segundo, CA 90245

Los Angeles Rams, 2327 W. Lincoln Ave.,

Anaheim, CA 92801

Miami Dolphins, Joe Robbie Stadium, 2269 N.W. 199th St., Miami, FL 33056

Minnesota Vikings, 9520 Viking Dr., Eden Prairie, MN 55344

New England Patriots, Foxboro Stadium, Route 1, Foxboro, MA 02035

New Orleans Saints, 1500 Poydras St., New Orleans, LA 70112

New York Giants, Giants Stadium, East Rutherford, NJ 07073

New York Jets, 1000 Fulton Ave., Hempstead, NY 11550

Philadelphia Eagles, Veterans Stadium, Broad St. and Pattison Ave., Philadelphia, PA 19148

Phoenix Cardinals, P.O. Box 888, Phoenix, AZ 85001-0888

Pittsburgh Steelers, Three Rivers Stadium, 300 Stadium Circle, Pittsburgh, PA 15212

San Diego Chargers, San Diego Jack Murphy Stadium, P.O. Box 609609, San Diego, CA 92160

San Francisco 49ers, 4949 Centennial Blvd., Santa Clara, CA 95054

Seattle Seahawks, 11220 N.E. 53rd St., Kirkland, WA 98033

Tampa Bay Buccaneers, 1 Buccaneer Pl., Tampa, FL 33607

Washington Redskins, Redskin Park Dr., Ashburn, VA 22011

Pro Football Hall of Fame, 2121 George Halas Dr. N.W., Canton, OH 44708

Canadian Football League, 110 Eglinton Ave. West, 5th Floor, Toronto, Ontario M4R 1A3, Canada

World League of American Football, 540 Madison Ave., New York, NY 10022

Arena Football League, 2200 E. Devon Ave., Suite 247, Des Plaines, IL 60018

NCAA, 6201 College Blvd., Overland Park, KS 66211

YOUTH FOOTBALL

Kids ages 7 to 15 may compete in a program called Pop Warner football, named after the legendary coach and innovator Glenn "Pop" Warner. This league divides players by age and weight to be sure that the game is played as safely as possible. Current NFL stars like John Elway and Emmitt Smith got their start by playing Pop Warner football.

Football is played at more than 14,000 high schools nationally. The National Federation of State High School Associations is in charge of school sports. Current Dallas Cowboy star Emmitt Smith posted the third-highest career rushing and scoring totals in U.S. high school history, with 8,804 yards and 106 touchdowns at Escambia (Florida) High.

GOLF

A great thing about golf is that amateurs can play on the same courses as the pros. You might never hit a home run in Yankee Stadium, but you can play golf at Pebble Beach — if you mow a lot of lawns to pay for it! The cost to play one round is $225 per player.

History

Golf probably had its origin in *paganica*, a game played by the Romans around the year 400. They played it with a bent stick and a feather-filled leather ball.

The game of golf as we know it today was first organized in Scotland. There, in 1754, a group of golfers called the Society of St. Andrews Golfers set down the rules of the sport. St. Andrews was the site of one of the first golf courses in the world.

The British brought golf to the United States, where golf courses were first built in the late 1880's. Those were Dorset Field Club in Dorset, Vermont; Foxburg Country Club in Foxburg, Pennsylvania; and St. Andrews Golf Club in Yonkers, New York.

The Amateur Golf Association of the United States, now named the U.S. Golf Association (USGA), was formed in 1894. Championship golf in America began the next year at the Newport (Rhode Island) Country Club, where the first U.S. Amateur championship was held, followed the next day by the U.S. Open championship. (An *open* championship means that professionals compete with amateurs.) One month later, the first Women's Amateur championship was held at the Meadow Brook Club in Hempstead, New York.

In 1916, the Professional Golfers Association of America (PGA) was formed. The first PGA Championship (for pros only) was held that year.

The first professional women's tour was organized in 1944 and was called the Women's

TEXT BY DAVID FISCHER

In 1930, amateur Bobby Jones won four major tournaments to get a Grand Slam.

Professional Golf Association (WPGA). In 1946, the first U.S. Women's Open was held.

By 1950 the WPGA was replaced by the Ladies Professional Golf Association (LPGA). The first LPGA Championship was played in 1955.

Equipment

The basic pieces of golf equipment are clubs and balls. Golf balls are usually white, but they can be orange or yellow-green to stand out against the green grass of the golf course. They weigh 1.62 ounces and measure 1.68" in diameter.

Early golf balls were a solid mass of tough rubber. Today, two types of golf ball are made: *wound* and *two-piece*. The wound ball, invented in 1898 by Coburn Haskell, was made by tightly wrapping a long rubber thread around a small rubber ball. The result was a ball that flew a longer distance than any other. The two-piece ball, introduced in the late 1960's, has no rubber thread. Its advantage is that it's easier for less skilled players to hit well. Covering both types of ball is a hard plastic shell that has numerous tiny round dents, called *dimples*, which affect the ball in flight (*see Cool Facts, page 142*).

Golf clubs are thin sticks, with a *head* at the bottom for hitting the ball and a *grip* at the top where the golfer holds the club. Connecting the grip to the head is the club *shaft*. In the early days of golf, the shaft was made

HOW TO PLAY

The golfer's goal is to get the ball into each hole with as few hits as possible. On each hole, the golfer must choose the right club, hit the ball the right way, and correctly judge the distance to the hole.

As he plays a hole, the golfer will normally hit long shots first, then take shorter and shorter shots as the ball gets closer to the hole. The long shots are hit with the longer *woods*, and the short shots are hit with the shorter *irons* (*see Equipment*).

The first shot or stroke is called a *drive*. The ball is placed on the *tee*, a small peg that balances the ball just above the ground. Only the drive may be hit off the tee. After the *tee shot*, a golfer must hit the ball as it lies, or wherever it lands, on the course.

As the ball gets closer to the hole, the player is likely to hit a short, high shot called a *chip* to get the ball onto the green. This is done with an iron with a high number, or a club called a *wedge*. Finally, the player strokes the ball into the hole. This is called *putting*.

COOL FACTS

Why do golf balls have dimples? In the late 1890's, golf equipment makers discovered that a ball flew longer and was easier to control if it had been nicked a bit. Then they discovered the ball flew even better if those nicks were sunken, circular dents. Finally, they learned that the more of these *dimples* a ball had, the farther a ball would fly. Today, a golf ball may have as many as 440 dimples!

Before clubs were numbered, they were called by names such as *brassie* (the equivalent of a 2-wood), *spoon* (3-wood), *baffy* (5-wood), *cleek* (2-iron), *mashie* (5-iron), and *niblick* (9-iron).

of wood. Today, the shaft is usually steel, but it can also be made from lighter materials, such as graphite, fiberglass, or aluminum. The length and weight of the club depend on the person. Golfers pick the club that feels best.

The two types of clubs commonly used are *woods* and *irons*. The main difference between these clubs is the head, where the club strikes the ball (*see The Clubs, page 143*). Woods have a large, thick head, which was originally made of a solid block of wood. Now the head of a "wood" is usually made of graphite or steel. Woods are used to hit long, straight shots that stay low. They are numbered 1 through 7, although a 2 or 6 is rare.

Irons have a smaller, thin head made of steel. Irons are used to hit high-arcing, shorter shots that require more accuracy. They are numbered 1 through 9. There are also the wedges: the *pitching wedge*, used for a short, accurate shot called a *chip*, and the *sand wedge*, used to chip out of sand traps. The *putter* is the shortest club, used to roll the ball into the hole. Players have 7 different woods and 12 different irons to choose from. In competition, a player can carry up to 14 clubs in his bag.

Keeping Score

A golfer's score for a hole is the number of times he hits the ball to get it from the tee at the beginning of the hole, to the *cup* or hole at the end. It usually takes three, four, or five shots to get the ball from the tee into the hole.

Par is the accepted number of shots or *strokes* a good player should need when hitting the ball from the tee into the hole. A par-3 hole should take three strokes, a par-4 hole four strokes, and so on. The par number for a hole is based on how difficult that hole is to play. Longer and more difficult holes usually

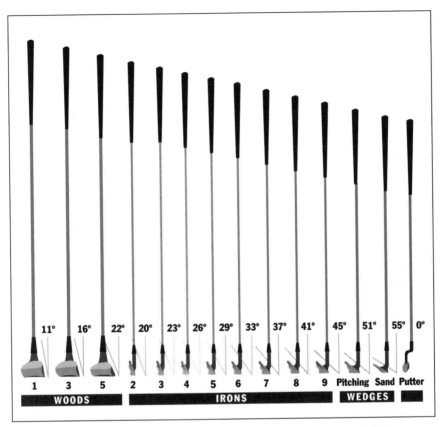

11°	16°	22°	20°	23°	26°	29°	33°	37°	41°	45°	51°	55°	0°
1	3	5	2	3	4	5	6	7	8	9	Pitching	Sand	Putter
WOODS			**IRONS**							**WEDGES**			

will require more strokes.

Golfers hope to score par or under par for a hole. A score of one under par for a hole is called a *birdie*. A score of two under par is an *eagle*. A *hole-in-one* is scored when the golfer's first shot goes into the hole. Also called an *ace*, a hole-in-one is rare.

When golfers need more shots to complete a hole, they are playing above par. A score of one above par for a hole is called a *bogey* *[BOH-ghee]*. Two strokes over is a *double bogey*; three strokes over is a *triple bogey*. Better golfers will score more pars and birdies and fewer bogeys.

Golfers can compete against the golf course by trying to beat the par score. Or golfers can compete against themselves by trying to bet-

THE CLUBS

In competition, golfers can carry 14 clubs. There are 7 woods and 12 irons to pick from. The differences among them are in the lengths and the club face angles. (The club face is the front of the head where the club hits the ball.) To make the ball fly long and low, woods and low-numbered irons have long shafts and barely angled club faces. High-numbered clubs and wedges have short shafts and greater angles to make the ball rise. The putter is short, with a straight face.

BLAST FROM THE PAST

Golfers yell "Fore!" when other players are in danger of being hit by a ball. The term probably comes from "Beware before!" a command given to soldiers dating back to the 1500's. It warned them to drop to the ground so that guns could fire over them.

●

Golf courses are sometimes called golf links. Links courses historically are courses that run along the seashore and have few trees. The first golf courses, in Scotland, were links courses. The British Open is the only one of the majors always played on a links course.

ter their score each time. Golfers can also compete against an opponent in *stroke play* or *match play*. Most professional tournaments use stroke play. In stroke play, the golfer who finishes all holes in the fewest number of total strokes is the winner. Teams competing against each other use match play. In match play, a hole is won by hitting the ball into the cup in the fewest number of strokes. Each hole won counts as a point. In a tie, both teams get half a point. The team that wins the most holes wins the match.

Big Events

Women pros compete on the LPGA Tour. In 1996, the LPGA Tour will cover 39 tournaments worth more than $25 million in prize money. The major events for women are the Nabisco Dinah Shore in March, the LPGA Championship in May, the U.S. Women's Open in July, and the du Maurier Classic in August.

Men pros compete on the PGA Tour. In 1996, the PGA Tour will have 54 events worth more than $66 million in prize money. After age 50, golfers may join the Senior PGA Tour.

The highlights of the men's golf season are the four major championships: the Masters, played in April; the U.S. Open, played in June; the British Open in July; and the PGA Championship in August. Except for the Masters, which is always played at Augusta National Golf Club in Georgia, the majors are played at different golf courses each year.

A player who wins all four major tournaments in a single year is said to win the *Grand Slam*. No professional golfer has ever won the Grand Slam, but in 1930, amateur Bobby Jones *(see Legends, page 146)* of the United States won the U.S. Open, U.S. Amateur, British Open, and British Amateur titles. He is considered to have won a Grand Slam.

Cup Competitions

In 1926, the best pro golfers from the U.S. played a tournament against the best pros from Great Britain. The next year, a trophy was donated by Samuel Ryder, a golf-loving Englishman who became wealthy by selling garden seeds, and the competition was then called the Ryder Cup. Matches are played every two years, alternating between the United States and Great Britain. In 1979, the British team was expanded to include players from Europe. After 31 events, the U.S. has won 23, lost 6, and tied twice.

In 1990, a similar competition for women was started called the Solheim Cup. It is held every two years. The U.S. has won twice and Europe has won once.

The amateur version of the Ryder Cup is called the Walker Cup. Named after George Herbert Walker (the grandfather of former U.S. President George Bush), the Walker Cup was first played in 1922 and is held every two years. The United States leads with a 31–3–1 record.

The amateur version for women is called the Curtis Cup. Named for Margaret and Harriot Curtis, sisters who both won the U.S. Women's Amateur, the Curtis Cup has been played every two years since 1932. The United States' record in this is 20–5–3.

The major amateur competitions for men and women include the U.S. Amateur and the U.S. Junior Amateur for players under 18 years of age. College golfers compete for the National Collegiate Athletic Association (NCAA) team championship.

Records

MEN

Most wins, one year: 18, by Byron Nelson, in 1945.

Most wins, career: 81, Sam Snead, 1936–55.

THE COURSE

A regulation course consists of 18 holes numbered 1 to 18. Each hole starts on the *tee* and ends on the *green.* The distance from tee to green is usually between 150 and 450 yards.

The *fairway* is a wide path of mowed grass that connects the tee to the green. Keeping your ball on the fairway is the surest way to the green.

A ball hit too far right or left will land in unmowed grass or beneath trees. This is called the *rough.* There are also *hazards* along the way, such as *sand traps* (pits filled with sand).

At the end of the fairway is the *green*, a small area of low-cut grass. On the green is the *hole*, which is 4 ¼" wide and 4" deep. Sticking up out of the hole is the *pin.* The pin is pulled from the hole when a golfer puts.

AMAZING FEATS

Jo Ann Washam scored two holes-in-one at the 1979 Kemper Open tournament! She aced the 16th hole in the second round and the 7th hole in the fourth round.

●

Eldrick "Tiger" Woods is the best young golfer in the United States. He played in his first tournament when he was 4. At 15, he became the youngest winner of the U.S. Junior Amateur championship, and won it three years in a row, from 1991–93. At 16, he became the youngest player to compete in a PGA tournament, where he was eliminated after two rounds. He attends Stanford University and plans eventually to join the PGA Tour.

Most consecutive wins: 11, Byron Nelson, 1945.

Youngest winner: Johnny McDermott, 1911 U.S. Open, 19 years, 10 months.

Oldest winner: Sam Snead, 1965 Greater Greensboro Open, 52 years, 10 months.

Lowest score for one round: 59, Al Geiberger, 1977 Memphis Classic; and Chip Beck, 1991 Las Vegas International.

Widest winning margin, in strokes: 16, Bobby Locke, 1948 Chicago Victory National Championship.

WOMEN

Most wins, one year: 13, Mickey Wright, 1963.

Most wins, career: 88, Kathy Whitworth, 1962–85.

Most consecutive wins: 5, Nancy Lopez, 1978.

Youngest winner: Marlene Hagge, 1952 Sarasota Open, 18 years, 14 days.

Oldest winner: JoAnne Carner, 1985 Safeco Classic, 46 years, 5 months.

Lowest score for one round: 62, Mickey Wright, 1964 Tall City Open; Vicki Fergon, 1984 San Jose Classic; Laura Davies, 1991 Rail Charity Golf Classic; and Hollis Stacy, 1992 Safeco Classic.

Widest winning margin, in strokes: 14, Louise Suggs, 1949 U.S. Women's Open; and Cindy Mackey, 1986 MasterCard International Pro-Am.

Legends

Patty Berg, U.S.: Patty did much to build the Ladies Professional Golf Association. She was the LPGA's first president and her 57 tour victories rank third on the all-time list. Patty won 16 majors. She became an LPGA Hall of Famer in 1951.

Walter Hagen, U.S.: Golf's first true professional, Walter entertained crowds with his shot-making skill and psyched-out opponents

Jack Nicklaus of the U.S. has won an unmatched 20 major championships.

with his trash talk. But Walter backed up what he said, winning 40 events and 11 major titles. Walter won the British Open four times and set a record by winning the PGA title four years in a row from 1924–27. He was inducted into the PGA Hall of Fame in 1940.

Ben Hogan, U.S.: Ben's 63 victories make him the third-winningest player in men's golf. In 1953, four years after he had suffered injuries in a serious accident, Ben won three of the four Grand Slam events, missing only the PGA, in which he did not play. That same year, Ben was named to the Hall of Fame.

Bobby Jones, U.S.: Bobby was golf's best amateur player, but he beat professionals, too. During the years between 1922 and 1930, Bobby won the U.S. Amateur five times, the U.S. Open four times, and the British Open three times. After winning golf's only recognized Grand Slam in 1930 (the U.S. Open, U.S. Amateur, British Open, and British Amateur), Bobby retired at age 28. He never played professionally. He then created the Masters tournament and helped design its golf course, Augusta National, which is one of the most famous in the world. He was elected to the PGA Hall of Fame in 1940.

Nancy Lopez, U.S.: Nancy burst onto the golf scene in 1978 to win nine tournaments, including a record five in a row, and the first of her three LPGA Championships. She

CHAMPIONS

MEN

THE MASTERS
1995	Ben Crenshaw
1994	J.M. Olazabal
1993	Bernhard Langer
1992	Fred Couples

UNITED STATES OPEN
1995	Corey Pavin
1994	Ernie Els
1993	Lee Janzen
1992	Tom Kite

BRITISH OPEN
1995	John Daly
1994	Nick Price
1993	Greg Norman
1992	Nick Faldo

PGA CHAMPIONSHIP
1995	Steve Elkington
1994	Nick Price
1993	Paul Azinger
1992	Nick Price

WOMEN

NABISCO DINAH SHORE
1995	Nanci Bowen
1994	Donna Andrews
1993	Helen Alfredsson
1992	Dottie Mochrie

LPGA CHAMPIONSHIP
1995	Kelly Robbins
1994	Laura Davies
1993	Patty Sheehan
1992	Betsy King

U.S. WOMEN'S OPEN
1995	Annika Sorenstam
1994	Patty Sheehan
1993	Lauri Merten
1992	Patty Sheehan

DU MAURIER CLASSIC
1995	Jenny Lidback
1994	Martha Nause
1993	Brandie Burton
1992	Sherri Steinhauer

QUICK HIT

Payne Stewart of the U.S. is the game's best-dressed player. He wears traditional loose-fitting pants that gather at the knee, called "knickers," that golfers wore 50 years ago. The knickers worn by golfers are called *plus fours* because they are made four inches longer than ordinary knickers.

won Player of the Year honors as a rookie, and three more times after that. Nancy has won 43 career titles for more than $3 million in prize money. In 1987, at age 30, she became the youngest golfer ever elected to the LPGA Hall of Fame.

Jack Nicklaus, U.S.: No other golfer has played better longer than Jack. "The Golden Bear," as he is called, has won more major championships (20) than any other golfer. He won six Masters titles, his first in 1963 and his last in 1986. At age 46, he was the oldest player ever to win the event. He also won five PGA titles, four U.S. Opens, and three British Opens. Jack has won 70 titles during his career, earned more than $5 million in prize money, and been named Player of the Year five times. He now plays on the Senior Tour.

Greg Norman, Australia: The popular Australian golfer is in the hunt more consistently than any other player today. Greg has won the British Open twice — in 1986 at Turnberry and in 1993 at Royal St. George's — but his heartbreaking defeats are more famous than his victories. "The Shark" has had the misfortune of losing all four major tournaments in a playoff. For the first time in his career, he won three Tour events in one season, in 1995.

Arnold Palmer, U.S.: Probably the most popular golfer ever, Arnie's many fans were called "Arnie's Army." He won 60 titles during his career and became the first golfer to earn $1 million. Arnie won the Masters four times and the British Open two straight years. He became a Hall of Famer in 1980 and currently plays on the Senior PGA Tour.

Payne Stewart, U.S.: The winner of the 1989 PGA Championship and the 1991 U.S. Open always gets noticed on the course. As a tribute to his father, Payne dresses the way golfers did 50 years ago *(see Quick Hit)*.

Tom Watson, U.S.: The PGA Player of the

Year a record six times, Tom has won eight major titles, including the British Open five times. During his career, Tom has won 32 tournaments for $6 million. His most spectacular shot was a chip-in from the rough on the 17th hole to win the 1982 U.S. Open over Jack Nicklaus.

Kathy Whitworth, U.S.: The winner of more tournaments (88) than any other golfer, male or female, Kathy won titles during the 1960's, 1970's, and 1980's. Her reliable putting led her to the top of the money list for eight years. She won Player of the Year honors seven times and entered the Hall of Fame in 1975.

Mickey Wright, U.S.: Using a swing that experts called perfect, Mickey won 82 career titles to rank second on the all-time list. She also won 13 majors, including the U.S. Women's Open and the LPGA Championship four times each. When TV began showing women's golf in 1963, audiences often saw the Wright stuff; she won a record 13 times that year. Mickey made it into the Hall of Fame in 1964.

Babe Didrikson Zaharias, U.S.: An all-around great athlete, Babe won gold medals in the hurdles and javelin throw at the 1932 Summer Olympics. She took up golf at the age of 20, and went on to win 31 career titles, including the U.S. Women's Open three times. Babe was one of the founders of the LPGA and was elected to the Hall of Fame in 1951.

Where to Write

Ladies Professional Golf Association, 2570 W. International Speedway Blvd., Suite B, Daytona Beach, FL 32114

Professional Golfers Association, Sawgrass, 112 TPC Blvd., Ponte Vedra, FL 32082

PGA World Golf Hall of Fame, PGA Blvd., Pinehurst, NC 28374

GREAT MATCHES!

U.S. Open, 1960: Arnold Palmer was seven shots behind leader Mike Souchak going into the final round. Arnie's first shot of the par-4 first hole landed on the green, and he got six birdies over the first seven holes to finish with a 65 and the title.

British Open, 1977: Tom Watson and Jack Nicklaus matched scores of 68-70-75 through the first three rounds. On the final day, Tom birdied four of the last six holes, shot a 65, and won by one stroke.

U.S. Women's Open, 1981: Pat Bradley and Beth Daniel had been co-leaders since the 6th hole. On the 15th hole, Pat sank a spectacular 70' birdie putt for a one-stroke lead that proved to be the winning margin. Her final-round score of 66 and total score of 279 were both tournament records.

The Masters, 1987: Greg Norman and Larry Mize were tied at the end of play, so there was a sudden-death playoff: The first player to win a hole wins. Larry sank an amazing 140' chip shot to win the tournament.

GYMNASTICS

Vaulting, tumbling, jumping, twisting — all of these acrobatic movements, as well as graceful dance movements, are part of the exciting sport of gymnastics.

History

Gymnastics began in ancient Greece and Egypt around 2600 B.C. There are drawings from that time that show people doing a form of tumbling and acrobatic-type movements.

Modern gymnastics began much later. Friedrich Ludwig Jahn, a German schoolteacher, is considered the "father of modern gymnastics." He began teaching gymnastics to strengthen the children in his country, and formed the first outdoor *gymnasium* in 1811. The first modern gymnasium was a place where people practiced gymnastics!

Friedrich Jahn also invented many of the pieces of equipment that are still used today, such as the parallel bars, horizontal bar, balance beam, horse, and rings.

Gymnastics became popular in Europe, and Europeans who moved to the United States brought their love of the sport with them. They formed sports schools that taught gymnastics, such as the German Turner clubs, the Czech Sokol clubs, the Polish Falcon clubs, and the Danish clubs.

Two German immigrants who were followers of Friedrich Jahn played an important role in American gymnastics history. Charles Beck started the first gymnastics program at an American school, in Massachusetts in 1825. One year later, Charles Follen started a program at Harvard, the first one at an American university.

THE FIRST COMPETITIONS

The International Gymnastics Federation

TEXT BY BRAD HERZOG

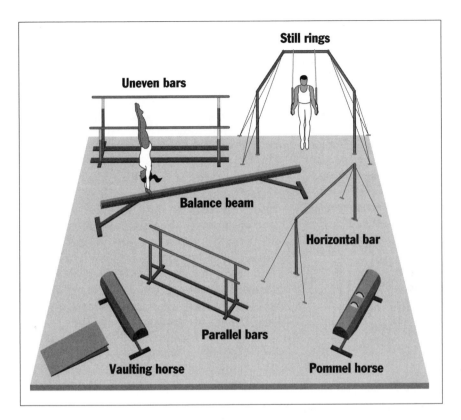

Still rings

Uneven bars

Balance beam

Horizontal bar

Parallel bars

Vaulting horse

Pommel horse

was formed in 1881. Men's gymnastics was an event in the first modern Olympic Games, in 1896. Seventy-five gymnasts from five countries competed, but the Germans dominated the competition, winning three of the six individual events.

The first world championship was held in 1903. Men competed at first only for the all-around and team titles. In 1924, the sport adopted its modern form of competion, with championships on each *apparatus* (piece of equipment), too.

The first women's event, the team combined exercise, was held at the 1928 Olympics. The first time a U.S. women's gymnastics team competed at the Olympics was in 1936. In those days, women competed separately in some events held at men's competi-

THE APPARATUS

Here's the gear: The vaulting horse is 5' long and 14" wide and set 4' off the ground. The balance beam is 15' long, 4" wide, and 4' high. The uneven bars are 7' 9" and 5' 2" above the ground. The horizontal bar is 8' 6" high. The parallel bars are 11' 6" long, 17" apart, and 6' off the ground. The pommel horse is a vaulting horse with two wooden handles on top. It is 5' 4" long and 3' 10" high. The rings are 8' 6" above the ground and 20" apart. The floor exercise mat (not shown) is 40' by 40'.

BLASTS FROM THE PAST

tions. It wasn't until the 1952 Summer Olympics that women's gymnastics was recognized as a different sport with its own events.

Big Events

The United States Gymnastics Federation, now called USA Gymnastics, was formed in 1963. It supports clinics, training camps, and team competitions, including programs to determine the national team.

Most members of the U.S. men's team are college gymnasts, but the best female gymnasts are teenagers from private clubs around the country. The U.S. team competes in international events such as the Olympic Games, the World Gymnastics Championships, the Pan-American Games, and the World University Games (for top college gymnasts). The Olympic, Pan-American, and World University Games are held every four years. The world championships are held every year.

Women's Events

There are four events in a women's gymnastics meet. They are, in the order in which they are competed: the *vault, uneven bars, balance beam,* and *floor exercise.*

VAULT

The vault, also called the *side horse vault,* is an event in which women perform acrobatic moves while jumping over a padded piece of equipment called a *vaulting horse.* The horse is 5' long, 4' high, and 14" wide. Women vault over the width of the horse.

The gymnast starts by sprinting down an 82'-long *runway,* then jumping off a *springboard.* The springboard is called a Reuther board, after the man who invented it. It enables the gymnast to launch herself into the air. She momentarily places her hands on the

Shannon Miller of the United States is a two-time world champion in the all-around competition.

horse and pushes off before vaulting over it.

Judges score a vault based on the gymnast's form, the height and distance she travels in the air, the number of flips and turns she does, and whether she *sticks* the landing (lands on her feet and stands still, without stepping). In most competitions, the gymnast vaults twice, but only her highest-scoring vault counts.

UNEVEN BARS

The uneven bars are two wooden bars connected by cables or wooden poles. One bar is 7' 9" high. The other is 5' 2" high. Each gymnast performs required movements in a routine that usually lasts less than 30 seconds.

HOW IT'S SCORED

The perfect score for any gymnastics event is 10.00, but each gymnast begins a routine with a score less than that. Women start with a 9.4, and men start with a 9.0.

Judges can add bonus points when the gymnast performs especially difficult elements. (Each skill is classified according to how difficult it is.) They can also subtract a certain amount of points for any flaws in the routine or for missing required moves.

In women's competition, there are seven judges (six judges plus one head judge) scoring each performance. In men's competition, there are five judges (four judges plus one head judge). The highest and lowest scores from the judges are dropped. The final score is the average of the remaining scores.

A gymnast's all-around score is compiled by adding together his score in each event. At college and international meets, each team's top five individual all-around scores are added together to get the team score.

AMAZING FEATS

The gymnast swings around one bar at a time, but she must switch quickly back and forth between them. She is constantly moving, using many grip changes, direction changes, *releases*, *regrasps*, and *circle swings* during her routine. Strength, concentration, and split-second timing are needed. Courage is also important, especially when the gymnast performs a difficult *dismount*.

BALANCE BEAM

A balance beam is 15' long, 4' high, but only 4" wide. The routine must last between 70 and 90 seconds, during which a gymnast must cover the entire length of the beam.

Athletes perform many difficult moves on the balance beam, including running steps, jumps, leaps, full turns, and *handstands*. The most talented gymnasts can do somersaults, cartwheels, and back *handsprings* on the balance beam. Points are deducted for missteps, falls, form breaks, wobbles, steps on dismounts, and missing elements.

FLOOR EXERCISE

The floor exercise combines acrobatic (tumbling) and gymnastic (dance) elements on a 40'-by-40' mat. Each routine is performed to music and should use the entire floor space. The routine lasts between 70 and 90 seconds.

The gymnast is expected to blend many elements, such as turns, handsprings, leaps, and *pirouettes* into one graceful routine. She should show strength, flexibility, and balance, along with artistic expression.

Men's Events

The six events in a men's meet are, in order: *floor exercise, pommel horse, still rings, vault, parallel bars,* and *horizontal bar.*

FLOOR EXERCISE

Male gymnasts compete on a 40'-by-40' mat

in the floor exercise, just like female gymnasts. In a span of 50 to 70 seconds, the gymnasts perform three or four *tumbling passes* (a series of flips or somersaults) in at least two directions (forward, backward, or sideways). Men do not perform to music and are not expected to dance. However, they must demonstrate strength (a straight-arm press to a handstand), flexibility (doing splits), and balance.

POMMEL HORSE

This is a horse with a slightly different look. Also called the *side horse*, the pommel horse is a padded piece of equipment about 14" wide and 5' 4" long. The gymnast grabs two wooden handles called *pommels*, which are about 50" off the floor. He then swings his legs in circles around the sides and top of the horse without stopping or touching the horse.

The gymnast's routine, which usually lasts 30–50 seconds, must cover the entire horse. Aside from the circular leg movements, he must also perform a move called the *scissors*. In the scissors, he begins with one leg on each side of the horse, then switches the positions of his legs from side to side. Often during his routine, the gymnast will support himself with only one hand while he raises his other hand to swing his leg past and reach for a new hold on the horse.

STILL RINGS

The still rings are two wooden rings suspended from cables about 8' 6" above the floor. Balance and strength are extremely important in this event, as the gymnast grabs the rings and tries to keep them motionless while performing various movements. His routine, which usually lasts up to a minute, must include circular swings and at least two types of handstands.

The athlete is required to perform *holding*

GREAT MOMENTS!

1976 Summer Olympics: Nadia Comaneci was just 14 years old when she became the first gymnast to score a perfect 10 at the Olympics. She scored her first 10's in the uneven bars and balance beam in the team events. By the end of the Games, she had seven 10's and three gold medals, a silver, and a bronze.

1984 Olympics: Going into the final event of the all-around competition, 16-year-old Mary Lou Retton of the U.S. trailed Ecaterina Szabo of Romania by just .05 of a point. Mary Lou needed a perfect 10 in the vault to become the first American ever to win the all-around. And she got it! It was her second 10 of the competition, and it won her the gold medal.

1984 Olympics: The U.S. and China were battling for the men's team gold medal, when Mitch Gaylord of the U.S. attempted a maneuver on the high bar that only he had ever tried: a flyaway backflip with a half-twist. He did it perfectly, scoring a 9.95 and leading his teammates to victory.

QUICK HIT

positions, which means he must remain still for several seconds without moving. He also performs several *strength positions*, such as the *cross*, a difficult move in which he stays upright with his arms extended sideways.

VAULT

While female gymnasts vault over the width of the vaulting horse, male gymnasts vault over the length of the horse. After taking a running start and jumping off a springboard, the gymnast pushes off the horse and performs several movements in the air, such as twists or somersaults.

The gymnast is scored on his speed heading into the vault, the height of the vault, the distance he travels before landing, and how well he can stick his landing. In some competitions, the gymnast's final score is the average score of two vaults. In international meets, he is only allowed one attempt.

PARALLEL BARS

In this event, the gymnast performs on two wooden bars, which are 11' 6" long, about shoulder-width apart, and 6' off the ground. He uses arm power to support himself on the bars while performing such moves as twists, swings, and handstands.

Flight movements are required, such as releasing and regrasping the bars with both hands. During a front flip or backflip, he may even lose sight of the bars for a moment.

HORIZONTAL BAR

The horizontal bar is a flexible steel bar fixed about 8' above the floor. In this event, the gymnast holds the bar with one or both hands and swings repeatedly around it without stopping. He often changes his grip, reverses his direction, and even releases and regrasps the bar. The routine usually lasts 30–45 seconds and often ends with an excit-

Kurt Thomas performs on the still rings. Kurt won three straight U.S. championships from 1978–80.

ing dismount, in which the gymnast does acrobatic moves in the air before landing on his feet.

Competition

Gymnastics in the Olympics and other international competitions, such as the world championships, is made up of three types of competition.

The first is the team competition. Each of the team's six members performs one *compulsory routine* and one *optional routine* in each event. (Beginning in 1997, there will be no more compulsory routines.)

The International Gymnastics Federation decides what the compulsory routine will be for each event, and each athlete performs the same routine. Optional routines are created by the individual gymnasts, and usually consist of the most exciting and difficult skills.

A team's five best scores are counted for each event. When all events are complete,

AWESOME ATHLETES

The powerhouses in U.S. college gymnastics are the University of Nebraska for men and the University of Utah for women. Nebraska won 8 of the 16 National Collegiate Athletic Association (NCAA) Division I men's championships held from 1979 to 1994. Utah won nine NCAA Division I women's titles from 1982 to 1994.

●

John Roethlisberger, who attended the University of Minnesota, is the first gymnast ever to win three NCAA all-around titles and three USA Gymnastics all-around championships. John's sister, Marie, was an alternate on the 1984 women's Olympic team. His father, Fred, was an Olympic gymnast in 1968.

each team's scores from all events are added. The team with the most points wins the team competition.

The 36 highest-scoring individual gymnasts in the team competition then compete in the individual all-around event. Only three gymnasts per country, however, are permitted to advance. The gymnasts start over with no points. Each gymnast performs one optional routine in each event. The gymnast with the highest total score from all events wins the gold medal and earns the title of all-around champion.

The third and final competition is the individual event finals. The top eight finishers in each event in the team competition qualify. Each country is allowed up to two competitors per event. The gymnasts in each event perform an optional routine, and the athlete with the highest score in that event wins.

Legends

Nikolai Andrianov, Soviet Union: Nikolai participated in three Olympic Games (1972, 1976, and 1980) and won more medals than any other male athlete in Olympic history. In 1976, he won the all-around gold medal. He also took the gold in the floor exercise, rings, and vault; silver in the parallel bars; and bronze in the pommel horse.

Vera Caslavska, Czechoslovakia: Vera won seven gold medals and four silver medals in Olympic competition. She won the all-around gold medal in both the 1964 and 1968 Olympics. In 1968, though she was 26 (old for a female gymnast), she won golds in the vault, uneven bars, and floor exercise. All together, Vera won 22 world, Olympic, and European titles between 1959 and 1968.

Nadia Comaneci, Romania: No gymnast had ever earned a single perfect 10 in Olympic competition before 14-year-old Nadia Comaneci came on the scene in 1976 *(see*

Great Moments!, page 155). At the Summer Olympics in Montreal, Canada, Nadia earned *seven* perfect 10's and became the youngest Olympic champion in history! She won three gold medals, a silver, and a bronze. At the 1980 Games, Nadia won two more gold medals.

Bart Conner, U.S.: At the 1979 world championships, Bart won a gold medal in the parallel bars, a bronze medal in the vault, and another bronze as a member of the third-place U.S. team. Five years later, he won a gold medal in the parallel bars at the 1984 Olympics, as the U.S. also took the team gold medal. He is currently a television commentator for gymnastics events.

Bela Karolyi, U.S.: In 1981, Bela defected from Romania to the U.S., where he continued to be perhaps the world's most successful gymnastics coach. In 30 years of coaching, he has trained 27 Olympians, 7 Olympic champions, and 15 world champions. His pupils have included Nadia Comaneci, Mary Lou Retton, Phoebe Mills, and Kim Zmeskal.

Olga Korbut, Soviet Union: Olga, then age 17, became a beloved Olympic athlete at the 1972 Games in Munich, Germany. She earned three gold medals and a silver medal. Olga also became the first person to perform a backflip on the balance beam. She started a trend toward more athletic and acrobatic routines for female gymnasts.

Larissa Latynina, Soviet Union: No Olympic athlete in history has won more gold medals than Larissa, who earned nine gold, five silver, and four bronze medals in 1956, 1960, and 1964. She won the all-around gold in 1956, and the all-around silver in 1960 and 1964. In those last two Olympics, she won medals in all four women's events.

Mary Lou Retton, U.S.: Mary Lou was the first gymnast to be elected to the U.S. Olympic Hall of Fame. Only 4' 9", she was

MEN'S OLYMPIC CHAMPIONS

Japan and the former Soviet Union have dominated men's Olympic gymnastics. Japan won five straight team gold medals from 1960–76. The Soviet Union (and later the Unified Team) won team golds in 1952, 1956, 1980, 1988, and 1992. The U.S. won the team gold in 1904 and 1984. Since 1900, nine U.S. men have combined to win a total of 12 individual gold medals. Here are all the 1992 male gold medalists.

ALL-AROUND
Vitaly Scherbo, Unified Team
HIGH BAR
Trent Dimas, U.S.
PARALLEL BARS
Vitaly Scherbo, Unified Team
VAULT
Vitaly Scherbo, Unified Team
POMMEL HORSE
Vitaly Scherbo, Unified Team
Pae Gil Su, North Korea
RINGS
Vitaly Scherbo, Unified Team
FLOOR EXERCISE
Li Xiaosahuang, China
TEAM
Unified Team

AMAZING FEATS

Shannon Miller won more medals (five) at the 1992 Summer Olympics in Barcelona, Spain, than any other American athlete. She won silver medals in the all-around competition and on the balance beam, as well as bronze medals in the uneven bars and floor exercise. Her fifth medal was a bronze medal as part of the third-place U.S. team. Shannon also won the all-around title at the 1993 and 1994 World Championships, becoming the first American gymnast to win back-to-back world titles. In addition, she won individual world titles in floor exercise and uneven bars in 1993, and in balance beam in 1994. She was the 1995 U.S. vault champion and is trying to make the 1996 U.S. Olympic team.

still strong enough to win the all-around gold medal at the 1984 Olympics in Los Angeles. Her feat that summer included one silver and two bronze medals in individual events. She also twice scored a perfect 10 in the vault *(see Great Moments!, page 155)*.

Cathy Rigby, U.S.: Cathy was the first American woman gymnast to win a medal in international competition. Though she was born with collapsed lungs and spent her first five years in and out of hospitals, Cathy went on to win a silver medal on the balance beam at the 1970 world championships. Her performance at the 1972 Olympics (she placed tenth overall) gave a big boost to the popularity of gymnastics in the United States.

Kurt Thomas, U.S.: Kurt was an All-America gymnast at Indiana University who went on to win three straight U.S. championships from 1978–80. In 1978, he became the first American in nearly 50 years to win a gold medal at the world championships. The following year, he won two gold medals and two silver medals in individual events at the world championships, plus an all-around silver medal. Because the U.S. stayed out of the 1980 Summer Olympics to protest the Soviet Union's invasion of Afghanistan, Kurt never competed in the Olympics.

Glossary

Aerial: When the gymnast turns completely over in the air without touching the piece of equipment with his hands.

Apparatus: A piece of gymnastics equipment.

Arch position: When the body is curved backward.

Compulsories: Mandatory routines that contain specific movements required of all gymnasts.

Composition: How each movement is arranged into a routine.

Dismount: To leave an apparatus at the end of a routine.

Execution: The style and technique in the performance of a routine.

Flic-flac: A back handspring common in the floor exercise and balance beam events.

Flip: Turning over one full rotation in the air without the support of the arms.

Giant swing: A move on the horizontal bar, in which the body is fully extended and completely rotating around the bar.

Handspring: A spring off the hands, achieved by putting the weight on the arms and using a strong push from the shoulders.

Kip: A move on the uneven parallel bars or horizontal bar, in which the gymnast moves from a position below the equipment to a position above it.

Layout position: A position in which the body is perfectly straight, like a pencil.

Optionals: Personal routines created by a gymnast to show off his or her skills.

Pike position: When the body is bent forward more than 90 degrees at the hips, while the legs are kept straight.

Pirouette: To change direction by twisting in a handstand position.

Release: To let go of the horizontal bar or one of the uneven bars to perform a move before regrasping the bar.

Routine: A combination of movements.

Salto: A flip or somersault.

Tuck: A position in which the knees are bent and drawn up to the chest.

Virtuosity: The artistry and rhythm displayed during a routine.

Where to Write

USA Gymnastics, Pan American Plaza, 201 South Capitol Ave., Suite 300, Indianapolis, IN 46225

Gymnastics Hall of Fame, 227 Brooks St., Oceanside, CA 92054

RHYTHMIC GYMNASTICS

Rhythmic gymnastics was added as a medal sport to the Summer Olympic Games in 1984. Only women compete in this sport. It combines body movement with the handling of small equipment: a rope, hoop, ball, ribbon, and clubs. Each is a separate event. There is also a group exercise, in which six athletes work together, exchanging equipment and performing similar movements.

Individual events run 60 to 90 seconds. Group exercises last 2 to 2 ½ minutes. The competition area is a 40'-by-40' floor mat.

Each piece of equipment has its own typical movements, such as high tosses, rolls, and swings. Each exercise also requires elements from four different categories of body movement: leaps, turns, balances, and flexibility. The athlete must use the entire floor area and both sides of her body.

The 1992 Olympic gold medalist in rhythmic gymnastics was Alexandra Timoshenko from the Unified Team.

ICE HOCKEY

Ice hockey has been called "the world's fastest sport." It's packed with swift skating and passing, blazing shots, rough-and-tumble play, and raucous celebrations when a goal is scored.

History

Exactly when and where hockey was invented is not known. As long ago as 500 B.C., the Greeks played a version of it. Iroquois Indians living in the St. Lawrence River valley in eastern Canada during the 1700's liked to hit hard balls along the ground with sticks. When players got hit by shots, they'd yell "Ho-gee!" That meant, "It hurts!"

Ice hockey as it is known today might have begun in England during the 1850's. Field hockey was popular during the warm-weather months. In winter, kids played the game on ice. In the United States, an ice game called *shinny* was popular. Players controlled a ball with a stick, avoided defenders, and scored by shooting the ball between two piles of stones placed four or five feet apart.

Ice hockey became very popular in Canada in the late 1800's. During the long, cold winters, thousands of kids played on frozen ponds. They used field hockey sticks to shoot *pucks* made from pieces of wood, tin cans, or even chunks of frozen horse manure! Boards were placed around the ice to keep the puck in play. The playing area became known as a *rink,* which is the Scottish word for course.

Early hockey games were wild and disorganized. Sometimes there were as many as 30 players on each team. Rules were changed or added as years went by. By the 1890's, organized leagues and teams were playing across Canada and in the northern United States. Ice hockey is now a major sport in North America, Europe, Scandinavia, and the coun-

TEXT BY JOHN ROLFE

NHL all-time scoring leader Wayne Gretzky (center) played on four Stanley Cup winners with Edmonton.

HOW TO PLAY

The object is to shoot the *puck* into the opposing team's net. A *goal* is worth one point.

A team has 20 players, but only 6 are on the ice at a time: 3 *forwards* (a *left wing*, a *center*, and a *right wing*), 2 *defensemen*, and a *goaltender*. The center leads a team's attack. Each wing covers a side of the ice. All three forwards can skate anywhere and also help defend their team's goal.

Defensemen mainly cover attacking skaters, but can also help their team score. The goaltender tries to block or catch shots at the goal.

During a game, forwards and defensemen play in *shifts* that last about two minutes. Play continues while players are being substituted.

Games consist of three 20-minute periods. If the score is tied, there can be overtime. The first team to score wins. If no one scores, the game ends in a tie. The NHL uses one 5-minute overtime period during the regular season and full 20-minute overtime periods in the playoffs until a team scores.

tries that once made up the Soviet Union.

Rules

The ice in the center of the rink *(see The Rink, page 165)* is called the *neutral zone*. Play begins there at a *face-off* circle when the referee drops the puck between the stick blades of two opposing players who are facing each other with their sticks on the ice. The players battle to control the puck and begin their team's attack.

Players are allowed to hit the stick or the body of the opposing player who has the puck. This is called *checking*. Forwards and defensemen can pass the puck only with their sticks or skates, but cannot kick the puck into the net. A pass that crosses a *blue line* and the *center red line* is illegal *(see The*

BLAST FROM THE PAST

In the early days of hockey, goalies wore baseball catchers' chest protectors and covered their shins with newspapers or magazines. The first goalie to wear a face mask was Jacques Plante of the Canadiens in 1959. After suffering four broken noses, two busted cheekbones, and a fractured skull, Jacques decided wearing a mask was a good idea!

Rink, page 165). If a player skates into the attacking zone before the puck enters it, he is *offside*. Play stops and the puck is brought to one of the four face-off spots in the neutral zone. If the puck is knocked out of the attacking zone, all offensive players must leave the zone until the puck is legally brought back.

Players cannot go in an opposing team's *crease* (the marked area immediately in front of the goal) unless they are playing the puck. Goals scored while an offensive player is in the crease do not count unless the player was pushed in by a defender.

Play is watched by two *goal judges*, two *linesmen* (who call illegal passes and offsides), and a *referee* (who calls penalties).

Penalties

Minor penalties include holding, tripping, and interfering with a player who is trying to get the puck. Minors are also given for illegal use of the stick, such as *hooking* (with the blade), *slashing*, and *cross-checking* (hitting an opponent with the stick held horizontally).

Except goalies, all players who receive minor penalties must leave the ice and sit in the *penalty box* for two minutes. (A goalie's penalty is served by a skater.) A team cannot replace the player unless it would be left with fewer than three skaters on the ice. A penalized player can return immediately if the opposing team scores.

Double-minor (four minutes) and five-minute *major* penalties are given to players who try to injure an opponent. These penalties include *charging* (delivering a check after taking more than two strides toward an opponent), *high-sticking* (swinging the stick above shoulder height), unnecessary roughness, and fighting. All five minutes must be served no matter how many goals the opponent scores.

Serious violations, such as threatening or hitting a referee, can result in 10-minute *mis-*

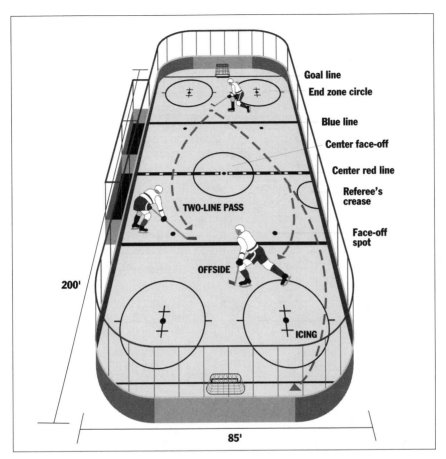

Goal line
End zone circle
Blue line
Center face-off
Center red line
Referee's crease
Face-off spot

TWO-LINE PASS

OFFSIDE

200'

ICING

85'

conduct, *game misconduct* (the player is ejected and a substitute takes his place), and *match* penalties (the player is ejected and a substitute serves his time in the box).

Equipment

Hockey players wear sweaters (jerseys), bulky shorts, and thick socks. Their skates are different from figure skates. The blade is curved along the bottom, and there are no teeth — called a *toe pick* — on the front. Skaters use an L-shaped, wooden stick. The handle must be 55" long or less. The blade can be no longer than 12 ½" and no wider than 3". A goalie's stick blade can be up to

THE RINK

Most rinks are 200' long and 85' wide. The ice is divided into zones by a red *goal line* at each end, two *blue lines*, and a red line at center ice. Each team defends a zone that stretches 60' from one of the blue lines to the goal line. Each goal line is 10' from the end of the rink. The 4'-by-6' goal is in the center of the goal line. There is also an 8'-by-4' square in front of the goal that is called the *crease*.

165

AMAZING FEATS

15 ½" long and 3 ½" wide.

Ice hockey is rough and dangerous, so players must be well protected. The hard, rubber pucks weigh 5 ½ to 6 ounces and can be shot at 100 miles per hour or more. Hard body-checks can break bones. All players must wear thick, padded gloves and a hard, plastic helmet. A goalie's helmet has a face mask. Some players also wear a cage-like mask or a clear visor to protect their eyes.

Under their uniforms, players wear pads on their shoulders, arms, elbows, knees, and shins. A goalie also wears a chest protector, 10"-wide pads on each leg, a big catching glove on one hand, and a blocker pad on the other. In all, a goalie's equipment weighs about 30 pounds.

Organized Hockey

The first ice hockey league was formed in Kingston, Ontario, Canada, in 1885. Ten years later, there were leagues all over Canada. Montreal had more than 100 teams!

In 1892, Canada's governor general, Lord Stanley of Preston, decided that a trophy should be awarded to the best team each year. He paid $48.50 for a silver bowl that is now the "Stanley Cup." When the Montreal Amateur Athletic Association club won the Amateur Hockey Association championship in 1893, it was the first team to win the Cup.

In the United States, the first league was formed in 1896. It was based in New York City and had four teams. All the players were amateurs. It wasn't until 1904 that a professional league was created: the International Pro Hockey League (IPHL). Based in Michigan, it attracted top American and Canadian players, who were paid $500 to $1,000 per game.

The IPHL went out of business in 1907, but other pro leagues popped up during the next 10 years. One of them, the Pacific Coast

Hockey Association (PCHA), did a lot to influence the way the game is played today. The PCHA was founded by Joseph Patrick and his sons, Frank and Lester. They were the first to put numbers on players' sweaters, use blue lines on the ice, and keep records of goals and assists. They also created a championship playoff series.

Teams from the PCHA and the National Hockey Association (NHA) played for the Stanley Cup from 1910 until the PCHA went out of business in 1926. In 1917, the NHA became the National Hockey League (NHL).

The NHL

The NHL began with four teams in Canada. They included the Montreal Canadiens and Toronto Arenas, who were later renamed the "Maple Leafs." Montreal and Toronto are the NHL's oldest teams. In 1924, the Boston Bruins became the NHL's first team in the United States. Two years later, the New York Rangers, Chicago Blackhawks, and Detroit Red Wings joined the league.

From 1942 to 1967, the NHL had only those six teams. Nearly all the players were from Canada and few people outside of the northern parts of the United States cared much about hockey. However, much has changed over the past 27 years. The NHL now has 26 teams, with some in such southern locations as Dallas, Miami, and Tampa Bay. American players such as defenseman Brian Leetch of the New York Rangers have become stars. So have top players from countries such as Sweden, Finland, and Russia.

The NHL's regular season lasts from October until mid-April. There are two "conferences" — the Eastern and Western — and each has two divisions. Each team plays 84 games. A win is worth two points in the standings. A tie is worth one. The eight teams with the most points in each confer-

NHL TEAMS

EASTERN CONFERENCE

Atlantic Division

Florida Panthers
New Jersey Devils
New York Islanders
New York Rangers
Philadelphia Flyers
Tampa Bay Lightning
Washington Capitals

Northeast Division

Boston Bruins
Buffalo Sabres
Hartford Whalers
Montreal Canadiens
Ottawa Senators
Pittsburgh Penguins
Quebec Nordiques

WESTERN CONFERENCE

Central Division

Chicago Blackhawks
Dallas Stars
Detroit Red Wings
St. Louis Blues
Toronto Maple Leafs
Winnipeg Jets

Pacific Division

Mighty Ducks of Anaheim
Calgary Flames
Edmonton Oilers
Los Angeles Kings
San Jose Sharks
Vancouver Canucks

QUICK HIT

NHL players are graded with a plus-minus rating that shows how much they help or hurt their team when they are on the ice. Players are given one rating point each time they are on the ice when their team scores a goal shorthanded or at even strength. If they are on the ice for an opponent's goal in the same situations, one rating point is deducted. A minus-30 rating means a player has been playing poor defense.

ence qualify for the playoffs. There are four rounds, including the Stanley Cup finals. In each round, a team must win four out of seven games to advance.

International Hockey

There are amateur and pro hockey leagues in about 30 countries. International rinks are 15' wider than NHL rinks, which is one reason why there is more skating and passing and less checking and fighting in international games than in the NHL.

A world championship tournament has been played each year since 1924 except during years when the Winter Olympics are held. Ice hockey became an Olympic sport in 1920 (see Olympic Champions, page 175).

Although players from Sweden and Finland have been in the NHL for years, the league now has more international stars than ever before. The breakup of the Soviet Union, in 1991, has allowed many Russian stars to come to the U.S. to play pro hockey. Former Olympic greats such as defensemen Viacheslav Fetisov and Alexei Kasatonov left to join the NHL's New Jersey Devils. Younger Russian players such as Sergei Federov (Detroit Red Wings), Alexander Mogilny (Buffalo Sabres), and Pavel Bure (Vancouver Canucks) have also become NHL stars.

Minor Leagues

There are five minor professional leagues with teams in the United States and Canada: the American Hockey League, International Hockey League, East Coast Hockey League, Central Hockey League, and Colonial Hockey League. Most of the 56 teams in these five leagues develop players for NHL clubs.

NHL Records
GOALS

Most goals scored in a game: 7, by Joe

Malone of the Quebec Bulldogs, on January 31, 1920.

Most times scoring three or more goals in one game: 49, Wayne Gretzky.

Most goals scored, season: 92, Wayne Gretzky, Edmonton Oilers, 1981–82.

Most goals scored, season, by a rookie: 76, Teemu Selanne, Winnipeg Jets, 1992–93.

Most goals scored, career: 803, Wayne Gretzky, 1979–present.

ASSISTS

Most assists, game: 7, done four times, three times by Wayne Gretzky with the Edmonton Oilers; most recently February 14, 1988.

Most assists, season: 163, Wayne Gretzky, Edmonton Oilers, 1985–86.

Most assists, career: 1,655, Wayne Gretzky, 1979–present.

SCORING

Most total points (goals plus assists) scored, game: 10 (six goals, four assists), Darryl Sittler, Toronto Maple Leafs, February 7, 1976.

Most total points scored, season: 215, Wayne Gretzky, Edmonton Oilers, 1985–86.

Most total points scored, career: 2,458, Wayne Gretzky, 1979–present

Most times leading the NHL in scoring: 10, Wayne Gretzky.

GOALTENDING

Most wins, season: 47, Bernie Parent, Philadelphia Flyers, 1973–74.

Most wins, career: 435, Terry Sawchuk, 1949–70.

Legends

Al Arbour: Al has coached 1,606 games, the most in NHL history. He won three Stanley Cups as a defenseman from 1953 to 1970, even though he had to wear eyeglasses on the ice. In 1973, he became head coach

CHAMPIONS

Hockey has had a lot of dynasties. The Pittsburgh Penguins won back-to-back Stanley Cups in 1990–91 and 1991–92. The Edmonton Oilers won five in seven years. The New York Islanders won four straight, from 1979–80 to 1982–83, and the Montreal Canadiens won four straight before that, from 1975–76 to 1978–79.

The Canadiens hold the record for most consecutive Stanley Cups won, with five between 1955–56 and 1959–60. They have also won the most Cups ever, with 24. The next-best mark is the Toronto Maple Leafs' 13.

The Stanley Cup champions of the past 10 seasons are:

1994–95
New Jersey Devils
1993–94
New York Rangers
1992–93
Montreal Canadiens
1991–92
Pittsburgh Penguins
1990–91
Pittsburgh Penguins
1989–90
Edmonton Oilers
1988–89
Calgary Flames
1987–88
Edmonton Oilers
1986–87
Edmonton Oilers
1985–86
Montreal Canadiens

BLAST FROM THE PAST

In 1972, a second major pro league was formed: the World Hockey Association (WHA). It had 12 teams. Some top stars such as Gordie Howe and Bobby Hull left the NHL to play in the WHA, but it went out of business in 1979. The Edmonton Oilers, Hartford Whalers, Winnipeg Jets, and Quebec Nordiques are former WHA teams that were allowed to join the NHL.

of a losing New York Islander team and led it to four straight Stanley Cups (1980–83). He coached the Islanders for 19 seasons.

Jean Beliveau: A great all-around center, Jean [zhon] was a star for the Montreal Canadiens from 1953 to 1971. He played in 13 NHL All-Star Games, and was NHL MVP twice. As team captain, he led Montreal to 10 Stanley Cups. He scored 507 goals, and was elected to the Hall of Fame in 1972.

Hector "Toe" Blake: In the 1940's, Toe was the left wing on Montreal's famous "Punch Line" with right wing Maurice "Rocket" Richard and center Elmer Lach. Toe played on three Stanley Cup winners. In 1955, he became Montreal's head coach, and went on to win eight Stanley Cups, including a record five in a row (1956–60). He was elected to the Hall of Fame in 1966.

Scotty Bowman: Scotty is the only coach in NHL history who has won more than 1,000 games in the regular season and playoffs combined. He has coached six Stanley Cup champions: the Montreal Canadiens in 1973 and 1976–79, and the Pittsburgh Penguins in 1992. He was elected to the Hall of Fame in 1991 and now coaches the Buffalo Sabres.

Francis "King" Clancy: He was only 5' 9" and weighed less than 150 pounds when he began his NHL career in 1921, but guts and speed made him a great defenseman for the Ottawa Senators and Toronto Maple Leafs until 1936. After retiring, he became an NHL referee, head coach, and team vice president. In all, King spent 66 years in the NHL! He was elected to the Hall of Fame in 1958.

Bobby Clarke: Bobby was a gutsy center for the Philadelphia Flyers, who were called "the Broad Street Bullies" for their tough play. He won three MVP awards and led the Flyers to Stanley Cups in 1974 and 1975. He scored 358 goals in 15 seasons even though he had diabetes, a disease that affects the

Gordie Howe won six NHL scoring titles and six NHL MVP awards in his 32 seasons in pro hockey.

GREAT GAMES!

The "King" Does It All: In the final game of the 1923 Stanley Cup championship, the Ottawa Senators had only eight skaters healthy enough to play. Defenseman King Clancy ended up playing shifts at every position, including goaltender! Ottawa went on to beat Edmonton, 1-0.

The Longest Night: At 8:34 P.M. on March 24, 1936, the Detroit Red Wings and Montreal Maroons faced off in a playoff game. After three regulation periods and five 20-minute overtimes, the score was still 0-0. Finally, with 3:30 left in the sixth overtime, Mud Bruneteau of Detroit scored to end the longest game in NHL history — at 2:25 A.M.!

The NHL vs. the Soviet Union: In 1972, Canadian NHL All-Stars played the Soviets in an eight-game tournament. After seven games, each team had won three and tied one. The final game was tied until, with 34 seconds left, Paul Henderson of Toronto scored to give the NHL the win. What a matchup!

body's ability to break down sugar. He was elected to the Hall of Fame in 1987.

Paul Coffey: A swift skater and dazzling passer, Paul holds the NHL career records for goals (344), assists (934), and points (1,278) by a defenseman. With the Edmonton Oilers from 1980 to 1987, he won three Stanley Cups. He won another Cup with the Penguins in 1991. An 11-time All-Star, Paul now plays for the Red Wings.

Ken Dryden: Ken made goaltending history in 1971, when he led the Montreal Canadiens to the Stanley Cup after playing in only six regular-season games. The next season, he became the first player ever to be named the NHL's top rookie *after* winning the playoff MVP award. He played eight seasons for Montreal, leading the team to six Cups in all.

COOL FACTS

One of hockey's most famous families is the Sutters. Since 1976, six Sutter brothers have played in the NHL: Brian (Blues, 1976–88), Darryl (Blackhawks, 1979–87), Duane (Islanders, Blackhawks, 1979–90), Brent (Islanders, Blackhawks, 1980–present); Ron (Penguins, Flyers, Canucks, Blues, Blackhawks, Lightning, Maple Leafs, 1982–present); and Rich (Flyers, Blues, Nordiques, Islanders, 1982–present). Ron and Rich are twins!

●

Roller hockey is now a popular sport. It is played in regulation-sized rinks without ice. Players use in-line roller skates. Each team has four skaters and a goalie. Games last for two 20-minute periods. A pro roller hockey league, Roller Hockey International, was created in 1993. It now has 18 teams competing in the U.S. and Canada.

He was elected to the Hall of Fame in 1983.

Phil Esposito: A center, Phil scored 717 goals in a career that lasted from 1963 to 1981. He won five scoring titles, two MVP awards, and two Stanley Cups. He played for the Chicago Blackhawks, Boston Bruins, and New York Rangers. He was elected to the Hall of Fame in 1984. His brother, Tony, is a Hall of Fame goalie who played in the NHL for 16 seasons.

Grant Fuhr: The NHL's first black goaltender, Grant was a big reason why Edmonton won four Stanley Cups between 1984 and 1988. A six-time NHL All-Star, he set a record by playing in 75 games during the 1987–88 season. He won 40 of them and was named the league's best goalie. He now plays for the St. Louis Blues.

Wayne Gretzky: A wizard with the puck, "The Great One" is the NHL's all-time leading scorer. He holds more than 60 NHL records. Since 1979, he has won 10 scoring titles, 9 MVP awards, and has scored 200 or more points in a season 4 times. He also led Edmonton to four Stanley Cups. Wayne joined the Los Angeles Kings in 1988 and the St. Louis Blues in February 1996. He plays center and Gordie Howe is his hero.

Gordie Howe: "Mr. Hockey" set pro records by scoring 975 goals and 2,358 points during an amazing 32 seasons! He won six NHL scoring titles, six MVP awards, and four Stanley Cups as a right wing for the Red Wings from 1946 to 1971. He came out of retirement in 1973 at age 45 to play with his sons Marty and Mark for the Houston Aeros of the WHA. He retired again in 1980 at 52! He was elected to the Hall of Fame in 1972.

Bobby Hull: "The Golden Jet" made the *slap shot* popular in the NHL. He starred at left wing for the Blackhawks from 1957 to 1972 and won three NHL scoring titles and two MVP awards. (Bobby then played in the

In 1959, Jacques Plante (right) became the first goaltender in the NHL to play with a face mask.

GREAT GAMES!

Miracle on Ice: At the Winter Olympics in Lake Placid, N.Y., on February 22, 1980, the U.S. hockey team pulled off a miracle when it upset the mighty Soviet Union. Team USA was down 3–2 midway through the final period when Mark Johnson scored to tie the game. Ninety seconds later, captain Mike Eruzione put the puck in the net to give the U.S. a 4–3 lead it never lost.

Fifty in 50: Mike Bossy of the Islanders needed 2 goals against Quebec on January 24, 1981, to tie Rocket Richard's record of 50 goals in 50 games, set in 1945. With 4 ½ minutes left in the game, he got one. The second came with just 1:31 on the clock!

The Great One Passes Mr. Hockey: Wayne Gretzky of the Kings needed to score 2 points to break Gordie Howe's NHL career record of 1,850 points. On October 15, 1989, against the Edmonton Oilers, his former team, Wayne tied the record with an assist in the first period and broke the record with a goal with just 53 seconds left in the game!

WHA for the Winnipeg Jets until 1979.) In Chicago, Bobby was a teammate of his brother Dennis, who played forward in the NHL for 14 seasons. Bobby's son Brett is a star with the Blues. Bobby was elected to the Hall of Fame in 1983.

Mario Lemieux: Since 1984, this 6' 4", 210-pound center has won four scoring titles, two MVP awards, and two Stanley Cups with the Penguins. Back injuries and a form of cancer called Hodgkin's disease have plagued him since 1989, but when he's well, "Super Mario" lives up to his nickname. He returned to All-Star form in the 1995–96 season.

Howie Morenz: Howie was one of the fastest skaters in NHL history. He began his career as a forward with Montreal in 1923 when low-scoring games were common. His speed made him a dangerous scorer. He won three MVP awards and two scoring titles, finishing his career in 1937 with 270 goals. He was elected to the Hall of Fame in 1945.

Bobby Orr: Bobby played for the Bruins and Blackhawks, and was the first NHL defenseman to become a top scorer. He won two scoring titles and was named best defenseman each year from 1968 to 1975. He set ca-

173

QUICK HITS

The NHL season achievement awards are usually referred to by their official names. Here's a translation. The league's most valuable player wins the Hart Memorial Trophy. The top scorer in the regular season takes home the Art Ross Trophy. The rookie of the year wins the Calder Memorial Trophy, the top defenseman the James Norris Trophy, the top goalie the Vezina Trophy, the best defensive forward the Frank J. Selke Trophy, and the playoff MVP the Conn Smythe Trophy. The NHL also honors the player who shows the best sportsmanship. He wins the Lady Byng Memorial Trophy.

reer records for defensemen with 270 goals and 915 points, and won two Stanley Cups. He was elected to the Hall of Fame in 1979.

Denis Potvin: Denis played for the Islanders from 1973 to 1988 and was the best all-around defenseman in NHL history. He threw ferocious bodychecks and also broke Bobby Orr's scoring records. Denis scored 310 goals and 1,052 points in his career, played on four Stanley Cup champion teams, and was elected to the Hall of Fame in 1991.

Maurice "Rocket" Richard: Wild-eyed and strong, Rocket terrorized goalies from 1942 to 1960. He scored 544 goals for Montreal and played for eight Stanley Cup champions. He was elected to the Hall of Fame in 1961. His younger, smaller brother, Henri, was called the "Pocket Rocket." Henri scored 358 goals in 20 seasons with Montreal and was elected to the Hall of Fame in 1979.

Terry Sawchuk: Terry was the first goalie to play in a crouch position. He started with the Red Wings in 1950 and allowed fewer than two goals per game during his first five seasons. When he retired in 1970, he had set career records for wins (435) and shutouts (103). He won four Stanley Cups and was elected to the Hall of Fame in 1971.

Georges Vezina: Each year, the NHL's top goalie receives the "Vezina Trophy." It is named in honor of Georges, who led Montreal to five NHL championships between 1910 to 1925. He once played in 373 games in a row and was called the "Chicoutimi Cucumber" because he was born in Chicoutimi, Quebec, Canada, and always kept his cool in big games. He joined the Hall of Fame in 1945.

Glossary

Assist: A player is credited with an assist (and one point) after passing to a teammate who scores a goal. Assists are given only to the last one or two players who touched the puck before the goal-scorer.

Changing on the fly: When a team substitutes players while the play is moving rapidly from one end of the ice to the other.

Bodychecking: Using the body to bump an opponent off-balance, away from the puck, or out of the play. Only the player with the puck or the last one to touch the puck can be checked. A team checking in the attacking zone is *forechecking*. When it checks in its defensive zone, it is *backchecking*.

Delayed penalty: When a penalty is called on a defending player, the action does not stop until his team touches the puck. The player then goes to the penalty box.

Dump and chase: A strategy in which a team shoots the puck into the attacking zone, chases after it, and tries to gain possession by checking the opposing players.

Hat trick: When a player scores three goals in a game. The term comes from the sport of cricket.

Icing: When a player shoots the puck all the way down the ice from his defensive zone across the other team's goal line *(see The Rink, page 165)*. Play stops and the puck is brought back for a face-off. Icing is not called if the player's team has fewer skaters on the ice than its opponent or if his team is the first to touch the puck after it crosses the goal line.

Penalty killing: The defensive style of play a team uses when, due to a penalty, it has fewer skaters than its opponent. The shorthanded team plays this way until the penalty time expires.

Penalty shot: A free shot that is awarded to a player who has been dragged down from behind before he could take a clear shot at the net. The player then skates alone with the puck into the attacking zone and shoots. The only defender allowed is the goalie.

Point: The place at each end of the attacking zone blue line where defensemen play

OLYMPIC CHAMPIONS

Teams from Canada won six of the first seven gold medals in Olympic hockey. But in 1956, the Soviet Union became the top Olympic hockey power. From 1956 through 1988, the Soviets failed to win the gold only twice — in 1960 and 1980 — when they were upset by the U.S. (The U.S. has also won the silver medal six times and the bronze medal once.)

Here are the recent Olympic champions. One team has played as the Soviet Union, the Unified Team, and now Russia, but it has been the best in the world.

1994	Sweden
1992	Unified Team
1988	Soviet Union
1984	Soviet Union
1980	United States
1976	Soviet Union
1972	Soviet Union
1968	Soviet Union
1964	Soviet Union
1960	United States

while their team is on a power play.

Power play: When a team tries to score while it has more skaters on the ice than its opponent because of a penalty.

Save: When a goalie stops a shot on goal by blocking or catching the puck.

Shorthanded: When a team has fewer skaters on the ice than its opponent.

Slap shot: A hard shot that is taken by drawing the stick way back and swinging it forcefully at the puck.

Slot: The area in front of the goal between the two face-off circles in each attacking zone.

Stick check: Using the stick to poke the puck away from an opposing player.

Wrist shot: A shot made without the stick blade leaving the ice.

Where to Write

National Hockey League, 650 Fifth Ave., 33rd Floor, New York, NY 10019-6108

Mighty Ducks of Anaheim, 2695 Katella Ave., P.O. Box 61077, Anaheim, CA 92803

Boston Bruins, Boston Garden, 150 Causeway St., Boston, MA 02114

Buffalo Sabres, Memorial Auditorium, Buffalo, NY 14202

Calgary Flames, Olympic Saddledome, Box 1540, Station M, Calgary, Alberta, Canada T2P 3B9

Chicago Blackhawks, 1800 W. Madison St., Chicago, IL 60612

Dallas Stars, 901 Main St., Suite 2301, Dallas, TX 75202

Detroit Red Wings, Joe Louis Arena, 600 Civic Center Dr., Detroit, MI 48226

Edmonton Oilers, Northlands Coliseum, Edmonton, Alberta, Canada T5B 4M9

Florida Panthers, 100 Northeast Third Ave., 10th Floor, Fort Lauderdale, FL 33301

Hartford Whalers, 242 Trumbull St., 8th Floor, Hartford, CT 06103

Los Angeles Kings, The Great Western

Forum, 3900 West Manchester Blvd., P.O. Box 17013, Inglewood, CA 90308

Montreal Canadiens, Montreal Forum, 2313 St. Catherine St. West, Montreal, Quebec, Canada H3H 1N2

New Jersey Devils, Byrne Meadowlands Arena, Box 504, East Rutherford, NJ 07073

New York Islanders, Nassau Veterans' Memorial Coliseum, Uniondale, NY 11553

New York Rangers, Madison Square Garden, 4 Penn Plaza, New York, NY 10001

Ottawa Senators, 301 Moodie Dr., Suite 200, Nepean, Ontario, Canada K2H 9C4

Philadelphia Flyers, The Spectrum, Pattison Pl., Philadelphia, PA 19148

Pittsburgh Penguins, Civic Arena, Pittsburgh, PA 15219

Quebec Nordiques, Colisée de Québec, 2205 Ave de Colisée, Quebec City, Quebec, Canada G1L 4W7

St. Louis Blues, St. Louis Arena, 5700 Oakland Ave., St. Louis, MO 63110-1397

San Jose Sharks, San Jose Arena, 525 West Santa Clara St., P.O. Box 1240, San Jose, CA 95113

Tampa Bay Lightning, 501 East Kennedy Blvd., Suite 175, Tampa, FL 33602

Toronto Maple Leafs, Maple Leaf Gardens, 60 Carlton St., Toronto, Ontario, Canada M5B 1L1

Vancouver Canucks, Pacific Coliseum, 100 North Renfrew St., Vancouver, B.C., Canada V5K 3N7

Washington Capitals, USAir Arena, 1 Harry S. Truman Dr., Landover, MD 20785

Winnipeg Jets, Winnepeg Arena, 15-1430 Maroons Rd., Winnipeg, Manitoba, Canada R3G OL5

Hockey Hall of Fame, BCE Place, 30 Yonge St., Toronto, Ontario, Canada M6K 3C3

USA Hockey (Olympic team), 4965 North 30th St., Colorado Springs, CO 80919

YOUTH HOCKEY

Hockey leagues for kids in the U.S. and Canada are organized according to age: mite (9 years old and under), squirt (10–11), pee wee (12–13), bantam (14–15), midget (16–17), junior (18–19), and senior (20 and older). Leagues for girls have also been created. They are: junior (8–12), teen (13–15), and open (16 and up).

Talented youth hockey players often move on to "major junior" teams in the Canadian Hockey League (CHL). Junior team players often play for teams far from home and must find time in a busy travel schedule to attend school. Each year, CHL teams compete for the Memorial Cup. The league's best players are drafted by NHL teams.

The best young players in the U.S. usually play in high school and college. Forty-six U.S. colleges and universities have hockey teams. A national tournament has been held since 1948. The University of Michigan has won the national championship a record seven times.

LACROSSE

Lacrosse has been called "the fastest game on two feet." It was created by Native Americans and has roots dating back as far as the 1400's.

ALL-BALL

Jim Brown was one of the greatest running backs in NFL history, gaining 12,312 yards and scoring 126 touchdowns with the Cleveland Browns from 1957–65. But he was also an All-America lacrosse player at Syracuse University in 1956 and 1957. He was the second-leading scorer in the country (43 goals, 21 assists) in 1957.

History

Lacrosse is the oldest team sport in North America. The game was called *baggataway*, which means "little brother of war." Players used sticks with pouches at the end to hurl a round object into the opposing team's goal. That is the way the game is played today.

In its early days, lacrosse was often extremely violent, and many games were played between Native American tribes to settle disputes. The contests would last several days and include hundreds of players. Often, the goals were located miles apart.

The Mohawk Indians introduced the game to the French Canadians in the 1750's. Lacrosse got its name from the fact that early French missionaries thought the players' sticks resembled a bishop's *crosier* (staff). The game became known as "La crosse."

By the mid-1930's, lacrosse had become one of the most popular sports in Canada. In the first international lacrosse match, in 1868, Canada defeated the United States. Soon after, lacrosse spread to England after a team of Iroquois Indians demonstrated the sport.

How to Play

Lacrosse is played by two teams. Each tries to throw a ball into the opponents' goal using long-handled sticks. The highest score wins.

A game is divided into four quarters. There is a face-off at the start of every quarter and after every goal. In the face-off, two opposing players crouch facing each other at the center line, and the referee places the ball on the

TEXT BY BRAD HERZOG

Gary Gait (#22) and twin brother Paul led Syracuse to three straight NCAA titles from 1988 to 1990.

A professional league, the Major Indoor Lacrosse League (MILL), was formed in 1987. The teams play box lacrosse, an indoor version played in an area about the size of a hockey rink. The field measures 200' by 85', and is surrounded by three-foot-high boards.

Box lacrosse is very popular in Canada. It combines the strategy of hockey, the fast break of basketball, and the contact of football.

Many of the best lacrosse players in the world compete in the MILL, which has six teams divided into two divisions. Each team plays four home games and four road games. The divisional winners compete for the North American Cup in April.

The league's form of lacrosse has six players to a side: five forwards and one goalie. There is a 30-second shot clock, which makes the game fast. The goal is smaller than in field lacrosse, measuring 4' wide and 4' 6" high. Games are divided into four 15-minute quarters.

ground between their sticks. He blows the whistle, and each player tries to gain control of the ball.

Players may use their sticks to pass the ball or run with it, but only the goaltender may touch the ball with his hands.

Equipment

Lacrosse players dress for both speed and contact. They usually wear short-sleeved shirts, short pants, shoulder pads, heavy leather gloves, and helmets with face masks.

The game is played with a hard rubber ball that is slightly smaller than a baseball. When it is thrown properly, it can travel up to 100 miles per hour.

The lacrosse stick, which is called a *crosse*, has a long handle and a head. The head is used to catch the ball. It is a leather and string pocket attached to a plastic frame.

Lacrosse sticks may range from 3' 6" to 6' long. Defensive players use longer sticks with wider heads than attacking players. The

AMAZING FEAT

head of a field player's stick may be 6 ½" to 10" wide, but the head of a goaltender's stick may be as much as 12" wide.

The Players

There are two basic kinds of lacrosse: *field lacrosse* and *box lacrosse (see Pro Lacrosse)*.

Field, or outdoor, lacrosse is played with 10 players to a side: a *goaltender*, three *defensemen*, three *midfielders*, and three *attackmen*.

Each team must always keep at least four players on the defensive end of the field (usually three defensemen and a goalie) and three players on the offensive end (usually three attackmen). If not, the team is called for being *offsides*. The midfielders play in both zones. Teams are allowed to substitute at any time.

The goalie protects the goal by blocking shots with his body or catching it in his stick. Defensemen use their long sticks and their bodies to *check* (legally bump into) opposing players who are carrying the ball. Body-checking is legal if the opponent has the ball or is within five yards of it. Defensemen attempt to regain control of the ball and move it out of the defensive zone.

Teams often use set plays that resemble strategies in basketball, hockey, and soccer. Midfielders help move the ball into the offensive zone. They are usually good passers and must be able to shoot accurately from long distances. Attackmen usually play behind or to the side of the goal. They use short sticks because they shoot from close to the goal. They must be able to shoot with either hand.

The Field

Men's field lacrosse is played on a grass or artificial-turf field 110 yards long and 60 yards wide. The goals are 6' high and 6' wide, and are centered between the sidelines, with 15 yards of playing area behind each net.

Surrounding each goal is an 18-foot circle

called the goal crease. A center line divides the field in half.

Rules

Attacking players may not enter the goal crease, but they may reach in with their stick to grab a ball. If a player is offsides, touches the ball, holds an opponent, or throws his stick, he is given a *technical foul*. If the team that was fouled had possession of the ball, the penalized player must sit out for 30 seconds. During that time, his team must play short a player. If the team that was fouled didn't have possession of the ball, it gets the ball.

A *personal foul* is called if a player uses an illegal bodycheck, slashes with his stick, trips an opponent, or is called for any unsportsmanlike conduct. He sits out for one to three minutes. Usually, if the opposing team scores when a team is playing shorthanded, the player's penalty time is over.

A game consists of four 15-minute quarters on the college level and four 12-minute quarters in high school. If the score is tied after four quarters, teams play four-minute sudden-death periods until a goal is scored.

College Lacrosse

In the United States, lacrosse is played by men and women in youth leagues, high schools, colleges, organized club leagues, and even at the professional level.

There are more than 150 colleges and universities across the U.S. that have varsity lacrosse teams and several more that feature lacrosse clubs. The college programs that are run by the National Collegiate Athletic Association (NCAA) are separated into three divisions, and each division holds its own national championship tournament in the spring. There is also a men's junior college championship every year.

From 1881 to 1970, teams won the national

WOMEN'S LACROSSE

The first known women's lacrosse game was played in 1886. Today, more than 22,000 women and girls in the U.S. play lacrosse at some level.

The women's game differs in many ways from the men's game. There is no official field size, though it is usually about 120 yards long and 70 yards wide, with 10 yards behind each goal. Games are divided into two 25-minute halves. Overtime periods last six minutes.

There are 12 players to a side, no offsides rules, and no body checking permitted. Fouls are penalized with a *free position*. That means a player on the team that has been fouled gets the ball in her stick at the place of the foul.

Today, there are more than 100 colleges in the country with women's lacrosse teams. NCAA Division I and II teams compete in one national tournament each spring, while the Division III teams hold their own national championship tournament.

181

AWESOME ATHLETES

At Syracuse University, stars (and brothers) Gary and Paul Gait invented an exciting scoring move called the "Air Gait." They take off from behind the goal and put the ball in the net before their feet land in the crease — without touching the goal or goaltender.

title by being voted the U.S. Intercollegiate Lacrosse Association champion. In 1971, the first NCAA Division I lacrosse tournament was played, and it was won by Cornell University. Johns Hopkins University has won the most Division I titles, with seven.

International Competition

The first International Lacrosse Federation World Championship was held in Toronto, Canada, in 1967. Since 1974, the event has been held every four years. At the 1994 world championship, which was won by the U.S., the Iroquois Nationals team competed. Native American teams had been banned from competition for 100 years and the Iroquois team didn't join international competition until 1990. The 1998 world championship will be held in Baltimore, Maryland.

Women compete in the World Cup, which began in 1982 in England. It has been held four times, and the U.S. has won three times and Australia once. The next World Cup will be held in Japan in 1997.

Legends

Evan Davis, U.S.: Evan played lacrosse at the University of Arizona from 1982–85. In 1984, he scored 130 points (goals plus assists), the most ever in one season by a Division I college player. The following year, he set another record by recording 19 points in one game. His 363 career points are yet another Division I record.

Francesca DenHartog, U.S.: Francesca played at Harvard University from 1980–83. She was the Ivy League Player of the Year in 1981 and 1982. She was a member of the U.S. World Cup team in 1982, 1986, and 1990.

Gary and Paul Gait, Canada: These twins led Syracuse University to three straight NCAA titles from 1988–90. Gary, who scored the second-most goals (192) in

NCAA history, was named College Player of the Year in 1988 and 1990. Paul was a three-time All-America. Both players have gone on to star with the Philadelphia Wings of the Major Indoor Lacrosse League.

Dave Pietramala, U.S.: Dave, currently a member of MILL's Baltimore Thunder, is considered one of the top defensemen in the world. He was a three-time All-America at Johns Hopkins University in Baltimore. Dave was the top player on the U.S. team that won the world championship in 1990.

John Tavares, Canada: John led the MILL in scoring in 1993 with 35 goals and 23 assists. He also led the Buffalo Bandits to two straight MILL championships in 1992 and 1993. In the 1992 MILL title game, he scored the game-winning goal in overtime.

Glossary

Clear: When defensive players move the ball downfield to get their team in attack position.

Free play: When the ball or a player with the ball goes out-of-bounds, the other team gets possession of the ball where it went out.

Groundball: A loose ball scooped up by a player.

Man-up situation: When a team has an extra player because the opposing team is one player short due to a penalty.

Ride: When attackmen prevent opponents from clearing the ball out of the defensive zone.

Where to Write

Lacrosse Foundation and Hall of Fame Museum, 113 West University Pkwy., Baltimore, MD 21210

Major Indoor Lacrosse League, 2310 West 75th St., Prairie Village, KS 66208

U.S. Women's Lacrosse Association, 45 Maple Ave., Hamilton, NY 13346

CHAMPIONS

MAJOR INDOOR LACROSSE LEAGUE

1995	Philadelphia Wings
1994	Philadelphia Wings
1993	Buffalo Bandits
1992	Buffalo Bandits
1991	Detroit Turbos
1990	Philadelphia Wings
1989	Philadelphia Wings

MEN'S NCAA DIVISION I

1995	Syracuse
1994	Princeton
1993	Syracuse
1992	Princeton
1991	North Carolina
1990	Syracuse
1989	Syracuse
1988	Syracuse
1987	Johns Hopkins
1986	North Carolina

WOMEN'S NCAA DIVISION I AND II

1995	Maryland
1994	Princeton
1993	Virginia
1992	Maryland
1991	Virginia
1990	Harvard
1989	Penn State
1988	Temple
1987	Penn State
1986	Maryland

RODEO

In the dramatic sport of rodeo, modern cowboys wrestle 600-pound steers and cowgirls ride bucking broncs in competitions that test their skill, strength, and courage.

History

More than 100 years ago, cowboys tended cattle on ranches in the West and often drove herds hundreds of miles to graze. Strength and skill were needed to control the cattle while the cowboys were riding on horseback.

In their spare time, cowboys started holding competitions among themselves to see who was the best at riding a *bronco* or catching a runaway bull with a rope *lasso*. In 1869, a bronc-riding competition was held in Deer Trail, Colorado. (A bronc or bronco is a wild horse or pony.) Before long, the sport of rodeo was born.

The first organized rodeos were held in the West in the 1880's. They tested horsemanship, skill at using a rope and tying knots, quick thinking, strength, and bravery. It takes guts to climb onto the back of an angry, bucking bull that weighs 2,000 pounds! Rodeo cowboys are often seriously injured. Some have even been killed.

In spite of the danger, hundreds of rodeos are held each year in the United States, Canada, and Australia. Men, women, and even kids compete.

Competitions

There are two main types of rodeo competitions: rough stock events and timed events.

In *rough stock*, riders try to stay on bucking bulls or horses for a set period of time. They are also awarded points for good form and how difficult the animals are to ride.

In *timed events*, competitors are judged ac-

TEXT BY JOHN ROLFE

Ty Murray, here riding a bull, was all-around champion five years in a row, from 1989 to 1993.

PRO RODEO

Top pros live a rugged and demanding life. They practice as much as eight hours a day. They travel thousands of miles all over the U.S. and Canada to compete in 100 or more rodeos each year.

Cowboys can choose which events they want to compete in and are ranked each year according to how well they do. The Professional Rodeo Cowboys Association awards one point for each dollar a contestant wins at the organization's official events. Timed event rankings are determined by the number of points each contestant wins at up to 100 events during the year. Rough stock rankings are computed with points earned at up to 125 events.

One of the first rodeos to offer prize money was held in Pecos, Texas, on July 4, 1883. The winners of the riding and roping contests received $25. In 1992, Billy Etbauer set a record by winning $101,531 at the National Finals Rodeo in Las Vegas, Nevada.

cording to how fast they complete a particular task.

ROUGH STOCK EVENTS

Bareback bronc riding: Without a saddle, riders try to stay on a bucking horse for eight seconds. Only one hand can be used to hold on to the handle of a *bareback rigging*, which is fastened around the horse just behind its shoulders.

The rider must keep his heels over the horse's shoulders as they leave the narrow starting pen called the *chute*. Each time the horse kicks up its hind legs, the rider brings his knees to his body, then stretches his legs out again. This motion is called *spurring*.

Judges award points based on how high and hard the bronc bucks and how well and often a rider spurs the horse. A rider is disqualified if he falls off, touches himself or the horse with his free hand, or fails to keep his

AWESOME ATHLETE

What a lot of bull! "Red Rock," one of the greatest bucking bulls in rodeo history, threw 312 riders in a row off his back between 1980 and 1988. On May 20, 1988, Lane Frost finally was able to stay on for the full eight seconds. "Red Rock" was inducted into the Pro-Rodeo Hall of Fame!

heels over the horse's shoulders while leaving the chute.

Saddle bronc riding: In this event, the rider sits in a saddle, holds a rein attached to a halter strap on the horse's head, and spurs by moving the lower half of each leg back and forth. The rider must also keep his feet in the stirrups, with his toes turned out.

Bull riding: This is the most popular — and dangerous — rodeo event. With one hand, the rider holds on to a rope wrapped around the bull just behind its shoulders. He tries to stay on for eight seconds by keeping his body close to his hand, with his legs forward and heels dug into the bull's sides.

TIMED EVENTS

Steer wrestling: Contestants slide off a running horse and grab a 600-pound *steer* (a young bull) behind its horns and wrestle it to the ground. The time stops once the steer is lying on its side with all four legs pointing in the same direction. A second rider, called a *hazer,* helps out by keeping the steer running in a straight line before it is tackled. This event is also called *bulldogging.*

Steer roping: A rider on a horse chases a steer and wraps a rope around its horns from one side. When the rider races around to the other side, the steer trips over the rope. The rider then jumps off his horse and ties the steer's hind legs together to stop the clock.

Team roping: Two contestants on horseback — a *header* and a *heeler* — work as a team. After they chase down a steer, the header ropes its horns, while the heeler ropes its hind legs. The clock stops when the header has wrapped his rope around his saddle horn, the heeler has tied the steer's legs, and both ropes have been pulled tight in a 90-degree angle.

Calf roping: A 300-pound *calf* (baby bull) is given a head start before a rider chases and ropes it. The rider then dismounts, picks the calf up, lies it on its side, and ties three legs together. The legs must point in the same direction and remain tied for five seconds after the rider has gotten back on his horse and allowed slack in the rope.

Barrel racing: This event is usually for women. Cowgirls are timed as they ride horses around three barrels in a cloverleaf pattern and then race back to the starting line. Judges add five seconds to a rider's time for each barrel she knocks over.

Organized Rodeo

Rodeo has many organizations, but the most important are the Professional Rodeo Cowboys Association, or PRCA (see *Pro Rodeo, page 185*), the Womens Professional Rodeo Association (WPRA), and the International Pro Rodeo Association (IPRA). Together, they organize more than 1,300 rodeos each year.

Cowgirls compete at all-women rodeos in almost all the standard events. The rules are slightly different in bareback bronc riding and bull riding. Women are allowed to hold on with two hands and the time limit is six seconds. Other events include goat-tying and steer undecorating (riding after a steer and snatching a ribbon off its back).

Amateur cowboys who enjoy performing at rodeos but are unable to make a living at it can compete in any one of the PRCA's 12 local "circuits." There is a circuit in just about every state. Point standings are used to determine circuit champions.

Kid rodeo riders can join the Little Britches circuit. Each year, some 18,000 boys and girls ages 8 to 18 compete at more than 100 Little Britches rodeos in 22 states.

Big Events

Rodeo's biggest event is the National

PRO RODEO CHAMPIONS

ALL-AROUND
1995　Joe Beaver
1994　Ty Murray
1993　Ty Murray

SADDLE BRONC RIDING
1995　Dan Mortensen
1994　Dan Mortensen
1993　Dan Mortensen

BAREBACK BRONC RIDING
1995　Marvin Garrett
1994　Marvin Garrett
1993　Deb Greenough

BULL RIDING
1995　Jerome Davis
1994　Daryl Mills
1993　Ty Murray

CALF ROPING
1995　Fred Whitfield
1994　Herbert Theriot
1993　Joe Beaver

STEER WRESTLING
1995　Ote Berry
1994　Blaine Pederson
1993　Steve Duhon

TEAM ROPING
1995　Header:Bobby Hurley
　　　　Healer: Alden Bach

STEER ROPING
1995　Guy Allen
1994　Guy Allen
1993　Guy Allen

BARREL RACING
1995　Cherry Cervi
1994　Kristie Peterson
1993　C. James-Rodman

COOL FACT

Rodeo clowns are a colorful feature at most events. Between competitions, the clowns entertain spectators with riding and roping stunts. They also help distract angry bulls and broncs that have thrown their riders until the riders can scurry to safety.

Finals Rodeo in Las Vegas, Nevada. It has been held each year since 1959 and is sponsored by the PRCA and WPRA.

The National Finals, held at the end of the year, are where the world champions in each event are determined. Only the top 15 ranked performers in timed, rough stock, and barrel racing events qualify to compete. There are 10 rounds of competition held during a 10-day period. The performer who has won the most money in two or more events by the end of the year is crowned the "World Champion All-Around Cowboy."

The PRCA also sponsors the annual Dodge National Circuit Finals Rodeo in Pocatello, Idaho. The 12 local champions in each event compete there.

The IPRA's big event is the International Finals Rodeo in Oklahoma City, Oklahoma. Other big events are the WPRA Finals, the national college rodeo championships, and the National Little Britches Rodeo Finals.

Records
HIGHEST SCORES FOR RIDES

Bull Riding: 100 points, by Wade Leslie on "Wolfman Skoal" at Central Point, Oregon, in 1991.

Saddle Bronc Riding: 95 points, Doug Vold on "Transport" at Meadow Lake, Sasketchewan, Canada, 1979.

Bareback Bronc Riding: 93 points, Joe Alexander on "Marlboro" at Cheyenne, Wyoming, 1974.

FASTEST TIMES

Calf Roping: 6.7 seconds, Joe Beaver at West Jordan, Utah, 1986.

Steer Roping: 8.4 seconds, Guy Allen at Garden City, Kansas, 1991.

Steer Wrestling: 2.4 seconds, by James Bynum at Marietta, Oklahoma, 1955; Carl Deaton at Tulsa, Oklahoma, 1976; and Gene Melton at Pecatonica, Illinois, 1976.

Team Roping: 3.7 seconds, Bob Harris and Tee Woolman at Spanish Fork, Utah, 1986.

Legends

Bob Askin: Bob was the original "Mr. Rodeo." He competed from 1923 to the early 1950's. He made history by successfully riding the "unrideable" broncs "Midnight" (in 1926) and "Five Minutes to Midnight" (in 1936). Both broncs are Hall of Famers.

Don Gay: Don is the greatest bull-rider of all time. Between 1974 and 1981, he was world champion every year except for 1978.

Charmayne James-Rodman: The winningest cowgirl in WPRA history, she has been the barrel-racing champion from 1984 to 1993. In 1990, she became the first cowgirl — and only the third rodeo competitor ever — to win $1 million in her career.

Ty Murray: In 1989, at age 20, Ty became the youngest all-around world champion in rodeo history. He won the title every year through 1993 and set a record for most money won in a single year ($258,750).

Jim Shoulders: Many people feel Jim was rodeo's greatest competitor. He won a record 16 PRCA world titles between 1949 and 1959, including five all-around, four bareback bronc riding, and seven bull riding championships.

Casey Tibbs: He was called the "Babe Ruth" of rodeo. He won nine world titles between 1949 and 1959, including six saddle bronc, two all-around, and one bareback bronc championships. He retired in 1964, but came back three years later and won 9 of his first 10 rodeos.

Where to Write

Professional Rodeo Cowboys Association/ProRodeo Hall of Fame and Museum of the American Cowboy, 101 Pro-Rodeo Dr., Colorado Springs, CO 80919

ONE MORE THING

Rodeo animals are carefully bred to be strong, spirited, and even wild. Top bucking broncs can cost as much as $15,000 and bulls as much as $20,000.

Broncs and bulls don't like having riders on their backs, and steers and calves don't like being tied up with ropes. However, rodeo athletes are careful not to hurt the animals.

There are also strict rules to make sure all animals are cared for properly. These rules are set by the American Humane Association

Great broncs such as "Midnight" and bulls such as "Red Rock" have their own place in rodeo history. These animals and others have even been elected to the Pro-Rodeo Hall of Fame.

ROLLER-SKATING

With the exploding popularity of in-line skates, roller-skating seems to be a new sport. But don't be fooled: It has been around for 200 years.

History

Roller-skating dates back to the 1760's in England. The first known pair of skates was developed by Joseph Merlin, an inventor from Belgium.

In the 1860's, James Plimpton, a furniture maker in the United States, invented the four-wheel roller skate. He also opened the first public roller-skating rink, in Newport, Rhode Island. Roller-skating became very popular and rinks began to open throughout the United States and around the world. In 1937, the first U.S. roller-skating championships were held.

The Skates

There are two types of roller skates. *Quads* are skates with four wheels, two in front and two in back. *In-line* skates have their wheels lined up in single file.

Although a type of in-line skates was patented in 1819, the modern version were invented in 1980 by Scott Olsen, a hockey player who wanted to develop an activity like ice skating for warm weather. After his new skate became a hit, Scott formed the Rollerblade company.

Competitions

There are two types of roller-skating competitions: *speed* and *artistic*. World speed competitions have been held every year since 1938, and have alternated between track racing (with banked turns on an oval track) and road racing. Events are held from 300 to

TEXT BY SCOTT WAPNER

Seven-time champion Dante Muse (in the lead) is the fastest American on eight wheels.

20,000 meters, and road racing also has a 42-kilometer marathon. There are individual and relay categories. There is also an overall competition, in which skaters earn points for how well they finish in each event. Each year, there are national and world championships. Skaters can compete in either quads or in-line skates.

Artistic competitions consist of figures (tracing patterns on the floor), singles (freestyle), and dance. As in figure skating *(see page 104)*, skaters perform programs to music, and there are events for singles and pairs.

Legends

Tina Kneisley, U.S.: Tina won the 1981, 1983, and 1984 world freestyle championships and three gold medals in pairs.

Dante Muse, U.S.: Dante has won seven U.S. overall men's speed titles. He won the overall world speed championship in 1990.

Alberta Vianello, Italy: Alberta won a record 19 world speed championships from 1953 to 1965, including 8 track and 11 road.

Where to Write

U.S. Amateur Confederation of Roller Skating/National Roller Skating Hall of Fame, 4730 South St., Lincoln, NE 68506

CHAMPIONS

SPEED SKATING: TRACK

WOMEN (continued)

5,000m	Cheryl Ezzell, U.S.
10,000m	Theresa Cliff, U.S.
5,000m relay:	United States
Individual overall	
	Cheryl Ezzell
Team	United States

MEN

300m	Ippolito Sanfratello, Italy
500m	Ippolito Sanfratello
1,500m	Chad Hedrick, U.S.
5,000m	Derek Downing, U.S.
10,000m	Chad Hedrick
20,000m	Christopher Luxton, United States
10,000m relay:	United States
Individual overall	
	Ippolito Sanfratello
Team	France

SPEED SKATING: ROAD

WOMEN

300m	Desly Hill, Australia
500m	Valentina Belloni, Italy
1,500m	Sandrine Plu, France
3,000m	Cheryl Ezzell, U.S.
5,000m	Theresa Cliff, U.S.
10,000m	Cheryl Ezzell
21K	Hilde Goovaerts, Belgium
Individual overall	
	Cheryl Ezzell
Team	Italy

MEN

300m	Derek Parra, U.S.
500m	Ippolito Sanfratello, Italy
1,500m	Derek Parra
5,000m	Scott Hiatt, U.S.
20,000m	Chad Hedrick, U.S.
42K	Chad Hedrick
Individual overall	
	Chad Hedrick
Team	United States

SKATEBOARDING

Skateboarding is an unofficial sport. Although there are competitions, there is no governing body and no national championship — just a lot of *thrashers* out there *shredding* like mad.

AMAZING FEAT

In 1990, Roger Hickey set two skateboard speed records, one while riding the board standing up (*upright*), and another while riding the board on his back (*prone*). In March, Roger raced 78.37 miles per hour while prone. In July, he went 55.43 m.p.h. while upright.

History

It's not surprising that skateboarding was invented by California surfers frustrated by bad waves. But in the 1930's? That's when someone first nailed roller-skate wheels onto boards and hit the sidewalks.

Nothing much happened with the sport until Frank Nasworthy invented the *urethane* wheel in 1973. Urethane is softer than the metal or hard clay that wheels had been made of, and it grips the road well. These wheels revolutionized the sport.

Competitions

Most *thrashers* aren't out there to be judged, they're out there to *shred*. But over the years, there have been competitions and world championships in events such as *freestyle* and *vert*. In freestyle, riders perform any moves or tricks they want, such as *Ollies*, while riding their boards on the streets.

Vert is done in *halfpipes* and *quarterpipes*. Halfpipe riders start their routines from the top of the pipe, or *ramp*. They race down one side and up the other, where they shoot into the air to perform tricks. Then, they turn around and race down the other side. Halfpipe riders can perform tricks continuously. Quarterpipe riders get a rolling start and shoot up the face of the ramp for their tricks. They must start their runs over each time.

The organization that had run competitions, the National Skateboard Association, went out of business in early 1994. There are still competitions, but no official events.

TEXT BY STEPHEN THOMAS

This well-protected skater is doing a trick off the lip of a halfpipe in a skateboard park.

The Boards

Ramp boards are large and have firm wheels mounted on wide *trucks* (the metal pieces on the bottom of the board) to make the board more stable. Firm wheels and wide trucks help the rider do tricks on the ramp.

Street boards are shorter and narrower and they have softer wheels. Soft wheels are slower, but slip less on dirty or sandy streets.

Freestyle boards are the easiest to maneuver because they're the smallest. They use harder wheels to give riders some speed.

Legends

Cara-Beth Burnside, U.S.: In 1990, Cara-Beth was the first woman to become a professional skateboarder.

Tony Hawk, U.S.: In the mid-1980's, Tony won 18 of 29 sanctioned pro events. Tony was the first skater to land a *720 aerial* on a halfpipe: He turned two full somersaults and landed back on his board.

SKATE TALK

Aggro: Totally aggressive skating.

Beat: A disappointment.

Bionic: The best.

Catching air: When a rider leaves the ground off of a halfpipe or quarterpipe.

Flapping: Hot, or radical, skating.

Grommet: See *Snoid*.

Halfpipe: A ramp that is a half-circle, like a drainpipe cut in half.

Hamburger: A bruise.

Lame: Uncool.

Ollie: The move skaters use to jump over a curb or fly high off a ramp. The whole board goes up in the air, level with the ground, with the skater's feet still on the board. The Ollie was created in 1978 by a skateboarder named Alan Gelfand, whose nickname was Ollie.

Poser: A person who dresses and talks like a skater but isn't one.

Quarterpipe: A ramp that is a quarter of a circle.

Shred: To skate.

Skate: To ride a skateboard.

Snoid: A young skater.

Thrasher: A skater.

Vert: A ride on a quarterpipe or halfpipe; catching air.

SKIING

Skiing is one of the big events of the Winter Olympic Games. It can be Nordic (cross-country and ski jumping), Alpine (downhill and slalom), or freestyle (aerials and moguls).

History

Skiing started in what is now Norway as far back as 7,000 years ago. The native people of that area, the Samis, used skis to cross the deep snows. Drawings on stone have been discovered from those days that show pictures of people wearing skis! The first ski poles probably doubled as spears for hunting.

It wasn't until many centuries later that skiing became a sport. The first cross-country ski races were held in Norway around 1840. In those days, skis were made of wood, which often came from barrels.

Skiing became popular after 1850, when a Norwegian named Sondre Norheim invented the first pair of ski *bindings*. Bindings hold boots onto skis. Sondre made his bindings by tying twisted pieces of tree roots around his boots. These gave him better control over his skis.

By the early 1900's, skiing had become a popular sport in many countries around the world. It was brought to the United States by immigrants from the Scandinavian countries (Norway, Denmark, Sweden, and Finland) who came to the U.S. and then moved west during the gold rush of the late 1800's.

Alpine ski racing developed in Switzerland, where the first organized slalom race was held in 1921. The invention of the ski lift in the mid-1930's helped to make Alpine skiing a popular form of recreation.

Cross-country skiing and ski jumping were part of the first Winter Olympics, in 1924. Alpine skiing events were added to the Win-

TEXT BY SCOTT WAPNER

ter Olympics at the 1948 Games, in St. Moritz, Switzerland.

At the 1948 Olympics, men and women each competed in three Alpine events: downhill, slalom, and combined. The giant slalom was added in 1952, the super-giant slalom in 1988 for men and 1992 for women. The combined was discontinued after the 1948 Games and brought back in 1988. Freestyle skiing was a demonstration sport at the 1988 Olympics and a medal sport for the first time in 1992.

Alpine Skiing

Alpine skiers ski down mountain slopes. *Alpine* comes from the Alps, the mountain

THE SLOPES

In downhill competition, skiers race as fast as they can down the mountain, following its natural slope. The course is about two miles long, with jumps and turns. Skiers can reach speeds up to 80 miles per hour.

Slalom racing requires a different technique. Skiers have to make a lot of sharp turns along a shorter, half-mile course. There are usually 55–75 gates on a course for the men's competition and 45–65 gates for women.

195

BLAST FROM THE PAST

The United States made its best Winter Olympic showing in Alpine skiing at the 1984 Games in Sarajevo, Yugoslavia. Bill Johnson became the first skier from the U.S. to win a gold medal in downhill, Debbie Armstrong became the second U.S. woman to win the giant slalom, and Phil Mahre became the first U.S. man to win the slalom. Phil's twin brother, Steve, won a silver in the slalom, making this the only time that brothers have finished first and second in an Olympic event.

chain that runs through Western Europe. There are five basic types of Alpine ski races: *downhill, slalom, giant slalom, super-giant slalom* (or Super G), and *Alpine combined* (which combines downhill and slalom races).

DOWNHILL

The downhill is skiing's version of the 100-meter dash. Skiers try to record the fastest time while streaking down a course that drops down between 500 and 800 meters.

The course is usually about two miles long. It is marked with *gates*, which the skiers must go around as they zoom down the mountain. Racers can go faster than 80 miles per hour. They fly into the air off of jumps and can sail as much as 50 meters before they land. In downhill competition, each skier takes one run down the course. The skier with the fastest time wins.

SLALOM

Slalom is what is known as a *technical* event. It demands speed, but also requires a lot of skiing skill. Skiers race down a half-mile course that is not as steep as the downhill course (about a 200-meter drop), but that is covered with gates: between 55 and 75 gates for men and 45–65 gates for women.

Skiers must make many short, quick turns around these gates, in the proper order, and reach the finish line as quickly as possible. In competition, slalom skiers take one run on each of two courses. The skier with the fastest combined time is the winner.

GIANT SLALOM

Giant slalom is a cross between downhill and slalom. The course, at about one mile, is longer and steeper than the slalom course. It has 48–60 gates, which skiers try to weave in and out of at speeds of up to 45 miles per hour. Skiers are timed the same as in slalom.

FREESTYLE SKIING

Freestyle is one of the most entertaining forms of skiing because of the acrobatic stunts involved. There are four categories.

In *ballet*, a skier performs a program set to music. The routine is a combination of jumps, spins, and steps.

Moguls is a fast-paced event that usually takes place on a steep hill with many packed mounds of snow, called moguls. Skiers go as fast as they can while performing stunts and jumps. They are judged on their time and how well they do their tricks.

Aerials is the wildest skiing event. Each skier takes two jumps off a platform and does flips, stunts, or acrobatic moves to music. Two types of aerials are done: inverted and upright. In the inverted, the skier performs flips. In the upright, he does not.

A *combined competition* consists of all three events, with the total score determining the winner.

Only moguls and aerials currently are Olympic events.

Ski jumpers, like Espen Bredesen of Norway, spread their skis in a V-shape to get more lift.

SUPER G

Super-giant slalom is a mix of the downhill and the giant slalom. As in downhill, racers really rocket (up to 50 m.p.h.) and the winner is determined after only one run. But technique is also important for manuevering through the gates.

A typical men's Super G course has 35 to 65 gates. A women's course has 30 to 50 gates.

ALPINE COMBINED

In the Alpine combined, skiers race in both a downhill race and a slalom race, and their times are added together. The two races usually are held on different days.

Nordic Skiing

Nordic skiing consists of three events:

COOL FACT

Bill Koch *[coke]* was the first American to win an Olympic medal in cross-country skiing. He won a silver medal in the 30-kilometer race in 1976. But Bill did more than that: He popularized the *skating* style of cross-country skiing. In that style, skiers take their skis out of the parallel tracks in the snow and push out with them as if they were ice skates. With his new style, Bill became the first U.S. cross-country skier to win the overall World Cup title, in 1982.

cross-country, ski jumping, and Nordic combined. The term *Nordic* comes from the word "north." Cross-country skiing originated in the northern European countries of Norway, Sweden, Denmark, and Finland.

CROSS-COUNTRY SKIING

Cross-country skiing is the most popular form of Nordic skiing. It combines speed and endurance. Unlike Alpine skiing, which is done down hills, cross-country is done on courses that are one-third uphill, one-third downhill, and one-third flat. Races can be from 5 to 50 kilometers in length. That's 3.1 to 30 miles!

There are two styles of skiing used by cross-country athletes: *classical* and *freestyle*. In the classical style, skiers keep their skis parallel in tracks cut in the snow. They move by thrusting one leg down and back, gliding forward on the other, and then thrusting the other leg back.

The term *freestyle* means skiers can choose any style they want, but most prefer the *skating* technique. This technique is fairly new *(see Cool Fact)*. In it, skiers use a motion much like ice-skating. They set one ski in the snow at an angle, then press that ski to the side and back while gliding forward on the other ski.

Cross-country skiers compete in races that require either freestyle or classical styles. They race against the clock. In most individual events, skiers start 30 seconds apart, and the finisher with the fastest time wins.

One different kind of race is the *two-day combined pursuit*. The pursuit combines a classical race on one day with a freestyle race on the other. The skier with the fastest time in the first race starts first on the second day. (All competitors start in order of how well they finished in the first race.) The first skier to finish on day two is the winner.

Cross-country teams also participate in four-person relays, with each team member racing a quarter of the total race distance.

SKI JUMPING

Ski jumping is one of the most exciting events in skiing. Competitors ski down a ramp (called an *in-run*), hit their takeoff point at about 55 m.p.h., then float down over a mountainside for as far as they can.

Although they appear on television to be high in the air, ski jumpers rarely are more than 10' off the ground. That's how far the takeoff point is from the ground. The jumpers' flight follows the slope of the hillside all the way down.

There are two types of ski jump courses: *normal hill* and *large hill*. At the 1994 Winter Olympics in Lillehammer, Norway, the normal hill was a 90-meter hill and the large hill was a 120-meter hill. Those meters measure the distance from the end of the ramp to the point near the bottom of the mountain where the ground begins to level out. That area, which is the landing area, is called the *K point* of the hill.

In normal-hill and large-hill competitions, each competitor takes two jumps. They are judged on the distance of their jump and their technique in the takeoff, flight, and landing. Style points are added to the distance points for each jump.

In a perfect jump, the skier holds his body nearly straight, with a slight bend in the waist. He lifts the front of his skis, spreading the tips to create an air pocket that helps him float down the mountainside. When he's ready to land, the skier lifts his head and arms. This forces his hips down, and his skis land softly. As he lands, he bends his right knee, dropping it nearly to the snow.

Besides individual jumping, there is a team event, which is held on the large hill. Four

ALPINE CHAMPIONS

At the 1994 Olympics, Tommy Moe became only the second U.S. skier to win an Olympic gold medal in the downhill. Diann Roffe became the first woman to win back-to-back Olympic gold medals in one event, the Super G. Here are the 1994 Alpine and freestyle gold medalists.

ALPINE

Men
Downhill Tommy Moe, U.S.
Slalom T. Stangassinger, Austria
Giant Slalom M. Wasmeier, Germany
Super G M. Wasmeier
Alpine Combined L. Kjus, Norway

Women
Downhill K. Seizinger, Germany
Slalom Vreni Schneider, Switzerland
Giant Slalom D. Compagnoni, Italy
Super G Diann Roffe, United States
Alpine Combined P. Wiberg, Sweden

FREESTYLE

Men
Moguls Jean-Luc Brassard, Canada
Aerials A. Schoenbaechler, Switzerland

Women
Moguls S. L. Hattestad, Norway
Aerials Lina Tcherjazova, Uzbekhistan

199

jumpers from each country take two jumps each. The three best scores from each team are combined to get the team score.

NORDIC COMBINED

Nordic combined consists of both a ski jumping event and a cross-country race. The sport is extremely difficult because a skier must develop two completely different techniques. Cross-country skiing is an endurance event, while jumping demands mostly speed and power.

The skiers who jump the farthest get a head start in the cross-country race. The racer who finishes first in the cross-country competition wins the event.

Equipment

Each type of skiing requires a different kind of equipment. The skis used vary in length, width, and weight for each event.

The shortest skis are aerial skis, which are just 63" long. The shorter length makes it easier for the skier to perform difficult stunts. Slalom skis are longer, at 78", but short enough to enable skiers to make quick turns around the gates. Downhill skis are 88–89" long and have sharp metal edges that allow the skier to make turns on the icy course. Cross-country skis are slightly shorter and have no edges. They are only 1 ¾" wide and weigh just 17.5 ounces — slightly more than a pound. Their light weight helps skiers in long, grueling races. Jumping skis are the longest, widest, and heaviest of all. They weigh 16 pounds each so they can support the jumper when he lands.

Poles are also shaped for each event. Alpine poles reach slightly above the skier's waist and are tapered to a point at the bottom. Three inches from the point is a plastic piece called a basket. The basket prevents a skier's pole from sinking too far down into the snow.

Tommy Moe is just the second American to win gold in the Olympic downhill.

Downhill and Super G poles are bent to wrap around the skier's body, cutting down the wind resistance. Freestyle poles are slightly longer and thicker because they must support a skier's weight during jumps and twists. Cross-country poles are like Alpine poles, except that the point is set at an angle to better grip the snow.

Both Alpine and freestyle skiers wear hard, durable plastic boots that fasten by buckles either in the front or in the rear. Cross-country skiers use a lightweight, comfortable, shoe-type boot.

Most skiers wear goggles. Skiers in downhill, Super G, aerial freestyle, and ski jumping wear helmets to protect their heads in case of a high-speed crash.

Legends

Lyubov Egorova, Russia: Skiing cross-country for the Unified Team (made up of the republics of the former Soviet Union), Lyubov won five medals — more than any other athlete — at the 1992 Winter Olympics. She followed that by winning three (two individual and one team) gold medals — more than any other woman athlete — at the 1994 Winter Games.

Jean-Claude Killy *[kee-LEE]*, **France:** Jean-Claude was one of the greatest Alpine skiers of all time. During the 1966–67 World Cup season, he won 12 of 16 World Cup

NORDIC CHAMPIONS

Nordic skiers shone at the 1994 Winter Olympics in Lillehammer, Norway. Lyubov Egorova led all Olympians with three gold medals. Manuela Di Centa led everyone with five total medals. Here are the 1994 gold medalists.

MEN

Cross-Country

10K classical
  Bjorn Daehlie, Norway

30K freestyle
  T. Alsgaard, Norway

50K classical
  V. Smirnov, Kazakhstan

Combined pursuit
  Bjorn Daehlie, Norway

4 x 10K relay
  Italy

Nordic Combined

Individual
  F.B. Lundberg, Norway

Team   Japan

Ski Jumping

Normal hill
  J. Weissflog, Germany

Large hill
  Espen Bredesen, Norway

Team, large hill
  Germany

WOMEN

Cross-Country

5K classical
  Lyubov Egorova, Russia

15K freestyle
  Manuela Di Centa, Italy

30K classical
  Manuela Di Centa, Italy

Combined pursuit
  Lyubov Egorova, Russia

4 x 5K relay
  Russia

AWESOME ATHLETES

Anders Haugen is the only American to win an Olympic ski jumping medal — and it took him 50 years to do it! In the 1924 Olympics, Anders finished fourth in the large-hill event. But in 1974, a researcher discovered that the scores had been added up incorrectly and that Anders should have finished third. Anders was 83 when he received his bronze medal. He was 33 when he made the jump.

●

Ulrich Wehling is the only male athlete to win the same event at three consecutive Olympics. Skiing for East Germany, he won the Nordic combined in 1972, 1976, and 1980.

events. At the 1968 Olympics, in his home country, he captured all three men's Alpine gold medals: downhill, slalom, and giant slalom. That tied Austrian skier Anton "Toni" Sailer, who had done the deed in 1956.

Franz Klammer, Austria: With 25 World Cup downhill victories, Franz was one of the world's greatest downhill skiers ever. He won the gold medal in downhill at the 1976 Winter Games.

Rosi Mittermaier, West Germany: Rosi was the first woman to win three Alpine medals at a single Olympics. She won gold medals in the downhill and slalom, and a silver in the giant slalom at the 1976 Winter Games.

Matti Nykanen, Finland: Nicknamed "Matti Nukes," this ski jumper was the overall World Cup champion in 1983 at age 19. At 20, he won a silver medal in the normal hill and a gold in the large hill at the 1984 Olympics. In 1988, he became the first athlete to win gold medals in three jumping events — normal hill, large hill, and team — at one Olympics.

Raisa Smetanina, Soviet Union: In four Olympics, from 1976 through 1988, Raisa won nine Olympic medals in Nordic skiing: three golds, five silvers, and one bronze.

Ingemar Stenmark, Sweden: Ingemar excelled in the slalom and giant slalom events. He swept to victory in both events at the 1980 Winter Olympics. He won the overall World Cup title three different times, and the slalom and giant slalom titles eight times each. By the time he retired in 1989, he had won a record 86 World Cup races.

Alberto Tomba, Italy: Alberto is the only skier in Olympic history to win back-to-back gold medals in an Alpine event. "Tomba la Bomba" won both the 1988 and 1992 giant slalom races. He also won the gold medal in slalom in 1988.

Hanni Wenzel, Liechtenstein: Skiing for one of the tiniest countries in Europe, Hanni won gold medals in the slalom and giant slalom, and a silver medal in the downhill at the 1980 Olympics. She joined Rosi Mittermaier as the only two women to win three Alpine skiing medals at one Olympics.

Glossary

Base: The running surface of a ski. Also, the packed snow under the surface.

Basket: A ring around the bottom of a ski pole that prevents the point from going too deep into the snow.

Binding: A device that fastens a boot to the ski.

Control gates: Sets of two flags positioned on a downhill course. They are to control and monitor the dangerous portions of the course.

Downhill: A race against time down a course 1 ½ to 3 miles long.

Edge: A piece of steel on a ski that helps to grip the snow when a skier makes a turn.

Helicopter: A full-twisting aerial stunt.

K point: The end of the "safe landing area" on a ski jump course. Beyond this point, the slope starts to level off. The size of the ski jump is measured from the end of the in-run to the K point.

Run: One trip over a ski course.

Snowplow: To ski with the tips of the skis pointed at each other in the form of a V. This is used to stop or slow down.

Tuck: A position that skiers try to stay in to allow the wind to flow freely by them. If a skier rises from his tuck, the wind slows him down.

Where to Write

U.S. Skiing, P.O. Box 100, Park City, UT 84060

U.S. National Ski Hall of Fame, Box 191, Ishpeming, MI 49849

WORLD CUP

Many skiers compete in the World Cup, a series of races held around the world in each of the Winter Olympic events.

World Cup races run from December until March. Competitors earn points based on how well they do at each World Cup event. The athlete with the most points at the end of the season is the World Cup champion in that event.

In addition to the Olympics and the World Cup, the other major international competition for skiers is the world championships. The world championships are contested for Alpine, Nordic, and freestyle events. The championships are competed in every odd year.

SNOWBOARDING

Snowboarding is a new sport that borrows from surfing, skateboarding, and skiing.

SNOW JOB

History

The sport of snowboarding started out with a toy called the Snurfer, a snow toy similar to a water ski with a rope on the front end. It was made by the Brunswick Sporting Goods Company in the 1960's. In the 1970's, a man named Jake Burton, who had been given a Snurfer when he was a kid, invented the snowboard by making his Snurfer wider and adding two *skegs* (fins) on the bottom. By the late 1970's, snowboarding had taken off.

By the late 1980's, more and more people were bringing their snowboards to ski areas, and there were professional competitions being held around the world. According to a 1993 poll, if snowboarding continues to grow at its current rate, it will be more popular than skiing by the year 2012!

The Board

An average snowboard is 6' long. Most are made of fiberglass or wood, and have metal edges to help the board cut turns through the snow. Many snowboarders wear special boots that fit into bindings on the snowboard.

How It's Done

Snowboarders ride sideways on the board through the snow, and turn by shifting their body weight, just as skateboarders do. They do not use poles.

Snowboarders and skateboarders have a lot in common. They share many terms, like *fakie,* which is a trick that you perform while moving with your back facing downhill. They

TEXT BY STEPHEN THOMAS

Snowboarding started out with a toy. Now it is the hottest sport at many ski slopes.

both do tricks in *halfpipes*, which in snow-boarding are long U-shaped tunnels packed with snow. Like skateboarders, snowboarders love to go fast, *grab air* (jump), and do tricks.

Competition

Professional snowboarders compete in *slalom*, *giant slalom*, *parallel slalom*, and *halfpipe* events. Slalom and giant slalom are similar to those events in skiing *(see Skiing, page 194)*. Snowboarders are timed as they go through gates on their way down the course. Parallel slalom is head-to-head racing.

Halfpipe is acrobatic, freestyle snowboard-ing. Snowboarders ride down one side of the halfpipe and up the other, doing tricks. Three or five judges grade competitors for difficulty, variety, landings, and overall style.

Pros earn some prize money but make most of their money from endorsing snowboarding clothes and equipment.

Where to Write

U.S. Snowboarding, c/o U.S. Skiing, Box 100, Park City, UT 84060

CHAMPIONS

1995 WORLD CUP
SLALOM
MEN Peter Pickler, Italy
WOMEN Marcella Boerma, Netherlands
GIANT SLALOM
MEN Mike Jacoby, U.S.
WOMEN Karine Ruby, France
PARALLEL SLALOM
MEN Mike Jacoby, U.S.
WOMEN Marion Posch, Italy
HALFPIPE
MEN Lael Gregory, U.S.
WOMEN Sabrina Sadeghi, U.S.

1995 U.S. CHAMPS
SLALOM
MEN Mike Jacoby
WOMEN Sondra Van Ert
GIANT SLALOM
MEN Rob Berney
WOMEN Sondra Van Ert
HALFPIPE
MEN Lael Gregory
WOMEN Aurelie Sayres

SOCCER

Outside of North America, soccer is known as *football*. It is the most popular sport — to watch and to play — in the world.

History

The Chinese and Japanese played games that were like soccer more than 2,300 years ago. The ancient Greeks played *episkyros*, a game that had kicking and throwing. The great Roman Emperor Julius Caesar wanted his soldiers to improve their physical fitness, so he had them play *harpastum*, a game developed from episkyros in which teams of 500 players would basically beat each other up.

According to legend, the Romans brought harpastum to the British Isles more than 1,500 years ago. But there is also evidence that kicking games were already present in the British Isles by then.

By the 1100's, kicking games were very popular in Britain. They were played by huge groups of people, sometimes over miles of land, and there were no real rules. These games were so popular that in 1314, King Edward II had to outlaw them because people weren't doing their work! The games weren't made legal again until the 1600's.

The *modern* game of soccer developed in England. By the 1800's, the game was being played at many English schools, although it was still quite rough. In 1862, a man named J. C. Thring wrote rules for what he called "The Simplest Game," and in 1863, the London Football Association was formed.

In 1871, the Football Association (FA) held its first cup championship, which was open to all amateur soccer clubs. By 1885, the FA Cup was opened to professional teams, too.

During the late 1800's, soccer was intro-

TEXT BY STEPHEN THOMAS

Pelé scored 1,281 career goals playing for Brazil, the Santos club, and the New York Cosmos.

In 1958, most people had never heard of Edson Arantes do Nascimento, a player on Brazil's World Cup team. But soon, most of the world would know about this soccer sensation, better known as Pelé.

That year, Pelé was just 17 years old, but he had already been playing professional soccer in Brazil for about a year. During the World Cup finals, he amazed teams with his play. But he saved some of his best for the championship game against Sweden.

About 10 minutes into the second half, a Brazilian defender cleared the ball toward Sweden's goal. Pelé raced to the ball. With his back to the goal, and surrounded by defenders, he stopped it with his right thigh, flicked it to his left and sent it over his head. In a flash, he spun around and rocketed a 10-foot shot with his foot into the net for a score.

Late in the game, Pelé scored again to help seal Brazil's 5–2 win. This was the beginning of the Pelé legend that would continue until he retired in 1977.

duced in countries all over the world. British sailors would play the game wherever their ships docked. By the end of the century, soccer had exploded all over Europe and South America. In 1904, the Fédération Internationale des Football Associations (FIFA) was formed. FIFA is the organization that runs soccer all over the world.

Soccer in the United States

Soccer has a long history in the United States. It was played at colleges as early as the 1820's and it became an organized college sport after the Civil War. In 1876, the Inter-

QUICK HITS

The modern form of soccer that became popular in England in the late 1800's was known as "association football." The name was shortened to assoc., then finally to soccer, which is how the game received its second name.

●

During the 1990 World Cup finals, 2.21 goals were scored in each of the 52 games. That's about one goal every 45 minutes — not exactly a shoot-out. For that, you need to go indoors. In 1993, an average of 14.5 goals per game were scored in the Continental Indoor Soccer League. That's about one goal every four minutes!

collegiate Football Association was founded. By 1913, the U.S. had been accepted as a member of FIFA. The U.S. even played in three of the first four World Cup tournaments, in 1930, 1934, and 1950 (it didn't qualify in 1938). But soccer has never been as popular in the U.S. as in other countries.

The most successful professional league, the North American Soccer League (NASL), started play in 1968, but went out of business in 1985. Although there are a few small professional leagues today, such as the American Professional Soccer League, no professional soccer league has had the success that the NASL did.

Among kids in the United States under the age of 18, soccer is the third most popular sport. And there are more than 600 National Collegiate Athletic Association (NCAA) Division I, II, and III college programs. Supporters of the Major Soccer League, a professional league with 12 teams that begins play in 1995, are hoping that some of that popularity will help professional soccer make a comeback in the United States.

The Field

Soccer is played on a rectangular field that must be between 100 and 130 yards long, and between 50 and 100 yards wide. In international competition, fields must be at least 110 yards long and 70 yards wide. The lines on the side of the field are called *touchlines*, and the lines at either end are *goal lines*.

The goals, which are 24' wide and 8' high, are centered on each goal line. The *goal area* is a rectangle that is 60' by 18'. Attacking players are not allowed to touch the goalie within this area unless the goalie has the ball and both of his feet are on the ground. Another rectangle, called the *penalty area*, is drawn around the goal area. It is 132' wide by 54' deep.

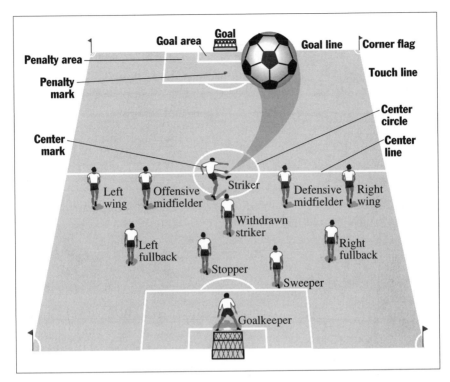

Inside the penalty area, 12 yards from the goal line, is the *penalty mark*. This is the spot from which *penalty kicks* are taken *(see page 212)*. The penalty mark is also the centerpoint of the *penalty circle*. If it were drawn on the field, the penalty circle would have a radius of 10 yards. But the only part of the penalty circle that shows is the part which falls outside the penalty area.

In each corner of the field, a quarter of a circle is drawn where the goal line and the touchline meet. This is the spot from which *corner kicks* are taken *(see page 211).*

The field is divided by the *center line*, which also divides the *center circle* in half. The center circle is where the game begins.

The Game

Soccer is played by two teams of 11 players each. The winner is the team that scores

THE PLAYERS ON THE FIELD

One of the basic soccer formations is the 4-4-2, which means a team has four *defenders*, four *midfielders*, and two forwards (plus the *goalkeeper*). Above, the defenders are the left and right *fullbacks*, the *stopper*, and the *sweeper*. The midfielders are the offensive and defensive midfielders and the two *wings*. The forwards are the *striker* and the *withdrawn striker (see The Positions, page 212)*. Other popular formations are the 4-4-3, designed to increase scoring, and the 4-5-1 used by the 1994 U.S. World Cup team.

BLAST FROM THE PAST

Until the 1870's, soccer players didn't pass the ball. Instead, a player who had the ball would dribble toward the other goal until it was knocked away from him. But in an 1872 game between Scotland and England, the Scottish players passed the ball back and forth. By working with their teammates, players realized, they could move the ball better. The new style revolutionized the game.

more goals. Games are 90 minutes long, divided into two 45-minute halves. Time is kept by the referee on the field, and the clock only stops when a player gets injured. In international soccer, each team may make only two substitutions during the game. After a player has left the game, he cannot return.

Soccer players may play the ball with their head, chest, thighs, and feet. The only time a player other than the goalie is allowed to use his hands is on a *throw-in (see below)*, which takes place after the ball has gone out-of-bounds.

Like American football, soccer begins with a coin toss. The winner can either kick off, or choose which end of the field to defend. The team kicking off plays the ball from the center spot.

At kickoff, all players must be in their own half of the field, and no opponent can enter the center circle until the ball has been played. The player who kicks off cannot play the ball again until it has been touched by another player. After goals are scored, the team that was scored upon restarts the game from the center circle.

To score a goal, the entire ball must pass over the goal line and into the net. Similarly, a ball is not out-of-bounds until it has completely crossed either the touchline or the goal line.

Here are some common plays that occur in soccer:

Throw-in: When the ball goes over the touchline, the team that *didn't* kick it out is awarded a throw-in. The ball must be thrown in with both hands, and must be thrown from behind and above the player's head. When the throw-in is released, both of the player's feet must be touching the ground and be outside or on the touchline. Goals cannot be scored on a throw-in.

Goal kick: If the attacking team kicks the

ball over the goal line, the defending team is awarded a goal kick. Goal kicks are taken from within the goal area, and must travel beyond the penalty area. They can be taken by any player but are usually taken by the goalkeeper.

Corner kick: If the defensive team kicks the ball over the goal line, the attacking team is awarded a corner kick. Corner kicks are taken from the quarter-circle mark on the side of the field where the ball went out-of-bounds. Many goals are scored on corner kicks. The team taking the kick sends the ball into the goal area, where most of the offensive and defensive players are usually positioned. The kicker's teammates try to get to the ball and head it into the goal.

Offside: Generally, if a player is in his opponent's half of the field without the ball, there must be at least two defenders, including the goalkeeper, between him and the goal, or he is offside. This is to prevent an offensive player from waiting by the goal. If the player is even with a defender, then he is not offside. If a player is onside when the pass is attempted, he can receive the pass when he is alone in front of the goalkeeper.

Free kicks: There are two types of free kicks, *indirect* or *direct*. Indirect free kicks are awarded after a player commits a violation (such as an offside), dangerous play, or obstruction. Direct free kicks are awarded after a player intentionally commits a major foul, such as tripping or hitting an opponent, or playing the ball with his hands.

Both kicks are taken from the spot of the foul. The opposing team must stand at least 10 yards from the ball before it is kicked, unless the kick is within 10 yards of the goal. If it is, then the players may stand between the goalposts to defend. Goals can be scored on a direct free kick. On an indirect

GREAT GAME!

In 1950, England entered the World Cup tournament as one of the favorites to win the championship. The United States was considered the longest of long shots.

England had some of the best professional players in the world. The U.S. had part-time players, most of whom had other jobs. Two of them were mailmen and one was a carpenter.

But somehow, these part-timers were able to beat England, 1–0, in what was called the most stunning upset in soccer history. Indeed, the United States wasn't able to beat England again until 1993!

COOL FACT

free kick, a goal cannot be scored until the ball has been touched by another player.

Penalty kick: A penalty kick is awarded when a player commits a major foul within his team's penalty area. On a penalty kick, all players except the goalie and the player taking the kick must stand at least 10 yards away from the penalty mark, which is where the kick is taken from. The goalkeeper must stand on the goal line and cannot move his feet until the player has kicked the ball.

If the goalkeeper stops the ball and it rebounds into the field, play continues. If the ball crosses the goal line but doesn't go into the goal, the attacking team is awarded a corner kick.

The Positions

Players on a team are divided into defenders, midfielders, and forwards (see The Players on the Field, page 209). The defenders are the last line of defense in front of the goalkeeper. After a defender has prevented his opponent from scoring by breaking up a play, he moves the ball to a midfielder to start an attack on the other team's goal. The midfielders link the offense and the defense. They score goals, handle the ball, and play defense. They are involved in almost every play. The basic job of the forwards is to score goals by attacking the other team's goal.

Within each one of those groups, there are specialists. In the defense, the sweeper is the person right in front of the goalkeeper. His job is to sweep the area clean of any offensive threat that has gotten by the other defenders. The stopper is the defensive player responsible for making sure that the other team's striker (see page 213) doesn't score. The left and right fullbacks, or backs, are the defenders who play on the outer edges of the field.

Among the four midfielders, the left and right wings are the two who play on the out-

Peter Shilton was the goalkeeper for England's national team 125 times between 1970 and 1990.

side edges of the field. The defensive midfielder must be creative on offense and also be good at tackling and taking the ball from an opponent. The offensive midfielder looks for scoring chances. He is a playmaker, and should have more chances to score than the defensive midfielder.

Among the forwards, the striker is the one who plays closest to the other team's goal. His job is to score. The withdrawn striker plays behind the striker. He either feeds the ball to the striker or shoots on his own.

Strategy

Unlike American football, soccer has almost no set plays. Teams cannot prepare for situations because, from moment to moment, there will almost never be two that are the

AMAZING FEAT

Only one U.S. soccer team has ever won an important world tournament: the U.S. women's team. In 1991, the U.S. women's team won the first-ever women's world championship, which was held in China. The team beat Norway in the final, 2–1. During the tournament, the U.S. outscored its opponents 25–5. Forward Michelle Akers-Stahl scored 10 goals to lead all players, and forward Carin Gabarra was named the tournament's most outstanding player. At the 1995 women's world championship, which was held in June, in Sweden, the U.S. won the bronze medal. Norway won the gold.

same. The only times that a team will attempt a play are on a free kick or a corner kick. On these two plays, no defensive player can affect the start of the play, but once the ball is played, defenders can get involved.

Teams might not have specific plays, but they do have a playing style. For example, the Brazilian teams of the 1950's had many talented scorers, so they had four players attacking the opponent's goal as often as they could. They were a very offense-minded team.

Other teams might play very defensive soccer, such as the 1994 U.S. national team. A defensive team will concentrate its players in front of its goal, hoping to prevent any scores. A defensive team's offense hopes to catch the attackers out of position and counterattack before the other team can recover.

Officials and Fouls

Soccer games are officiated by one referee and two linesmen. The referee is the highest-ranking official on the field. He is responsible for issuing *yellow* and *red cards*. A player who has committed a serious penalty, such as tripping an opponent or charging him in a dangerous manner, receives a yellow card from the referee. This is also known as a *caution*.

If a player receives two yellow cards, that is equal to a red card. The referee shows a player a red card if the player is being kicked out of the game. A player can receive a red card after one particularly bad foul.

The two linesmen assist the referee in decisions, but their main responsibilities are determining when the ball goes out-of-bounds on the touchline and when players are offside.

The World Cup

Every four years, 24 countries compete in the monthlong World Cup tournament, the most important international soccer tournament. The World Cup is the most popular sporting event in the world, even more popular than the Super Bowl. In 1990, each of the 52 games of the finals was watched on television by 500 million people. (The population of the entire U.S. is only about 250 million.) And the final game between Argentina and Germany was watched by 1.3 *billion* people!

Until 1928, the Olympics had been the most important soccer tournament in the world. But because most of the world's best players were professional, they could not play in the Olympics. So FIFA decided to begin another soccer tournament that would be the sport's official world championship.

The first World Cup tournament was held in Uruguay in 1930. Many of the world's best teams didn't take part in the competition because they couldn't afford to go to South America for two months. Only 13 countries competed, and Uruguay beat Argentina, 4–2. By 1992, 141 countries began playing World Cup qualifying matches, in hopes of becoming one of the 24 teams in the 1994 World Cup, held in the United States. *(See World Cup Champions, page 213.)*

The World Cup trophy, which goes to the winner, is kept in Zurich, Switzerland, by FIFA. The trophy is gold in color, and shows two soccer players holding up a large globe.

More Big Events

Soccer teams that compete in international tournaments like the World Cup are made up of a country's best players. They are an all-star team. But when the all-stars aren't playing for their national team, they are most likely playing in one of the many European or South American professional leagues.

Many countries, like England, Germany, and Italy, have more than one league for players to choose from. Aside from all the pro

OLYMPIC CHAMPIONS

As with the World Cup, countries must win regional qualifying tournaments to reach the Olympics. A country's Olympic team is not necessarily the same as its World Cup team. Professionals were not allowed to play in the Olympic soccer tournament until 1984. And in 1992, FIFA and the International Olympic Committee ruled that only players younger than 23 could play in the Olympics. Here are the champions since soccer joined the Olympics in 1900.

1992	Spain
1988	Soviet Union
1984	France
1980	Czechoslovakia
1976	East Germany
1972	Poland
1968	Hungary
1964	Hungary
1960	Yugoslavia
1956	Soviet Union
1952	Hungary
1948	Sweden
1944	Not held due
1940	to World War II
1936	Italy
1932	Not held
1928	Uruguay
1924	Uruguay
1920	Belgium
1916	World War I
1912	Great Britain
1908	Great Britain
1906	Denmark
1904	Canada
1900	Great Britain

leagues, practically every town has club teams that local people can play on.

As if all those league and World Cup games weren't enough, each year there are many tournaments for European and American teams that help keep their players sharp. Here's a look at some of those tournaments.

European Championship: The European Championship is held every four years, between World Cup years. It is a tournament for the national teams of Europe.

European Champion's Clubs' Cup: Known as the European Cup, this tournament is held every year for European teams that have won their league championship.

European Cup Winners' Cup: This annual tournament is for the winners of cup competition in each European nation.

Copa Libertadores (Liberator's Cup): This is the annual South American club championship. Each South American country is represented by two teams.

CONCACAF Gold Cup: The Gold Cup is played every two years by teams from North and Central America, as well as the Caribbean nations. The U.S. won this tournament in 1991 when it beat Honduras, 4–3. It was the first regional tournament victory ever for a U.S. team. (CONCACAF stands for Confederation of North, Central America, and Caribbean Association Football.)

Copa America: Held every two years in odd-numbered years, this is the South American national team championship.

Indoor Soccer

Indoor soccer has been played around the world since the 1930's. In 1978, the Major Indoor Soccer League (MISL) was launched. The next year, the North American Soccer League (NASL), the professional league that played conventional soccer, launched a competing indoor league. Many soccer fans out-

Midfielder Diego Maradona helped Argentina win the World Cup trophy in 1986.

side the U.S. felt that indoor soccer wasn't soccer at all. Some called it "pinball soccer."

Indoor soccer is played on hockey rinks, but on artificial turf instead of ice. Teams of six players play 60-minute games in four 15-minute quarters. Unlike regular soccer, there is free substitution. Anytime a player gets tired, he is replaced, so the action is nonstop. High-scoring games with 14 goals are not uncommon. And as in hockey, players are sent to a penalty box for major fouls, creating a man-advantage for the team that was fouled.

The two indoor leagues coexisted for three years, but they had to compete for players. In 1982, the MISL agreed to let some NASL teams play with them indoors, which they did for one season.

All of this helped the NASL go out of business in 1985. The MISL didn't do much better: It folded in 1992.

Today, there are two small indoor professional leagues: the National Professional Soccer League, which has 12 teams, and the Continental Indoor Soccer League, which started in 1993 and has seven teams.

GREAT GAME!

In the 1986 World Cup finals, Diego Maradona of Argentina showed that he was the world's most talented soccer player since Pelé. He showed that he was lucky, too.

In the quarterfinals, Argentina played England. Early in the scoreless second half, an English defender passed back to Peter Shilton, England's goalkeeper. Diego raced after the ball. He and Peter jumped after it, and somehow the ball went into the net — 1–0, Argentina. Replays showed there was no way Diego's head could have reached the ball before Peter's hands. He must have hit the ball with his hand. Still, the goal counted.

After the game, when asked about the goal, Diego said it was "a little the hand of God, a little the head of Maradona."

Legends

Franz Beckenbauer, West Germany: In 1990, Franz was voted the best European soccer player of all time. He played on three West German World Cup teams, including

BLASTS FROM THE PAST

During World War II (1939–45), Jules Rimet, one of the founders of the World Cup, kept the original World Cup trophy hidden under his bed at his home in Paris, France. He was afraid the Germans, who had invaded France, might seize it.

●

In 1966, a dockworker in London, England, stole the World Cup trophy. He took it from an exhibition in London about three months before the start of the tournament there. The trophy was missing for seven days, until a mongrel dog named Pickles found it while digging in a garden at his home.

the winning team in 1974. He also managed (coached) the 1990 team to the World Cup, becoming the only person ever to play for and manage a World Cup winner. Franz played for the New York Cosmos in the NASL, helping the league become popular.

Diego Maradona, Argentina: Widely seen as the greatest soccer player since Pelé, Diego, a midfielder, first played for Argentina in 1977, when he was just 16. In 1986, he led Argentina to the World Cup title, and helped the team return to the championship game in 1990. In 1987 and 1990, he led Napoli to the Italian League title, as well as to the 1990 UEFA (European Union of Football Associations) Cup. He was the South American player of the year in 1979, 1980, and 1990. He was disqualified from the 1994 World Cup because he failed a drug test.

Lothar Matthaus, Germany: Lothar is a dangerous midfielder who was the 1990 European soccer player of the year. He has played for the last three West German/German World Cup teams. In 1990, he helped West Germany win the Cup. He has more *caps* than any German player ever: 108 since 1980.

Pelé, Brazil: Pelé was the greatest soccer player in history. He helped Brazil win two World Cups, the first time in 1958 as a 17-year-old *(see Great Games!, page 207)*, the second in 1970. During his career, he had 97 goals in 111 international games for Brazil. He also led Santos, his Brazilian club, to the World Club Championships in 1962 and 1963. Near the end of his career, Pelé played for the New York Cosmos of the NASL and helped make professional soccer popular in the United States.

Peter Shilton, England: Peter is the most capped player in the world. Between 1970 and 1990, he was England's goalkeeper in 125 international matches. He first played professional soccer in England when he was 16. In 1979 and 1980, he led his pro team in England to the European Cup. During his career, Peter made a record 1,374 appearances.

Marco Van Basten, Netherlands: Marco, a striker, was named European soccer player of the year in 1988, 1989, and 1992, tying the record for most times winning that honor.

Glossary

Booking: If a player is ejected from a game, he has been booked. The player is not replaced by a teammate.

Cap: When a player plays for his national team in international competition, he is awarded a cap. Many years ago, players were given an actual cap, but they aren't today.

Dribbling: Advancing the ball by controlling it with your feet.

Foul: Any rule violation, but usually used to describe physical aggression.

Pitch: The British name for the field.

Stopper: A defender whose job is to stop the other team's top scoring threat.

Striker: A forward whose main job is to score.

Sweeper: A defender who moves around behind his own defense, picking off stray passes. Sweepers are the last line of defense in front of the goalie. Sometimes, sweepers move forward on offense.

Tackle: To take the ball from an opponent. Often, both players fall to the ground.

Trap: To control the ball by stopping it with your chest, feet, thigh, or head.

Wingers: The midfielders who play nearest the touchlines.

Where to Write

U.S. Soccer, 1801-1811 South Prairie Ave., Chicago, IL 60616

National Soccer Hall of Fame, 5-11 Ford Ave., Oneonta, N.Y. 13820

YOUTH SOCCER

Some 200 million kids under the age of 18 play soccer around the world. About 12 million of those play in the United States, where only basketball and volleyball are more popular with this age group. For U.S. kids under 12, only basketball is bigger.

The American Youth Soccer Organization (AYSO) is one of the largest soccer organizations in the United States. The AYSO was started in California in 1964 with nine teams. Today, there are more than 25,000 AYSO teams in 38 states!

There are also international competitions for kids' teams. FIFA holds three world championships for juniors: one for players under age 17; one for those under 20; and the Olympics, for players under 23.

SOFTBALL

S oftball is base-ball's popular cousin. More than 42 million Americans of all ages participate each year in leagues, high schools, colleges, and at picnics.

History

Softball was invented in Chicago, Illinois, on Thanksgiving Day in 1887. A group of men were clowning around in a gym, when one man threw a boxing glove and another guy hit it with a pole.

That gave George Hancock an idea. He tied the glove up into a ball and drew a baseball diamond on the floor. The men then played a game of "indoor baseball." George later wrote a set of rules, and the game became popular both indoors and out.

In 1933, the name "softball" was formally adopted for the sport, and a national championship tournament was held at the Chicago World's Fair. Softball is now played in 70 countries around the world.

Rules and Equipment

Softball is played like baseball (see *Baseball, page 26*), but games are seven innings long, pitchers throw underhand, and stealing bases is usually not allowed. Softballs can be 12", 14", or 16" around, which makes them bigger than baseballs (9"). Bats must not be longer than 34" or wider than 2 ¼".

There are many different kinds of softball.

In *slow pitch*, bases are 65' apart and teams use four outfielders. Pitchers stand 50' from home plate and throw the ball in a 10'-to-12'-high arc. That means the pitch sails 10' to 12' into the air but must cross home plate between the batter's knees and chest in order to be called a strike. This is a hitter's game. One team, the Men of Steele from

TEXT BY JOHN ROLFE

Pitcher Joan Joyce won more than 500 games, including 105 no-hitters!

Tampa, Florida, belted 3,730 homers in the 1989 season! In *fast pitch*, bases are 60' apart and teams use three outfielders. Pitchers stand only 46' from home plate in men's competition and 40' away for women. They throw the ball straight and often as hard as a big-league fastball. Bunting and stealing are important because batters rarely hit the ball. In 1949, Herb Dudley of the Clearwater Bombers struck out 55 batters in a 21-inning national championship game!

In *modified pitch*, the base paths and pitching distance are the same as in fast pitch. The ball is thrown without an arc, but not at top speed.

In *16-inch*, a larger ball is used and fielders do not wear gloves.

Big Events

National championship tournaments in all kinds of softball are held each year. The National Collegiate Athletic Association Women's College World Series has been held since 1982. Women's fast-pitch softball will be a medal sport at the 1996 Olympics.

Where to Write

Amateur Softball Association/National Softball Hall of Fame, 2801 Northeast 50th St., Oklahoma City, OK 73111

LEGENDS

Eddie Feigner: Eddie, whose real name was Meryl King, formed a four-man team called "The King and His Court" in 1946. He is still famous for beating nine-man teams while pitching one inning blindfolded and another from second base!

Joan Joyce: The top female softball pitcher of all time, Joan could throw 100 miles per hour. Her amateur career record was 507–33 with 105 no-hitters. In 1962, she faced baseball slugger Ted Williams in an exhibition. He was able to hit only 2 of her 40 pitches!

Mike Macenko: Playing for the Men of Steele, Mike belted 3,143 homers between 1983 and 1989. He hit 844 of them in 1987 to set a national single-season record.

Raybestos Brakettes: This team, from Stratford, Connecticut, is the greatest women's fast-pitch team in history. Since they were founded in 1947, they have won 24 national titles. Joan Joyce was their star pitcher for many years.

SURFING

To surf, men and women stand on a board and use the power of waves to ride toward shore. Surfers need great balance, agility, and strength.

SURF SUIT

In the late 1950's, the wetsuit was pioneered by a surfer named Jack O'Neill. A wetsuit is a skintight rubber suit that keeps you warm in cold water. It allows people to surf all year long, as long as the water isn't ice cold. Some of Jack's first wetsuits were jackets that he sprayed with water seal!

History

In 1778, a British ship captain named James Cook discovered Hawaii and surfing at the same time. While sailing around the islands that make up Hawaii, Captain Cook was surprised to see the natives riding the surf on long wooden boards. In his diary, Captain Cook said the people "appeared to be flying over the water."

But what was new to the captain had been a way of life for Hawaiians for centuries. As early as the 1100's, Hawaiians carved surfing pictures in rocks. The ancient Hawaiians were serious about surfing: If the waves weren't big enough, they would pray to a *kahuna* (sorcerer) and ask for big surf.

In the 1800's, surfing — and the Hawaiian people — almost disappeared. When Captain Cook first came to Hawaii, there were about 300,000 people living on its six major islands. By the 1880's, there were only about 40,000. Diseases brought by the explorers killed most of the island's people.

In the 1820's, missionaries arrived in Hawaii to bring Christianity to the natives. The missionaries thought surfing was immoral and discouraged people from participating. Not only were the Hawaiians not supposed to surf, but there were fewer and fewer of them alive who even knew *how* to surf.

Surfing never completely disappeared, however. In 1907, Jack London, a famous American author who had gone to Hawaii, wrote a story about surfing that helped make the sport popular in the United States. (Hawaii

222

HOW IT WORKS

Waves are formed by wind, which causes the surface of the water to ripple. The longer and harder the wind blows, the larger those ripples become. As the ripples become waves and move toward shore, and as the ocean floor becomes more shallow, the lower part of the wave slows down. This causes the top of the wave, which is still going fast, to spill over onto itself. This is how whitecaps are formed.

Usually, the ocean floor becomes shallow gradually, so waves form slowly. But in Hawaii, which has some of the best surfing in the world, the ocean floor is flat and deep until it gets close to shore. Then, it gets shallow very quickly, causing the waves to get big very quickly.

At the *Banzai Pipeline*, one of Hawaii's best surfing areas, waves hit two sets of submerged reefs that slow the bottom of the wave, making the front rise up and get steeper. Then, the top of the wave comes crashing forward, creating a *tube* of air inside which brave surfers try to ride.

Four-time world champion Wendy Botha of Australia is one of the greatest women surfers ever.

was a U.S. territory, and it did not become a state until 1959.)

Mr. London wrote about an Irish-Hawaiian surfer named George Freeth. Later, George was invited to California to put on the first surfing demonstrations in the United States.

Duke Kahanamoku

George Freeth was the first person to surf in the United States, but Duke Kahanamoku, another Hawaiian, made surfing popular around the world.

At the 1912 Olympics in Stockholm, Sweden, Duke won a gold medal for the U.S. in the 100-meter freestyle swim. (He would win two more gold medals and two silvers in future Olympics.)

When Duke returned to the U.S., he was asked to give swimming demonstrations around the country. But Duke, who had been surfing since he was 4 years old, didn't just swim. If there were waves, he surfed. That year, Duke surfed in Florida, New Jersey, and Southern California.

In 1915, Duke was invited to Sydney, Australia. When he saw the huge waves, he de-

AMAZING FEAT

In July 1917, at Waikiki Beach in Honolulu, Hawaii, Duke Kahanamoku made what has been called the greatest ride in surfing history. Starting over a mile out, Duke rode waves that were reported to be as high as 30' all the way back to shore.

cided he had to surf. There was just one problem: He didn't have a surfboard! So Duke made one of his own out of sugar pine. The board is still on display at the Freshwater Beach Surf Club in Sydney.

Thanks to Duke, more and more people around the world learned about Hawaii's number one sport.

Equipment

Surfers today don't just ride the waves straight to shore as they did in the early days. Instead, they zip up, down, and all over the waves doing difficult tricks.

In 1935, surfing changed when a Californian named Tom Blake added a *skeg* to his surfboard. A skeg is a fin that attaches to the bottom rear of the surfboard. It helps the rider turn the board and ride across the *face*, or front, of the wave, parallel to shore.

Until the 1940's, surfboards were made of wood. Some were as long as 18' and weighed as much as 150 pounds. Many people didn't surf because they couldn't handle the huge board.

But after World War II, surfboard companies began to experiment with much lighter materials, such as fiberglass and polyurethane. These materials made the boards much easier to control, and that made surfing more popular. By the early 1980's, an average surfboard was about 6' long and weighed about eight pounds.

Longboard vs. Shortboard

Today, two types of surfboards are used: the *longboard* and the *shortboard*. A longboard is between 8–10' long. Shortboards are usually between 5–7' long.

Longboards float better than shortboards because they contain more foam. They give a smoother ride in rough water, just as a larger car does on a rough road. It is easier to catch

224

waves on a longboard than on a shortboard. Shortboards were invented in Australia in the late 1960's. The biggest difference between a longboard and a shortboard is maneuverability. Shortboards are much easier to control.

Longboards, which were popular from the 1940's through the 1960's, are being widely used again as some older surfers have returned to the sport. In 1986, the Association of Surfing Professionals (see Big Events) created a competition division just for longboard surfers.

Big Events

Surfing competitions became serious as surfboard designs improved and surfers' abilities improved. In 1954, the first Makaha International surf contest was held in Hawaii. In 1964, the first official world championships were held at Manly Beach, in Australia. And in 1966, the first Duke Kahanamoku Invitational was held in Hawaii.

In 1969, the Duke Kahanamoku Invitational awarded $1,000 in prize money to the winner. Many surfers were unhappy that surfing was becoming a professional sport. They felt that surfing was an art form, and that it was impossible to judge if one surfer had done better than another. These surfers were known as "soul surfers," because they preferred to surf for the good of their souls, rather than money or fame.

Still, professionalism became a part of the surfing scene. The International Professional Surfing (IPS) circuit was founded in 1976. By the late 1970's, the IPS was holding competitions in Hawaii, South Africa, and Australia.

In 1983, the Association of Surfing Professionals (ASP) replaced the IPS as the main governing body of professional surfing. The ASP runs events for men and women in Japan, France, and the United States, and

CHAMPIONS

There is no single "world championship" event in professional surfing. The man or woman who leads the World Championship Tour in overall points is considered the world champion.

MEN

1995 Kelly Slater, Florida
1994 Kelly Slater, Florida
1993 Derek Ho, Hawaii
1992 Kelly Slater, Florida
1991 Damien Hardman, Australia
1990 Tom Curren, California
1989 Martin Potter, Great Britain

WOMEN

1995 Lisa Anderson, Florida
1994 Lisa Anderson, Florida
1993 Pauline Menczer, Australia
1992 Wendy Botha, Australia
1991 Wendy Botha, Australia
1990 Pam Burridge, Australia
1989 Wendy Botha, Australia

BLAST FROM THE PAST

In the early 1960's, the number of surfers around the world grew from the thousands into the millions. Movies and music helped. A series of successful movies featured a young California girl named Gidget who loved to surf. And people all over the country heard the Beach Boys sing songs about California and surfing. In one of their most popular songs, "Surfin' USA," the Beach Boys sang: "Catch a wave and you're sitting on top of the world!"

awarded more than $1.4 million in prize money in 1994. Its biggest competition is the World Championship Tour (WCT).

The WCT is made up of 12–15 events and features the top 44 surfers from the previous year's rankings and 4 wild cards. WCT surfers earn points for how well they finish in each event. The surfer with the most points at the end of the season is the world champion. There are separate competitions for men and women. *(See Champions, page 225.)*

Scoring

There are four steps to winning an event on the ASP tour: 1. Find the biggest wave. 2. Do the best tricks. 3. Surf with speed and power. 4. Ride your wave longer than anyone else.

In the top division of an ASP event, surfers compete first in three-person heats, most of which last for 25 minutes. Each surfer rides 10 waves. His overall score is the combined score of his four best rides. The following rounds are head-to-head matchups. The two-person final is 30 minutes long, and surfers are scored on the best 4 of 15 rides. Judges score each surfer from 1 to 10, and use tenths of a point.

Some of the more amazing tricks done by surfers are *aerials*, in which surfers leave the wave on their board, catch air, and return to the wave to continue surfing; and *floaters*, in which surfers ride over the back of a wave, into the whitewater, and then back to the face of the wave, making a full circle.

Legends

Wendy Botha, Australia: Wendy is one of the greatest women's surfers ever. She is an artist on the water, making amazing turns on huge waves. She has been the world champion four times, most recently in 1992.

Pam Burridge, Australia: Pam was the first professional female surfer in Australia.

She turned pro when she was 17. In 1990, she was the world champion. In 1993, Pam was ranked Number 2 and won two events.

Phil Edwards, U.S.: Many people think to be a great surfer, you need to make a name for yourself in Hawaii. In 1961, Phil Edwards did. Phil, who learned to surf in California, took his longboard to Hawaii and became the first person to ride the Banzai Pipeline *(see How It Works, page 223).*

Kelly Slater, U.S.: Kelly is one of the best young surfers in the world. In 1992, he became the world champion at just 21 years of age. Kelly has also appeared on the TV show *Baywatch.*

Glossary

Barney: A clumsy surfer.

Chalk people: People who live far from the water.

Gnarly: Messy or sloppy; used to describe the surf.

Goofy-footer: A person who surfs with his right foot toward the front of the board, instead of the usual left foot forward.

Kelphead: A beginning surfer.

Kook: An outsider who shows up on the local beach.

Latronic: "See you later," as in "Latronic, dude."

Leash: A cord that attaches the surfboard to the surfer's ankle, so that he doesn't have to swim too far to catch up to the board after a wipeout.

Skegs: The fins on the bottom of the surfboard that help the surfer steer the board.

Wipeout: When a surfer falls off his board before finishing a ride.

Where to Write

National Scholastic Surfing Association, P.O. Box 495, Huntington Beach, CA 92648

ONE MORE THING

The *bodyboard* was invented in the early 1970's by a surfer named Tom Morey. Tom was looking for an easier — and less painful — way to ride the waves.

A bodyboard is shorter and wider than a surfboard. Bodyboards are 24–44" long and 18–24" wide. Some bodyboarders stand on their boards, but most lie on their stomachs. And bodyboards are softer than surfboards, so they don't hurt as much when they conk you on the head.

Today, bodyboards aren't just ridden for fun: In 1994, there were eight professional events held in California and Hawaii, and a world championship!

SWIMMING

Long before the invention of the familiar strokes used in swimming today, people swam by using their hands and legs to imitate the way dogs and other animals moved through the water.

History

It is believed that the first swimmers were the people who lived in the ancient countries of Greece, Rome, Assyria, and Egypt. The earliest reference in history books to swimming *races* dates back to 36 B.C. in Japan.

Swimming has remained popular throughout history, except between the years 500 to 1500. During this time, there was a great deal of disease, particularly a bacterial disease that became known as the plague. People feared, with good reason, that germs were spread through the water, and stayed away from water activities.

During the late 1700's and early 1800's, however, swimming regained its popularity. In England, the Metropolitan Swimming Clubs Association was established in 1791 to set up swimming clubs. That led to the creation of the National Swimming Society, which was founded in the 1830's. One of its main purposes was to hold swimming competitions.

The date of the first international swimming meet is hard to pin down. In 1844, a group of Native Americans competed in London, England, and received a medal from the National Swimming Society. The winner was Flying Gull, who defeated Tobacco by swimming the length of a 130' pool in 30 seconds.

When competitive swimming began, most swimmers used the *breaststroke (see How It's Done, page 230).* It wasn't until the late 1800's that the ancestor of the stroke used most often today — the *Australian crawl* —

TEXT BY SCOTT WAPNER

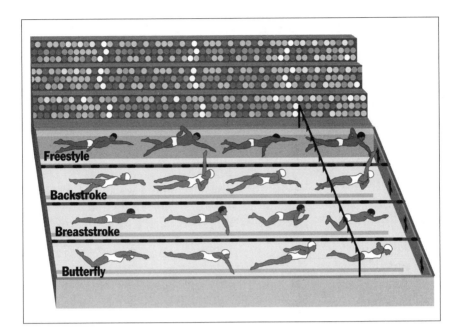

Freestyle

Backstroke

Breaststroke

Butterfly

was developed by Australian swimmer and coach Frederick Cavill. The stroke got its name because a swimmer using it looks as if he is crawling through the water.

An American version of the crawl was created by swimmer Charles Daniels. Charles experimented with his kicking, timing it to the stroking of his arms. The crawl enabled swimmers to cut through the water faster than they could with the breaststroke or *backstroke*, and soon swimming instructors were teaching it as the main way to swim.

Swimming was an event in the first modern Olympic Games, in Athens, Greece, in 1896, and it has been included in the Games ever since.

In those first Olympics, the only swimming events held were men's *freestyle* (basically, the crawl) at 100, 500, and 1,200 meters. In 1904, events based on strokes began to be held, as the backstroke was added to the competition.

The first American to win an Olympic

THE STROKES

Races are held in four strokes: freestyle, backstroke, breaststroke, and butterfly. In the freestyle, swimmers can choose any stroke but nearly always choose the crawl because it is the fastest. The backstroke is similar to the crawl, but is done with the swimmer on his back. The breaststroke is the most relaxing of all the strokes, while the butterfly is one of the most difficult because it requires precise timing and great energy.

BLAST FROM THE PAST

Olympic swimmers did not always compete in a pool. In 1896, they swam in the Bay of Piraeus in Athens, Greece, and had to battle 12' waves. In 1900, they raced down the River Seine in Paris, France, pushed by a strong current. In 1904, they swam in a lake in St. Louis, Missouri, where the starting line was a raft that kept sinking!

swimming medal was the father of the American crawl, Charles Daniels, in 1904. Breaststroke became an Olympic competition in 1908.

In 1912, swimming events for women were added to the Olympics. Fanny Durack of Australia won the first women's Olympic swimming event, the 100-meter freestyle. Her biggest struggle came before the Games, when she had to convince the Australian team that it wouldn't be a waste of time and money to send her to the Olympics. At one time, Fanny owned every world record in women's swimming, from 50 yards to one mile.

The *butterfly* is the most recent swimming stroke. The earliest form of the butterfly was created in the 1930's, when breaststrokers discovered they could swim faster if they lifted their arms out of the water at the end of each stroke to recover for the next stroke. In 1952, the *dolphin kick (see The Kicks, page 231)* was added. Four years later, swimmers were competing in the butterfly at the 1956 Summer Olympics in Melbourne, Australia.

The *individual medley* became an Olympic event in 1964.

How It's Done

There are five basic strokes: the backstroke, breaststroke, butterfly, crawl, and *sidestroke*. The sidestroke, however, is not usually used in competitive swimming.

Backstroke: The backstroke is performed with the swimmer lying on his back with his face out of the water. The arms are started at the side as if the person were standing at attention. The swimmer then alternates the arms, extending back, and then pulling down to the side again. It is as if the swimmer were doing an upside-down version of the crawl. The legs are kicked up and down in a *flutter kick*.

Johnny Weissmuller went from gold medals to playing Tarzan in movies and on TV.

Breaststroke: The breaststroke is the most relaxing of all the strokes used in competition. The swimmer floats on his stomach, with the legs bent slightly. The arms begin outstretched, with the hands almost touching, and push outward from each other in a circular motion. At the same time, the knees are brought toward the chest and then kicked outward in a frog kick. The process is then repeated. The swimmer breathes when the hands are pushed down to the sides of the body.

Butterfly: The butterfly requires precise timing and great energy; it is a very tiring stroke to do. In the butterfly, both arms are thrown forward out of the water and then pulled down into the water toward the legs. As the arms come out of the water behind the swimmer, so does the head. This is when the swimmer takes a breath. The butterfly is done with the dolphin kick.

Crawl: In freestyle competition, any stroke can be used, but nearly all swimmers use the crawl because it is the fastest stroke. The arms move forward alternately, reaching out and pulling back. To breathe, the swimmer turns his head to the side with the arm that

THE KICKS

Dolphin kick: Used in the butterfly stroke, this kick closely resembles the flutter kick, except that instead of alternating the legs up and down, they are moved at the same time, with knees slightly bent as the legs move up. Imagine a dolphin moving its tail to propel itself.

Flutter kick: The flutter kick is used with the crawl and backstroke. The legs are moved up and down alternately. The power from the kick comes from the upper leg. The feet are thrust outward as if a gooey substance were being kicked off the feet.

Frog kick: This is used with the breaststroke. To start, the legs are fully extended and the toes pointed toward the rear. The heels are then pulled toward the hips just under the water's surface. When the feet are near the hips, the knees are slightly bent and extended outward. Then, without pausing, the feet are pushed backward and the legs are pulled together until the toes point to the rear. It's like the way a frog kicks its feet in the water.

AWESOME ATHLETE

Duke Kahanamoku of Hawaii is the man who popularized surfing as a sport (see *Surfing, page 222*). But before he became a world-famous surfer, Duke was a world-famous swimmer. He won the gold medal in the 100-meter freestyle in the 1912 and 1920 Olympics and a silver medal in 1924.

has just pulled back. The crawl is done with a flutter kick.

The Pool

Competitive races are held in two types of pools: long-course and short-course. Long-course pools are 50 meters long (about 55 yards) and 25 meters wide (about 27 yards). This is also known as an *Olympic-size* pool.

All international meets are held in long-course pools. This includes the Olympics, the Pan American Games, and the world championships. The pool is divided into lanes, and at the end of each lane is a touch pad that electronically measures a swimmer's time to the hundredth of a second.

Short-course pools are 22.9 meters long (about 25 yards) and 16 meters wide (about 17 ½ yards). Short-course pools are used in many high school and college competitions.

The lanes in both types of pools keep the swimmers separate while they are racing. Plastic markers called *lane-lines* run the length of the pool. Besides dividing the pool into lanes, they absorb the waves the swimmers create. This helps keep the surface of the water calm. Long-course pools may have 6, 8, or 10 lanes, and short-course pools have either 6 or 8 lanes.

In national and international competitions, the water must be between 78 and 80 degrees Fahrenheit, and at least 4' deep. The pool at the Olympic Games is always about 8' deep (2.5 meters).

Competitions

Swimming competitions are called *meets*, and are held on many levels, from local to international.

Because there are so many competitors in major meets, qualifying *heats* are held. The winners of the heats go on to a final race. The swimmers with the fastest qualifying times swim in the centermost lanes, and the slowest swimmers get the outside lanes.

At the sound of the starting gun, swimmers in freestyle, breaststroke, and butterfly events dive off raised *starting platforms* into the water. For the backstroke, swimmers start in the water and push off the wall when the gun sounds.

In an Olympic pool, every race over 50 meters requires the swimmer to make a turn in order to swim back the other way. Quick turns can make the difference between first place and last place. To turn, freestyle and backstroke swimmers use a *flip turn*. The swimmer does a somersault underwater to reverse his direction.

Butterfly and breaststroke swimmers use an *open turn*. They keep their heads above water while making the turn.

In Olympic freestyle competition, swimmers race 50, 100, 200, and 400 meters. Women also swim 800 meters and men swim 1,500 meters.

The backstroke, breaststroke, and butterfly are all contested at 100 and 200 meters. In another race, called the individual medley (IM), the swimmer completes 50 or 100 meters in each of the four strokes, usually in the following order: butterfly, backstroke, breaststroke, and freestyle.

Relay races are also held in international and national meets. In a relay, a team has four swimmers who each swim the same distance. In a medley relay, each swimmer swims the same distance but with a different stroke.

Big Events

Amateur swimming is governed by the Federation Internationale de Natation Amateur (FINA). About 100 countries make up the association. Each country has its own swimming association that is a member of

WOMEN'S CHAMPIONS

Here are the women who won gold medals in swimming at the 1992 Olympics.

FREESTYLE
50m   Yang Wenyi, China
100m   Zhuang Yong, China
200m   Nicole Haislett, U.S.
400m   Dagmar Hase,
       Germany
800m   Janet Evans, U.S.

BACKSTROKE
100m   Krisztina Egerszegi,
       Hungary
200m   Krisztina Egerszegi,
       Hungary

BREASTSTROKE
100m   Elena Roudkovskaia,
       Unified Team
200m   Kyoko Iwasaki,
       Japan

BUTTERFLY
100m   Qian Hong, China
200m   Summer Sanders,
       U.S.

INDIVIDUAL MEDLEY
200m   Lin Li, China
400m   Krisztina Egerszegi,
       Hungary

RELAYS
4x100m medley
       United States
4x100m freestyle
       United States

233

COOL FACTS

Every fraction of a second counts in swimming, so swimmers try to make their bodies as smooth as a dolphin's. They wear skintight swimsuits made of slick materials, swim caps, and they shave the hair off their bodies so there will be less resistance between their skin and the water. Their only other equipment is a pair of goggles. Goggles allow them to keep their eyes open at all times as they race through the water.

FINA. In the U.S., that organization is the United States Swimming Association.

Swimming's major international meets include the Olympics, Pan American Games, Goodwill Games, and world championships. Like the Olympics, the swimming world championships, Pan American Games (open only to athletes from North, Central, and South America), and Goodwill Games are held every four years.

The U.S. national championships are held twice a year, in April and around July–August. The other major meets in the United States include the World University Games, the U.S. Open, and the Alamo Challenge.

Records

MEN'S EVENTS

Freestyle

50 meters: 21.81, by Tom Jager of the United States, in 1990.

100 meters: 48.21, Alexander Popov, Russia, 1994.

200 meters: 1:46.69, Giorgio Lamberti, Italy, 1989.

400 meters: 3:43.80, Kieren Perkins, Australia, 1994.

800 meters: 7:46.00, Kieren Perkins, Australia, 1994.

1,500 meters: 14:41.66, Kieren Perkins, Australia, 1994.

Backstroke

100 meters: 53.86, Jeff Rouse, U.S., 1992.

200 meters: 1:56.57, Martin Lopez-Zubero, Spain, 1991.

Breaststroke

100 meters: 1:00.95, Karolyi Guttler, Hungary, 1993.

200 meters: 2:10.16, Mike Barrowman, U.S., 1992.

Butterfly

100 meters: 52.32, Denis Pankratov, Russia, 1995.

Janet Evans of the United States holds world records in three freestyle events.

200 meters: 1:55.22, Denis Pankratov, Russia, 1995.

Individual medley
200 meters: 1:58.16, Jani Sievinen, Finland, 1994.
400 meters: 4:12.30, Tom Dolan, U.S., 1994.

Freestyle relay
400 meters: 3:15.11, United States, 1995.
800 meters: 7:11.95, Unified Team, 1992.

Medley relay
400 meters: 3:36.93, United States, 1988.

WOMEN'S EVENTS

Freestyle
50 meters: 24.51, Jingyi Le, China, 1994.
100 meters: 54.01, Jingyi Le, China, 1994.
200 meters: 1:56.78, Franziska Van Almsick, Germany, 1994.
400 meters: 4:03.85, Janet Evans, U.S., 1988.
800 meters: 8:16.22, Janet Evans, U.S., 1989.
1,500 meters: 15:52.10, Janet Evans, U.S., 1988.

Backstroke
100 meters: 1:00.16, Cihong He, China,

MEN'S CHAMPIONS
Here are the men who won gold medals in swimming at the 1992 Olympics.

FREESTYLE
50m Aleksandr Popov, Unified Team
100m Aleksandr Popov
200m Evgueni Sadovyi, Unified Team
400m Evgueni Sadovyi, Unified Team
1,500m Kieren Perkins, Australia

BACKSTROKE
100m Mark Tewksbury, Canada
200m Martin Lopez-Zubero, Spain

BREASTSTROKE
100m Nelson Diebel, U.S.
200m Mike Barrowman, U.S.

BUTTERFLY
100m Pablo Morales, U.S.
200m Melvin Stewart, U.S.

INDIVIDUAL MEDLEY
200m Tamas Darnyi, Hungary
400m Tamas Darnyi Hungary

RELAYS
4x100m medley United States
4x100m freestyle United States
4x200m freestyle Unified Team

AMAZING FEAT

One of the greatest distance swimmers of all time was Pedro Candiotti of Argentina. He was nicknamed "The Shark of Quilla Creek," and his longest swim was 281 miles from Santa Fe to Zarate in Argentina. He was in the water for 84 hours!

1994.

200 meters: 2:06.62, Krisztina Egerszegi, East Germany, 1991.

Breaststroke

100 meters: 1:07.69, Samantha Riley, Australia, 1994.

200 meters: 2:24.76, Rebecca Brown, Australia, 1994.

Butterfly

100 meters: 57.93, Mary T. Meagher, U.S., 1981.

200 meters: 2:05.96, Mary T. Meagher, U.S., 1981.

Individual medley

200 meters: 2:11.65, Lin Li, China, 1992.

400 meters: 4:36.10, Petra Schneider, East Germany, 1982.

Freestyle relay

400 meters: 3:37.91, China, 1994.

800 meters: 7:55.47, East Germany, 1987.

Medley relay

400 meters: 4:01.67, China, 1994.

Legends

Matt Biondi, U.S.: Matt won five gold medals, one silver, and one bronze at the 1988 Olympics in Seoul, South Korea. His 11 medals tie him with swimmer Mark Spitz and shooter Carl Osburn for the most medals ever won by a U.S. Olympian. Matt is one of only six male swimmers from the U.S. to make three Olympic teams. He was a member of the 1984, 1988, and 1992 teams.

Charles Daniels, U.S.: Charles was the father of the American crawl, modifying the famous stroke that began in Australia. He won five medals at the 1904 Olympic Games (three gold, one silver, and one bronze), all in freestyle events.

Gertrude Ederle, U.S.: Gertrude was the first woman to swim across the English Channel, swimming from France to England in 1926. Because of bad weather and rough

Mark Spitz won a record seven gold medals at the 1972 Olympics, and 11 total medals in his career.

DISTANCE SWIMMING

Distance swimming has long been a popular form of sport as well as a challenge of human endurance. Distance swims, such as crossing the English Channel, all five Great Lakes, or swimming around Manhattan Island in New York City, attract swimmers eager to test themselves.

The English Channel was first crossed by Captain Matthew Webb in 1875. Captain Webb took 21 hours and 45 minutes to complete the 20-mile swim from Dover, England to Cape Griz Nez, France. The first woman to swim the Channel was Gertrude Ederle, who swam from France to England on August 6, 1926. She did it in 14 hours, 31 minutes, beating the men's record at the time by more than two hours.

Shelley Taylor Smith has won the Manhattan Island Marathon four times. In 1989, she swam the 28 ½ miles in 7 ½ hours.

The Great Lakes were crossed (one at a time) by Vicki Keith of Ontario, Canada, in 1988.

seas, she swam an extra 10 miles and still beat the men's record by two hours! At the 1924 Olympics, Gertrude won bronze medals in the 100-meter and 400-meter freestyle events. She also won a gold medal in the freestyle team relay. As an amateur, she broke nine world records.

Kornelia Ender, East Germany: Kornelia was only 14 years old when she won three silver medals at the 1972 Olympics in the 200-meter medley and both medley relay events. At the 1976 Olympics in Montreal, Canada, she won four gold medals and a silver. By the time she retired in 1976, she had set 23 individual records.

Janet Evans, U.S.: At the 1988 Olympic Games, Janet won gold medals in the 400-meter and 800-meter freestyle races and in the 400-meter individual medley. She continued her winning ways at the 1992 Summer Olympics, by winning a gold medal in the 800-meter freestyle and a silver medal in the 400. Janet holds the world record in the 400-meter, 800-meter, and 1,500-meter freestyle events.

Mary T. Meagher, U.S.: When Mary was swimming competitively, she was known as

"Madame Butterfly" because she swam the 10 fastest 200-meter butterfly times ever! No one has even come close to breaking her records. Over four days in August 1981, she broke her own world record in the 200-meter butterfly by .41 seconds. Three days later, she crushed her own 100-meter butterfly world record by 1.33 seconds.

Kristin Otto, East Germany: Kristin was one of the most versatile swimmers ever. At the 1988 Olympics in Seoul, South Korea, she won a women's record six gold medals. She captured the 50-meter and 100-meter freestyle, 100-meter backstroke, 100-meter butterfly, 4x100-meter freestyle relay, and 4x100-meter individual medley relay. Kristin had been expected to win three to five gold medals four years earlier, but East Germany had boycotted the 1984 Summer Olympic Games in Los Angeles.

Summer Sanders, U.S.: In 1990, Summer became the first swimmer in four years to beat Olympic champion Janet Evans in the 400-meter individual medley. At the 1992 Olympics, Summer won a gold medal in the 200-meter butterfly, a silver in the 200-meter IM, and a bronze in the 400-meter IM. She retired from competitive swimming in January 1994, but came out of retirement in April 1995 to try for the 1996 team.

Mark Spitz, U.S.: Mark won a record seven gold medals at the 1972 Summer Olympics. His golds came in the 100-meter freestyle, 200-meter freestyle, 100-meter butterfly, 200-meter butterfly, 4x100 meter freestyle relay, 4x200-meter freestyle relay, and 4x100-meter medley relay. Mark also won two gold medals at the 1968 Summer Olympics, as well as a bronze and a silver, to give him a total of 11 medals.

Johnny Weissmuller, U.S.: Johnny was the first swimmer to crack the one-minute mark in a 100-meter freestyle race. At the

1924 Olympics, he won gold medals in the 100-meter and 400-meter freestyle events. He also won a gold medal in the 100-meter freestyle at the 1928 Olympics. After his swimming career was over, Johnny starred as Tarzan in the movies *(see Cool Fact, page 238).*

Glossary

Anchor: The final leg of a relay race, or the swimmer who swims that leg.

Flip turn: A tumbling turn in which the swimmer somersaults and twists his body as he approaches the pool wall and then pushes off the wall with his feet.

Heat: A qualifying competition to determine which swimmers will qualify to race in the finals.

Individual medley (IM): A race that requires swimming each leg with a different stroke. The order is usually butterfly, backstroke, breaststroke, and freestyle.

Lap: The length of a pool from one end to another.

Leg: One fourth of a relay swum by four different competitors.

Open turn: A turn in which the swimmer touches the wall with his hand, keeping his head above the water.

Split: A timed section of a race. For example, a 200-meter race might have four 50-meter splits.

Split time: The amount of time it takes to swim a certain part of a race.

Stroke: The combination of arm and leg movements the swimmer uses to propel himself through the water.

Where to Write

U.S. Swimming Association, 1 Olympic Plaza, Colorado Springs, CO 80909

International Swimming Hall of Fame, 1 Hall of Fame Dr., Ft. Lauderdale, FL 33316

SYNCHRONIZED SWIMMING

Synchronized swimming combines art, athleticism, and rhythm. In this sport, swimmers perform routines to music. It resembles ballet in many ways.

Three events are internationally recognized in synchronized swimming: solo, duet (two swimmers) and team (eight swimmers).Synchronized swimming has been an Olympic sport for women since 1984. Through the 1992 Games, competition was held in solo and duet. At the 1992 Olympics, all the gold medalists were from the United States.

At the 1996 Summer Olympics in Atlanta, the team competition will replace the solo and duet events.

TENNIS

In the early 1900's, tennis was played with heavy wooden rackets by men in long pants and women in full skirts. Imagine seeing that today!

History

Hundreds of years before Pete Sampras began slamming serves, people were playing games that looked like tennis. About 500 years ago, the French played an indoor game called *paume*, which means "palm," a form of handball. Soon after, players began using rackets to help improve their reach.

That sport became known as court tennis, an indoor game that is still played in some places today. Players must hit the ball over a net, but they can hit it off walls and onto ledges that surround the court on three sides.

Major Clopton Wingfield of England is considered the father of modern tennis. In 1873, he moved the game outside and played it on grass. *Lawn tennis*, as the sport was soon called, was less expensive to play than court tennis, which had to be played in special buildings. The Major also made the rules for his game simpler than those for court tennis.

Major Wingfield's game quickly became popular. By the late 1870's, there were tennis clubs all over the world, and many countries had national championships.

In the early 1900's, all tennis players were *amateurs* — they weren't paid prize money. But they were given money to help pay expenses, like hotel and travel costs.

That began to change in the 1920's, when a few players began playing the game for money. They traveled around the country, playing matches before small crowds. In 1927, the winner of the first United States Pro Championships earned $1,000. Being a pro then

TEXT BY STEPHEN THOMAS

Andre Agassi used an oversized racket to win Wimbledon in 1992.

meant traveling from town to town, facing the same players every night, and earning what you could from ticket sales. But players who turned pro could no longer play in the Davis Cup or in the four *Grand Slam* tournaments (*see Big Events, page 244*). Players would usually wait until the end of their careers to turn pro.

But in 1967, Lamar Hunt, an oilman from Texas, changed tennis. By offering a lot of prize money, he persuaded many top players to leave amateur tennis behind. In 1968, when officials at the important Wimbledon tournament in England realized that their event was going to be without the world's best players, they agreed to pay players, too.

As soon as Wimbledon offered prize money, almost all of the other tournaments did as well. That began the *open* era of tennis, with major events open to amateurs and pros.

Rules

The object of tennis is simple: Hit the ball over the net and onto the court one more time than your opponent, and you win the point. But there are rules that players must follow.

The serve: The player who is serving has two chances to put the ball into play. If the first serve is hit into the net, or doesn't land in the service box on the opposite side of the net (*see The Court, page 243*), a *fault* is called. If a player serves two faults, he has *double-faulted* and loses the point. If the ball brushes the top of the net but lands in the

HOW TO PLAY

In tennis, you can play singles or doubles. In singles, one player plays against another. In doubles, two teams of two players each compete.

The object of the game is to hit the ball over the net and prevent your opponent from returning the ball by forcing him to make errors, such as hitting the ball into the net.

One player, the *server*, starts the ball in play by hitting the ball into a box on the opposite side of the net, the service box *(see The Court, page 243)*. The server has two chances to get the ball into the box at the start of a point.

To win a game, a player must score four points and win by at least two *(see Scoring, page 242)*. Matches are divided into *sets*, and the first player to win six games wins the set, but he must win by two games. If a set is tied after six games, a *tiebreaker* is played.

Most women's and many men's matches are best-two-of-three set matches. In major tournaments, men play best-three-of-five set matches.

BLASTS FROM THE PAST

The first organized tennis tournament was held in 1877 at the All-England Croquet and Lawn Tennis Club, the site of Wimbledon.

●

In 1933, American Helen Jacobs shocked officials at a tournament by wearing shorts that showed her lower legs. Play was halted until she changed her clothes.

service box, a *let* is called, and that serve is done over.

The server must have both feet behind the baseline and must hit the ball while it's in the air. If his feet touch the inside of the court before the ball is hit, a *foot fault* is called, and the player loses a point.

Players alternate serving games. In tournaments, players must change ends after every odd-numbered game.

The receiver: When *receiving* the serve, a player may not hit the ball before it bounces. However, he may do so during a *rally*, when players are hitting the ball back and forth. Players must return the ball before it bounces on the court twice.

The rally: Players may hit the ball with any part of their racket, but they cannot hit the ball with their hands or body. If a ball strikes a player, he loses the point. Players cannot hit the ball twice on one shot.

If the ball lands on the sideline or baseline during play, it is good. During a rally, players may not touch the net.

Scoring

Since the beginning of tennis, one point in a match has been counted as 15, two points as 30, and three points as 40. If a player has no points, the score is called *love*.

Some tennis historians believe that early players based their scoring on the 60 degrees of a *sextant*, an instrument used in astronomy. No one knows why "five" was dropped from the third point, but people think it is because forty is easier to say than forty-five.

If two players are tied 40–40, the score is called *deuce*, from the Latin "a due," which means two. When the score is deuce, a player must score two points in a row to win. Whoever wins the first, or deuce, point is said to have the *advantage*. If that player wins the next point, he wins the game. Sometimes, a

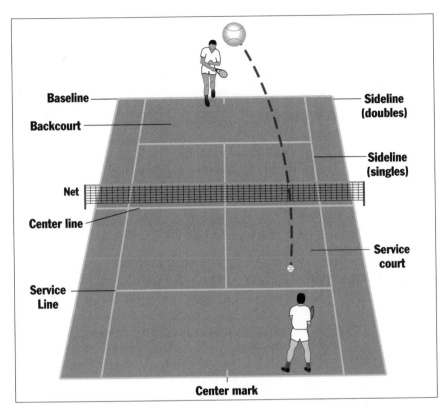

Baseline
Backcourt
Net
Center line
Service Line
Sideline (doubles)
Sideline (singles)
Service court
Center mark

game will go back and forth many times before a player wins the final two points.

Rackets

Before the 1960's, all tennis rackets were made of wood. Although there are no rules requiring a racket to be a certain length or weight, most weighed about 14 ounces. The old rackets had a small *face*, or hitting area.

Players tried to use steel rackets in the 1940's and 1950's, but most people found it difficult to control the ball. Metal rackets were lighter than wooden rackets, which meant that people could swing faster. But metal is stiffer than wood. Therefore, although their swings were more powerful, players were spraying balls all over the court.

In the late 1960's, aluminum rackets were

THE COURT

A tennis court is 78' long. The lines on the ends are called *baselines*. Those on the sides are *sidelines*. The net divides the court into 39' halves. Singles courts are 27' wide. Doubles are 36' wide.

Between the baseline and the net is the *service line*. From the service line to the net is the *center line*. Those lines mark the box into which the server must hit the ball.

On the baseline is the *center mark*. The server stands on one side of the mark and serves into the box on the opposite side.

AWESOME ATHLETE

Jimmy Connors is the only player to win the U.S. Open on three court surfaces. Jimmy won on grass in 1974, when the tournament was held in Forest Hills, New York. He won on clay in Forest Hills in 1976 and 1978. And he won on hard court in 1982 and 1983, after the Open had moved to the National Tennis Center in Flushing Meadow, New York.

used more and more. Many players became convinced that the added power of a metal racket was worth a little loss of control. By the late 1970's many of the world's top players were using metal rackets.

Soon companies began making rackets out of fiberglass and graphite. These materials are lighter and stiffer than metal, so players were able to hit with even more power.

In 1976, the tennis world was changed forever when the Prince racket was introduced. The Prince was made of aluminum and its face was about 60 percent larger than the strung portion of older rackets. That created a larger hitting area.

Not only did the Prince pack power, but its *sweet spot* was about 70 percent bigger than the sweet spot on the old rackets. The sweet spot is the area on the strings that produces the most powerful shot. Players didn't have to hit the ball perfectly to hit it hard.

Big Events

Women professionals compete on the Women's Tennis Association (WTA) tour. In 1996, they will compete in 55 tournaments and earn more than $36 million. Men compete on the IBM/ATP (Association of Tennis Professionals) tour. In 1996, they will compete in 87 tournaments and earn about $76 million.

The highlights of the tennis season are the four major tournaments. These are the Australian Open, which is played in Flinders Park-National Tennis Centre in Melbourne, Australia, in January; the French Open, played at Roland Garros Stadium in Paris, France, in May; Wimbledon, played at the All-England Club beginning in June; and the United States Open, played at the National Tennis Center, in Flushing Meadow, New York, beginning in late August.

These tournaments are also called the Grand Slam events. A player who wins all four in a year is said to win the Grand Slam. Only five players have ever done that: Don Budge (U.S., 1938), Rod Laver (Australia, 1962 and 1969), Maureen Connolly (U.S., 1953), Margaret Smith Court (Australia, 1970), and Steffi Graf (West Germany, 1988).

Cup Competitions

The Davis Cup is a tournament between men's teams from different countries. It was started in 1900 by Dwight Davis, a tennis player from Harvard University, as a competition between the U.S. and Great Britain.

Davis Cup competition helped make tennis a popular international sport. In 1905, six countries competed for the Cup. By 1928, 33 countries were trying to win this trophy. The U.S. has won the Cup a record 31 times.

In 1920, Hazel Hotchkiss Wightman created the Wightman Cup as a Davis Cup-type competition between the *women* of the U.S. and Great Britain. The tournament was played from 1923 to 1989. It ended with the U.S. leading, 51–10.

In 1963, the Federation Cup was begun as another women's tournament. In 1992, 32 countries competed. The U.S. has dominated here too, winning 14 times through 1995.

Olympic Tennis

Tennis was an Olympic sport until 1924, when it was dropped because it was too hard to tell the amateurs from the pros. In 1988, tennis returned to the Games. Steffi Graf of West Germany and Miloslav Mecir of Czechoslovakia won the first Olympic tennis gold medals in 64 years!

Records
WOMEN

Most singles tournaments won, career: 166, by Martina Navratilova of the United States, 1975–1994.

COURT SURFACES

Grass: There are very few grass courts in the world, because they are expensive to maintain. Wimbledon is the only major tournament still played on grass. Grass courts are very fast. A ball will skid on grass and take strange bounces.

Clay: The French Open is played on clay. Clay courts are soft, and play is slower than on grass. When a ball is hit onto clay, it slows down and bounces higher than it does on grass.

Hard: Most tennis courts are hard courts. The United States and Australian Opens are played on hard courts. This surface is faster than clay, but slower than grass. A ball still moves pretty fast on a hard court, and it takes a true bounce.

COOL FACTS

Nobody knows for sure how tennis got its name. The most popular theory is that it comes from the French word *tenez,* which means "take it."

●

Have you ever wondered why tennis balls are fuzzy? That fuzz, which is actually the material *felt,* is there for two reasons: 1) It slows the ball down, making it easier to return a shot; 2) It allows the racket strings to grip the ball, helping players to hit with topspin or backspin.

Most Grand Slam singles titles, career: 26, Margaret Smith Court, Australia, 1960–1977.

Most money won, career: $20,337,902, Martina Navratilova, U.S., 1975–1994.

MEN

Most singles tournaments won, career: 109, Jimmy Connors, U.S., 1972–1992.

Most Grand Slam singles titles, career: 12, Roy Emerson, Australia, 1959–1973.

Most money won, career: $21,859,428, Pete Sampras, U.S., 1988–present.

Legends

Arthur Ashe, U.S.: Arthur was the first African-American man to win both the United States Open (1968) and Wimbledon (1975). Before he died, in 1993, he became as well known for his civil rights work as he was for his tennis achievements.

Bjorn Borg, Sweden: Bjorn dominated men's tennis in the late 1970's. He won 62 tournaments during his career, including a record five straight Wimbledon titles.

Don Budge, U.S.: In 1938, Don became the first player to win the Grand Slam. In Davis Cup play, his record was 19–2.

Maureen Connolly, U.S.: In 1951, "Little Mo," as she was known, became the second-youngest woman to win the U.S. Women's Tournament (now called the U.S. Open). In 1953, she became the first woman to win the Grand Slam. Between September 1951 and July 1954, she lost only one tennis match. In her career, she won nine Grand Slam titles.

Margaret Smith Court, Australia: In 1970, Margaret won the Grand Slam. During her career, she won the singles, doubles, and *mixed doubles* (teams of one man and one woman) titles at every Grand Slam tournament, and a record 26 Grand Slam singles titles. In four other years, Margaret won three of the four Grand Slam titles. She finished

Helen Wills Moody shows the look and the small racket of tennis's early days.

the year ranked Number 1 seven times.

Chris Evert, U.S.: With her steady baseline game and calm attitude, Chris won 18 Grand Slam singles titles and 157 tournaments. From 1972 until she retired in 1989, Chris was never ranked below Number 4 in the world, and ended a year ranked Number 1 four straight times.

Althea Gibson, U.S.: Althea was the first African American to win a Grand Slam singles title. In 1956, she won the French Open. In 1957 and 1958, Althea won Wimbledon and the U.S. Open. After she retired in 1958, she became a professional golfer.

Steffi Graf, Germany: Steffi was ranked Number 1 from August 1987 until March 1991, longer than any other man or woman in history. In 1988, she won the Grand Slam. During her career, Steffi has won 18 Grand Slam titles, including three in 1995.

Billie Jean King, U.S.: Without Billie Jean, there might not be women's professional tennis. In 1973, she beat former tennis champion Bobby Riggs in an exhibition match, proving that women could compete with men and should earn the same amount of money that men were earning. In 1973, she helped found the Women's Tennis Association. Billie Jean won 12 Grand Slam titles, including six at Wimbledon.

Rod Laver, Australia: "The Rocket," as he was known, is the only player to win the

CHAMPIONS

AUSTRALIAN OPEN

MEN
1996	Boris Becker
1995	Andre Agassi
1994	Pete Sampras
1993	Jim Courier

WOMEN
1996	Monica Seles
1995	Mary Pierce
1994	Steffi Graf
1993	Monica Seles

FRENCH OPEN

MEN
1995	Thomas Muster
1994	Sergi Bruguera
1993	Sergi Bruguera

WOMEN
1995	Steffi Graf
1994	Arantxa Sanchez Vicario
1993	Steffi Graf

WIMBLEDON

MEN
1995	Pete Sampras
1994	Pete Sampras
1993	Pete Sampras

WOMEN
1995	Steffi Graf
1994	Conchita Martinez
1993	Steffi Graf

U.S. OPEN

MEN
1995	Pete Sampras
1994	Andre Agassi
1993	Pete Sampras

WOMEN
1995	Steffi Graf
1994	Arantxa Sanchez Vicario
1993	Steffi Graf

Grand Slam twice. He won it as an amateur in 1962, and again as a professional in 1969. As a pro, he couldn't play in the Grand Slam tournaments between 1963 and 1967.

Suzanne Lenglen, France: From 1919 until 1926, Suzanne lost only one singles match. She won both the French and U.S. Championships six times. Suzanne's great personality helped make tennis popular.

John McEnroe, U.S.: John was the best player in the world in the early 1980's. His powerful serve and ability to win points by charging the net carried him to seven Grand Slam wins, including four at the U.S. Open.

Helen Wills Moody, U.S.: Helen was called "Little Miss Poker Face" because of her lack of emotion on the court. At the 1924 Olympics, she won gold medals in singles and doubles. She won 19 Grand Slam titles.

Martina Navratilova, U.S.: Martina is the greatest woman player in history. She has won 18 Grand Slam singles titles, including a record 9 Wimbledon titles, and holds the record for most doubles titles won, with 163. Martina was born in Czechoslovakia.

Monica Seles, U.S.: In 1990, Monica won the French Open at age 16 ½. Since then, she has won eight other Grand Slams. In March 1991, she became the top-ranked woman in the world, a spot she held until April 1993, when she was stabbed by a crazed fan and forced to leave the tour. She returned in 1995. She reached the final of the 1995 U.S. Open and won the 1996 Australian Open. Born in Yugoslavia, Monica is now a U.S. citizen.

Bill Tilden, U.S.: Many people consider Bill the greatest player ever. From 1920 through 1925, Bill was 66–0 in major tournaments. He won 10 Grand Slam titles. His serve was once clocked at 130 miles per hour!

AMAZING FEAT

In 1984, at the Ginny of Richmond (Virginia) tournament, Vicki Nelson-Dunbar beat Jean Hepner 6–4, 7–6 (13–11 in the tiebreaker). Their match lasted 6 hours and 31 minutes! One point took 29 minutes to finish!

●

In 1993, Pete Sampras became the first player to serve more than 1,000 aces in a season. Pete clubbed winning points with one stroke of his racket 1,011 times!

Glossary

Ace: An ace is a serve that is so fast or so

well-placed that the receiver is unable to touch it with his racket.

Backhand: One of the two most common groundstrokes. A right-handed player uses a backhand to hit a ball that lands to his left.

Backspin: Players use two types of spin when they hit the ball: topspin and backspin. To hit with backspin, a player swings down on the ball, from high to low, causing it to spin backward as it moves forward. Backspin causes the ball to float. It hits the court softly and doesn't bounce very high.

Forehand: The other common groundstroke in tennis, right-handed players use it to hit any ball that lands to their right.

Groundstrokes: Shots hit from baseline to baseline in a rally.

Lob: A high-arcing shot designed to go over the head of an opponent at the net.

Tiebreaker: A sudden-death finish that is played when a set reaches 6–6. A tiebreaker is won by the player who scores seven points first, though he must win by two.

Topspin: A type of spin that players can put on a ball when they hit their groundstrokes. To hit with topspin, a player begins his swing very low and finishes very high. He brushes up the back side of the ball, making it spin forward as it moves forward. Topspin causes the ball to drop very quickly, hit the court hard, and bounce high.

Volley: When a player hits the ball before it bounces, he has hit a volley. Most volleying occurs when a player is standing at the net.

Where to Write

Association of Tennis Professionals, 200 ATP Tour Blvd., Ponte Vedra Beach, FL 32082

Women's Tennis Association, 133 First St. Northeast, St. Petersburg, FL, 33701

International Tennis Hall of Fame, 194 Bellevue Ave., Newport, RI 02840

GREAT MATCHES!

1937 Davis Cup: Don Budge vs. Gottfried Von Cramm. Don had beaten Gottfried, of Germany, one week earlier in the Wimbledon Final. This time, Gottfried won the first two sets, but Don managed to win the next two. In the final set, Gottfried raced to a 4–1 lead but Don came back, leading the U.S. into the Davis Cup final.

1980 Wimbledon Final: Bjorn Borg vs. John McEnroe. John evened the match by winning the fourth set in a tiebreaker, 18–16, that lasted 20 minutes. But Bjorn won the fifth set, and a record fifth straight Wimbledon.

1985 French Open Final: Chris Evert vs. Martina Navratilova. Chris had beaten Martina only once in their last 14 matches. In this see-saw match, Chris won the first set, and Martina won the second. Chris jumped to the lead in the third, but Martina roared back, and was on the verge of victory when she missed an easy shot. Chris won the final two games, and the match.

TRACK AND FIELD

In track and field, athletes try to run faster, jump higher, and throw farther than anyone else. It may be the world's oldest sport — and it remains one of its most competitive.

History

Track and field was part of the first ancient Olympic Games, in Athens, Greece, in 776 B.C. In fact, a sprint race was the only athletic event at those Games.

But people had been getting ready for track and field competition since the beginning of time. In those days, you were either fast, strong, and accurate with a rock or spear, or you were a meal for a hungry animal. Eventually, people started competing to see who was the fastest or the strongest.

Other track and field events, such as the discus, javelin, and long jump (as well as other sports), eventually became part of the ancient Olympic Games. In 393 A.D., the last ancient Olympics were held. The Games were banned by Emperor Theodosius of Rome for political and religious reasons. Without the Olympic Games, track and field meets disappeared for almost 1,500 years.

People continued to compete in track-and-field-like events in Europe, sometimes in chivalrous or military tournaments. These competitions eventually evolved from occasional contests and minor events into something much larger and more organized.

What we now know as modern track and field took shape in England in the 1800's. In 1837, Eton College held a track meet between two classes. And in 1864, Cambridge University and Oxford University, both in England, competed in the first track and field meet between two colleges. Most of the rules used in those early track meets are still used today.

TEXT BY STEPHEN THOMAS

An eight-time gold medalist at three Olympics, Carl Lewis is a living legend on the track.

In 1896, the first modern Olympic Games were held in Athens, Greece. The Olympics were brought back largely because of the work of Baron Pierre de Coubertin, of France. Baron de Coubertin wanted to promote international friendship through athletic competition.

Track and field wasn't the only sport at those Olympics. The Games also included swimming and even figure skating!

In 1912, 16 countries agreed to form the International Amateur Athletic Federation (IAAF), the organization that still governs track and field. In the 1920's and 1930's, athletes such as Finland's Paavo Nurmi, who ran his way to 35 world records, and the United States' Babe Didrikson Zaharias, who won two golds and one silver medal at the 1932 Olympics, helped make track and field popular all over the world.

Competition

Track and field is sometimes called *athletics*. It includes many different events.

The *track* events are running races, ranging from *sprints* (shorter races, from 50 to 400 meters long) to *middle-distance* races

INDOOR VS. OUTDOOR

There are many differences between indoor and outdoor track. Indoor tracks usually have only four lanes, and outdoor tracks have eight. While all outdoor tracks are 400 meters long, many indoor tracks are about one third as long.

There are not as many field events indoors. The javelin and the discus are not held, because people could be hurt by the flying objects!

Indoor races are shorter than outdoor races. Instead of 100 meters, the indoor sprint is 50, 55, or 60 meters long. The longest indoor race is 5,000 meters.

The size of the track also affects the way the races are run. Indoor straightaways are very short, and there are many more turns than in an outdoor race. Most indoor records are slower than outdoor records because it's easier to run fast in a straight line.

It also helps to be aggressive indoors. Runners are bunched together, so they must be ready to charge ahead if someone gets in their way.

Thomas Burke
(1896)
12.0 seconds
59' behind

QUICK HIT

Track events are held on an oval track that is 400 meters around. Why? Ask the English. Like Americans, they measure things in feet and yards. As they developed track and field, they laid out quarter-mile (440-yard) tracks. But because most of the world uses the metric system for measuring, it was later decided to make all tracks 400 meters long, which is about two meters less than a quarter mile. Historians believe that if track and field had been developed in continental Europe, the track might have measured 500 meters, or a half kilometer.

(from 800 to 5,000 meters) to *long-distance* races (from 10,000 meters to the *marathon*, which is 26.2 miles long).

The *field* events are made up of the *high jump, long jump, pole vault, shot put, discus throw, hammer throw*, and *javelin*. In addition, all-around athletes compete in the *decathlon* and *heptathlon*. These are called *multi-event* sports, because they combine 10 events in the decathlon and seven events in the pentathlon.

Big Events

The Summer Olympic Games, held every four years, is the Number 1 competition in track and field. The world championships are a close second.

The world championships were started by the IAAF in 1983, to be held every four years during the year before the Olympics. The first outdoor world championships were held in Helsinki, Finland, in 1983. The first indoor world championships were in Indianapolis, Indiana, in 1987. The indoor world championships are held every two years.

Track and field athletes also compete in outdoor and indoor track seasons. The indoor track season is only three months long, from January to March. Meets are held in North America, Europe, and Japan. The most important group of meets, in which athletes

| Florence Griffith Joyner (1988) 10.49 seconds 20' behind | Jesse Owens (1936) 10.2 seconds 11' behind | James Hines (1968) 9.95 seconds 3' behind | L. Burrell (1994) 9.85 seconds Winner |

compete for prize money, is the USA/Mobil Indoor Grand Prix circuit. At each meet, athletes earn points based on their performance. At the end of the indoor season, prize money is awarded according to how many points athletes earned in their event. In addition, the overall points leader wins money, too.

The outdoor season lasts from about April to September. As on the indoor circuit, athletes who compete on the USA/Mobil Outdoor Grand Prix circuit can earn prize money based on their season-long performance in their event and by being the overall leader.

Sprints

The sprint at the first Olympic Games in 776 B.C. was called a *stadion*, and it was about 192 meters long. Today, the sprints are all races from 50 to 400 meters, including hurdles *(see Hurdles, page 258)* and relays.

Starting blocks are used at the beginning of all sprints. These came into wide use after World War II. The blocks are placed on the track and have footholds against which the runner pushes off at the start. They help the runner blast forward down the track. Before starting blocks were invented, runners used to dig footholds in the tracks, which were made of cinder.

Runners' shoes are different today, and so is the track. Sprinters' shoes are lightweight

FAST, FASTER, FASTEST

Performances in every track and field event have gotten faster over the years, as athletes have improved their training techniques and used better equipment. This is particularly true in the sprints. Starting blocks, lighter shoes, and harder, faster tracks have taken tenths of seconds off times. That might not sound like much, but in a race decided by hundredths of a second, one-tenth of a second is a ton! The winning time in the first Olympic 100-meter sprint, in 1896, was 11.8 seconds. The current world record is nearly two full seconds faster.

COOL FACT

Most indoor tracks were made of plywood. That's why running indoors is known as running on "the boards." Irish miler Eamonn Coghlan, who holds the indoor mile record (3:49.78), was known as the "Chairman of the Boards" because he ran so well inside.

and little more than holders for the spikes. Middle-distance shoes are also light and offer only slightly more support. Outdoor tracks are made of a rubberized material. It is harder than cinder and doesn't give as much underfoot. Running on a cinder track compared to a modern track is like running on the beach versus running on the grass.

The sprinting events have been dominated by American athletes for almost 40 years. These events require incredible reflexes (to get a fast start), blinding speed, and great upper body strength. Sprinters pump their arms to help power themselves as they streak toward the finish line.

100 meters: The 100-meter race is the most famous sprint. It is a race of pure speed. Sprinters explode out of the starting blocks, try to reach full speed as quickly as possible, then try to hold on until the finish. The winner of this race at the Olympics or world championships also wins the title of the "World's Fastest Human."

60 meters: This race is the indoor equivalent of the 100 meters. A great 60-meter runner won't necessarily be a great 100-meter runner, though. Both races require blinding speed, but 100-meter runners must be able to maintain that speed over a longer distance.

200 meters: The 200-meter race is run around one curve of the track, and is equal to one half of a lap. Runners in this event have almost as much pure speed as 100-meter runners, but they must keep up their speed as they go around the turn and into a straightaway. As in the 60 and 100 meters, competitors must run in lanes. But in the 200, runners have a *staggered start*. In a staggered start, runners in the outside lanes start a little farther down the track. This is to make up for the fact that they must run a longer distance around the turn.

400 meters: In the 1800's, the 400 meters

Jesse Owens, a four-time Olympic gold medalist in 1936, had to start from footholds dug in the track.

THE AMATEURS

Track and field athletes once were all unpaid amateurs. They competed just for the love of the sport.

IAAF rules said that track athletes weren't allowed to earn money. If they accepted any money, even for commercial endorsements, they no longer would be permitted to compete.

As far back as the 1800's, many top athletes broke the rules by secretly accepting money to support themselves. This came either as "appearance money" (to show up at a meet) or prize money (if they won their event or set a world record).

In 1981, the IAAF changed its rules to allow athletes to earn money if it were paid through the IAAF and used for training expenses. Then, in 1985, the IAAF made it legal for athletes to be paid directly for competing.

Today, there are meets sponsored by large companies that award prize money. Because they can earn a living in their sport, track and field athletes can compete longer than in the past.

was considered a middle-distance event, which meant that runners tried to pace themselves during the race. Now, the 400 is a flat-out sprint, and perhaps the toughest of the track races. As in the 200 meters, runners get a staggered start and must stay in their lane for the entire race — one lap of the track.

Relays: Frank Ellis and H. L. Geyelin, both of the University of Pennsylvania, are the fathers of the four-person relay race. In 1895, they organized the first Pennsylvania (or Penn) Relays. The Penn Relays, held every April, is made up almost exclusively of relay races. It is one of the most important outdoor meets in the world.

In relay races, each member of a relay team runs one *leg* of the race carrying a *baton*. At the end of his leg, he hands the baton to the next runner. The two runners have an area 20 meters long in which to exchange the baton. If they don't exchange the baton within this area, the team is disqualified. Teams work very hard to make sure their baton passes are smooth and that the person receiving the baton is at almost full speed when the baton is placed in his hand.

BLAST FROM THE PAST

In the early days of track and field, many races were started "by mutual consent." This meant that the runners took off when they all were ready. Sometimes, starts were delayed for a long time because one runner would try to out-fox the other to get a better start. In fact, an early rule required the use of a starter's pistol only if the start by mutual consent didn't occur within an hour!

Sprint World Records

OUTDOORS

100 meters, men: 9.85 seconds, by Leroy Burrell of the U.S., in 1994; **women:** 10.49, Florence Griffith Joyner, U.S., 1988.

200 meters, men: 19.72, Pietro Mennea, Italy, 1979; **women:** 21.34, Florence Griffith Joyner, U.S., 1988.

400 meters, men: 43.29, Butch Reynolds, U.S., 1988; **women:** 47.60, Marita Koch, East Germany, 1985.

4x100-meter relay, men: 37.40, United States, 1992 and 1993; **women:** 41.37, East Germany, 1985.

4x400-meter relay, men: 2:54.29, United States, 1993; **women:** 3:15.17, Soviet Union, 1988.

INDOORS

50 meters, men: 5.61, Manfred Kokot, East Germany, 1973, and James Sanford, U.S., 1981; **women:** 5.96, Irina Privalova, Russia, 1995.

60 meters, men: 6.41, Andre Cason, U.S., 1992; **women:** 6.92, Irinia Privalova, 1993.

200 meters, men: 20.25, Linford Christie, Great Britain, 1995; **women:** 21.87, Merlene Ottey, Jamaica, 1993.

400 meters, men: 44.63, Michael Johnson, U.S., 1995; **women:** 49.59, Jarmila Kratochvilová, Czechoslovakia, 1982.

4x200-meter relay, men: 1:22.11, Great Britain, 1991; **women:** 1:32.55, SC Eintracht Hamm, West Germany , 1988.

4x400-meter relay, men: 3:03.5, Germany, 1991; **women:** 3:27.22, Germany, 1991.

Sprint Legends

Lee Evans, U.S.: At the 1968 Olympics, Lee won the 400-meter sprint. His world-record time of 43.86 wasn't beaten until Butch Reynolds ran 43.29 in 1988. Lee also anchored the 4x400-meter relay team to the world record and another gold medal.

Michael Johnson, U.S.: At the 1995 world championships, Michael won both the 200m and 400m. It was his fourth world championship 200m and his fifth 400m. Michael hopes to run both distances at the 1996 Summer Olympic Games.

Florence Griffith Joyner, U.S.: "FloJo," as she was known, still ranks as the world's fastest woman. At the 1988 U.S. Olympic *Trials* (tryouts), she ran the 100 meters in 10.49, shattering the world record. At the 1988 Olympics, FloJo won the 100 and 200 meters, setting the world record in the 200.

Carl Lewis, U.S.: Carl is perhaps the greatest track and field athlete ever. He's also the world's fastest human. At the 1991 world championships, he won the gold medal and set the world record by running 9.86 seconds. In the 4x100-meter relay, Carl has anchored 10 of the top 17 U.S. relay teams, including the team that set a world record of 37.40 at the 1992 Olympics. Carl is also one of only four men to long jump farther than 29'. He has won eight gold medals and one silver medal at three Olympics.

Merlene Ottey, Jamaica: Before the 1993 world championships, Merlene had won nine Olympic and world championship medals, all of them bronze. But at the 1993 worlds, she won a gold medal in the 200 meters and a silver in the 100. In February 1994, Merlene ran 6.03 and set a world record in the 50-meter dash. At the 1995 worlds, she won a gold medal in the 200m (after Gwen Torrence was disqualified) and a silver in the 100m.

Jesse Owens, U.S.: In 1936, Jesse won Olympic gold medals in the 100 and 200 meters, the 4x100-meter relay, and the long jump. At a meet in 1935, he set four world records in 70 minutes, and tied two others.

GREAT RACE!

On May 6, 1954, a 25-year-old medical student named Roger Bannister ran a mile in 3:59.4. It was the first time anyone had run a mile in less than four minutes! The world record that Roger broke — 4:01.4 — had been set by Gunder Hagg of Sweden in 1945. Many runners had just figured that man could not possibly break the four-minute barrier.

On a very windy and cool Thursday in Oxford, England, Roger did the impossible. He ran the first quarter mile in 57.5, and the half in 1:58.2. At three quarters of a mile, his time was 3:00.5, which meant that he had to run the last lap in less than 60 seconds. He ran 58.9.

Once Roger had broken four minutes, it didn't take long for others to do the same. In fact, just six weeks after Roger's historic race, Australia's John Landy ran 3:58!

Later that year, Roger beat John in "The Mile of the Century," a famous race that took place at the British Empire & Commonwealth Games.

QUICK HIT

Butch Reynolds, U.S.: In 1988, Butch smashed one of the oldest track and field world records when he ran the 400 meters in 43.29 seconds. Two years later, he tested positive for *steroids* and was suspended from competition for two years. Butch denied that he had used steroids and challenged the IAAF in court. After years of fighting, he won his case and came back in 1993 to finish the year as the Number 2-ranked 400-meter runner in the world. At the 1995 world championships, Butch finished second to Michael Johnson in the 400 meters.

Wilma Rudolph, U.S.: When Wilma was a kid, she had polio, a disease that can cause paralysis. She wore a brace on her left leg until she was 12 years old. By the time she was 20, Wilma was an Olympic gold medalist. At the 1960 Olympics, she won the 100 and 200 meters, and the 4x100-meter relay. She was the first woman to win three gold medals at one Olympics!

Hurdles

Hurdling first appeared in England in the early 1840's. Back then, hurdles were sheep fences that were staked into the ground. Hurdlers hopped over them with their legs gathered up beneath them and their chests straight up and down.

In the late 1870's, an American named Alvin Kraenzlein developed the hurdling technique used today. He leaped over the hurdle with his front leg straight. The next important change came around 1900 with the introduction of the moveable hurdle, which looked a bit like an upside down T.

Today's hurdles look more like an L. When a runner hits the top of the L with his foot, the hurdle falls safely out of the way. But hitting hurdles slows a runner down and leads to a slower time for the race.

Hurdlers combine awesome speed with

great flexibility, agility, and courage. Just imagine running full speed at a low wall and leaping over it in one smooth motion. Now do that ten times at almost the same speed that Carl Lewis runs a *flat* (no hurdles) 100 meters or Michael Johnson runs a flat 400.

Indoor hurdles races are either 50, 55, or 60 meters long. Outdoors, men race 110 meters, women race 100 meters, and both compete in the 400-meter intermediate hurdles.

Men's hurdles are 42" high in the 110-meter race and 36" high in the 400-meter race (also known as the *intermediate* hurdles). Women's hurdles are 33" high in the 100 meters, and 30" high in the 400 meters. There are 10 hurdles in each of these races.

Hurdling World Records
OUTDOORS
110-meter hurdles, men: 12.91, Colin Jackson, Great Britain, 1993; **100-meter hurdles, women:** 12.21, Yordanka Donkova, Bulgaria, 1988.

400-meter hurdles, men: 46.78, Kevin Young, U.S., 1992; **women:** 52.61, Kim Batten, U.S., 1995.

INDOORS
50-meter hurdles, men: 6.25, Mark McKoy, Canada, 1986; **women:** Cornelia Oschkenat, East Germany, 1988.

60-meter hurdles, men: 7.30, Colin Jackson, Great Britain, 1994; **women:** 7.69, Lyudmila Narozhilenko, Russia, 1990.

Hurdling Legends
Gail Devers, U.S.: Gail won every race she entered in 1995, including the 100-meter hurdles at the 1995 world championships. She finished 1995 ranked Number 1 in the world in that event, in which she also won the gold medal at the 1992 Olympics. She hopes to win another gold at the 1996 Summer Olympics in Atlanta.

CHAMPIONS

These men won gold medals in the track events at the 1992 Summer Olympics in Barcelona, Spain.

100m	Linford Christie, Great Britain
200m	Mike Marsh, U.S.
400m	Quincy Watts, U.S.
800m	William Tanui, Kenya
1,500m	Fermin Cacho, Spain
5,000m	Dieter Baumann, Germany
10,000m	Khalid Skah, Morocco
110m hurdles	Mark McKoy, Canada
400m hurdles	Kevin Young, U.S.
3,000m steeplechase	Mathew Birir, Kenya
20k walk	Daniel Plaza, Spain
50k walk	Andrei Perlov, Unified Team
4x100m relay	United States
4x400m relay	United States
Marathon	Hwang Young Cho, South Korea

Edwin Moses, U.S.: Edwin was the greatest intermediate hurdler ever. From 1977–87, he won 122 straight races, and held the world record (47.02) for nine years. (At the 1992 Summer Olympics, American Kevin Young shattered the record when he ran 46.78 and won the gold medal.) Edwin also won two Olympic gold medals, in 1976 and 1984.

AWESOME ATHLETE

Three months after she began running, 15-year-old Maria Mutola of Mozambique, Africa, competed in the 800-meter run at the 1988 Olympics. She didn't make the final. In 1993, 21-year-old Maria was undefeated and ranked Number 1 in the world — the youngest woman in 24 years to earn the top ranking. She lives and trains in Oregon.

Middle Distance

The races between 800 and 5,000 meters are known as middle-distance events (5,000 meters is 3.1 miles). Athletes who compete in these events combine speed with endurance.

When you run, your muscles need oxygen. If your muscles don't get enough oxygen, you will slow down. In middle-distance events, runners must run fast, but not so fast that their muscles won't get enough oxygen to work well. Even an athlete in great shape can run full speed for only about 100 meters before his muscles use all the available oxygen.

800 meters: The 800-meter race is the shortest of the middle-distance races. It is about the same distance as a half mile. The pace is a few seconds slower than a sprint, making the 800 almost a two-lap sprint.

1,500 meters/mile: The 1,500 meters is known as the "metric mile" because it is only about 300' shorter than a mile. It is the most famous middle-distance race. In major international meets like the Olympics, the 1,500 meters is run. But at indoor meets like the Millrose Games or some outdoor meets like the Bislett Games, the mile is run.

3,000 meters/5,000 meters: The women's 3,000 meters wasn't run at the Olympics until 1984! Before that, the longest race for women was 1,500 meters. Olympic officials believed that women weren't strong enough to handle the longer races. There is still no Olympic 5,000-meter race for women.

Steeplechase: If it hadn't been for a clum-

Joan Benoit won the first Olympic marathon for women.

sy horse, steeplechase might not have been invented. In 1850, English college students were racing their horses over fences in the woods. One of the horses fell, and the rider told his friends that he'd rather run than ride his horse again. The steeplechase was born.

The steeplechase is a 3,000-meter race in which runners jump over 28 hurdles and seven *water jumps*. (Water jumps combine 36-inch-high hurdles, or barriers, and a water pit.) Unlike regular hurdles, steeplechase barriers are solid and won't move. This means that a runner can help himself over by placing his front foot on top of the hurdle and pushing off, which is what steeplechasers do to clear the seven water jumps. They hurdle the other 28 barriers, however.

Middle-Distance World Records
OUTDOORS

800 meters, men: 1:41.73, Sebastian Coe, Great Britain, 1981; **women:** 1:53.28, Jarmila Kratochvílová, Czechoslovakia, 1983.

1,500 meters, men: 3:27.37, Noureddine Morceli, Algeria, 1995; **women:** 3:50.46, Qu Yunxia, China, 1993.

Mile, men: 3:44.39, Noureddine Morceli, Algeria, 1993; **women:** 4:15.61, Paula Ivan, Romania, 1989.

3,000 meters, men: 7:25.11, Noureddine

GREAT RACE!

In 1983, Joan Benoit won the Boston Marathon and set a women's marathon world-best when she ran 2:22:43. Joan also hoped to win the first-ever women's Olympic marathon, which was to be held in 1984. But she almost didn't even make it to the starting line. Seventeen days before the 1984 United States Olympic Trials, she had knee surgery.

Joan still made the team, and she and Grete Waitz of Norway were co-favorites heading into the Olympics. Joan had beaten Grete only once in 11 previous races.

When the Olympic marathon began, Joan opened up a big lead only 14 minutes into the race. Grete figured that Joan would get tired and fall back to the pack. Grete's only problem was that Joan didn't get tired. By nine miles, Joan's lead was almost one minute, and by 15 miles, it was up to 1:51!

Joan won the first women's Olympic marathon by almost 1:30! (She later married and changed her last name to Samuelson.)

AMAZING FEATS

In 1993, Wang Junxia, an unknown runner from China, quickly became one of the greatest female runners ever. Competing in the Chinese National Championships, Wang shattered the women's 10,000-meter record. Her time of 29:31.78 was almost 45 seconds, or about two seconds per lap, faster than the previous world record. Five days later, she destroyed the women's 3,000-meter world record by more than 16 seconds. Her time was 8:06.11. At that meet, Chinese women broke three world records.

Morceli, Algeria, 1994; **women:** 8:06.11, Wang Junxia, China, 1993.

5,000 meters, men: 12:44.39, Haile Gebrselassie, Ethiopia, 1995; **women:** 14:36.45, Fernanda Ribiero, Portugal, 1995.

Steeplechase: 7:59.18, Moses Kiptanui, Kenya, 1995.

INDOORS

800 meters, men: 1:44.84, Paul Ereng, Kenya, 1989; **women:** 1:56.40, Christine Wachtel, East Germany, 1988.

1,500 meters, men: 3:34.16, Noureddine Morceli, Algeria, 1991; **women:** 4:00.27, Doina Melinte, Romania, 1990.

Mile, men: 3:49.78, Eamonn Coghlan, Ireland, 1983; **women:** 4:17.14, Doina Melinte, 1990.

3,000 meters, men: 7:35.15, Moses Kiptanui, Kenya, 1995; **women:** 8:33.82, Elly van Hulst, Netherlands, 1989.

5,000 meters, men: 13:20.4, Suleiman Nyambui, Tanzania, 1981; **women:** 15:03.17, Liz McColgan, Scotland, 1992.

Middle-Distance Legends

Said Aouita, Morocco: Said was the first man to run 5,000 meters in less than 13 minutes. In 1987, he ran 12:58.39, which was the record until 1995. He once held the 1,500-meter world record. At the 1984 Olympics, Said won the gold medal in the 5,000 meters.

Roger Bannister, Great Britain: Roger was the first person to run a mile in less than four minutes *(see Great Race!, page 257).*

Sebastian Coe, Great Britain: Sebastian holds one of the oldest records in track and field. In 1981, he set the 800-meter world record, when he ran 1:41.73. At the 1984 and 1988 Olympics, Sebastian won gold medals in the 1,500 meters and 800 meters. In 1992 he was elected to the British Parliament.

Noureddine Morceli, Algeria: Noureddine, at age 26, is already the greatest middle distance runner in history. He is the only man to be ranked Number 1 in the world in the mile and 1,500 for four straight years. In 1995, Noureddine set world records in both the 1,500m and the 2,000m. He holds the indoor and outdoor world records for 1,500 meters.

Paavo Nurmi, Finland: Paavo, who was known as the "Flying Finn," dominated running in the 1920's. He set 29 world records at distances from 1,500 to 20,000 meters. Paavo won nine gold medals at the 1920, 1924, and 1928 Olympic Games.

Mary Decker Slaney, U.S.: Mary was one of the greatest middle-distance runners ever. In 1983, she won the 1,500 and 3,000 meters at the world championships. At one time, she held U.S. records in five events, ranging from 800 to 3,000 meters.

Long Distance

Long-distance runners can run amazing distances. One reason is that their muscles are different from other runners' muscles.

A distance runner's muscles are made up of what are called *slow-twitch fibers*, while sprinters and middle-distance runners have *fast-twitch fibers*. Slow-twitch muscles function very well at a slower pace for a longer time. Fast-twitch muscles function better at a faster pace for a shorter time. Most people are born with one type of muscle or the other.

The two most important long-distance races are the 10,000 meters and the marathon. Neither is run indoors. The 10,000 meters is about 25 laps around a track. The marathon is run on a road course, often through city streets. At competitions like the Olympics or the world championships, the marathon begins and ends with a lap of the stadium track.

Other famous marathons, such as the Boston Marathon (in April) and the New York City Marathon (in October), are run entirely on the streets of those cities, on the same

CHAMPIONS

These women won track events at the 1992 Summer Olympics.

100m	Gail Devers, U.S.
200m	Gwen Torrence, U.S.
400m	Marie-Jose Perec, France
800m	Ellen Van Langen, Netherlands
1,500m	H. Boulmerka, Algeria
3,000m	Elena Romanova, Unified Team
10,000m	Derartu Tulu, Ethiopia
100m hurdles	P. Patoulidou, Greece
400m hurdles	Sally Gunnell, Great Britain
4x100m relay	United States
4x400m relay	Unified Team
10k walk	Chen Yueling, China
Marathon	Valentina Yegorova, Unified Team

AMAZING FEAT

One of the more unusual events in track and field is the hour run, in which men run as far as they can in an hour's time. The holder of the world record for this event is Arturo Barrios of Mexico, who ran 21,101 meters in 1991. That's 13.1 miles per hour!

course every year. Because all marathon courses are different, the IAAF doesn't recognize a world marathon record. Instead, it keeps track of the "world best" performance in the marathon.

Long-Distance Records

OUTDOORS

10,000 meters, men: 26:43.53, Haile Gebrselassie, Ethiopia, 1995; **women:** 29:31.78, Wang Junxia, China, 1993.

20,000 meters, men: 56:55.6, Arturo Barrios, Mexico, 1991; **women:** 1:06:48.8, Izumi Maki, Japan, 1993.

30,000 meters, men: 1:29:18.8, Toshihiko Seko, Japan, 1981; **women:** 1:47:05.6, Karolina Szabø, Hungary, 1988.

Marathon (world bests), men: 2:06:50, Belayneh Densimo, Ethiopia, 1988 (Rotterdam); **women:** 2:21:06, Ingrid Kristiansen, Norway, 1985 (London).

Long-Distance Legends

Ingrid Kristiansen, Norway: At one time, Ingrid held the 5,000- and 10,000-meter world records, and had the world's best marathon. In 1985, she won the London Marathon and ran 2:21:06. In 1986, she set the 5,000- and 10,000-meter world records.

Yobes Ondieki, Kenya: At the 1993 Bislett Games in Oslo, Norway, Yobes ran 26:58.38 and became the first man to break 27 minutes in the 10,000 meters. His wife, Lisa, was a world-class marathoner.

Joan Benoit Samuelson, U.S.: In 1984, Joan won the first-ever women's Olympic marathon *(see Great Race!, page 261)*.

Frank Shorter, U.S.: The year 1972 was a great one for Frank. He won the Olympic marathon and the Fukuoka marathon in Japan, another important international race. He also won the Sullivan Award as America's top amateur athlete. Frank won the silver

Roger Bannister, a medical student, was the first person to run a four-minute mile.

medal in the marathon at the 1976 Olympics. In the mid-to-late 1970's, he helped road racing (5-kilometer and 10-kilometer races) become very popular in the United States.

Grete Waitz, Norway: Without Grete, there might not be a marathon race for women at the Olympics. She proved that women could run 26.2 miles. From 1978 through 1990, she won 13 of the 19 marathons she entered, including the first women's world championship in 1983. She won the silver medal in the first women's Olympic marathon in 1984. Grete also won the New York Marathon a record nine times.

Emil Zatopek, Czechoslovakia: At the 1952 Olympics, Emil won the 5,000- and 10,000-meter runs, and the marathon. No one before — or since —has won those three races at one Olympics. As if that wasn't incredible enough, the Olympic marathon was the first marathon he had ever run! During his career, Emil won an incredible 261 of 334 races at all distances and set 18 world records.

Jumps

High jump: The object of the high jump is to leap over a bar that rests on two supports. Jumpers run toward the bar, gaining momen-

CROSS-COUNTRY

Cross-country runners run fairly long distances (men usually run more than 10 kilometers, and women about 5K). But they don't run them on tracks or on roads. They run on wooded trails or across fields.

Some people say that cross-country is the most difficult type of running. The ground can be very rough and uneven, and the trails can be in terrible shape if it rains. Plus, there are always plenty of hills.

Cross-country was an Olympic event until 1924. That year, the race was held on a very difficult course in Paris, France, and close to a power plant that was spitting out horrible fumes. Many runners collapsed and ended up in the hospital. Only 15 of 38 runners finished.

In the United States cross-country is a fall sport. In Europe, it's more of a winter sport. The most important meet is the world championships. In 1994, William Sigei, of Kenya, won his second straight world title, and Helen Chepngeno, also of Kenya, won her first.

BLAST FROM THE PAST

The marathon is one of the oldest races in track and field. Some people believe the first marathoner was a Greek messenger who ran from Marathon to Athens in ancient Greece to tell people the story of a great military victory. At the end of his 26-mile run, the messenger told his story — and then dropped dead.

tum that will lift them up and over. Jumpers are out of the competition if they have three misses at one height. The best height cleared is the one that counts in the final standings.

Long jump: The long jump was the only jumping event of the ancient Olympics. Back then, jumpers held weights in their hands, which they swung back and forth while they were in the air to help propel them farther.

In the modern long jump, athletes just leap as far as they can after a running start. It helps to be a fast runner, and most long jumpers are also fine sprinters.

Jumpers sprint down a *runway*. At the end of the runway is a *takeoff board*. The jumper tries to hit this board with his foot and launch himself into the air. If his foot goes beyond the edge of the takeoff board, the jump does not count. The length of the jump is measured from the edge of the takeoff board to the closest mark made in the *sand pit* where the athlete lands. Each jumper has six attempts in which to leap his farthest. His best jump is the only one that counts.

Triple jump: The triple jump, which used to be known as the hop, step, and jump, is divided into three parts.

The jumper takes a running start, then leaps and lands on the same foot (the *hop*). He continues his motion but must land on the other foot (the *step*), which he then uses to push off for the *jump*. Triple jumpers use the same runway as long jumpers, but start from much farther back. They also must launch themselves from a takeoff board.

The length of a jump is measured from the takeoff board to the closest mark made in the sand pit, where the jumper lands. Triple jumpers also can take six jumps in most competitions, and only their best jump counts.

Pole vault: The ancient Greeks used poles in battles to get across rivers or over walls. In track and field, poles were first used to jump far, not high. But around the mid-1800's, members of an athletic club in England developed the sport as we know it today.

Pole vaulters race down the runway carrying a pole, which they ram into a *box*. The pole is typically between 16' 6" and 17' long, and is hollow. The combination of speed and body weight makes the pole bend. As it straightens, it carries the athlete over the bar. Like high jumpers, pole vaulters are disqualified if they cannot clear a height in three tries, and only their best height counts.

Jumping World Records
OUTDOORS

High jump, men: 8' ½", Javier Sotomayor, Cuba, 1993; **women:** 6' 10 ¼", Stefka Kostadinova, Bulgaria, 1987.

Long jump, men: 29' 4 ½", Mike Powell, U.S., 1991; **women:** 24' 8 ¼", Galina Chistyakova, Soviet Union, 1988.

Triple jump, men: 60' ¼", Jonathan Edwards, Great Britain, 1995; **women:** 50' 10 ¼", Inessa Kravets, Ukraine, 1995.

Pole vault, men: 20' 1 ¾", Sergei Bubka, Ukraine, 1994; **women:** Emma George, Australia, 14' ½".

INDOORS

High jump, men: 7' 11 ¼", Javier Sotomayor, Cuba, 1989; **women:** 6' 9 ½", Heike Henkel, Germany, 1992.

Long jump, men: 28' 10 ¼", Carl Lewis, U.S., 1984; **women:** 24' 2 ¼", Heike Drechsler, East Germany, 1988.

Triple jump, men: 58' 3 ¾", Leonid Voloshin, Russia, 1994; **women:** 49' 3 ¾", Yolanda Chen, Russia, 1995.

Pole vault, men: 20' 2", Sergei Bubka, Ukraine, 1993; **women:** 13' 7 ¼", Sun Calyon, China, 1995.

Jumping Legends
Bob Beamon, U.S.: Bob's long jump of

OLDEST, YOUNGEST . . .

<u>Oldest Olympic gold medalist:</u> Patrick "Babe" McDonald, U.S., 42 years, 26 days; 56-pound weight throw, 1920.

<u>Oldest Olympic medalist:</u> Tebbs Lloyd Johnson, Great Britain, 48 years, 115 days; bronze medal in the 50-kilometer walk, 1948.

<u>Youngest Olympic gold medalist:</u> Barbara Jones, U.S., 15 years, 123 days, 4x100-meter relay, 1952.

<u>Most world records equaled or set in a day:</u> 6, Jesse Owens, U.S., May 25, 1935. Jesse set or tied what were world records in the 100-yard dash, long jump, 200-meter dash, 220-yard dash, 220-yard hurdles, and 200-meter hurdles.

<u>Most world records in a season:</u> 10, Gunder Hagg, Sweden, 1941–42; in the 1,500 to 5,000 meters.

<u>Most world records in a career:</u> 34, Sergei Bubka, pole vaulter, Ukraine.

<u>Youngest person to set a world record:</u> Carolina Gisolf, Holland, 15 years, 5 days; in the high jump, 1928.

<u>Oldest person to set a world record:</u> Carlos Lopes, Portugal, 38 years, 59 days; in the marathon, 1985.

<u>Longest lasting record:</u> 26' 8 ¼" long jump by Jesse Owens; lasted 25 years, 79 days (from 1935 to 1960).

AWESOME ATHLETES

In recent years, African runners, many of them from Kenya, have dominated men's distance running events. At the end of 1995, African runners held 12 of the 15 men's world records at the distances between 800 and 10,000 meters.

●

In 1989, Javier Sotomayor of Cuba became the first person to high-jump eight feet. In 1993, he broke his own record when he jumped 8' ½". Javier won the 1992 Olympic gold medal and the 1993 world championship in the high jump. He finished 1995 with his fourth Number One high jump ranking, and record sixth title overall.

29' 2 ½" at the 1968 Olympics was almost 2' farther than anyone had ever jumped before, and was the world record until Mike Powell broke it at the 1991 outdoor world championships. (At that meet, Mike and teammate Carl Lewis became only the third and fourth jumpers in history to leap more than 29'.)

Sergei Bubka, Ukraine: Sergei is the greatest pole vaulter ever. He was the first, and is still the only, vaulter to clear 20'. His indoor world record is 20' 2", and his outdoor record is 20' 1 ¾". Sergei has won the outdoor world championships five times and the indoor championships seven times

Heike Drechsler, Germany: In 1995, Heike competed 22 times and lost only three times. She has been the Number 1-ranked women's long jumper in the world a record nine times! She won a silver medal at the 1988 Olympics and a gold at the 1992 Games.

Dick Fosbury, U.S.: In 1968, Dick revolutionized high jumping when he developed the Fosbury Flop. Before the flop, jumpers used to try to get a leg and an arm over the bar and roll sideways over the top, facedown. This was called the Western Roll. With the flop, jumpers go over the bar headfirst with their backs to the bar.

Throws

There are four throwing events: the *discus*, *shot put*, *hammer throw*, and *javelin*.

In ancient Greece, the winner of the discus was honored for his strength and was considered the greatest athlete in the land. The javelin was also contested at the ancient Olympics, but it developed into its modern form in the 1800's in Germany and Scandinavia. Finland still produces many of the world's best javelin throwers.

The hammer throw and the shot put probably began more than 900 years ago in Ireland and Scotland. But it wasn't until the mid-

The greatest pole vaulter of all time, Sergei Bubka of Ukraine has broken the world record 30 times!

RACE WALKING

Race walking is a little more complicated than putting one leg in front of the other. One foot must touch the ground at all times, and the walker must straighten his leg for a moment on each stride.

Historians give most of the credit for the creation of race walking to two men, Foster Powell and Robert Barclay Allardice, both of England. In 1789, Mr. Allardice walked 100 miles in 22 hours, and in 1809, Mr. Powell walked 1,000 miles in 1,000 straight hours. The first competitive race-walking event was held in 1866 at the English Championships.

World records can only be set in races held on the track. Most men's races are 20 or 50 kilometers long and women's are 5 and 10 kilometers. Most indoor race-walking events are between 1,500 and 5,000 meters.

Race-walkers can really motor. The men's world record in the 10K (6.2 miles) is 38:31.3, only about two minutes per mile slower than the world record for the men's 10K run.

1800's that these two events became what they are today. In the early days of the hammer throw, contestants threw a sledge hammer, which is how the event got its name.

In the shot put, hammer throw, and discus, athletes must throw from inside a *circle*. (The shot put and hammer throw circles are 7' wide, and the discus circle is about 8' wide.) If the thrower steps out of the circle, the throw does not count. Throws are measured from the inside edge of the circle to the front edge of the spot where the object hits.

Shot put: Shot-putters need to be strong and agile. They begin each effort bent over at the waist, balancing on one leg. Then, without stopping, they bounce toward the front of the circle on the same leg, turn their upper body, and heave the shot as far as they can.

BLAST FROM THE PAST

The first event at the first modern Olympic Games in 1896 was the triple jump. It was won by James Connolly of the United States, who jumped a little less than 45' to win the gold medal. The current world record, held by Willie Banks of the U.S., is 58' 11 ½".

The men's shot is a metal ball that is about 4 ¾" in diameter and weighs 16 pounds. The women's shot is about 4" in diameter and weighs a bit less than 9 pounds.

Competitors hold the shot in one hand and begin each attempt with the shot pressed to their neck beneath their chin. The shot cannot drop below shoulder level. They then *put*, or push, the shot as far as they can.

Hammer throw: The hammer is a 16 pound metal ball attached to a handle by steel wire, all of which is heaved together.

Throwers begin by swinging the hammer in an arc, so that it passes above their heads and below their knees. Then, to help generate more force, they spin around a few times before releasing the hammer.

Throwers from the Soviet Union and the Unified Team have won seven of the last eight Olympic gold medals in the hammer throw. In 1976, 1980, 1988, and 1992, they swept all three Olympic medals in the event.

In indoor meets, the hammer throw is replaced by the 35-pound weight throw. The weight looks like the hammer, but is heavier and doesn't travel as far.

Discus: The discus looks a bit like a flying disk: It's shaped like a circle and is flat. The men's discus is about 9" in diameter and weighs a bit less than 4 ½ pounds. The women's discus is about 7" in diameter and weighs a bit more than 2 pounds. The center and the edge of the discus are metal, while the rest is wood.

The thrower holds the discus flat, against his palm and forearm, and releases it with a sidearm motion. Like a hammer thrower, a discus thrower spins to generate power.

When it leaves the thrower's hand, the discus rises and spins around in circles. This motion helps it float through the air. A gust of wind will help it fly even farther.

Javelin: The javelin looks like a spear. In

ancient times, it was thrown for accuracy. Now it is thrown only for distance.

The men's javelin must weigh a little more than 1 ¾ pounds and be between 8' 6 ¼" and 8' 10 ¼" in length. The women's javelin weighs a bit more than 1 ½ pounds, and must be between 7' 2 ½" and 7' 6 ½" long. Most javelins are made of metal, and the tip must always be steel. But javelins can have wooden shafts.

Javelin athletes are the only throwers who wear spikes. That's because they're the only ones who do any running. They sprint down a runway toward the foul line. (If they cross the line, the throw doesn't count.) Just before they reach the foul line, they turn and pull back the arm holding the javelin. When they reach the line, they let the javelin fly.

Like the discus, the javelin rotates as it flies in the air, which helps it soar. It can also be helped by a gust of wind. The front tip of the javelin must break the ground's surface. The throw is measured from the edge of the foul line to the point where the javelin breaks the ground. All throwers have six attempts in which to do their best.

Throwing World Records
OUTDOORS

Shot put, men: 75' 10 ¼", Randy Barnes, U.S., 1990; **women:** 74' 3", Natalya Lisovskaya, Soviet Union, 1987.

Discus, men: 243' 0", Jurgen Schult, East Germany, 1986; **women:** 252' 0", Gabriele Reinsch, East Germany, 1988.

Javelin throw, men: 313' 10", Jan Zelezny, Czech Republic, 1993; **women:** 262' 5", Petra Felke, East Germany, 1988.

Hammer throw, men: 284' 7", Yuri Syedikh, Soviet Union, 1986; **women:** 223' 7", Olga Kuzenkova, Russia, 1995.

INDOORS

Shot put, men: 74' 4 ¼", Randy Barnes, U.S., 1989; **women:** 73' 10", Helena

CHAMPIONS

The following athletes won gold medals in the field events at the 1992 Summer Olympics.

MEN

High jump
Javier Sotomayor, Cuba

Long jump
Carl Lewis, U.S.

Triple jump
Mike Conley, U.S.

Pole vault
Maksim Tarassov, Unified Team

Shot put
Mike Stulce, U.S.

Discus
Ramas Ubartas, Lithuania

Javelin
Jan Zelezny, Czech Republic

Hammer throw
Andrey Abduvaliyev, Unified Team

Decathlon
Robert Zmelik, Czech Republic

WOMEN

High jump
Heike Henkel, Germany

Long jump
Heike Drechsler, Germany

Shot put
Svetlana Krivaleva, Unified Team

Discus
Maritza Marten, Cuba

Javelin
Silke Renk, Germany

Heptathlon
Jackie Joyner-Kersee, U.S.

271

COOL FACTS

Until the 1950's, pole vaulters used stiff bamboo poles and landed in sawdust-filled pits. But in 1960, Herb Jencks, an American who built fishing rods for a living, introduced the first fiberglass vaulting pole. The fiberglass, which bent and rebounded much more than bamboo, sent people flying through the air with the greatest of ease.

●

Each time a shot is put, it loses a little weight because tiny particles chip away when it hits the ground. To make sure that everyone is throwing a legal shot, officials weigh the shot before each throw. If the shot is too light, some weight is added through a hole in the shot which is usually covered with a plug.

Fibingerová, Czechoslovakia, 1977.

Weight throw, men: 84' 10 ¼", Lance Deal, U.S., 1995; **women (American record):** 62' 10", Sonja Fitts, 1992.

Throwing Legends

Huang Zhihong, China: In 1995, Zhihong won the silver medal in the shot put at the world championships. She has been the world's top-ranked shot-putter three times, finished 1995 as third-ranked, and won the silver medal at the 1992 Olympics.

Al Oerter, U.S.: Al was the first man to throw the discus over 200'. He won the discus at four straight Olympics (1956, 1960, 1964, and 1968), setting an Olympic record each time. In 1980, at age 40, Al made a comeback and qualified for the Olympic team.

Babe Didrikson Zaharias, U.S.: In 1950, Babe was named the Greatest Woman Athlete of the Last 50 Years by the Associated Press. At the 1932 Olympics, she won gold medals in the 80-meter hurdles and the javelin, and a silver in the high jump. Between 1930 and 1932, Babe set world records in these three events. She went on to play professional golf *(see Golf, page 140)*.

Multi-Events

Multi-event competitions were held in some of the ancient Olympic Games. The original *pentathlon* included five events (*penta* means five in Greek): a run, long jump, discus, javelin, and wrestling. The two most important multi-events today are the decathlon (for men) and the heptathlon (for women). Both are two-day events.

In both competitions, athletes earn points based on their performance in each of the events. The athletes compete against one another, but they also try to perform as well as they can to earn the greatest amount of points. The competitor who scores the most

Al Oerter of the U.S. won the discus event at four straight Olympics, setting a record each time.

FIRSTS

Track-and-field athletes try to push the limits of athletic achievement. Here are some important breakthroughs.

MEN

First sub-10-second 100-meter dash: 9.95 seconds, by Jim Hines, U.S., 1968.

First sub-four-minute mile: 3:59.4, Roger Bannister, Great Britain, 1954.

First 20' pole vault: 20' 0", Sergei Bubka, Soviet Union, 1991.

First 70' shot put: 70' 7 ¼", Randy Matson, U.S., 1965.

First 200' discus throw: 200' 5", Al Oerter, U.S., 1962.

WOMEN

First sub-11-second 100-meter dash: 10.88, Marlies Oelsner, East Germany, 1977.

First sub-4:00 1,500-meter run: 3:56.0, Tatyana Kazankina, Soviet Union, 1976.

First sub-4:20 mile: 4:17.55, Mary Decker, U.S., 1980.

First sub-2:30 marathon: 2:27:33, Grete Waitz, Norway, 1979.

First 6' high jump: 6' 0", Iolanda Balas, Romania, 1958.

First 70' shot put: 70' 4 ½", Nadyezhda Chizhova, Soviet Union, 1973.

First 200' discus throw: 201', Liesel Westermann, West Germany, 1967.

First 7,000-point heptathlon: 7,148, Jackie Joyner-Kersee, U.S., 1986.

points in all the events combined wins. The winners of these events earn the title, "The World's Greatest Athlete."

Decathlon: The decathlon is a 10-event competition (*deca* means 10 in Greek) for men. The first day's events are the 100-meter dash, long jump, shot put, high jump, and 400-meter run. The events on the second day are the 110-meter hurdles, discus, pole vault, javelin, and 1,500-meter run.

There is no indoor decathlon. Instead, men sometimes compete in a form of the heptathlon. The events in the men's indoor heptathlon are the 60-meter sprint, long jump, shot put, high jump, 60-meter hurdles, pole vault, and 1,000-meter run.

Heptathlon: The heptathlon is a seven-event competition for women (*hepta* means

273

QUICK HIT

seven in Greek). The first day's events are the 100-meter hurdles, high jump, shot put, and 200-meter dash. The second day's are the long jump, javelin, and 800-meter run.

From 1964 to 1980, the women's multi-event competition consisted of five events, and was called the pentathlon. Women sometimes compete in the pentathlon indoors. The events are the 60-meter hurdles, high jump, shot put, long jump, and 800-meter run.

Multi-Event World Records

OUTDOORS

Decathlon: 8,891 points, Dan O'Brien, U.S., 1992.

Heptathlon: 7,291 points, Jackie Joyner-Kersee, U.S., 1988.

INDOORS

Heptathlon: 6,476 points, Dan O'Brien, U.S., 1993.

Pentathlon: 4,991 points, Irina Byelova, Unified Team, 1992.

Multi-Event Legends

Bruce Jenner, U.S.: Between 1974 and 1976, Bruce won 12 of the 13 decathlons he entered. At the 1976 Olympics in Montreal, Canada, he set a world record of 8,618 points and won the gold medal. Bruce won the Sullivan Award in 1976 as the United States' top amateur athlete.

Jackie Joyner-Kersee, U.S.: Jackie was the first woman to score 7,000 points in the heptathlon and is the world-record holder with 7,291 points. She won gold medals in the heptathlon at the 1988 and 1992 Olympics and a silver medal in 1984. She won a gold medal in the long jump at the 1988 Games and a bronze in 1992. Jackie holds the American indoor records in the 50-, 55- and 60-meter hurdles. She finished 1995 as the top-ranked American long jumper and second-ranked heptathlete.

Jackie Joyner-Kersee has won Olympic gold medals in the long jump and the heptathlon.

Bob Mathias, U.S.: Bob won the decathlon in 1948 when he was just 17 years old. (He had learned how to pole-vault and throw the javelin only a few months before.) Bob won the decathlon again at the 1952 Olympics.

Dan O'Brien, U.S.: Dan became the world's greatest athlete after he won the decathlon at the 1993, 1994, and 1995 world championships. He didn't make the 1992 Olympic team, but he broke the world record later that year.

Glossary

Anchor: The fourth and final leg of a relay. The first leg is called the *leadoff*.

Baton: The hollow stick that is passed between runners in relay races. It is about 12" long and weighs about two ounces.

Leg: One fourth of a relay. There are four *legs* in a relay.

Steroids: An illegal drug that can improve performance by allowing athletes to train harder. It can also damage their health.

Where to Write

USA Track & Field/National Track & Field Hall of Fame, P.O. Box 120, Indianapolis, IN 46206

ULTRA-MARATHONERS

There are some people for whom running 26.2 miles just isn't enough. These awesome athletes are known as ultra-marathoners. They compete in 50-mile road races, 100-kilometer (62-mile) road races, or 24-hour-long road races. In the 24-hour race, athletes run as many miles as they can in one day.

In 1993, Konstantin Santalov of Russia won the World Challenge 100K, in a time of 6:26:26. Carolyn Hunter-Rowe of Great Britain won the women's race in 7:27:19. Also in 1993, Kevin Setnes of the U.S. ran 258.181 kilometers (about 160 miles) to win the 24-hour championship. American Sue Ellen Trapp won the women's race, with 233.816 kilometers (about 145 miles).

VOLLEYBALL

Volleyball was invented 100 years ago as a combination of several popular games. Today it is played indoors and outdoors; on wooden floors, sand, grass, and concrete; and by 800 million men, women, and children all over the world.

HEADS UP!

At the 1992 Olympics, the members of the U.S. men's volleyball team shaved their heads to protest a decision about a match. They then won six of seven matches to take the bronze medal.

●

In 1993, the University of Washington (in St. Louis, Missouri) women's team set an NCAA record with its 59th straight victory.

History

William G. Morgan invented volleyball in 1895 at a YMCA in Massachusetts. He combined elements of basketball, baseball, tennis, and handball to create his new game.

Volleyball spread internationally during World Wars I and II. The *set* and the *spike*, two important elements of volleyball, were developed in the Philippines in 1916.

In 1922, the first United States national tournament was held, and six years later, the United States Volleyball Association was formed. Today, that organization is called USA Volleyball.

Men competed in the first-ever world championships in 1949, and women began competing in their own world championship three years later. Volleyball first appeared as an Olympic event, for both men and women, at the 1964 Summer Olympics in Tokyo, Japan.

Competition

Each year, national tournaments are held for teams of players of all ages. USA Volleyball sponsors a number of events, including the U.S. Open Volleyball Championships, at which the best men's and women's volleyball teams in the country compete; a national co-ed tournament called the U.S. Mixed Six Championship; and the U.S. Outdoor (grass and sand) Championships.

USA Volleyball also selects the members of the U.S. men's and women's national teams. The teams compete in the Olympics and world championships, and in annual interna-

Karch Kiraly led the U.S. national team to gold medals at the 1984 and 1988 Olympics.

BEACH VOLLEYBALL

Another kind of volleyball — *beach volleyball* — is one of the fastest-growing sports in the world. Two-person men's and women's beach volleyball will be an Olympic event for the first time in 1996 at the Summer Olympic Games in Atlanta, Georgia.

There are three major professional beach volleyball tours. Karch Kiraly, Kent Steffes, Randy Stoklos, and Sinjin Smith are among the best players on the Association of Volleyball Professionals (AVP) men's tour.

Karolyn Kirby and Liz Masakayan are the top players on the Women's Professional Volleyball Association (WPVA) tour. The AVP began a women's circuit in 1993.

Four-person teams also compete professionally in the Bud Light four-man and four-woman tours.

tional tournaments for prize money. The men compete in the $3 million World League. The women compete in the $1 million Grand Prix.

At the college and university level, almost 2,000 schools sponsor women's volleyball programs and 60 sponsor men's programs. Championship tournaments are held in three divisions of the National Collegiate Athletic Association (NCAA) and for junior colleges.

Some 320,000 girls and 23,000 boys nationally compete on high school teams.

Rules

The object of volleyball is to use any part of the body above the waist to send the ball over the net and onto the other team's court. The opposing team must return the ball over the net in three or fewer hits without letting it touch the ground.

Players can use one or both hands to hit the ball, and hands may be open, fisted, or clasped together. No player may throw, catch,

QUICK HITS

lift, or scoop the ball, and no player may hit the ball twice in a row. If the ball touches the top of the net and then goes over, it is still in play, except on a serve.

A high-level volleyball game is usually watched over by five or seven officials: a first referee, second referee, scorer, and two or four linesmen. A rule violation is called if a player tries an illegal serve, is out of position on the court, participates in an illegal substitution, or commits a *personal penalty*. After a minor penalty, a player is given a *yellow card* as a warning. After a second minor or a more serious offense, he gets a *red card* and his team either loses the serve or loses a point.

Scoring

Points can only be scored by the serving team, except in the deciding game of a match, when points are scored on every serve. The serving team scores a point when the opponents commit a *fault* by allowing the ball to touch the floor on their side, holding or throwing the ball, hitting the ball more than three times in a row, or hitting it out-of-bounds. One player keeps serving until his team fails to score a point, which is called a *side-out*.

A player loses his serve if he commits a *service fault*, which occurs if the ball hits a teammate, goes under or touches the net, or lands out-of-bounds.

The first team to score 15 points wins. A team must win by at least two points until one team reaches 17. Matches are best two-out-of-three or three-out-of-five game sets.

Teams change sides of the court after every game, and the last receiving team in one game becomes the first serving team in the next. In the deciding game of a match, teams switch sides after one team scores 8 points.

Equipment

The net is 32' long and 3' wide. For men, the

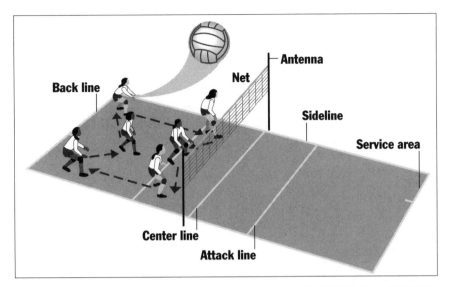

Labels on image:
Back line | Net | Antenna | Sideline | Service area | Center line | Attack line

net is 7' 11 ⅝" high. For women, it is set at 7' 4 ⅛". There are 32"-high *antennas* on each side of the net which act as out-of-bounds markers above the net.

The standard volleyball has a leather cover, weighs 9–10 ounces, and measures 25–27" around.

How to Play

Serving: The player in the right back position on the court serves, using either an underhand motion, which is easy to do but also easy to return, or an overhand motion.

Passing: Once a ball is served, the opposing team must either return it or set up an attack. In competitive volleyball, most service returns are actually passes to teammates. Players often use the forearm pass, or *bump* pass, in which the player joins his hands and lets the ball strike both forearms. The object is to get the ball under control, allowing the *setter* to set up the attack.

Setting: The setter tries to take a bump pass and turn it into a ball that can be hit by a teammate into the opponent's court. A setter usually gets under the ball, faces a team-

ON THE COURT

An official indoor volleyball court is 59' long and 29' 6" wide. (Most outdoor courts are 60' by 30'.) A net with a center line below divides the court into two equal 29' 6" squares. Each square has an attack line 9' 10" from the center line.

In six-player volleyball, teams use three players in a row near the net (*front line*) and three players behind them (*back line*).

When a team wins the serve, each player moves clockwise one position. This is called *rotating*. The center forward becomes the right forward, the right forward becomes the right back, and so on. Players can move out of position once the ball is in play.

COOL FACTS

There are also several variations of volleyball, including *newcomb* and *wallyball*. Newcomb is basically volleyball without the volley. Instead of hitting the ball, players catch it and throw it back over the net. If the ball hits the floor, touches more than one player on a side, or goes out of bounds, a point is scored. Wallyball is volleyball played on a racquetball court. The ball may be played off any wall except the back wall.

mate, and hits the ball at different heights and speeds, according to which teammate he is setting it for.

Hitting: The team member who plays the ball from the setter is called the *hitter*. His job is usually to *spike* the ball over the net. He jumps up and reaches the ball above the net in order to drive it downward into the opponent's court. A spike requires excellent speed, timing, and jumping ability.

The hitter's goal is either to place the ball where an opposing player is not or to hit the ball so hard that it cannot be returned. Front-row hitters can attack the ball from anywhere on the court, but back-row players must be behind the attack line when they hit the ball over the net.

Playing Defense: Attacks are usually defended by *digs* and *blocks*. A dig is similar to a bump pass, but the player is "digging" the ball off the court, often rolling or diving to reach the ball. A block occurs when a front-line player standing close to the net leaps with his arms held high to block an opposing hitter's spike. It does not count as one of a team's three hits.

NCAA Records

Most kills in a match, men: 55, by Jason Mulholland of USC in 1993, and Dave Goss, Stanford, 1992; **women:** 52, by Angelica Jackson, San Diego State, 1987.

Most aces in a match, men: 11, Eric Wenstrom, New Jersey Tech, 1992; **women:** 16, Suzanne Negrotta, Southeast Louisiana, 1990.

Most blocks in a match, men: 27, Mark Wellborn, USC, 1979; **women:** 25, Lisa Smith, Louisiana State, 1987.

Most digs in a match, men: 32, Craig Geigel, Ohio State, 1993, and Adam Lockwood, Hawaii, 1989; **women:** 56, Catalina Suarez, Missouri-Kansas City, 1989.

Most assists in a match, men: 128, Jason Watson, BYU, 1993; **women:** 109, Lori Endicott, Nebraska, 1988.

Legends

Flo Hyman: Flo, one of the greatest women players ever, led the U.S. team to a silver medal at the 1984 Olympics. She was also named the world's best spiker at the 1981 World Cup. Flo, who was 6' 5" tall, died due to a rare genetic disorder called Marfan's Syndrome at the age of 31 in 1986.

Karch Kiraly: Karch led the University of California at Los Angeles (UCLA) to three NCAA championships (1979, 1981, and 1982). He was named MVP of the team four times. Karch has also won three beach volleyball championships (1979, 1981, and 1988).

Glossary

Ace: A serve that cannot be returned.

Dink: To push the ball softly over or around blockers.

Kill: A successful attack that results in a point or a side-out.

Rally: An exchange of hits over the net.

Set attack: When a setter tries to score rather than pass the ball.

Stuff: To block someone so effectively that it results in a point or side-out.

Where to Write

U.S. Volleyball Association, 3595 East Fountain Blvd., Suite I-2, Colorado Springs, CO 80910

Association of Volleyball Professionals, 330 Washington Blvd., Suite 600, Marina Del Rey, CA 90292

Women's Professional Volleyball Association, 1730 Oak St., Santa Monica, CA 90405

Volleyball Hall of Fame, 444 Dwight St., Holyoke, MA 01040

CHAMPIONS

Olympics, Men
1992 Brazil
1988 United States
1984 United States

Olympics, Women
1992 Cuba
1988 Soviet Union
1984 China

NCAA Division I, Men
1995 UCLA
1994 Penn State
1993 UCLA

NCAA Division I, Women
1995 Nebraska
1994 Stanford University
1993 Long Beach State

AVP Beach Volleyball, Men
1995 Adam Johnson and José Loiola
1994 Karch Kiraly and Kent Steffes
1993 Karch Kiraly and Kent Steffes

AVP Beach Volleyball, Women
1994 Holly McPeak and Cammy Ciarelli
1993 Holly McPeak and Cammy Ciarelli

WPVA Beach Volleyball, U.S.
1995 Holly McPeak and Nancy Reno
1994 Karolyn Kirby and Liz Masakayan
1993 Karolyn Kirby and Liz Masakayan

WPVA Beach, World
'94–'95 Sandra Pires and Jackie Silva, Brazil
'93–'94 Karolyn Kirby and Liz Masakayan, U.S.
'92–'93 Karolyn Kirby and Nancy Reno

WRESTLING

When it comes to wrestling, the first thing people think of today is Hulk Hogan, the Macho Man, or the Undertaker. But wrestling's origins go back much further than the World Wrestling Federation.

KING PINS!

The University of Iowa men's wrestling team, coached by wrestling great Dan Gable, won nine straight collegiate national championships from 1978 to 1986.

History

Cave drawings show that wrestling dates back to 2,600 B.C. and the ancient Egyptians. The ancient Greeks adopted the Egyptian style of wrestling, which later became known as *freestyle* wrestling *(see Types of Wrestling, page 283)* and was the most popular sport at the ancient Olympic Games. The ancient Romans took the Greek version and developed a different form of wrestling that today is called *Greco-Roman (see Types of Wrestling, page 283)*. Both forms of wrestling later spread throughout Europe.

European immigrants brought wrestling to the United States. The sport was practiced by troops during the Civil War for entertainment. The first organized wrestling tournament, which was freestyle, was held by the Amateur Athletic Union in New York City in 1888. Wrestling also found a place in colleges. In 1903, four Ivy League schools founded the Intercollegiate Wrestling Association.

Greco-Roman wrestling was part of the first modern Olympic Games, in 1896, but it didn't catch on in the U.S. at first. The first Greco-Roman meet in the U.S. wasn't until 1953. Freestyle wrestling became part of the Olympics in 1904.

The sport's main governing body, the International Wrestling Federation (FILA), was formed in 1912 at the Olympic Games in Antwerp, Belgium. The U.S. Wrestling Federation was created in 1969, and became the governing body of the sport in the United States.

TEXT BY SCOTT WAPNER

In Olympic-style wrestling, athletes wear singlets and try to win points for holds on a mat.

Types of Wrestling

Freestyle: In freestyle, wrestlers may use their legs to grasp the opponent's arms or legs. Tripping or tackling by using the legs is also allowed. Wrestlers are also permitted to use an opponent's legs to lift and control him.

Greco-Roman: In Greco-Roman wrestling, a wrestler may not hold his opponent below the waist, or grip the opponent's legs. A wrestler also may not hook, trip, or lift an opponent with his legs. The legs can only be used to brace one's body or for support. The Greco-Roman style requires wrestlers to have enormous upper body strength and agility.

Rules

Wrestlers compete in weight classes, so that they are matched up with opponents who are the same size. A wrestler may not weigh more than the maximum weight for his class, but he can weigh less.

The rules of amateur wrestling differ for high school, college, and international (such as Olympic) matches.

High school: In high school, athletes wres-

CHAMPIONS

Here are the 1992 Olympic wrestling champions.

FREESTYLE

Light flyweight (105.5 lbs.)
  Kim II, North Korea
Flyweight (114.5)
  Li Hak Son, North Korea
Bantamweight (125.5)
  Alejandro Puerto Diaz, Cuba
Featherweight (136.5)
  John Smith, U.S.
Lightweight (149.5)
  Arsen Fadzaev,
  Unified Team
Welterweight (163)
  Park Jang Soon,
  South Korea
Middleweight (180.5)
  Kevin Jackson, U.S.
Light heavyweight (198)
  Makharbek Khadartsev,
  Unified Team
Heavyweight (220)
  Leri Khabelov, Unified Team
Super heavyweight (over-220)
  Bruce Baumgartner, U.S.

GRECO-ROMAN

Light flyweight (105.5)
  Oleg Koutcherenko,
  Unified Team
Flyweight (114.5)
  Jon Ronningen, Norway
Bantamweight (125.5)
  An Han Bong, South Korea
Featherweight (136.5)
  Akif Pirim, Turkey
Lightweight (149.5)
  Attila Repka, Hungary
Welterweight (163)
  Mnatsakan Iskandarian,
  Unified Team
Middleweight (180.5)
  Peter Farkas, Hungary
Light Heavyweight (198)
  Maik Bullman, Germany
Heavyweight (220)
  Hector Millan, Cuba
Super heavyweight (over-220)
  Aleksandr Karelin,
  Unified Team

BLASTS FROM THE PAST

tle on a mat that is at least 32' square. (College mats are 33' square and international mats are slightly larger.) Matches are three rounds of two minutes each. There are 13 weight classes, from 103 to 275 pounds.

College: Collegiate matches are also three rounds, but they begin with a three-minute period, followed by 2 two-minute periods. There are 10 weight classes, ranging from 118 to 275 pounds.

International: In both freestyle and Greco-Roman international matches, there are 10 weight classes ranging from 105.5 (48 kilograms) to over-220 pounds (over-100 kg.). Wrestlers in each class are separated into two groups, or *pools*. The two pools have separate tournaments and the winners meet in a championship final. Each match is a single five-minute period.

How It's Done

The object of wrestling is either to outscore your opponent or to *pin* him by touching his shoulder blades to the mat.

High school, college, and international matches begin with the wrestlers standing and facing each other. In high school and college matches, a coin is flipped before the second and third periods to determine which wrestler gets the choice of starting the round in the top, bottom, or *neutral position.*

Wrestlers receive points for such moves as *takedowns, near falls, reversals, rides,* and *escapes (see Holds and Positions).* A wrestler can also get points when the other wrestler commits a penalty.

In Olympic wrestling, a match ends if one wrestler pins the other, or builds a lead of 10 points. Otherwise, the wrestler with the most points at the end of a match wins.

Holds and Positions

In a takedown, one wrestler gains control

over his opponent from a neutral position and forces him to the mat. In the neutral position, neither wrestler has control.

A wrestler who is taken down is awarded a point for an escape if he can get back to the neutral position.

In a ride, a wrestler controls how his opponent moves by holding his leg and his arm.

A reversal is when a wrestler goes from a defensive position to an offensive position.

A near fall happens when a wrestler almost pins his opponent. To complete a fall successfully and get a pin, a wrestler must keep his opponent's shoulders on the mat for three seconds.

Equipment

Wrestlers wear headgear and outfits that allow them free motion. The uniform, called a *singlet*, is usually made of a tight-fitting, stretchy material. The headgear covers the ears and has a strap under the chin.

Big Events

The Olympics, Pan American Games, and world championships are the most important events in international amateur wrestling.

The Olympics are the largest of the international competitions for both freestyle and Greco-Roman wrestling. All three competitions are held every four years. In addition, wrestling has its own World Cup, which is held annually and has team and individual events.

Records

Most Olympic gold medals: 3, by Carl Westergren of Sweden (1924, 1928, 1932); Ivar Johansson, Sweden (1932, 1936); and Aleksandr Medved, Soviet Union (1964, 1968, 1972).

Most total Olympic medals, country: 119, Soviet Union.

AROUND THE WORLD

There are other forms of wrestling that are popular in different countries. Among them are *sumo* wrestling and *sambo* wrestling.

Sumo wrestling began in Japan about 1,200 years ago. These matches pit two massive opponents, each weighing as much as 556 pounds, against each other in duels of great strength and balance. The matches take place inside a circle more than 14' in diameter. The circle is covered by a roof, which symbolizes a shrine. Sumo wrestling grew out of the Shinto religion.

The object is to try to knock the other wrestler out of the ring or to the ground. The wrestler who steps out of the circle or touches the ground with any part of his body other than his feet loses the match.

Sambo wrestling originated in the Soviet Union around the 1930's. Sambo is a mixture of many different forms of wrestling, but is most like judo. Wrestlers score points by throwing their opponents.

Most total Olympic medals, individual: 5, Wilfried Dietrich, West Germany (1956–68).

Most world championships: 10, Aleksandr Medved, Soviet Union, 1962–64, 1966–72.

Most NCAA Division I titles: 29, Oklahoma State University.

AWESOME ATHLETES

In 1972, Dan Gable and Wayne Wells became the first wrestlers from the United States to win titles at both the world championships and the Olympic Games.

●

In 1984, the United States won its first Olympic Greco-Roman gold medals when Jeff Blatnick and Steve Fraser each claimed titles.

Legends

Bruce Baumgartner, U.S.: Bruce won gold medals in the freestyle super-heavyweight division at the 1984 and 1992 Olympics and a silver medal in 1988.

Jeff Blatnick, U.S.: No American wrestler had ever won a medal of any kind in a Greco-Roman Olympic competition until Jeff won the gold in the super-heavyweight (over-220 pounds) class at the 1984 Olympics. Even more amazing is that Jeff was diagnosed with a form of cancer called Hodgkin's disease before the Games. Jeff was outweighed in the final match by 35 pounds, but his determination carried him to an upset victory.

Wilfried Dietrich, West Germany: Wilfried participated in both freestyle and Greco-Roman wrestling and won a total of five individual Olympic medals from 1956 to 1968.

Dan Gable, U.S.: Dan won every major tournament available to a wrestler, including a gold medal at the 1972 Olympics. During his college career at Iowa State University, he won 100 matches in a row. After his wrestling career, Dan became the coach of the University of Iowa's wrestling team, which went on to win nine straight NCAA Division I titles.

Aleksandr Medved, Soviet Union: Aleksandr was the most accomplished freestyle wrestler in the world, with three Olympic gold medals and ten world championships. He won the Olympic gold medal in the light-heavyweight division (198 pounds) at the

1964 Olympics, then won gold medals in the super-heavyweight class (over-220 pounds) at the 1968 and 1972 Games.

John Smith, U.S.: John is the most successful wrestler from the United States. Wrestling in the freestyle featherweight class (136.5 pounds), he won Olympic gold medals in 1988 and 1992, and five consecutive world championships, from 1987 to 1991.

Glossary

Anchor: To firmly hold an opponent to prevent or restrict movement.

Body press: When a wrestler positions all of his weight on top of his opponent.

Cradle: A hold in which the opponent is held in a doubled-up position as a result of his head and one leg being caught between the joined hands of the other wrestler.

Decision: If no fall occurs, a wrestler wins the match on the basis of having the most points.

Escape: To free yourself of a hold and get back to the neutral position.

Fall: A match-ending move in which a wrestler pins the shoulders of his opponent against the mat — for two seconds in high school, one second in college, and one half to one second in international competitions.

Grappling: Two wrestlers trying to apply holds while lying on the mat.

Hammerlock: A hold in which an opponent's arm is held behind his back.

Reversal: A move from a defensive position to an offensive position.

Stalemate: When neither wrestler can gain an advantage over the other.

Where to Write

USA Wrestling, 6155 Lehman Dr., Colorado Springs, CO 80918

National Wrestling Hall of Fame, 405 West Hall of Fame Ave., Stillwater, OK

PROFESSIONAL WRESTLING

A wild and crazy form of wrestling known as "professional" wrestling is one of the most popular forms of the sport, partly because it is shown on TV. Bouts often pit a "good" wrestler against an "evil" opponent in a staged match that is more entertainment than athletics.

These matches take place inside a boxing ring instead of on a mat. Competitors wear bright costumes, sometimes with masks over their faces, and have stage names like The Million Dollar Man, Johnny B. Badd, The Nasty Boys, and Lex Luger.

Some of the titles for which they compete are the heavyweight, intercontinental, and tag team (when two wrestlers are partners and take turns during the match) championships.

PHOTO CREDITS